Innocence
BETRAYED

Secrets on the Fox River

RICHARD C. GOVE

ISBN: 1490491031
ISBN 13: 9781490491035
Library of Congress Control Number: 2013911496
CreateSpace Independent Publishing Platform,
North Charleston, South Carolina

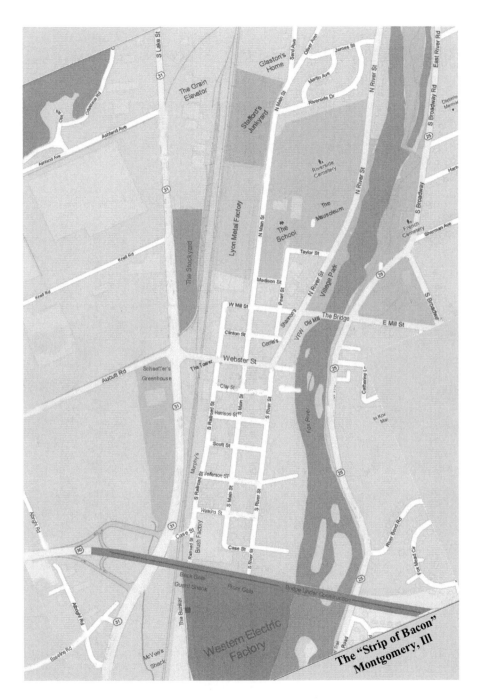

Montgomery, Ill 1958

Dedication

With love in my heart and a host of fond memories, I am dedicating this book to the memory of Helen and Clyde Gove, my mom and dad. The Lord knows they deserve it. I gave them more trouble and heartache than any parent deserves.

Thanks – without friends nothing would be accomplished.

Three people were incredibly instrumental in motivating me to complete this work:

First, **Alex Lizzi, Jr.**, a fellow author and a good friend; without his inspiration I would have never written the first line.

Secondly, **Jim Touvell**, my brother-in-law (more like a brother), clarified some of the details of old Montgomery and helped me recapture the events and places mentioned in this novel. He had no idea why I was asking. The last I checked, he still serves as an officer in the Montgomery Volunteer Fire Department.

Finally, **Helen Baker**, a literary angel, read this novel numerous times to bring it to its final draft. For years Helen and I have compared notes on books we had read mutually. Little did I know that she would be my most valuable critic. Thank you, Helen.

"Steppin' off this dirty bus – first time I've understood –
it's got to be the going - not the getting there that's good.
That's a thought for keeping if I could –
it's got to be going - not the getting there that's good."

Final lines of "*Greyhound*"
Harry Chapin

Foreword

It has been said that it takes a village to raise a child. Maybe so, but is it the village or the child that receives the credit for the good or the bad that results? If all goes well and the child becomes the pride of the community - I suppose the village takes credit. But, should things take that unwanted turn toward delinquency, or even worse; well, something tells me that child faces the music alone. Fair or unfair, that is the fate of the village - and the fate of the child.

Prologue

Things aren't always as they seem. A calm exterior may exude calmness, but it might also mask a turbulent interior, or that which appears to be peaceful on the outside, might in fact be brewing a storm on the inside. Storms stir the soul. Storms can awaken a part of us that we might not welcome.

What he didn't see was dark, foreboding and hiding in the shadows that are ever-present. What he did see was the bright blue sky flecked with high cumulus clouds, the warm humid air hung revealing the hint of fresh tar, fully leaved oaks, elms and maples created canopies over the streets, and the lazy river ambled by; that is what he saw as he stepped from the front stoop of the old house.

This environment excited him. It was summer, the best season of the year; no coats, no school and no limits. The smell of the closest factory, though offensive to some, smelled good and provided him a sense of familiarity – a feeling of home and contentment.

At 12 years old in 1958, Nicholas Lewis (Nick) Corrie was confident that the entire world was nothing more than that which he could see and explore. Nick's job was to explore it. He was an explorer charged with the responsibility to see where it came from, where it was going, what it was made of, and how it could be entertaining.

He'd seen exotic places like Chicago and New York City on television, but they were mere flashes of light on a glass screen; his world, the world within a five-mile radius of where he stood right at this moment, was real; touchable, exciting and capable of filling days and nights with adventures that a young boy would remember the rest of his life. Unfortunately, it was capable of creating memories that a young boy wished he could forget.

CHAPTER 1

This was not how it should end. She struggled, she didn't understand. It wasn't supposed to be this way.

She was young and anxious to learn about the mysteries of life, anxious to find the keys that would unlock the answers to her many questions. Her mom had told her to stay home, but she disobeyed.

Why was he doing this? Why didn't he just let her go home? She could just go home and forget this ever happened. She pleaded. She wished she had stayed home.

Everything that seemed to have order was now out of order. It wasn't right. She didn't mean for this to happen. She tried to detach herself from her surroundings and what was happening to her; she tried to will him out of her life. She wanted to fight, but knew it would be futile. When he was near, she felt her skin recoil. He was disgusting.

She wanted to be home, she wanted things to be normal again. Her eyes saw nothing but blackness, and then they closed.

CHAPTER 2

He rode away from the old house on his Monarch fat tire bicycle, heading west on Clinton Street toward the railroad tracks; Nick was searching for other explorers.

His Monarch was a gift from his parents a year ago. Nick made changes to the Monarch to make it his own. He removed the fenders and raised the handlebars, but he kept that orange and black thing on the cross bar that made it look like a motorcycle gas tank. Everyone knew this was Nick's bike.

At nine in the morning, finding fellow explorers didn't take long. Two bikes carrying explorers approached Nick on Main Street. The first was ridden by Stan - reliable, compliant Stan; the other by Butch - a gelatinous boy who chose to avoid common sense behaviors. These three explorers have been friends a long time, relying on each other's exploring skills to keep them occupied with adventure.

Before the bikes stopped rolling, Nick began the exchange: "Hey Stan – hey Butch."

Without a greeting, Butch belched out "Hey man, did you hear?"

"Hear what?"

"About old man Murphy?"

"No – what about him?"

"Man, you aren't going to believe this, his house was trashed, he has vamoosed, cops and cop cars are all over the place, and they have ropes strung all around to keep everyone out!"

"Say whaaat?"

"You heard me. We've got us a real thing going on. Montgomery is on the map, man!"

Excitedly, Nick spun his bike in the direction of old man Murphy's, and said, "Let's ride down there."

"No man, they shagged us out and said don't come back. Right Stan?"

Stan replied with a nod.

Nick hesitated before saying: "They can't do that – this is a free country."

Baiting Nick, Butch's smile grew as he said, "Yeah. Go tell them that – we'll wait for you. But be firm Nick. Let them know you mean business."

Nick slumped slightly, "OK, OK I dig it. Man, this must be big, this must be really big. How do you know old man Murphy has vamoosed?"

"We heard all the sirens and commotion and rode down there, only to be kicked out by Rively. When we were leaving we ran into one of the firemen, you know the guy that lives on Main near the church, I think his name is Jim something-or-other, I asked him if Mr. Murphy was alright; I was trying to show my community concern – it always works for my mom when she gets nosey. He said old man Murphy wasn't in there."

"Was the place on fire too?" asked Nick, excitedly.

"No man! You know they always call in the fire department any time anything happens. Maybe they're afraid someone will fart too close to a lit match – I don't know why, they were just there. Hey do you remember when someone dumped a bag of dog crap in Principal Favaro's car? The fire department showed up then, and for what?"

Sensing that this would likely lead to one of Butch's endless diatribes, Stan interjected, "Nick, you're right, this is big. We've got to get closer so we can get an eyeball on what everyone is doing. We've got to figure out what's happening." Looking at Butch, then toward Nick, he added, "How do we get closer?"

Silence hung like a fog until Nick said: "Old man Murphy's place is next to the railroad tracks on the east side of the tracks, what if we ride west cross the tracks at Webster Street, hoof it the few blocks and climb the hill? We can lie on the rocks next to the tracks and watch. I don't think anyone will notice us."

Butch grinned and said, "Great idea, Nick! You always come up with a plan. Man, how do you do it?"

The three explorers were different in their own ways, but typical. Nick's hair was medium length on top, short on the sides. Each day began with his hair parted on the right side, but eventually what was combed to the left fell onto his forehead for the rest of the day. Stan, or maybe Stan's parents, preferred the crew cut, which eliminated grooming responsibilities. Butch sported a flat top, which he meticulously held in place with none other than "Butch Wax," that pink, stinky goop with a consistency thicker than axle grease.

They wore rolled up jeans and well-worn T-shirts. The T-shirts rarely remained clean for more than an hour each morning.

Nick and Stan wore Converse All-star gym shoes, those purchased the previous fall for gym class, while Butch wore slip-on sneakers.

Butch was the first of the three to own a genuine pair of Levi's with a button fly from the Army Surplus Store in Aurora. The older boys in Montgomery wore Levi's, but the parents of the younger boys were reluctant to spend the three dollars and seventy-five cents for Levi's, when a trip to Sears & Roebucks or Montgomery Ward could produce jeans for two dollars. Nick and Stan couldn't pass the opportunity to make fun of Butch when his Levi's were new. "Man you're walking like you have a pole up your butt." The stiff canvas material of Levi's definitely required a break-in period.

Riding across the tracks presented no problem to any of them, but the hoofing and climbing took a toll on Butch's conditioning, or actually, the lack thereof. Huffing, he kept imploring the others to wait up. "Come on guys, I have a stone in my shoe." Of course, no stone existed, but he felt sympathy might serve his purpose; Nick and Stan continued to trudge. The twenty foot high man-made hill is made of dirt at the lower level, then of track ballast, consisting of two to three inch jagged metamorphic rock, and the cinders from the steam engines.

The metamorphic rock absorbed the vibration of the fifty-ton rail cars, provided adequate drainage while establishing stability, and softened the clattering derived from the wheels riding on the rails. Whether or not the stones served their intended purpose was of little concern to the climbers. Climbing the hill was neither easy nor fun. Each upward step on the rocks resulted in slippage causing ragged edges to dig into the sides of their canvas shoes, and some slippage was significant enough to make it necessary to use one's hands to provide balance.

Near the top of the hill, Nick and Stan sat awaiting the lumbering Butch. They both smiled as Butch plopped down next to them, breathless.

"Butch, you either didn't eat your Wheaties this morning, or you ate them all, box included."

"Funny Nick; real funny. You guys are thinner than I am (huffing). I carry more of a load, and I am big-boned."

"Did your Mommy tell you that?"

"Shut up Nick. Leave my mom out of it."

"Ok, Ok. Sorry. Do you think your big bones can make it to the top?"

Standing, Nick warned, "Once we get to the top we'll need to crouch down 'til we get into position. We should lie flat on this side of the tracks. If we get seen . . . it's doomsville."

CHAPTER 3

Flying high above Montgomery reveals an unusual geographic layout; something like a strip of bacon. The heart and lifeblood of Montgomery is located in a space three blocks wide with the Fox River bordering on the east side and the multi-rail CB&Q (Chicago, Burlington and Quincy) railroad tracks bordering on the west. Factories, commercial buildings and homes all strung together with utility poles and wires.

The world's largest "hump yard" for sheep and cattle is on the west side of the tracks. This is where the unsuspecting live-stock make their final stop before their fateful trip to the Chicago slaughter houses. It takes only slight imagination to see hundreds of animals just standing, eating, drinking and all that follows. It is the all-that-follows that suggest a problem. The problem is always down-wind.

Fortunately, the wind varies. If the wind is from the north, the air that passes through Montgomery, east of the tracks, hosts fairly acceptable aromas of the factories and occasionally the blooming vegetation; however, if the wind is from the west, well . . . one simply gets used to it after a while.

Montgomery is known as an industrial village and is home to numerous factories, large and small; Caterpillar, All-Steel, Lyon Metal, National Brush and Western Electric to mention a few. Some of them are not located on the strip of bacon, but close enough. All these factories employ far more workers than the village's entire population of eighteen hundred. Folks from miles around drive to the factories every morning, and depart from the factories every afternoon, creating temporary traffic congestion.

During these times one can see, feel, smell and experience all the joys of rush hour, though it usually lasts less than an hour.

One bridge crosses the river at Mill Street going east, and two streets cross the railroad tracks going west; Webster and Case Streets. No road goes south thanks to the large Western Electric factory that occupies all the land between the river and the railroad tracks. Do the math; lots of cars with only limited access routes to get off the strip of bacon. On especially hot days the bacon tends to sizzle with automobile exhaust, short tempers and long lines of cars.

Other than the factories, Montgomery's commerce is basic and service-related; a grocery store, a diner, a bakery, auto repair shops, gas stations, a church, a Laundromat and a village police station that serves as the town hall, the jail and the courtroom (not capable of doing all three at the same time).

Oh yes, and three neighborhood watering holes - one of them being the local VFW. The watering holes are in close proximity to one another right in the middle of town all vying for thirsty patrons.

The Montgomery police force consists of Bob Woodyard and John Rively. Bob is the chief and John is everything else. Together, they split the shifts and care for the needs of Montgomery. Other than the usual police attention required by the local watering holes on Friday night, policing is pretty routine - pretty routine until 6:45am Wednesday morning, July 30th, 1958.

The morning rush-hour was underway; though song birds entertained, it was doubtful that anyone was listening. John, leaning back in the wooden swivel chair in the police station, was waiting for Bob to show up at seven o'clock to end his night shift. His face reflected fatigue, but his dark blue police uniform looked crisp; the creases in the pants stood out; John kept them that way. He took pride in his uniform, but refused to wear the uniform hat with the shiny leather bill; it just wasn't him. Around his midsection a leather belt sported a police pistol, loops for additional ammo, handcuffs and other police gadgets.

Willy Smith, a local with lots of time on his hands, burst into the police station as the door banged against the wall, "John, you got to get down to Murphy's place!" Willy was panting.

Startled, John sat forward, "Willy, what's going on?"

"I don't know John, it just ain't right!"

"What isn't right, Willy? Slow down and take your time."

"Murphy's front door is wide open and blowing in the breeze. You know Murphy – he plays his cards close to his vest and doesn't really invite anyone into his world, let alone his house. I've lived here for over 20 years, his door is never open. Something just ain't right!"

"Alright Willy, calm down. You want to ride down with me?"

"Sure."

They rode away from the station in the 1955 Ford Fairlane police car.

Willy asked, "Hey, is it true that this thing has a special cop car engine?"

"It's true Willy; it has a 312 cubic inch V8 engine, the same as the Thunderbird engine, with other special equipment. We consider it absolutely necessary to chase down and apprehend our notorious speeders."

"We have speeders?"

John smiled and gave a slight wave with his right hand, "No, Willy, I was pulling your leg about the speeders."

Murphy's house was the only house on the west side of Railroad Street with no close neighbors. Low bushes separated his place from the railroad tracks that parallel his backyard. Large mushrooming trees provided shade on both sides of the house and the back yard. The garage, a single stall ancient structure, was located on the south side and to the rear. Murphy didn't drive a car, so the weeds and grass reclaimed what once was a two rut-driveway. As John and Willy approached the house, John could see why Willy was alarmed.

Though the large front porch shielded the front entrance to the house, it was obvious the front door was wide open. John stopped at the porch, rather than pulling toward the garage. Willy waited for John to come around the car before opening his door, and he made sure John was well ahead of him before starting toward the porch.

John climbed the three concrete steps and began striding across the wooden porch as he called out, "Mr. Murphy, its John Rively with the police department." No Response. "Mr. Murphy?" Again no response.

John thought of Mr. Murphy as one might consider a dog on a chain in front of a house. Stay away from the house and the dog was merely an ornament; inch closer to the house and the dog's eyes begin to narrow, his head dips lower, the message is clear – come no closer. That's how John thought of Mr. Murphy; and John was mired in the dog's territory.

John approached the door and peered in hoping to see or hear something that would convince him that Murphy was alright and he could go back to the station, bid farewell to Bob and head for home. The morning's bright sunlight prevented him from seeing beyond the threshold. He pulled his flashlight and turned it on to see inside. "Holy crap!"

"What is it?" Willy blurted out –backing away, more than proceeding.

"Well, it's a lot of stuff."

"What kind of stuff?"

"Get in here and see for yourself. I'm going find my way to the back of the house." John called out as he stepped forward, "Mr. Murphy?"

What Willy and John saw was a collection of . . . things – stacked from floor to ceiling. The absence of light was not due to closed curtains or blinds, but rather, to the stacks and piles of boxes, newspapers, magazines, old furniture, and lots of junk piled so tightly most items blended together and could not be identified without close examination. Light from the windows had no chance of penetrating the mass.

A narrow pathway snaked through the junk leading to the back of the house. John headed that way stepping carefully. He called, "Mr. Murphy?" - no response.

John followed the path veering to the left and ended up in the small kitchen. Ambient light came through a window that was positioned unusually high over a kitchen sink. The sink, like the counters and most of the floor space, was piled with more junk. The small table and two wooden chairs, relatively free of junk, provided the only semblance to human occupation. The entire house smelled musty and stale, like one might imagine the contents of an old box in an attic. John used his flashlight to locate a light switch. The single fixture in the ceiling illuminated the room, but not much more than the flashlight. A door led to the backyard, John checked it and it was unlocked.

Wide-eyed, Willy wormed his way to the kitchen, "What do you make of this, John?"

"Well Willy, Murphy obviously likes to collect . . . things. That's his business. There has to be more rooms than this, did you see any?"

"Nope."

"Let's look again."

Retracing his steps toward the front of the house, John found a crevice separating the junk leading off the main path to the right. He took it. The crevice was so narrow he had to turn sideways to prevent his shoulders from hitting the stacks. It led to another room of stacked treasures. John assumed this to be a bedroom. The beam of his flashlight revealed an exposed window with a heavy shade pulled down. John surmised that Murphy kept the window clear so he could check on the weather in the morning.

He opened the window shade. What his flashlight had not revealed was Murphy's bed in the far corner of the room, tucked in among the piles. The single bed was unmade with graying sheets and an old green blanket; the sight of the pillowcase was not inviting.

Willy stuck his head in the room, "What do you see, John?"

"More of the same Willy."

Leaning to one side to see around John, Willy pointed, "What's on the side of the mattress?"

John turned. The ambient light from the window revealed dark brown stains on the edge of the mattress, each about the size of a quarter. John squatted to look. It looked like dried blood. Instinctively, he ran his forefinger lightly across one of the spots and drew it up for examination. He looked at it, smelled it and told Willy to back out without dragging his feet.

"Why?"

"Willy, do exactly what I tell you do – I'll explain in a minute. Now do it."

Before moving, John pointed the flashlight at the floor next to the bed. The floor was constructed of hardwood, but was hidden under layers of grime and dirt accumulated over the years. A small crocheted rug in front of the bed blended in with the grime. John used the beam of the flashlight to examine the rug: on it was another stain barely visible. Not wanting to disturb any blood on the floor, he slowly directed the beam in a 360 degree pattern around him revealing another dark stain. John kept the beam directed at the floor as he carefully made his way through the crevice to the main path leading back to the front porch where he found Willy sitting on the porch rail smoking a cigarette.

"John, this is creepy."

"I know Willy, but we need to find Murphy. I think he's hurt."

"Was that blood on that mattress?"

"Yeah, I think so. Willy, don't most of these old houses have coal furnaces in the cellars?"

"Well, yeah, I suppose they do."

"Ok then, go around that side of the house (pointing to the south), and I'll go around this side. Look for an exterior cellar entrance - one of those with the slanted doors covering the staircase."

"Wouldn't it be better if we both looked together so we don't miss something, John?"

"Willy, if you see anything, yell – I will come – but don't do anything, just yell."

John stepped off the front porch turning left. Willy slowly exited to the right.

The area that should have been lawn was wild grass, weeds and dirt. The shade from the mature trees prevented excessive vegetation growth. The sun was beginning to bake the creosote that coated the railroad ties and the smell was evident for another day. As John skirted the side of the house he saw a subterranean window-well filled with years of rotting leaves, indicating the existence of a cellar, but no entrance. He was about to turn along the back of the house, when Willy yelled, "John, I've got it!"

John sprinted to find Willy standing erect and proudly pointing at the cellar doors. The wooden doors were weathered and free of any leaves or debris suggesting they had been opened recently. "Come on Willy, give me a hand."

They pulled the doors up and let them fall to the open position, creaking as they landed on each side of the staircase. Looking down, John noted the disturbance of the dust on the steps confirming the stairs were used recently.

"Willy, wait here. I'll be back in a minute."

John descended on the right side of the stairs trying not to disturb the existing tracks. At the bottom he waited for his eyes to adjust. He took two steps into the darkened cellar. As his vision sharpened he used the flashlight to methodically scan the contents of the cellar, starting from the left to the right. Mid-way in his scan, his reflexes caused him to jerk backward. An involuntary "Oh Shit!" filled the basement's silence.

"What is it John?"

Silence.

"John, are you all right? John - John can you hear me?"

"Yeah . . . yeah Willy, I can hear you." John was attempting to recover from the visual display.

Without further dialog, Willy inched his way down the stairs without regard to the footprints in the center.

John, not aware of Willy nearing the last step on the bottom, called up without turning around, "Willy, you stay put; I'll be up in a minute."

"I'm right here" said Willy, causing John a jolt of surprise.

"Willy, go back up!"

As John addressed Willy, he inadvertently turned to the side, though his flashlight revealed a portion of the sight in the cellar to Willy. Willy's response was both spontaneous as well as dramatic. "What the hell?! Holy Christ! Oh my God!" All stated without pause before he bent forward and vomited. John's pant legs caught the over-spray.

John caught Willy before he collapsed and assisted him up the stairs.

Once he got Willy situated in a seated position against the garage, he ran to the car to radio Bob.

CHAPTER 4

Railroad tracks are the blood veins of American commerce, and are, much to the chagrin of parents, a ready-made playground for boys; granted a dangerous playground, but a playground full of adventure and surprises. I say it's for boys, but occasionally an exceptionally courageous girl will join in, but only rarely. Girls have a tendency to avoid the dirty stuff and everything to do with exploring the tracks involves dirt of one kind or another.

Even the old cabooses that were stored by the hump yards had the grime of cinder ash and the residue of their pot-belly stoves ground into their souls. That which was ground into their souls would become part of anything that touched them; and good explorers touch everything. To sit on the wooden benches with the cracked leather cushioning was to carry a remnant of the caboose on your butt for the remainder of the day. But what a fine way to spend a day playing cards and smoking cigarettes. Occasionally, an explorer would steal a girly magazine from an older brother; the caboose conversation was always livelier and more imaginative on that day.

Hobos, the truly unanchored, free spirited beings of the era, ride the rails like the cowboys of the west ride their horses; full of stories, yarns, and songs, all of which speak to the explorer's heart.

Trains stop in Montgomery infrequently to load or unload the livestock. It would be during the infrequent Montgomery stops that the lonesome hobo might exit and be available for the pleasure of eager explorers wanting to learn what exists beyond the horizons.

All in all, the tracks provide an escape, a refuge, a frontier, an adventure and a challenge for explorers.

Stan was the first to the top of the ballast hill. Crouching low, he motioned Nick and Butch to go farther down the tracks before cresting the hill. They misjudged the location of Murphy's house on the other side. Stan stayed low and scrambled another 75 feet and motioned Nick and Butch to come up. Lying flat on their bellies, they had good cover. The rails were mounted to the railroad ties. The ties were partially buried in the ballaSt. From the opposite side of the tracks, one would have to be looking specifically in their direction to notice them.

In order to observe Murphy's house and the activity around it, the boys craned their necks upward to see over the rails. Their neck muscles would cooperate for a while, but would begin to cramp and ache, resulting in frequently needed rest periods.

Nick was continually relaying what he saw to Butch, whose rest periods were needed more frequently.

"So Stan, what do you make of it?" asked Nick.

"Nick, this is something, man. I mean, look at all those cop cars. There's Rively's, and Chief Woodyard's - a County car and a County van – both of our fire trucks." Stan stopped, "I've never seen those cop cars over there."

Nick looked in the direction Stan was looking, "Oh, those are State cops, you can tell because they have a different gumball on top, and the siren is mounted next to the gumball."

"Is that a meat wagon by the bush?"

"It's not ours – I don't know."

Butch, having gained strength from a lengthy rest period, was peering over the rails and said, "Hey – that's from the Coroner's Office. I read about that in a magazine. The cops call in the coroner to pronounce people dead. Man, that's what that has to be – did old man Murphy murder someone? Oh man, this is boss!"

"Slow down Tonto - rushing into the wrong canyon can get you dead. We need to just watch and figure out what's going on" replied Nick. "Stan, do you know the little guy standing by the garage?"

Stan squinted and craned his neck higher and said, "Yeah, that's Willy Smith – what is he doing there?"

Butch was quick to offer, "I'll bet he's an undercover cop! I'll bet he's been casing the joint for a long time, today they swooped in for an arrest."

Nick said, "Butch, will you relax? If you talk any louder we're going to have company. Why don't you lay back and watch for trains? We'll keep you posted on anything that changes over there."

Dejectedly, Butch asked, "So what do you want me to do if I see a train coming? Just keep my mouth shut?"

"No stupid, say *train* and then concentrate on getting your big bones down that hill."

Resenting being reproved for his creative thinking, Butch remained on his belly looking down the tracks. He imagined how foolish Nick and Stan were going to feel when the story really came out and he, Butch, the reader of Police Gazette magazine, was right.

Stan and Nick continued to take in what they could see, but to no avail. Men walking around, looking at things, talking to one another, and smoking cigarettes, none of it seemed informative. Complicating matters even more, most of the activity was on the side of the house near the garage, which was partially blocking their view.

With Stan and Nick concentrating on the house, and Butch relishing the eventual glory of being deemed right, a thunderous voice boomed, "WHAT ARE YOU BOYS DOING HERE!?"

Startled, wide-eyed and frightened, all three jumped, thrusting their knees into the ballast, almost causing a three-way simultaneous bladder release. They spun their heads around to see their captor, Phil - Phil the pill, cool guy Phil, one of those guys that has all the answers, but none of the solutions, to every problem ever created. Philip Girrard Glaston.

"Phil, you asshole!" said Stan, lying flat again.

17

Nick looked at Phil with a scowl and said, "Phil, you're a jerk. Get yourself down. We're not supposed to be here! There are more cops over there than at Stateville Prison."

Butch never uttered a word for fear that his bladder would actually release.

Crouching low, but not so low as to lie on the dirty rocks, Phil asked in a low voice, "What are you girls doing lying on the rail-road tracks? I saw you all the way from Webster Street."

Still aggravated by Phil's sick joke, Stan said, "Why Phil, I thought you knew everything. If you did, then you'd know a high profile investigation is going on right here in our hometown. Really Phil, I'm disappointed in you."

Phil responded, "I know what's going on over there; I didn't know what was going on over here." With sarcasm he added, "Have you seen them carry out any bodies yet?"

Missing the sarcasm, Stan responds, "No – but Butch thinks the panel truck is from the Coroner's Office."

"Girls, girls, girls – lets blow this gig and go talk about it where you don't look like you're getting romantic with the rocks."

Nick's chest was getting sore from the rocks poking at his T-shirt.

Stan said, "I think they probably heard Phil the foghorn, so we better get out of here anyway." Butch was recovering from his near bladder release episode and said, "Damn you Phil, that wasn't funny."

Phil responded as he began his slow descent, "For you, or for me?"

"Jerk!"

Phil Glaston was an enigma; the youngest of a family of four boys, really big boys, who lived north of town, beyond the junk-yard, on Sard Avenue. Phil was two years older than Nick, six feet tall, broad shouldered, with a ruddy look that was accentuated by the early onset of facial hair and a deep resonant voice.

His dark pompadour haircut emulated none other than Elvis the pelvis, who was in the Army without his pompadour; it added significantly to Phil's overall persona. His looks and his voice claimed respect, until his obnoxious manner of being a know-it-all, speaking to others as if he was in on something they weren't, and his obsessive habit of demeaning others openly took over. The respect dissipated and was replaced with general disdain.

Phil hung out with the boys at the diner, but it was as if Phil was always on the outside looking in. They did not understand why Phil hung around with them, rather than other fourteen year olds, but they tolerated it. None of them trusted Phil with any personal information for fear of finding out that Phil shared it with others outside the group.

All four boys made it down the hill without a major event and walked to Webster where they left their bikes by the "railroad tower," which wasn't really a tower at all, but rather a two-story wooden structure, with lots of windows on all sides. Unfortunately, the new electronic signal system resulted in the tower having outlived its usefulness a decade earlier; thus it sat vacant, rotting and peeling in the sun; simply a reminder of days gone by.

"Let's head to the park" Phil barked, as if he had assumed command.

The boys rolled their eyes and rode their bikes in that direction.

They headed toward the river on Webster for two blocks. In those two blocks they passed the post office, two filling stations, the church, the grocery store, the Laundromat and the diner. They ignored the stop sign when they turned left on River Street.

River Street, as the name implies, parallels the river, as Railroad Street parallels the railroad tracks. Times must have been pretty simple in the mid 1800's as Montgomery grew its roots. We can be thankful that the founders hadn't erected a public outhouse. Who would want to live on "Crapper Street?"

The wind felt invigorating while zipping down the hill. They could feel the cracks in the pavement as their tires plinked across them. The speed plastered their T-shirts to their chests and caused the backs to puff out. Speed is always exciting.

Phil was in the lead with the others trailing behind. It was easy to recognize Phil's bike; raccoon tails tied on either side of his handlebars flapped in the breeze. They passed the barber O.K. shop and VFW on the right, then came to Shannon's Tavern on the left. Nick noticed something that caused him to put on the full brake action. With Nick's back tire screeching and the bike sliding to the right, Stan and Butch followed suit not knowing why, but not objecting. Nick nearly came to a stop and pedaled over to the front of Shannon's.

On the front stoop of the concrete building sat another friend. Only, this friend was somewhat unlikely.

There sat Charlie - Charlie, the town drunk. Parents warned the boys, "You better stay away from that old man!" The boys figured Charlie had been around forever. He sat on those steps for as long as they could remember – never bothering anyone – he was a fixture.

Two years ago Nick was afraid of Charlie, thinking of him as an ogre under the bridge. One day Nick went to Shannon's with his dad. His dad addressed Charlie in a friendly manner, and Charlie responded in like. This surprised Nick – he was expecting a grunt or a growl, or whatever noise an ogre makes. Before leaving, Charlie said, "Paul, who's that quiet guy next to you?"

"Charlie, this is my boy, Nick."

Nick sensed pride welling up in his dad's statement.

"Nick, it is my pleasure to make your acquaintance." Charlie offered a liver-spotted hand.

Nick couldn't remember being greeted like this before. Most of the time it was a ruffling of his hair and a "good looking boy, Paul," but Charlie focused on Nick, not his dad's fine job of creating him. The ogre disappeared and Charlie was a friend.

Since that day, Nick found time to sit on those steps and talk with Charlie. They would talk about school, sports, fishing, what was happening in Montgomery, girls that Nick was noticing, and most importantly, Charlie told great stories; stories of riding the rails, of big cities, of being a cowboy out west, and of gangsters in Chicago. Whether or not the stories were true didn't matter to Nick. Charlie told them like a man of experience and that was good enough for Nick. Charlie became the older brother Nick didn't have. Nick trusted Charlie to the utmost. Nick had a good friend.

Some folks in town alerted Nick's parents that their son shouldn't be hanging around a tavern with the likes of Charlie, the town drunk, but Nick's parents just suggested that Nick should talk with Charlie in the park across from Shannon's. Nick agreed but never mentioned it to Charlie.

Music drifted from the screen door of the tavern, "*People see us everywhere. - They think you really care, - But myself, I can't deceive, I know. . .*" Conway Twitty belted out "*It's Only Make Believe.*" The sour smell of spilt beer and the accumulation of years of cigarette and cigar smoke wafted from the tavern.

Nick pulled up to the concrete steps and said, "Hey Charlie?"

"Hey, Nicky-boy, I was sitting here thinking how nice it would be if you happened to stop by today. So what are the Mayor and his court up to this fine day?"

Nick never understood why Charlie referred to him as "the Mayor" – he didn't feel like a mayor, or a leader, but it tickled Charlie to call him the Mayor in the presence of the other guys, so he went along.

"Charlie, there's trouble down at old man Murphy's place."

"So I hear. I'm glad you boys are here to give me the straight poop."

The three boys straddling their bikes looked at each other, and Nick said, "We don't really have any poop. What did you hear, Charlie?"

Charlie looked toward the screen door, paused and said, "What say we stroll over to the wonderful park the city has groomed for our enjoyment? It's cooler over there, and we can talk without interruption."

CHAPTER 5

Bob Woodyard, the longtime Chief of Police, and a longer time resident of Montgomery, arrived at Murphy's exactly fourteen minutes after John's radio call. He pulled behind John's Village car and was walking before the car door slammed shut. Bob took long fast strides paying no attention to Willy sitting against the wall of the garage. He asked John, "What the hell is going on John, you sounded like your underwear was too tight."

"Yeah, sorry, I guess I was too excited. It's down in the cellar, but let me brief you before we go down."

"Have you radioed the County yet?"

"Yeah, they're on their way. I asked them to radio the State too, just in case."

"The State? Fantastic, can't wait to learn more from those boys. According to them, you'd think we just fell off the turnip truck."

"Sorry boss, but I think we're going to need help with this one."

"Forget it, John; just fill me in."

John proceeded to brief Bob, from the time Willy showed up at the station to the point John needed to assist Willy to the side of the garage.

Bob removed his billed uniform hat, his forehead wrinkled in concentration as he tried to assimilate all that he just heard. It wasn't much; the facts didn't seem to make sense. He asked, "Are you sure Murphy's not around anywhere?" motioning with his hat toward the house.

"Pretty danged sure, Bob. He's not in the house, not in the cellar, not in the garage; I checked the tracks, the fields on both sides of the house – I'm pretty sure he's gone."

"That's the most confusing part of the story. I've known Murphy a long time. He might leave this property to buy groceries or to walk to Aurora, but he walks fast and he's back fast."

"I know Bob, but what can I tell you? When the County gets here we can spread out and check more thoroughly, but I think he's gone."

Bob sighed, "Let's wait on the County before heading for the cellar. Have you talked with Mrs. Bartlett across the street?"

Looking in that direction, John said, "No, I've been watching for signs of movement, but haven't seen any and I didn't want to wake her. She's got to be eighty."

"Yeah, and she couldn't hear a bomb go off in the next room, let alone 100 yards down the street. We'll check with her later."

Willy, still affected by the cellar discovery, walked slowly to where Bob and John were talking, "Aren't you going down Bob?"

"Not yet Willy, the County boys will be here in a minute. John said you had a rough go of it. Why don't you head for home? "

"I was fine helping John – but, that cellar . . ." his voice trailed off.

"Willy, go home and get some rest."

Willy walked back to the side of the garage and sat down.

The scream of sirens cut through the air long before the vehicles were in sight. They came south on Route 31 on the west side of the tracks, crossed at Webster and turned on Railroad Street. Bob thought that they should have shut off the sirens when they turned on Railroad - but they didn't. The sirens became a beacon for everyone within earshot to come running. There was already a small group gathering in front of Murphy's. Bob thought, "It's their town; I guess they have a right."

Two County vehicles, a car and a van, arrived by skidding to a stop in front of the house.

The lead car was occupied by Kane County's Lead Investigator. Bob and John knew him from other joint efforts – his name was Conner, Henry Conner. He was a likable guy and competent at his job. He respected local cops and listened to their commentary and analysis.

The van was driven by another County investigator that John had met, but couldn't remember his name. He was tall, had a pock-marked face and was carrying a tool box. John tried to remember his name, but nothing was coming.

Henry threw out his hand, "John, good to see you." Turning, he offered his hand to Bob, "Bob. So what do you have?"

John hoped the tall investigator would offer his name, but that didn't come, so he initiated by offering his hand to the investigator. They shook without speaking.

Bob responded to Henry's query, "Well Henry, we don't have a clue as to what we have, or what we don't have." He proceeded to inform Henry of everything that had been relayed to him and concluded by pointing toward the open doors. "According to John, we have a mess in the cellar."

Henry added, "According to John, you have a mess in the house as well. What is it with the junk?"

Bob answered, "Henry, I have no idea. Murphy has been here since Christ was a corporal; I have never set foot in that house. I don't know anyone who has."

Turning to John, Henry asked, "Besides the blood on the mattress, did you see any other signs of struggle?"

"Not really, but it's kind of hard to tell; you'll see when you go in" responded John.

"We'll do that later. Let's deal with the cellar first."

Turning back to Bob, Henry asked, "Have you been in the cellar yet, Bob?"

"No. I figured I'd wait for you guys to avoid the possibility of disturbing the scene."

"Good call."

The group instinctively began walking in the direction of the cellar. The County investigator asked, "Who's the little guy by the garage?"

Bob responded, "That's Willy. He was the one who originally reported the front door being open; he rode down here with John. Best I can figure, John thought it was going to be routine. Unfortunately, Willy's first experience in crime fighting has taken a toll."

The investigator snickered.

The entrance to the cellar was as John and Willy left it. John said, "It's not roomy. It has a low ceiling and I didn't look for lighting."

Henry turned to his investigator and said, "Process what you can with the steps. John, are those your footprints?"

"Those on the right are mine, I purposely walked down the right side to avoid prints that appeared in the center, however, Willy followed me down, and I helped him out. I think we boogered up anything that might be helpful."

The tall investigator replied, "Maybe, maybe not. Let me see what I can find."

He began working on the steps and asked, "John, did you drag, carry or pull the little guy up the steps?"

"No, I had my hands under his armpits and guided him."

"Did either of you ever sit or kneel on the steps?"

"Nope."

The investigator continued, "Henry, I doubt that any discernible footprints can be captured, they've been walked on too many times, however, if you'll look at the three steps closest to the top you'll make out significant drag marks. The drag marks are wider than the normal foot pattern. I'm not sure what's been dragged, we better get the camera in here before we go down."

He walked up to his tool box extracting his camera and chrome flash unit. Flash, pause, flash, pause, flash. Changing the bulb for every shot, the investigator said, "OK, got it."

Extending professional courtesy to Bob, Henry suggested, "Bob, why don't you and I go down to get the lay of the land, afterwards we'll start the investigative procedures. We'll look, take in what we can and come out to talk about it."

Henry went first, with Bob following. Their flashlights were powered by four "D" batteries; the large lenses cast a broad illumination. Henry ducked as he entered the threshold of the cellar and stepped to the left allowing Bob to enter. Bob, not realizing it, stepped directly into Willy's breakfast. Henry looked over and said, "That'll knock the shine off."

The flashlights lit up the cellar. Though emotionally moved by the display of blood, neither expressed it. Without changing their positions, they surveyed the cellar, each looking for the key that could explain what they were seeing.

The cellar was damp, and eerie; the faint smell of coal dust and mildew filled the single 25 feet deep by 34 feet wide room. Occupying most of the far right corner was a coal furnace covered with sheet metal. Next to it was the coal hopper, and in the near right corner was a depleted supply of coal.

To the left was a makeshift work area with a bench, a stool and electronic devices of varying types; radios, tuning devices, antennas, and speakers. Bob and Henry noticed the light over the bench. Not wanting to inadvertently destroy evidence neither moved in the direction of the string hanging from it.

What held their attention the longest was straight in front of them on the floor, a blanket or tarp covered with blood – lots and lots of blood. The blood was dark brown, well into the drying process, but isolated pools still glistened in the artificial light. Against the far wall, partially hidden by a metal crate or cabinet, was a contributor to the bloody scene.

Bob, staring hard at the object said, "Henry, what in God's name, is it?"

"I don't know Bob."

"Whatever it is, it looks like it's been skinned or scrubbed with a wire brush, Henry."

They both did an additional scan of the entire cellar and headed for daylight.

As they ascended the final steps, the breeze and sunlight was welcoming. They noticed the crowd was growing. Henry recognized Pete Morantz from the State Police, but no one else. He pulled John aside, "John, unless they have an official capacity in this investigation, they are no closer than the street. Got it?"

"You bet, Henry. The fire department is here, do you need them?"

"John, do you smell smoke?"

"No. Sorry Henry."

"That's OK John; I didn't mean to snap at you, I'm a little rattled."

John walked off to direct people away from the front and side yards and thought to himself, "Whew, I'm glad to hear that I'm not the only one."

Henry walked over to where Bob was engaged in conversation with Pete Morantz. Pete was smiling at Bob and saying, "Bob, what have you gotten yourself into? This sort of thing never happened in Montgomery before you were chief."

"Yeah, that's been 27 years, Pete. The place is falling apart" said Bob.

Henry jumped in extending his hand to Pete and said, "Hey Pete, thanks for coming."

"Always a pleasure to lend a hand, Henry."

Henry continued, "Let's get everyone together for a briefing. We need to strategize how we're going to handle this investigation. That cellar is going to be a challenge. Hell, we got something pretty awful on the back wall that we can't identify, and we can't get to it without swimming through blood. We can't screw this up."

CHAPTER 6

The City Park is located on the northeast corner of River and Mill Streets. Shannon's Tavern sits on the southwest corner. The Mill Tavern, the last of the three watering holes, occupies the northwest corner. An out of place three-story vacant stone building looms on the southeast corner. The old stone building was a water-driven grist-mill built in the mid 1800's to grind wheat into flour; thus Mill Street gained a name; thank you founders.

The Fox River establishes the entire east boundary of the park. The park goes north for three blocks. To prevent cars from pulling onto the grass in the park, heavily tarred logs, twelve inches in diameter, lined the park along River and Mill Streets. Eight-foot long horizontal logs stood perched on two shorter vertical logs sunk into the ground. The horizontal logs, car bumper height, were spaced so foot traffic or a bicycle could barely squeeze between them.

The boys rode their bikes between the parking logs and on to the grass in the park where they found Phil, smoking a cigarette, waiting for them on a picnic table near the river. "What kept you, girls? Am I too fast for you?"

"No" answered Nick, laying his bike down, "Charlie has news about old man Murphy. He's coming over."

"News? The only news that old codger has is bottled and distilled."

Nick responded, "Hey, back off, we want to hear what he has to say. Here he comes."

Charlie moved at his own comfortable pace and gracefully sat at the picnic table. Phil wandered off to the river.

With excitement in his voice, Stan turned to Charlie and said, "So Charlie, fill us in on old man Murphy. What do you know?"

Charlie, enjoying the moment, sat straighter and smiled. "I don't mean to be a burden, but would one of you gentlemen happen to have a coffin nail you are willing to share?"

Nick looked at Butch and said, "Did you steal any of your mom's Kools this morning?"

Butch replied, "No, man, I think she's catching on. I heard her tell my dad that she has to slow down because she's smoking too much. I keep this up and I am going to be in deep shit."

Stan called out, "Hey Phil, can we have one of your fags?"

Phil walked over slowly, "Who's it for?"

"Charlie."

"Man, these things cost me money, I can't be handing them out to the neighborhood. I could go broke, and then what?"

With a slightly deeper than normal voice, Nick asked, "Phil, may I have one of your cigarettes, please?"

"Who's it for?"

"Me, Phil, why else would I ask?"

Taking one of Lucky Strikes from the pack, Phil handed it to Nick.

"Thanks, Phil." Turning, he handed it to Charlie.

"Hey, I thought it was for you?"

"It was, but I decided to give it to Charlie. Thanks again, Phil."

Phil gave him the finger and walked back toward the river.

Charlie pulled a Zippo lighter from his shirt pocket. When he flipped it open, the top wobbled so badly Nick thought it was coming off; it didn't. Charlie lit his cigarette. He pulled an exceptionally long drag from the Lucky, inhaling so deeply it held the rapt attention of all three boys. As he exhaled, it was a release for all of them.

Thoughtfully, Charlie said, "This thing has you boys pretty worked up, wouldn't you say?"

"Yeah it does!" said Stan. "We've been down to old man Murphy's and got kicked out by Rively. We climbed the tracks to spy from the west side, but didn't really see anything, except for Willy Smith, and . . ."

Charlie cut in, "Willy Smith?"

"Yeah, Willy's right there in the mix, go figure."

"Well, well, a real stumper. I guess we better pool our resources to figure this one out" states Charlie.

Nick chimed in, "Charlie, tell us what you know."

Charlie smoked the cigarette down so low Nick wondered why it wasn't burning his fingers. Charlie put it out on the sole of his shoe and said, "Chuck Morgan came in a little while ago and was talking to Shannon. I wasn't supposed to hear, but I have better ears than most give me credit for. Chuck said he talked to someone who saw a lot of blood and something dead in the cellar."

"Blood! Something dead! Are you shitting me?" cried Butch. "Right here in Montgomery? Man, I told you guys that truck was from the Coroner's Office. Old man Murphy's murdered someone!" More reflectively, he asked, "But, who? And where is old man Murphy?"

Nick, shaking his head, said, "Butch, you are wearing thin. We don't know if anyone has been murdered, yet."

"Yeah, but, they saw something dead."

"Yes, Butch, something dead, not someone dead; now shut up and let Charlie talk. What else do you know, Charlie?"

"Sorry boys, that's about all I have to offer to your investigation. Chuck and Shannon headed for the backroom and that's all I heard."

"Damn" said Nick.

"What do you know about old man Murphy, Charlie?" asked Stan.

"When you get to be as old as I am, you get to know a lot about nothing. Some of it has a bearing on the big picture; the rest of it is as useless as tits on a boar. I think Thad Murphy fits in between."

Repeating what he heard, Nick said, "Thad?"

"Yes, Thad is short for Thaddeus. Mr. Murphy's first name is Thaddeus. I knew Thad many years ago. He was a different man back then."

"What do you mean a different man back then?" asked Stan.

"How would you boys describe Mr. Murphy today?"

"Weird" offered Stan.

"Strange" came from Butch.

"A hermit" Nick said.

Not realizing that Phil had wandered back from the river, everyone was surprised to hear, "He's a crazy old bastard that lives by himself and collects junk."

Charlie rubbed his multi-day stubble and said, "Well, you summed him up pretty good. From your point of view, he's all that you said he is. But, we have to be careful, because things aren't always the way they seem."

Looking confused, Butch asked, "What?"

"How old are you, Butch?" asked Charlie.

"I'm twelve."

"OK, how long have you been observing Mr. Murphy?"

"I don't observe him, hell, I don't care about him; at least, not until today."

Patiently, Charlie continued, "What I mean is how many of your twelve years do you think you have noticed that he is even alive?"

Realizing that Butch was having difficulty following Charlie, Nick said, "Let's say six years."

"Fair enough," agreed Charlie. "During those six years he has been pretty consistent in his behavior, hasn't he?"

"Yeah, consistently strange" said Butch.

"How old do you think Mr. Murphy is?"

The boys looked at one another with shrugging shoulders, offering no answer.

Charlie said, "Let's say he is sixty; that's close enough, give or take a few years. You have only seen him the last six of those sixty years. You have no idea of the previous fifty-four years, and what circumstances, events, relationships or hardships brought him to the last six years. I am suggesting that you keep an open mind before you rush to judgment."

Phil chimed in again, "This is getting too complicated for me. People are people. Some are screwy, some aren't."

"Phil, you're right, people are people. I wanted you boys to know a little bit about the main character of your mystery" said Charlie.

"But Charlie, all we've learned is that his name is Thad. What else do you know about him?" asked Nick.

Sheepishly, Charlie turned to Phil and said, "Phil, if you could be kind enough to give me one more of your nails, I'd surely be obliged. This nicotine addiction is demanding."

With less reluctance this time, Phil removed a Lucky and handed it to Charlie. After Charlie took his, Phil said, "Let's all smoke, I have more at home."

One by one, they each removed a cigarette from Phil's pack and lit up.

Nick hadn't come to grips with sucking the smoke into his lungs yet, while the others did it with ease. Nick held the smoke in his mouth for a while and blew it out.

Charlie continued, "A long time ago, probably thirty years or so, Thad Murphy was, as I said before, a different man than what you see now. He came into money when his parents died. He flaunted himself as the life of the party. Unlike most of us, he'd been to college, and often spoke of his fraternity. If a party was hosted anywhere in town, you could bet Thad was not only in attendance, but right in the middle, having a good old time. Some folks felt he was a braggart, I heard others say he was arrogant, but, that was Thad. He married the prettiest girl I have ever seen; her name was Sara. Thad met her in college and brought her home with him. Boys, I know you have seen pretty girls, but Sara was so beautiful she could cause a man to stumble over his own feet. When she smiled, the heavens opened up and the angels sang. She was something, and, she was Thad's. Thad and Sara made a striking couple. To see them, you would have thought they had roped the moon together. Sara gave birth to a baby girl almost right away. Aside from Sara and that little girl, Thad's pride and joy was his Durant Touring car. Most of us were still walking, riding bicycles, or at best, driving a Model-T Ford, but Thad drove a Durant. It was a yellow convertible and was fast for its day. Thad drove it fast too. If he had been to a party, he'd be kicking up dust wherever he went, whooping and hollering in that yellow Durant. Do you boys know that big old stately house this side of the brush factory?"

They all nodded.

"That house is kind of run down, but in its day it was festive. One Saturday night Thad and Sara attended a lawn party at that house. It went late into the night. I didn't attend, but I knew a fellow that did. He told me he thought that Thad was too drunk to drive when he saw Thad and Sara leaving. He watched Thad spin the tires of the Durant coming out on Watkins Street and barreled across the railroad crossing at Case. That was all anyone saw of Thad and Sara that night. The next morning Mitchell Camp, a farmer out on Orchard Road, found Thad's Durant upside down in one of his fields. When Mitchell got to the Durant, he found Sara. She was dead, having been rolled on as the Durant turned over and over. Mitchell said he sat down and cried right there, he couldn't help himself. After recovering from finding Sara, he searched for Thad. He found Thad unconscious, about 100 feet away. He must have been thrown free, while Sara wasn't."

The boys sat in silence, not really knowing what to say. Reflectively, Stan said, "Thad obviously lived, but what happened to his little girl? I've never seen any family around that house of his."

"Good question, Stan," said Charlie. "Thad was in the hospital a long time in Aurora, but eventually got out. He sold the family house he and Sara lived in and bought that house by the railroad tracks. We all assumed that the little girl went to live with family, and as the years went by we figured she'd come to visit if she was living with family, but no one I know of is aware of any visits. Most of us knew Thad vowed to never get in a car again. Boys, to the best of my knowledge, he hasn't broken that vow, so he hasn't gone to visit her either. So, I don't know what happened to her."

Everyone sat, collecting their thoughts when Phil broke the mood, "I don't care what you say, old man Murphy is a kook! He was a kook back then and he's still a kook. I see him walking to Aurora on the tracks behind my house. He's just an old kook."

Nick responded, "He might be a kook, Phil, but Charlie sure helped us answer questions about Murphy. I didn't know any of this."

"OK, now you know. So what? I think I'm going to chase girls with real curls." Phil headed for his bike. He said over his shoulder, "Don't let your skirts get caught in your spokes - girls."

Once Phil was out on River Street, Butch said, "Man, what is with him? He's like having the runs, he comes when you don't expect him, and he's a pain in the ass while he's here."

They all laughed, including Charlie. Nick said, "That is the most intelligent thing you've said all day, Butch. Good one."

Stan got more serious and said, "Charlie, thanks for the story, but do you think old man Murphy could be a murderer? I mean, that's what we're talking about, isn't it?"

Charlie thought for a moment, and said, "You know, I have never had any inkling that Thad has a violent side to him. But, for thirty years he has been, as Nick said, a hermit. I think when a person gets driven into his own house, and into his own mind for that long, anything is possible. I don't know, Stan."

Butch asked, "Charlie, where does old man Murphy get his money? He doesn't work."

"I don't know if any of the money he once had is still left, but I do know he tinkers with radios for other people. I've taken a couple of radios to him for Shannon."

"You've been in his house?" asked Nick.

"No, I haven't. When I go down to his place it seems almost magical. He doesn't know I'm coming, but I no sooner hit the front porch and he's coming out the front door to meet me, closing the door behind him. I don't know how he does it."

"So then what?" asked Nick.

"I hand him the radio and he tells me when to come back to get it. Then it's the same all over again, he meets me before I ever get to knock."

"Do you talk to him?" asked Stan.

"Small talk, 'How you been, Thad?' or something like that, but no real conversation."

"This is getting very strange" said Butch.

Charlie stood up, "Yes it is. Shannon is probably looking for me. I'm going to head back over, boys."

"Thanks Charlie" offered Nick.

"Anything for the Mayor and his court, Nicky-boy," Charlie said as he walked away.

"Charlie – we'll be back if we pick up on anything."

"You do that. I'll be waiting."

Nick looked at the other two boys and said, "You guys want to go to the diner?"

Before Nick finished 'diner', Butch said, "Yeah, I'm hungry!"

"Let's head up" said Nick grabbing his bike by the handlebars.

CHAPTER 7

The car crash in 1928 demolished more than just the car; it took Sara Murphy's life and left Thad Murphy in the St. Charles Hospital in Aurora, Illinois for two months. Sally Murphy, age six months, was placed in the custody of Kane County as a ward of the court.

Kane County notified Betty Thomas of Mystic, Iowa, the only relative to Thad, a cousin, that could be located. When the officials explained the circumstances, Betty Thomas and her husband, Grover, drove to Illinois to pick up Sally.

Betty and Grover visited Thad in the hospital. Betty cried for the loss of Sara and pledged that they would care for Sally as long as Thad needed. The Thomases returned to Mystic with Sally.

During Thad's hospitalization, Betty wrote to him on numerous occasions wishing him a quick recovery and assuring him that when he recovered, she and Grover would drive to Illinois to return Sally to her home. Her letters were never answered.

Betty contacted St. Charles Hospital in Aurora, to inquire as to Thad's condition and to learn of his anticipated release date. She was surprised and dismayed to learn that Thad had been released a week earlier. Dismayed that Thad had not notified them.

She mailed a letter to Thad's home, expressing her gratefulness for his healing and asked when it would be convenient to make the trip to Illinois to return Sally. That letter was returned "Addressee Refused."

Over the months that followed, additional letters addressed to Thad were returned. On one occasion, Betty solicited the help of Kane County to deliver a letter to Thad personally. The County assured Betty the letter was delivered, but no reply was received.

With all logical thought processes failing them, Betty and Grover assumed the long-range responsibility of parenting Sally.

Sally became a blessing to Betty and Grover; their own attempts to have children were unsuccessful. They considered adopting, or not to have children at all. The call from Kane County concerning Thad's accident changed everything. Betty and Grover came to the conclusion that they were Sally's parents.

They chose to delay telling Sally about her father and her deceased mother, or anything else that would, or could, distract from their joy. Sally Murphy became Sally Thomas.

Sally delighted the Thomases with her developing intellect. She did well in school, participated in the few after-school activities. Her parents were not only proud of her, but they centered their lives upon her.

Betty taught Sally to cook, to serve hospitable meals to guests, to sew, to crochet rugs and Afghans, and to clean; Betty loved preparing Sally for a future that Betty hoped would be full and productive.

In the week following Sally's high school graduation, Betty and Grover discussed how they were going to tell Sally about her father, the accident that had taken her mother, and the circumstances that led to her becoming their child. Throughout the years, Betty and Grover broached the content of the imminent discussion, but never concluded with a strategy or a sincere desire to follow through. Their lives were good, Sally's life was good, why complicate things with a story that didn't make sense. But the time was at hand; they felt that Sally had the right to know.

Early on a Saturday evening Grover asked Sally to join him and her mother on the screened-in back porch of their home. Grover, a lifelong resident of Mystic, felt summer evenings in that small Iowa town made the rest of the year worthwhile; the winters could be brutal, but the summers, especially the summer evenings, softened the soul and made one thankful for life in Iowa.

Betty prepared lemonade for them as they sat in wicker chairs and looked out at the expanse of farmland that began beyond the barbed wire fence at the edge of their property. The breeze was warm, the faint aroma of alfalfa drifted in from a field not far away. Grover sucked it in with a deep breath and exhaled with a prayer of thankfulness. He was blessed. But right this moment he would be even more blessed if he did not have to engage in a conversation that felt so cumbersome.

Grover began, "Sally, your mother and I love you more than life itself."

"I know Daddy, I love you too."

"Well Pumpkin, I guess it's time for us to have a talk about how you came to us."

With this, Sally immediately sensed that this was not a conversation of general sorts and sat forward in her chair. "What do you mean, Daddy?" Her heart beat faster as she awaited her father's response.

Grover, with Betty filling in when necessary, told the entire story of Thad and Sara Murphy, the accident, Thad's hospitalization, and with remorse, they told of the many and various attempts to make contact with Thad following his release from the hospital. Sally squirmed as she tried to absorb the unbelievable; she was Sally Thomas, everyone knew her as Sally Thomas, her parents were Grover and Betty Thomas, Grover ran the hardware store and Betty is a housewife, but . . . most importantly, they were Sally Thomas's mom and dad!

Dabbing her eye with a tissue, Betty said, "Honey, we could not love you more. We have always felt that God gave you to us since we could not have children of our own. We delayed this conversation because we wanted to make sure you were old enough to understand, and . . ." Pausing a moment to blow her nose, she continued, "Frankly, we wish we could have gone without ever having this darned conversation at all."

Sally rose, went to Betty, leaned down and wrapped her arms around her mother and hugged her deeply. She went to Grover and sat in his lap and hugged him. After a while she stood and walked over to the screen, she saw the familiar farm land that stretched out before her and smelled the alfalfa, but none of it registered. She tried to take it all in and said, "You've really delivered a wallop tonight. I guess you could say I am stunned, but you should also know that my love for both of you has not changed. I need a little time to let it soak in. Do you mind if I go for a walk?"

"Of course not Pumpkin; if it would help, I would be happy to go with you" responded Grover.

Sally walked to Grover, bent down and kissed him on the cheek. "Daddy, I always want to be with you, but right now I just want to think." She turned to Betty and kissed her on the cheek and said, "I won't be long."

CHAPTER 8

The area around Murphy's place was abuzz with activity. The leaves in the trees could be heard as the breeze came across the tracks. The only other noise was the tension that reverberated off of everything.

As the group of investigators gathered for Henry's briefing, another car pulled onto the grass in front of the house. Pete Morantz recognized it and said, "I asked for additional State investigators when I got the call, I hope you don't mind Henry."

"No Pete, but make sure they know this is County jurisdiction. Fair enough?"

"Fair enough."

The two State investigators made their way to the group. Pete introduced them. Following the introductions, and for Henry's benefit, Pete said, "We're here to help. This is County jurisdiction. What they say goes."

The state investigators looked quizzical, but said, "Sure Pete."

Henry gathered everyone. He wasn't really sure of a strategy, but he wanted to maintain control of the situation, so he began with a review of the facts:

"We know a man named Murphy lives here by himself, a bit of a recluse, with no social connections or activity. He is nowhere to be found, which the locals find extraordinary. Early this morning, around 6:45am, John was sent here to investigate why the front door was open. His investigation revealed blood on a mattress in the old man's bedroom. The house is full of . . ." he paused to find the right word, 'junk', and is definitely going to make our job a challenge. John's investigation eventually took him to the cellar, where he found what we are pretty sure is a crime scene. It's ugly".

He pointed to the cellar doors, "To the right is a big furnace, to the left a work area and bench, between the two and on the floor is a tarp, or a covering, that is covered with blood. On the floor next to the far wall, something is dead. Neither Bob nor I could see it well enough to identify it. It might not be human, but we can't make that assumption at this time. Getting to that corpse is going to be critical, but only after we clear the way by securing all the evidence. I suggest that we send down two of you with cameras. Take shots of everything, but don't go more than two to three feet beyond the entrance at this time. Time your shots so we don't over-expose with a double flash. Oh yeah, watch where you step, a junior G-man", he nodded toward Willy who was sitting by the garage, "followed John down the steps during the initial investigation; he left his breakfast on the floor. That is not a part of the investigation. Any comments or suggestions?"

A state investigator asked, "Does the old man drive a car?"

"Not for the last 25 years or more" Bob responded.

"What's in the garage?"

"According to John, nothing significant, but give a look."

Henry said, "Let's get the shots going in the cellar; and Pete, why don't you and one of your guys start in the house. John will brief you on what to expect. From what I understand, you'll need it."

John had broken off to manage the crowd. He put up ropes along the road to prevent onlookers from moving on to the property. When John lifted the ropes to allow the State investigators to park, the onlookers became more aggressive and began to inch their way closer. John told two of the younger residents who had become too aggressive in their curiosity to leave the area.

Henry called out, "Hey John, we need you over here."

John walked over. Henry told him to brief Pete on the layout of the house.

John replied, "No problem, but you need to get someone on the ropes, those folks are persistent."

"I'll take care of it" replied Henry.

Henry secured help from the volunteer firemen to keep folks back and walked back to Bob, "So what do you think, Bob, are we on the right track?"

"Yeah, it seems so. What do you want me to do?"

"Just keep me out of trouble, Bob. My wife says that's a fulltime job."

Bob looked in the direction of the tracks and said, "I'm troubled about Murphy. For him to leave this place is like having your nose disappear from your face."

Henry replied, "We've got to get to him, but I think the more we can find out about this place, the better equipped we'll be to locate him."

Bob asked, "What's your gut telling you?"

"If pressed to the wall – I'd say he snapped and did something he really didn't want to do, turned tail and ran to get away from it."

Bob thought for a moment, "Ok, let's run with that for a moment. He did something in the cellar, then ran; right?"

"Yep."

"I think we can both agree that whatever happened down there involved more than whatever is wedged between that metal crate and the wall. Right?"

Henry gave this thought, "Probably . . . no, I agree. That is a lot of blood."

"Ok, Murphy runs, but he carried something out; assuming what is against the wall didn't create all that blood. Are you with me?" urged Bob.

"Yes. And, there are drag marks on the steps" added Henry.

"True. But Murphy is around sixty years old, five six or seven, maybe 140 pounds. – how much could he carry and how far?"

Shaking his head contemplatively, Henry said, "I don't know, Bob. Your points are valid, but stranger things have happened."

Bob responds, "Stranger things have happened, but we need to get folks out on a grid search before any signs are trampled or rained on."

"You're right, Bob. Let me call to see if I can shake loose any more bodies from the County."

The investigation proceeded with John assisting Pete and the State investigator in the house, and the investigators lit up the cellar like the fourth of July with the constant flashes.

Bob and Henry made a cursory appraisal of the garage and found nothing out of place; spider webs connected everything, gardening tools that had likely hung on the wall for years, a couple of tires from a Model-A or a Model-T, an old bench with odds and ends.

They walked back to the tracks searching for signs that could support the theory that Murphy left carrying a load. The only thing that was remotely inconsistent was recent scuff marks in the dirt close to the ballast and the tracks. The scuff marks could have been caused by a lot of things. There aren't many deer, but there are a few. Kids play on the tracks all the time. Trainmen will exit a stopped train to stretch their legs. The scuff marks weren't much.

As Bob and Henry headed back to the house, they noticed the investigators emerging from the cellar. Picking up their pace, they got back as the two investigators sat on a piece of log not far from the garage. Willy was talking to them.

"How are you guys doing?" asked Henry.

"We shot the hell out of that cellar; every nook and cranny, every spider, every inch. When the photos are developed, we should have a lot to look at."

"Good job, guys" said Henry. "What's your initial take on the scene?"

"Pretty much the same as yours, however, that corpse, as you called it, is tucked in behind that metal cabinet, it reminds me of the farm at slaughter time. It looks like a side of beef, or hog. I hope like hell it isn't human, because it's not big enough to be an adult human."

Turning toward the front of the house, Henry said, "Yeah, I hope not. When you guys are ready, let me know and we'll advance the investigation. I think we'll send one of you in to start. I'm going to check with the guys in the house."

"We won't be long, we're going to put the camera gear away and secure the film."

Henry walked up the three steps and across the porch. Someone had found the switch to a ceiling light in the front room. Henry's response was as spontaneous as John's initial response. "Holy Jumping Jehoshaphat! Damn, is any of this going to fall on us?" Not really saying it to anyone in particular.

Pete heard Henry and came forward from the back of the house. "Welcome to Shangri-La, Henry. And no, I don't think anything will fall, but don't start climbing."

Examining a particular stack, Henry said, "What in the world was he doing with this?"

"Hey, old fashion bonfires can be fun, Henry. Maybe he has a big one planned for the end of summer."

"That could be. So, what have you boys found so far?" asked Henry.

"They're still at it; John, Bob's man, is assisting in the bedroom. Those two guys (referring to John and his investigator) are both small enough to negotiate the entrance easily. We took pictures of everything, including the bedroom and the rest of the house. They moved the mattress and rug to the van; you can imagine how much fun that was. Henry, guess what we found on the far side of the bed on the floor?"

"No telling" answered Henry.

"A Colt Peacemaker forty-five caliber revolver; my guess is Murphy inherited it from his old man. Heck of a handgun" offered Pete.

"Strange he didn't take it with him" said Henry.

"I'll say; I'd love to own one those peashooters" said Pete. "We discovered another trail through this rubble on the opposite side. It leads to a small bathroom, and . . . get this, a small door off the bathroom leads to another bedroom."

"And you found Murphy napping through this whole thing" offered Henry.

"No, no. Not that. But it was surprising. The bathroom and the other bedroom are reasonably neat. No junk; a bathroom and a bedroom with normal furnishings - and fairly clean. Come on, I'll show you."

Pete walked back disappearing to the right - Henry followed. A narrow slit between the stacks took them to a bathroom, well-lit with ambient light. It was neat and clean, as Pete said, but basic. The commode, the sink and the bathtub were old; claw feet on the bath tub, a pedestal holding up the sink and four pronged handles on the water controls. All were cleaned recently, no rust stains.

The door leading to the bedroom was exceptionally narrow, not more than twenty inches wide. They slipped through it to a small bedroom. The room was to the rest of the house, like a nun is to a brothel. Unlike the rest of the house, jammed with junk, the small bedroom sported a dresser, a quilt covering a single bed, a small table, two wooden chairs with cloth cushions, and a window with thin lace curtains. The curtains were open.

Pete was observing Henry for his reaction.

Henry shook his head and said, "Well, well, well, doesn't this throw everything catawampus?"

"I know Henry, that's how I felt when I saw it. Maybe Murphy needed an escape from the rest of the house and reserved this room for his sanity."

"Have you found anything indicating occupancy by another person?" asked Henry

"Not so far. The drawers are empty. The small closet is empty; no one is hiding under the bed" replied Pete.

"Good work, Pete. I need to get back to the cellar. The shots are done and we are going to start phase two."

Henry made his way from the bathroom and through the narrow pathways of the house. He walked across the porch and to the side of the house.

The tall County investigator was impatiently waiting on him. He said, "Hey boss, I'm ready to go, how do you want me to go about it?"

Sensing he was holding him up, Henry said, "Look, I appreciate the fact that you are a professional and don't need me to tell you what to do, but I'm trying to make sure we use our collective minds to prevent a screw up. So, tell me how you want to do it and we'll use that as the starting point."

"Fair enough. I think I should split the basement in two; I'll do one side . . ." he said while nodding toward the left side of the cellar, "then I do the other. I will start where we were standing for the shots and work both sides methodically gathering anything I think will help and take kits for testing. I'll do my best to avoid contact with the blood, if possible. Once I've worked both sides, I'll try to identify the dead thing and extract it at that time."

"Good plan. I'll watch from the doorway, if you don't mind" said Henry.

"Don't mind at all."

CHAPTER 9

The diner is a meeting place. Food is served, but is the byproduct for many of its visitors. The diner was a place to discuss just about anything; a place to talk and to hear other views of current events. It was a place to go when every other place didn't seem right.

Crafted right out of a magazine ad; the diner's long counter of worn white Masonite had little chrome fence devices holding salt, pepper, ketchup and mustard containers that lined the back edge. Tattered-edged, food-stained menus stuck up from the fences like weathered billboards. The seats of the chrome stools were covered with red shiny Naugahyde, as were the seats of three small booths that were positioned along the windows on the right. The multi-colored Wurlitzer juke box in the corner brought Buddy Holly, The Coasters, Elvis, The Diamonds and other musical brilliants to the patrons of the diner. The presence of the grease-laden grill permeated the air like an invisible fog. Yep, this was a diner.

Nick grabbed the booth farthest from the door, Stan and Nick on one side facing the door, with Butch comfortably spread out and occupying the other side.

The waitress adorned with the pocketed white apron wrapped around her bulging waist and the white waitress-hat pinned to her hair, approached the booth with her order pad and almost paid attention to them: "What'll it be boys?"

Nick said, "Cherry coke please."

Butch said, "Aren't you going to eat, Nick? Man, I'm hungry."

"No, you go ahead and order, Butch."

Butch glanced up at the chalkboard hanging behind the counter revealing the daily specials. "I'll have a California cheeseburger, fries, and a chocolate malt."

Stan said, "A Seven-up and fries. Thanks."

After the waitress was behind the counter, Nick said, "Man, what did you guys think about what Charlie said about old man Murphy?"

Butch's eyes grew excited. "I knew it involved serious shit. Like Charlie said, for thirty years this guy's been letting it build up, and one day – POW, it all breaks loose. I mean, all those cop cars and the Coroner, come on, they don't send that many cars without a dead body."

"No, Butch, that's not exactly how I heard it, but I mean about old man Murphy being one guy years ago, and another guy now, and his pretty wife gets killed – that stuff."

"Oh, yeah, I'm not sure I got all that. I mean it was a good story, but what did it have to do with old man Murphy killing somebody? Don't take me wrong, Charlie's great, man, but, well, I wish he could have told us more about what was going on. You know what I mean?" answered Butch.

Stan thought for a moment and said, "I think Charlie knew that guy pretty well way back then. Don't you?"

Nick responded, "Yeah, he was pretty clear on the story he was telling. Old man Murphy, weird or not, wouldn't vamoose without a reason. And, to Butch's defense, Murphy's place is getting a lot of attention. This is exciting, but in a sick kind of a way. Did you guys ever imagine when you woke up this morning that we'd be chasing down anything this big? This whole thing is getting hard to figure out."

The waitress returned with Butch's burger and fries in one hand and balancing all three drinks in the other arm. Placing the items on the table top, she said, "Anything else, boys?" and turned back toward the counter without waiting for a reply.

Once she was gone, Butch whispered, "Yes, you can kiss my ass if you call us "boys" again. She is such a bitch!"

They laughed. Nick said, "Butch, you are on a roll today. First you compare Phil to the runs, and here you have your pants down in the diner waiting to get a kiss."

"Hey, I'm a funny guy, you know that." Butch look genuinely surprised that anyone would doubt his obviously humorous talents.

"Yeah, you're funny to look at. Besides, she forgot my fries" added Stan.

Butch concentrated on consuming the cheeseburger, slurping the malt in between bites. Nick and Stan sat lost in their thoughts.

At the other end of the diner, the door opened, Nick recognized Andy Durham as he walked in. Andy was three years older than them, and attended the Junior High in Aurora, and unlike some of the older boys, he always treated them with respect. His folks farmed a small parcel of land on the west side of the tracks on Baseline Road.

Andy looked around the diner. When he saw the three boys, he walked straight to them. "Hey guys, how ya doing?"

Nick answered, "Doing good, Andy, how you doing?"

"Oh, fair to midlin', I guess - you know I'm working at the sheep yards, don't ya?"

"No man, I didn't. Making a lot of money?"

"Not really; it's nasty work. Besides, I have to help out my folks with a part of my earnings, but we'll be back in school in another month. This is my day off."

"Hey, sit down and join us" offered Nick. "Slide over Butch."

"Naw, I can't, but thanks. Do you guys know Beth McVee?"

Nick was surprised by the mention of Beth's name. "Yeah, she goes to school with us. Why?"

"Her folks are worried cause they don't know if she was home last night, but she wasn't in her room this morning. They're getting all twisted up about it; they told my folks, and they sent me out to find her. You haven't seen her have you?"

Nick answered, "No, not since I saw her at a Little League game a couple of weeks ago. What do you mean her folks don't know if she was home last night?"

"Her folks don't have much; they live in that ramshackle house not far from the tracks; the old man is the night watchman at Miller's Tool & Die and he leaves for work at, like, six at night. Her mom waits tables at that truck stop on Route 34, and doesn't get home until eleven. When her mom got home last night she figured Beth was in bed, so she turned in herself. The old man got home around seven this morning and looked in on Beth, but she wasn't in her room. They came to our place hoping she was playing with our goats. She likes them goats. Damn, this is my day off and I'm chasing a dizzy schoolgirl because her parents can't keep track of her. You guys have any ideas?"

"Where have you been so far?" asked Stan.

"I rode up to the school, rode up through the New Addition, I checked the grocery store, and rode the streets toward Western Electric. I don't know where else to look. She's probably at a friend's house playing with dolls, and I rode right by her and didn't know it. Hey, what's going on over on Railroad Street?"

That was what Butch was waiting for, "Oh man, we think old man Murphy murdered someone in his cellar. We've been scoping it out all morning. Did you see all the cops?"

"What? Who got murdered?" asked Andy.

Stan jumped in, "Please disregard the clown sitting across from me, Andy. We don't know that anyone has been murdered, but we do know a big investigation is going on. Old man Murphy is missing, and Willy Smith said he saw a lot of blood in the cellar."

"And something dead!" blurted Butch.

"Yeah, and something dead; but, really, that's all we know right now" offered Stan.

With a suspicious look, Andy asked Nick, "Are these yokels pulling my leg?"

"No, 'fraid not Andy" answered Nick, "But let's get back to your problem. Does Beth get lost often?"

"I don't think so, but I don't really know, Nick. I see her around my place. Like I said, she likes to play with our goats; she'll help

Mom with the other critters on the weekend. She doesn't seem like the type that would run away, or do something real stupid" replied Andy.

"Have you checked the cemetery and the mausoleum?" asked Nick

"No. Why would she be in a mausoleum?"

Stan interjected, "It's a hang out. The mausoleum has been locked up for years, but we've found a way in. It's kind of cool; spooky as hell on Halloween. Some say it's haunted, but I've never seen a ghost. We need to check it."

Nick added, "Yeah, what about Jefferson Street by the river? Someone built a neat hut down there and it's getting a lot of attention lately."

Butch quickly offered, "I'll say, Robby Morgan said he caught Gerry Percasky and Jack Bennet making out in that hut last week."

"Thank you Hedda Hopper, for the latest in social encounters and sexual activities in, and around, the greater Montgomery community" Stan offered sarcastically.

Butch responded defensively, "Well, it's true, man. Robby doesn't lie."

Nick said, "Ok, Ok, we have the cemetery and we have Jefferson; where else?"

"Do you think she knows any of the girls that live in the small apartments on River near Western Electric?" asked Stan.

Andy shrugged his shoulders.

Nick began to slide out of the booth, "Let's start with what we have. Andy and I will head to the cemetery, you guys head to Jefferson and on to the apartments. It's going to take us longer to check the whole cemetery, so when you're done, ride up and we'll meet on the west side of the cemetery across from the junkyard."

"Hey, wait a minute. What about old man Murphy's?" asked Butch.

"What about it? It's not going anywhere; you guys can ride past it when you're heading our way. Ride real close to it Butch, maybe they'll arrest you" answered Nick while smiling.

They left the money on the table for the food and drinks; exact change – no tip.

CHAPTER 10

Leaving the diner, Butch and Stan headed to Jefferson Street, Nick and Andy took Webster and turned right on Main Street which runs between and parallels Railroad and River for the entire length of Montgomery. After they traveled a couple of blocks, the majority of the west side of Main Street is occupied by Lyon Metal, a large factory. On the right is a cinder covered parking lot for the factory, the ball field for the school, the school, and the west edge of the cemetery. The factory on the west side ends, and the intriguing junkyard begins.

The junkyard with its stacks of old cars, the mean dogs on heavy chains and a few cars for sale out front was a natural attraction for an explorer. Nick's dad had taken him to the junkyard a few times to find parts for cars that his dad was repairing. Nick was looking forward to his next opportunity to explore the junkyard.

On the right side of Main Street, Riverside Cemetery occupied all the land between Main and River, with most of the gravesites being on the River Street side. The west side was being reserved for future inhabitants.

Nick and Andy rode their bikes onto the gravel road entering the cemetery. They skirted the edge of the school property and quickly became surrounded by trees, bushes, gravesites, and a labyrinth of gravel roads leading to different sections of the cemetery. Positioned in the central portion of the cemetery was an ominous stone mausoleum, surrounded by tall bushes. It seemed out of place. Due to its age, it was condemned; chains and locks secured the large brass doors on the side facing River Street.

A couple of years ago, Nick, and others, crawled beneath the bushes on the backside of the mausoleum and found a window at ground level with bars across the outside. It didn't take long to bend and remove the bars, and voila, they were in. It became the place to play cards, or to take girls to scare them, to smoke cigarettes, or to simply hang out.

After Nick and Andy rode the majority of the gravel roads, they headed to the back of the mausoleum and stashed their bikes behind the bushes. They did this for two reasons: First, if the cemetery caretaker happened along, the bikes would be a dead giveaway that the boys were in the condemned building; secondly, because some explorers saw this opportunity to demonstrate their sick sense of humor, they liked to snatch haplessly discarded bikes and hide them. Though this usually proved to be only a momentary period of panic, it was a pain in the ass to find the hidden bikes.

Nick led the way to the point of entry, "Hang on, I have to piss like a racehorse." Andy joined him, only aiming in another direction. When they both finished, they entered the bushes.

Down on all fours they crawled beneath the bushes and came to the window. Nick warned, "When we get in you'll have to wait for your eyes to adjust to the darkness, the only light is from the windows up high along the roofline."

Nick and Andy crawled in. Nick called out, "Hey Beth, you in here?" His voice bounced off the stone walls and brass markers, reverberating for seconds, but with no response.

Andy was awed, not to mention spooked by the sight of the brass covered drawers that presumably held dead bodies, said, "And you guys actually hang out in here?"

"Yeah, it takes a while to get used to, but it's cool because adults aren't going to be crawling in here. I've got to tell you a story. Do you know Carol Purdy and Shelly Bates?" asked Nick.

"Yeah, I think I do, why?"

"Well, earlier this spring, Stan and I coaxed them into this place. It was dusk and we used flashlights. They wanted to smoke cigarettes; we just wanted to get them in here. We sat right over there." Nick pointed at the corner to the southweSt. "They were comfortable in this place, and more importantly they were comfortable sitting pretty close by us. Things were progressing and would have progressed faster if I'd known what to do, but we were enjoying ourselves. Then . . .walk over here Andy, I'll show you something." They walked around the center drawers.

The entire center of the building was occupied by a bank of drawers. Each drawer is 26" high by 34" wide stacked four drawers high on each side. The caskets in the drawers were arranged so that the feet of the body in the north row met the feet of the body on the south row. The brass plates stated the name, dates of birth and death, and personal comments about the occupant in the drawer.

When Nick and Andy rounded the corner of the center drawers, Nick said, "See that?" pointing at a brass plate on the concrete floor in the northeast corner.

"Yeah" said Andy.

Nick continued, "We were sitting in the corner, smoking cigarettes and planning on something more entertaining and – KAPOW!! That brass plate picked that moment to fall off the drawer. Andy, it sounded like an explosion in here. We all scrambled for the window. I was surprised that Stan and I let the girls go out first; instead of knocking them aside to escape from whatever made that noise. Pushing the girls, we were on their tails to get out of here. Carol was the first out. By the time I got out she was already pedaling her bike out of the cemetery. Shelly was gasping for breath blaming us that it was bad joke. We swore it wasn't. She believed us and we rode after Carol. We never caught her; by the time we got to her house, her bike was in her front yard and she was out of sight. We were worried that she would tell her parents and we'd all be in trouble. We found out later that she didn't ride home because of fear; she wet her pants and didn't want any of us to know it. She ended up telling Shelly and Shelly told us." Nick shook his head while smiling.

"Andy, it was a couple of weeks before we mustered the courage to climb back in to find out what made the noise. When we saw the brass plate and the big nick in the concrete we knew right away. Butch was with us and said the guy in the drawer pushed the plate off."

"This is a pretty creepy hang out" said Andy.

"No kidding. I don't think Carol and Shelly would accept an invitation to an ice cream social at the church, if we asked them."

"Can you blame them? We're all looking for good make-out places, but a mausoleum, Nick?"

"Hey, we tried" answered Nick sheepishly.

Turning toward the window, Andy said, "She's not here, and I'm not getting used to the creepy place, so let's head out."

Once outside and brushing off the dirt, Nick said, "Sorry, but at least we checked, and we know where she isn't."

"Damn it! This is my day off."

"Hey, we'll find her. Let's go wait for Stan and Butch."

Shortly after arriving at the west side, they saw the bikes heading their way. Based on the lack of enthusiasm, the results did not seem promising. "Well?" asked Nick "Any luck?"

"No way" responded Stan. "I think everyone in town is over on Railroad Street gawking at Murphy's place."

"Did you look there?" asked Andy.

"Yeah, but I had to keep track of bungling Butch here. Every time I turned around he was off trying to get one of the gawkers to tell him about the murder. The fact is no one on the outside knows any more than we do, and most have no idea of a murder. I got him out of there."

Butch was quick to add, "Hey, that's how you solve crimes, by asking questions. You never know what you'll learn 'til you ask."

Stan and Butch laid their bikes down and joined Nick and Andy on the grass. They sat in silence each hoping that someone else would have something constructive to say.

Andy broke the silence, "Hey guys, I appreciate your help, but I'm heading for home. I don't know where else to look, and it isn't my problem. She's probably home by now anyway."

Feeling unusually compassionate for Andy's dilemma, Butch offered, "Phil lives not far from here, why don't we ask him to help?"

"Phil Glaston?" Andy asked.

"Yeah, Phil the pill" said Butch

"Does he hang around with you guys?"

"Yeah, why?" answered Nick.

"It's nothing. I just feel really sorry for him" said Andy.

"Sorry? Holy crap! Why would you feel sorry for him? " asked Butch.

"What do you know about him?" asked Andy.

"Well, Phil is the man with the plan. Phil is a legend in his own mind. If you don't believe it, just ask Phil; he'll tell you" snapped Butch.

"No, I mean do you know anything about his family life?" urged Andy.

"Not much. He lives right over there on Sard" . . . pointing toward the Glastons. ". . . as Butch said, he can be obnoxious at times, but he's OK" answered Nick.

"Don't take me wrong, I don't know much about him either, but his brothers are king-sized assholes" said Andy. "Earlier this spring, a couple of us guys met up with Kurt and Benjy, Phil's older brothers. I think there are four in all, and I heard the oldest is in jail, but I don't know that for sure. Anyway, we met up with them. They drive that souped-up black '49 Ford with the fender skirts and louvered hood."

"Yeah, I've seen it around town. They drive like maniacs" added Stan.

"Yeah, they do more than drive like maniacs. Anyway, we thought it would be cool to ride around rather than pedal when they offered to take us for a spin. Phil was tagging along with them. We piled into the backseat with Phil. We cruised up to Aurora to a hole-in-the-wall liquor store. Benjy, the bigger of the two assholes, asked everyone to kick in money for beer. We gave him a couple of bucks and he went in and came out with three six packs of beer. At that point, I thought, 'Assholes, or not, this was going to be a good day.'"

"Are they old enough to drink?" asked Butch.

"Hell no" answered Andy. "But, Benjy bought it, and we were going to drink it. Have you guys ever been in the old deserted Mill?"

Nick answered. "Yeah, from the river side; we waded through the water and the muck and crawled through the hole in the back."

Andy continued, "You can avoid the muck if you slither through a loose plank this side of that hole. That's what we did. We went in and climbed up to the ground floor and broke out the beer. Benjy gave each of us a beer and we were sucking them down like there was no tomorrow. After a couple of beers, Kurt said to Phil, 'Hey, do you want to see some magazines of naked ladies?'"

Phil had to be feeling the beer, because I was, so he said, 'Sure.'

Kurt led him to that small room in the back that doesn't have windows, and said, "You'll find a stack of them on the floor at the back wall, go get them and bring them out for all of us."

"Phil went in to get the magazines; Kurt shut the door and wedged a two-by-four between the handle of the door and floor; he and Benjy, the moron, began laughing like crazy. I could hear Phil pleading with them to open the door, but that made them laugh even more. Here's the part that makes me sick; Benjy and Kurt grabbed the rest of the beer and made for the ladder. As they passed the closed door Benjy asked, "Is the snake still in there?" Kurt responded, 'You bet your ass it is!' I really didn't know what to do, and frankly, I wasn't thinking real straight anyway, so we left with the assholes. When we got to the car, I asked, "Are you going to leave him locked up?" That made them laugh again and they said, "No man, we'll come back and get the pussy." "What about the snake?" I asked, because we see water moccasins in the river all the time. Kurt answered, "There ain't no snake, man. We just wanted to give him something to think about." They dropped us off and that was it. It was starting to get dark so I rode home and thought about it all night; to be in a room without light and to wonder where the snake was. Damn! I happened to see Phil the next day, so I knew they let him out, but what assholes! Can you imagine doing that to your brother?"

The three boys shook their heads.

"No man, I can't. We all do weird shit from time to time, but that is some gone shit" said Stan.

"I wonder why Phil has never told us about that?" asked Butch.

Nick offered quickly, "Why would he do that? It is his family. Would you want the world to know that you live with screwed-up assholes like that? I wouldn't. Sometimes I have a hard time with Phil, but maybe this explains some of it."

Getting up and heading toward his bike, Andy said, "Thanks again, guys. I'm sorry I wasted your time."

"Don't mention it" said Nick. "Could you let us know if Beth's parents find her?"

"Yeah, I'll get word to you somehow. Do your parents have a phone?"

"Yep."

"I'll have my mom call yours."

"Thanks Andy" said Nick.

Andy was already pedaling when he said, "See you cats later."

CHAPTER 11

Nick's interest in Beth McVee was more than general interest. About a month before school let out, Nick stayed after school to help his football coach, Coach Lee, rearrange the equipment room. It wasn't a big job and he finished in an hour. On his way out of the building, he saw Beth McVee, who was twenty or thirty feet ahead him.

Nick had been noticing Beth in school. She was a tiny thing, with auburn hair, a pretty face, long eye lashes and eyes that were like pools. Nick was smitten with her beauty. He remembered times he said Hi to her, but didn't have the nerve to talk with her. Some of Nick's friends were girls and he wasn't reluctant to talk with them, but his feelings toward Beth were different. He even talked to Charlie about her.

Sitting on the steps of Shannon's tavern, Nick began asking Charlie how to approach the unapproachable. Charlie knew right away that Nick was "sweet on her," as Charlie put it. Nick denied it at first, but, realized Charlie was going to see through it, so he admitted that he liked her, but didn't know how to approach her.

Charlie, who knew how to get to the root of the matter in seconds, simply said, "Nick, if you care about someone, you have to let them know, or they will skate through life never knowing they missed out on a good friend."

"But I don't know what to say to her" explained Nick.

"That's a good point, Nicky-boy. If you say the wrong thing, you could drive her off. If you don't say anything at all, she won't know how you feel. So, that leaves us with finding the right thing to say so you both feel good about what has been said."

"And what is the right thing, Charlie?" asked Nick.

"I don't know Nick; you're the one that knows her, not me. What do you know about her?"

"Well ..." feeling embarrassed, Nick said, "I know she's pretty."

"That's a start, Nick, but some ladies might think you are being forward if you start by discussing their beauty. At her age, I can almost guarantee that she doesn't think of herself as being pretty. Do you think you are handsome, Nick?"

"No!"

"Chances are her self-appraisal is equally as critical as yours."

"So what do I say?"

"Come on, Nicky-boy, you're a bright fellow. What else do you know about her? Does she drive a car?"

Knowing Charlie was fooling with him, Nick said, "No."

"What does she do?"

"Well, she seems to read a lot cause she tells about the stories she reads."

"OK Nick, that is getting us somewhere. Now what was the last story she told?"

"I ... I'm not sure?"

"Think Nicky-boy, your love life is dependent upon it. Think."

"Let me see ... oh yeah, she was telling about a big earthquake in California. It brought down buildings and left huge cracks in the earth, and people were stranded, without homes, without water, and ..."

"That's good enough, Nick, you have found a temporary key to her heart."

"What do you mean?"

"Nick, she was proud to share with you and her other class-mates what she read about earthquakes. My bet is that she could have gone on talking about it, but the teacher probably said that the class should move on, or another contributor needed to share about their reading."

"You're right, she did."

"Now you let her know that you would like hear what the teacher made her stop telling."

"Charlie, where'd you learn this stuff?"

"It's all a matter of observation and paying attention, Nicky-boy."

So, with Charlie's fine counsel in mind, Nick called out to Beth, "Hi Beth."

Surprised, Beth turned around. "Hi Nick, what are you doing here?"

"Helping Coach Lee down in the equipment room, how about you?"

"I stayed after to work with Miss Merrill on a story I'm trying to write" said Beth.

"A story; are you a writer?" Nick asked as they continued to walk down the sidewalk leading to Main Street.

"No, but maybe someday. Miss Merrill is encouraging me to write a story to be submitted to a kid's magazine. She says I have talent, whatever that means" she said with a shrug.

"Oh, you do have talent" Nick said, almost too quickly.

"How would you know, Nick Corrie? You've never read anything I've written."

Stuttering slightly, Nick said, "N-N-No, but I have heard the stories you tell in school, and they're really good."

"Like what?"

"Like the California earthquakes, the cracks they leave in the earth, and destruction of the buildings, and people going without water, that stuff." Nick felt his lungs tightening and his voice going up an octave.

Beth stopped walking and turned to face Nick, "I think you were actually listening to me, Nick."

"I was, Beth, and I'd like to hear more since Miss Merrill cut you off."

"Nick, she didn't cut me off. We ran out of time. She's a wonderful teacher."

"Yeah, I like her too, but she is tough."

"Would you like to hear about the earthquakes now?" asked Beth.

"You bet" responded Nick - silently thanking Charlie for the tip.

They walked down Main Street while Beth told of the disastrous effects of earthquakes. Nick heard most of what Beth said, but found himself enamored by her smell, her looks, her expressions, and, of course, by the very fact that he was walking with her, alone. He'd never walked with a girl before, well, he'd walked with girls before, but not like this walking. Man, did he like her. They walked on until they reached Watkins Street on the far south side of town.

When they stopped, Beth said, "Nick, you live way back there" pointing in the direction of the school "Did you mean to walk this far?"

Being caught off guard, Nick stammered and said, "Oh – well, my aunt lives down by the river and I thought I'd stop in to say Hi."

Beth gave him a playful smile and said, "Thanks for walking with me."

Feeling like he'd been caught in a lie, he offered, "That's OK, I really wanted to hear about the earthquakes. Hey, by the way, where do you live?"

With an almost unnoticeable dipping of her head in the direction of the railroad tracks, she said, "Over there."

"Hey, I'd, um, be glad to walk you the rest of the way" said Nick

"That's Ok, Nick, my folks are waiting on me, but thanks again for walking with me; I enjoyed it." With that she turned and began walking briskly west on Watkins and toward the tracks.

Not really sure of what happened, Nick yelled after her, "I liked it too - see you tomorrow."

Nick headed for home, more confused than ever. Did he screw this up? She was talking like a magpie and seemed to be enjoying it, but without warning, it was over like a bad ending to a movie. "Man, this girl's stuff is crazy stuff" he thought. ". . . and where was her house?" He quickly scanned his mind for the lay of the land in the direction she indicated; the brush factory, the back entrance to

Western Electric, which was guarded, the railroad crossing . . . that's it. No houses existed in the direction she indicated. Was she trying to mislead him, or play a game on him? The more he thought, the faster he walked. With no recollection of the walk home, he was suddenly entering his house.

The next day Nick was tired. He had a rough night replaying every minute of his walk with Beth the day before. He pictured her turning to him and saying, "Hi Nick, what are you doing here?" and every movement she made, and every word she said during every step of the journey. Those were precious, enchanting memories, but the Watkins flip-and-switch performance left him feeling empty. He kept thinking, What could he have done to cause the reversal? Just a moment before she gave him that cute smile that made him melt on the inside, then, BAM, she was gone.

When he arrived at school, he didn't head over to the basketball court where the guys would be horsing around, but instead, he headed up the steps into the school. He entered Miss Merrill's room, the first room on the left, thinking he would go to his desk and sit back and think some more. Entering, he saw Beth at her desk. His first thought was to quietly ease back out of the room without being noticed. Beth looked up. The room ignited with her smile, "Hi Nick." Beth said with enthusiasm.

"Hey Beth," Nick responded. "Working on your story?"

"Yes. When it's finished, would you like to read it?" she asked.

"Uh, sure. Absolutely. When is it going to be done?" Nick was thrilled; this was another opportunity to spend time with her.

"In a couple of days, maybe more, but to get it entered, Miss Merrill said I need to finish it."

"Yes, I really want to read it."

More kids were now entering the room. Nick wasn't sure he wanted to broadcast his new interest in Beth, so he went out to the drinking fountain. His heart was racing and he felt jittery. "What's going on?" He thought "I've got to get to Charlie!"

He found Charlie sitting on the steps that afternoon and gave him the blow-by-blow account of every step of his walk with Beth. When he came to the end, Charlie laughed as hard as Nick could ever remember seeing him laugh before. "What's so funny, Charlie?"

Charlie leaned back and looked at Nick, smiled broadly, and said "You are what is so funny, Nick."

"Me? What'd I do that was funny?"

"You were being a man, and that's always funny." Charlie was enjoying this.

"Charlie, you are really confusing me."

"Nick, I am sorry. I am not laughing at your expense, I am laughing because you are a man, and men are fragile beings capable of severe stupidity at times. You see, men think one way, and women think another. The problem is men can never think like women, no matter how hard they try. When they can't, they get frustrated and start blaming themselves, or blaming the woman; when in fact, blame isn't the problem at all. It's just the way it is. What happened yesterday is a perfect example of what I am trying to say. You were cruising along, walking on clouds, but suddenly your world hit the mat, Gorgeous George had you on your back and the ref was counting to three. Right?"

"Right."

"That's because something in Beth's mind told her it was time to go, and she was going, and you weren't going to stop her. That's all. Then today she is happy as a clam to see you. And you, you stagger around banging your head against the wall, feeling pretty stupid, wondering what the hell is going on." Charlie started laughing again.

"Charlie, I still don't get it. Why'd she have to go? Why didn't she want me to walk on with her?"

Charlie's laughing continued, "There you go again. Asking questions only a woman can answer, and they won't because they know they got us. First thing you have to get in your head is, when it comes to relationships, women are smarter than you. Maybe Beth realized she needed to go to the bathroom and she couldn't wait for your lollygagging butt, or maybe she remembered she had something to do, or maybe, she didn't want you to walk her to her house." Charlie paused before he said the last part.

"Well, why not?"

"For a bright boy, you are a slow learner on this subject, Nicky-boy - because that's the way they think. That's all. Don't try to figure it out, just roll with the punches and you'll stay somewhat sane. Keep asking those dumb questions and you'll end up like this dumb old man."

"Charlie, you're not a dumb old man, you're one of the smartest guys I've ever known."

"Nicky-boy, that's a nice compliment, but you haven't known many men yet."

"So, what do I do?"

"Nick, roll with the punches, and don't try to figure her out. She is in control."

"Thanks for your help, Charlie."

Nick walked home with Beth a few times before the end of the school year. He read her story and was impressed, he wondered how much she had written and how much Miss Merrill had written for her, but knowing Miss Merrill, he felt he was wrong about that. Miss Merrill would have guided her, but Miss Merrill would not have written for her. Beth was anxious to see if the story would get published.

Nick and Beth kept their interest in each other hidden from the schoolyard rumor mill. They witnessed the foolishness erupting when anyone got wind of a suspected romance, so they limited their time together during the walks to Watkins Street, purposely delaying them until the schoolyard cleared out.

During these walks they talked about school, the kids in school, Nick's friends, the adventures Nick and his friends created, but never a lot about Beth. Nick wanted to learn more about her, but she was clever. Whenever he would ask about her family, or her interests, beyond writing, she would get him talking about one of his screwy friends, or one of the crazy things that Nick had done. She'd laugh at the funny stuff and showed sincere interest in the stuff that was more serious. But inevitably, before Nick learned anything about her, Watkins Street came up and they both knew the conversation was over.

One time, as they were about to say goodbye, Beth took Nick's hand and said, "Nick, I want you to know how much I enjoy talking with you."

Nick didn't know what to do; he loved the touch of her soft skin and her tiny fingers. He could feel the joints of fingers and the palm of her hand, and her body heat; it was like touching something sacred and holy. He loved it.

Fumbling for words, he said, "Thanks."

Beth smiled that delicious smile, turned and headed west on Watkins.

Afterward, Nick stood dumbfounded. With the feel of her hand indelibly written in his mind, he thought, "Thanks? THANKS? That's the best you have to offer, you dumbshit, you cow-licking piece of dung, you dog humping dickhead? You are a moron! THANKS? Damn it!" He walked while emotionally giving himself a beating that kept him busy all the way home.

The next time they neared Watkins, Nick timidly took Beth's hand and said, "Beth, I don't think I responded . . ., well, what I mean is, when you took my hand I was, well, I liked it – a lot, but I wasn't expecting it, and I think I was tongue-tied."

"Really Nick, I didn't notice" Beth offered playfully.

"Oh come on, you must have noticed."

She paused, smiled and said, "Yes I did, but I chalked it up to you being shy."

Nick immediately responded as if he was defending his manhood, "I'm not shy!"

"You are around me. You act differently around me than you do the rest of the kids at school."

"I don't mean to, it's just that . . . well, you are different."

"How am I different?" she asked, knowing Nick was struggling terribly, "Do I have spinach on my teeth? Or do I smell funny?"

"No, no, that's not it, I . . . feel differently about you. I really like talking with you, and being with you. You make me feel . . . well, good, I guess."

With that, Beth leaned forward and placed a light kiss on Nick's cheek and said, "Nick Corrie, I like you too." She turned and was gone.

Nick floated home that day. He must have passed thirty houses, countless cars of people, crossed streets, but missed it all as he floated on his delirious dream.

Due to various reasons, that was the last time Nick walked home with Beth before the end of the school year. They talked privately when they could at school, and promised to look for each other during the summer vacation, but that happened only once, during the Little League game. Since then, Nick lived with the wonderful recollection of her brief kiss, which he replayed continuously in his mind. Next year would be easier for them; they would be in Franklin Junior High in Aurora, a much bigger school and much easier to get lost in all the commotion.

CHAPTER 12

After that fateful Saturday night talk in 1944 with her parents, Sally began to wonder about what life might have been if that accident, so many years ago, never happened. What would her real mom have been like, and what happened to her real dad? Is he alive? Does he care if she is alive?

She wanted to go back to life before that talk on that Saturday night; a life that was clean, simple, easy to understand and absent from these haunting questions. She tried to flush them away, but she couldn't. She felt that she needed answers to return to normalcy. The thoughts gnawed at her.

Even going to her dad's hardware store had changed. She used to love going to help her dad distribute new shipments of stock, price label items, and she was even helping with the books and inventory. Both Grover and Sally thought she might take over the business when Grover decided to retire, but neither ever voiced their thoughts to one another.

Now, going to the hardware store wasn't the same. The enchantment had been stolen; but by whom? Nothing in Mystic changed, only a conversation on a Saturday night between three people who loved each another. Those thoughts! Why was it important? Who cared what happened sixteen years ago that no one could control? Sally concluded that she cared, but she didn't know why.

Sally had been seeing Tom Shrader, a boy who lived on a farm a few miles from her house. They had gone to school together and recently graduated together.

Tom was eighteen while Sally just turned sixteen. Sally was bright. The school in Mystic blended students from four grades and advanced them on their academic achievement. Sally had skipped the third and seventh grades.

During their high school years Tom and Sally became friends, then closer friends and eventually became known as a couple. Sally really enjoyed her time with Tom. They attended school dances together, fished the creek out on Junction Road together, went to movies together and listened to the serials on the radio together on Sally's back porch. Occasionally, Sally would even help Tom with farm chores. They meshed their lives.

Sally and Tom were careful when it came to expressing their physical attraction for one another. Grover and Betty would have a kitten if they knew their little girl was exploring the sensual side of life, but it seemed natural, comfortable and fun.

Mystic was so small that everyone knew, not only everyone else, but what everyone else was doing on any given day of the week. Finding a place to spoon was difficult, but they managed. They managed in Tom's old car, before or after the movies; sometimes at Sally's house if Grover and Betty were gone, or in the barn at Tom's parents' farm.

Sally loved to hold Tom close to her and smell his masculine smell. He was strong, but gentle. Tom wanted to explore all aspects for sensuality, but Sally had reservations. She enjoyed it when Tom would slip his hand inside her bra and played with her breasts, and Sally was always pleased to see that she caused a bump in Tom's pants.

On one occasion, following a Saturday night movie, Tom and Sally were parked behind the hardware store. Sally was wearing a dress. She was engrossed in the kissing, the holding and Tom's touching. Without her realizing it, Tom slipped his hand up her dress and was touching her and she was enjoying it, absolutely lost in ecstasy, when abruptly she stopped him. She was more embarrassed by her own enjoyment than by his actions. Feeling guilty because Tom was confused, she wrapped her arms around his neck and said, "Later Tom, later." She wanted to go farther in the worst way, but she was going to wait.

Then that Saturday night discussion with Betty and Grover came. Everything changed. She wanted to be with Tom, but felt uncomfortable when she was. She wanted the splendor of holding a prolonged kiss with him, knowing his pants were growing tighter, but the splendor was stolen as well. He begged repeatedly to learn what was wrong, but she swore that everything was fine. Tom knew better and his visits were less and less frequent over the next four weeks.

Eventually, Sally learned that Tom was seeing Sherry Strong, another of their classmates. This should have been devastating for Sally, but it wasn't. She felt bad, but accepted it as a part of the change.

Late one afternoon, Sally walked out to the screened-in back porch to find Betty mending socks. Grover was still at the hardware store. Sally plopped down in one of the wicker chairs and said, "Mom, tell me about my real mom."

Betty was prepared for this conversation and put the mending kit aside. "I've been waiting for you to ask, honey. I wanted you to pick the timing. I guess now is the time. Where would you like me to start?"

"I don't know. Tell me what she was like, what did she look like, would have I liked her, did she have family . . . you know, that kind of stuff."

"You want to know it all, but I may not have all the answers, but I'll give it a whirl. Your mom was one of the most beautiful ladies I have ever known. She was five foot tall and weighed barely more than a feather. She had gorgeous light blond hair, and eyes that drew a person in. Sometimes they were blue and other times they were greenish blue, but always pleasant to look at. She was kind and personable. She told me that her folks had her late in life and had died. I think she came from stock a little higher than mine and your father's. I really think that had we lived closer, we would have become real friends."

"How much time did you spend with her?" asked Sally.

"Oh honey, hardly none at all. We were invited to Thad's wedding; that was the first time I met her. The wedding was filled with so much hubbub I didn't get to know her at all. But on another occasion, we drove to Illinois to meet with Thad's and my cousins. It was then that your mom and I spent time together. That's when I began to get to know her."

"Tell me about the wedding, please."

"What an affair, it was out of a storybook; it was 1926. Nothing in the entire state of Iowa can compare. Grover and I were so far out of our league that we kept looking at one another trying to figure out what we were supposed to do." Betty chuckled.

"The wedding took place in a big protestant church in Aurora, Illinois, I can't remember which one, but I remember the reception. How could I forget it? On an island in the middle of the Fox River, in the center of downtown Aurora, is a twenty-two story building called the Leland Hotel. It was just built; the largest building in Illinois, outside of Chicago. And on the top floor was a ballroom, and that is where Thad hosted the reception. Honey, it was regal! Everything was perfect; Thad even paid for an ice sculpture. It was beautiful, and Sara was beautiful, and Thad was Thad. And honey, the view from the ballroom on the top floor made me dizzy; I'll bet we could have seen Iowa we were so high."

"What did you mean when you said "Thad was Thad?" asked Sally.

"Well honey, I guess Thad was a lot different from me and the other cousins. We are down-home-spun folks that don't put on the airs. But, Thad broke all the barriers, he hobnobbed with the best, wore the best, drove the best and wanted everyone to know it. He was kind enough to all of us, but we knew our place and we knew his place."

"How come he had money and you didn't - I mean as much money – or I mean . . ?"

"Honey, I know what you mean; Thad's mom was my dad's sister. She married Artimus Murphy; he owned a business in Illinois and they had money, certainly more money than the rest of us, but he didn't flaunt it. They lived in a stately house by the river south of Aurora; we always felt welcome and comfortable when we visited them. In the early twenties, Artimus, Thad's dad, grew ill and died. Thad's mom went to pieces and most of us think she decided that she would rather be dead than to go on without Artimus. We received word that she indeed died; so, we drove over to attend a funeral for the second time within six months. Thad was twenty-three years old. He hadn't been to college yet, but none of us knew why. His dad could have afforded it, but Thad just worked in the business. Thad's relationship with his parents was peculiar. With Thad's parents gone, Thad inherited everything from his mom and dad. Attorneys sold the business. Thad went to college at the University of Illinois - I think it was the University of Illinois. That's where he met your mom. One of the guests at the reception told a story that Thad, an upperclassman, a senior, took advantage of an inexperienced freshman, your mom, and wrapped her up before anyone else could get to her. And frankly, that sounds like Thad. After Thad graduated, he secured a position with the Second National Bank of Aurora. He and your mom moved into his parents' house after the wedding."

"I get the feeling that you did not like Thad" stated Sally.

"Well . . . maybe I'm not being fair. Thad was flamboyant, boisterous and I think self-centered, but he treated your mom like a queen. What happened after the accident really turned me against him. Grover and I got the call and we rushed to Illinois to help any way we could. Bringing you home was such a treat. We doted over you and it was so much fun, but we were prepared to give you back. But we never heard from Thad. Like your dad told you, we wrote letters to Thad and then to the County, asking for help to get in touch with him; the County responded that Thad was notified, but nothing from Thad. We thought we deserved at least a letter to explain what his plans were, but none came. Eventually, we gave up trying to reach him and you became our daughter. For this, I owe Thad everything dear to me. You became our life – our blessing. But, I have always thought that Thad was too wrapped up with Thad to care about you or about us. So if I am critical of Thad, I hope you understand."

"I do."

"Honey, you and your mom could have been twins. You have all of her beauty. And you would have loved your mom, she was special. Like your mom, you can bring a room to a standstill by just walking into it."

"Mom, that's not true!"

"Yes it is honey; did you see Mr. Richardson nearly walk over the top of the folding chair after church on Sunday?"

"I heard a commotion, but didn't know what it was about."

"That's because you were walking away from him. I was still at the front of the church. I was watching you because I am so proud of you, when I saw Sam Richardson watching, or lusting after you so intently that he nearly broke his leg in the fall. I wanted to go and tell him that church is not the place to ogle a young woman's behind, but I didn't."

"Mom!"

"Sorry honey, but it's true. Grover told me when you're in the store with him he has men stop in and walk out with nothing at all. He thinks you are wonderful window dressing."

"Mom, you're embarrassing me."

"Don't be embarrassed for inheriting beauty from your mom; just don't let it go to your head." Betty paused and said, "Honey, I haven't seen Tom around lately, have things changed?"

Looking down at her interlaced fingers in her lap, Sally said, "Yeah, I hear he's seeing Sherry Strong."

Betty wanted to ask more, but sensed that it was not the time; she rose and went to Sally, sat on the arm of the chair, she wrapped her arms around Sally and said, "Sometimes things happen that way, honey."

"Yeah Mom, I guess things happen."

CHAPTER 13

After Andy left them sitting on the grass in the cemetery, Nick, Stan and Butch laid back with their hands behind their heads staring at the few clouds passing by. Butch said, "Andy seems like a pretty nice guy. I don't think he's ever hung out with us before."

After a slight pause, Nick said, "No, he's older and he seems to always be busy with his folks' place. I don't see him around much, but, when I do, he's always been a nice guy. Man, he did not like the mausoleum!"

"Why, what do you mean?" asked Stan.

"Well, we got in and called for Beth, and Andy was ready to leave. I think he was spooked," answered Nick. "I told him the story about Carol and Shelly."

"Did you tell him we were scared shitless?" asked Stan laughing.

"Yeah, but I think he was too spooked to appreciate it" responded Nick.

"I was spooked the first time too" said Butch.

"No shit, Sherlock. We begged and coaxed you to climb through the window. Once in, you froze" said Stan, while chuckling.

"Well, I felt strange, that's all."

"More, like you were going to pee your pants" said Stan.

"Hey, come on, we were all scared the first time in. I remember crawling through that window into the darkness wondering if I was going to wet my pants" offered Nick. "When my eyes adjusted to the dim light and I saw those brass plaques and the empty rooms in the corner with the barred doors, all I wanted to do was run. But, I didn't because no one else was running. It took a couple of times for me to get used to it. Hey, how come you weren't with us that time, Butch?"

"I think that was when I was having my tonsils taken out" answered Butch. And with that, Butch leaned over, grew red in the face and ripped a prolonged fart with pride.

"Oh man!" cried Nick. All of them jumped up and ran away from the infected area laughing.

Still laughing, Stan asked, "You been saving that one for us, Butch?"

"No, actually, I really wanted to leave it in the diner for Miss Personality, but it wasn't ready" said Butch.

"You should have told us" said Nick. "We could have stayed longer."

Still laughing, Stan un-cranked a surprise of his own that rivaled Butch's.

Once again, scrambling away for the lack of gas masks, they stood laughing.

"Hey, you guys keep this up and we're never going to get back to our bikes" said Nick.

Said Stan, "Sorry guys, I wasn't saving that one for Miss Personality; I was saving it for you."

"Thanks, you moron" said Nick. "Speaking of morons, how about Andy's story about Phil and his moron brothers?"

"Man, I can't . . . I don't know how they could be that mean to their own brother. Phil can be Phil, but come on" said Stan.

"Let's ride over and check on Phil," said Nick. And with that, Nick, not wanting to be outdone, unleashed a fart that would not rank with the previous displays of flatulence, but caused all three to run to the bikes to escape the impending after-effects."

They rode out of the cemetery, turned right on Main Street veering left onto Sard Avenue. The Glastons' place sat back off the road with a long driveway. Their property went all the way to the elevated train tracks and hill of ballast. A swamp separated their property from the rise to the tracks.

The house was a one-story structure running east to west. An out building served as a garage and storage shed. Numerous cars, in varying stages of ill-repair, were stationed throughout the yard.

They rode their bikes down the graveled driveway, noticing the black '49 Ford with fender skirts and a louvered hood sitting in front of the out building. Two legs protruded from under the front wheel well; they were not moving. They rode closer, their tires crunching on the gravel. The legs moved and emerged from under the car. Attached to the legs was one of the asshole brothers; Benjy or Kurt, the name didn't matter because an asshole is an asshole.

"Yeah?" is all the asshole offered.

Nick stopped his bike and said, "We're looking for Phil."

"He ain't here."

"Nice car" stated Nick, as he elongated 'nice'.

This struck the right note with the asshole and he said with a tender tone, "Yeah, she's my baby; she's cherry. I swapped out the flathead for a 292 mill with a four barrel." Looking thoughtfully at the front end of the car, he added, "I think she has a wheel bearing going bad." He said this as if a loved one was facing a serious medical condition. "But I'll take care of her."

"Really nice car," said Nick "Phil was with us earlier, do you know where he is?"

"I haven't seen the turd-bird since yesterday. But, I was out most of the night, so that don't mean nothing." Asshole got down and began sliding back under the car.

"Thanks" offered Nick. All three immediately spun their bikes around and headed out the graveled driveway.

Once they were on the asphalt riding side by side and easing onto Main Street, Stan said, "Whew, that guy is in love with that car."

"You ain't kidding! What the hell?" said Butch. Butch mimicked the asshole, "My baby's got a wheel bearing going bad, I think I'm going to have to pull her pants down."

Their laughter almost caused them to collide.

"He hasn't seen the 'turd-bird' since yesterday? Yeah, because he hasn't left the side of his ill baby" said Nick.

"Let's ride down to old man Murphy's" said Stan.

CHAPTER 14

Andy rode back to his place feeling bad and wishing he could deliver good news, but what more could he do? He'd looked everywhere, solicited the help of friends, even climbed into that eerie mausoleum, where else could he have looked?

He pulled his bike into the large open space between the house and the small barn. Mr. McVee's 1950 dark green Studebaker was parked by the back door of the house. The Studebaker, with its torpedo nose and wrap-around back window, reminded Andy of a spaceship. It was sitting near the back door to the house with all the rust, dents and bald tires included. He did not want to go in. This was his day off. He felt like he was letting his parents down, as well as the McVees, but he had to go in, he knew it.

With shoulders slumped and his eyes cast down, he entered the kitchen and shook his head.

"You didn't find her?" Margie Durham, Andy's mom asked.

"No Ma, I looked everywhere; rode every street, checked at the store, the school. I even got help from some other guys. They suggested that we check a hut down by the river on Jefferson and we even checked the cemetery." Andy did not mention the mausoleum; he was sure his parents would never understand why he'd entered a condemned mausoleum looking for a missing girl. "We rode everywhere, I don't know where else to look."

Beth's mom was at the kitchen table, leaning more than sitting; her normally attractive face was red and blotchy and her eyes were swollen. She looked at Andy and said, "Andy, you've been kind, thank you." Trying to conceal her continuing tears, she put her face in her hands.

Stuart McVee, Beth's dad, was standing next to her as a protector. He put his hand on her shoulder to comfort her and said to Andy, "Son, we thank you for your help. I'm sorry to put you through this."

"No sir, it's Ok. I'll do what needs to be done" responded Andy, feeling uncomfortable. Here he is complaining about this being his day off, and the McVees are wracked with pain; the joy of their lives is gone.

Stuart turned to Margie and said, "You have a good boy, Margie."

Margie reached out for Andy's arm and replied, "I know."

Harvey Durham, Andy's dad, must have been out working on equipment or on the tractor. Andy turned toward the door to find him when Mr. McVee said, "Son, I am out of ideas. I'm lost. We've checked every place this side of the tracks. Can you think where she might have gone, beside where you've looked?"

Andy slowly shook his head, he really wanted to help, but came up empty of new ideas. "No sir, I wish I did. Maybe you need to talk with the police; they can get the word out." Remembering what was going on at Railroad Street, he said, "But you won't find them at the station, they're all over on Railroad Street. A bunch of cops are investigating something."

This captured the attention of both ladies and they looked up. Mrs. McVee asked, "What's going on, Andy?"

"Mrs. McVee, I don't know. The guys that helped me look for Beth said it's an investigation; that's all I know. Mr. McVee, if you go over, you'll have to stop at the street and ask for help. They have it roped off." With that he reached for the door and left in search of his dad.

Stuart McVee drove his old Studebaker over the tracks. He could see the congestion of cars on Railroad Street. He parked a block away and walked up to the cordoned off area. He didn't know any of the people gathered, so he looked for someone with authority. A fireman stood on the other side of the rope, leaning against one of the police cars. Stuart made his way over to him and said, "Sir, I need to talk with a police officer, my little girl is missing."

"I don't think you're going to get to talk with anyone right now, they got themselves an investigation going on" replied the fireman.

"Please ask one of them to step over here, this has me and my wife real upset" Stuart said with urgency.

The fireman looked at Stuart, thought a minute, and said, "I'll do what I can. Wait here."

The fireman was uneasy approaching the gathering of cops, he didn't want anyone getting mad at him, but this guy was pretty upset. Looking around he spotted John Rively, one of the younger cops, standing near the garage. With his hand, he motioned to John to slide to the side, so they could talk.

"John, I'm sorry, but that guy over there . . .," nodding in the direction of rope, ". . . insists on talking to one of you right away. He said his little girl is missing and he and his wife are upset. I tried to tell him that you guys have your hands full with all this, but he was pretty persistent."

John sighed heavily and looked in the direction of the nod. The man on the other side of the rope was looking right back at John. John said to the fireman, "So he said it won't wait?"

"That's what he said" replied the fireman.

"Ok, tell him I'll be right over."

John walked back toward the house and pulled Bob aside. "Bob, I hate to do this, but that guy . . .," motioning toward the front of the house, ". . . claims his little girl is missing. I'm going over to talk with him. What do you want me to do if I think she really is missing?"

"Oh for Pete's sakes, it's probably going to be a matter of the girl being with a relative or friends, but go talk with him. If you think it's necessary to do some checking, go ahead. We don't have that much to do right now anyway; we're still waiting on the test results and the photos to get back from the County."

John lifted the rope up for Stuart to come under, and walked a few feet into the yard to provide privacy. He offered his hand and said, "John Rively. How can I help you?"

Stuart shook John's hand and said, "Stuart McVee. We - I mean my wife, my daughter and I, live across the tracks east of Baseline. I can see you don't need any more problems, but John, my 12 year girl is missing, and I think I'm going mad."

It was obvious to John that tears were close at hand, so he touched Stuart's arm and said, "Stuart, it's probably a matter of your little girl going out and she forgot to tell you that she was going."

"John, I want so badly to believe you, but that isn't my Beth; Beth is my daughter. She's been gone too long to just be off" said Stuart.

"How long has she been gone?" asked John.

"Since at least seven o'clock this morning and maybe before that" replied Stuart.

"Maybe before that?"

"Yeah, you see, Beth is our only child, and she is a really good girl; pretty level-headed and responsible. I work at Miller's Tool & Die, and my wife is a waitress at a café. I'm home until six in the evening when I have to leave for work. My wife gets a ride to and from work and is usually home around ten thirty or eleven. Beth knows she is to be in the house before dark. She never fails at it, we've checked on her. She's not allowed to bring friends to the house; but she doesn't have many friends anyway.

My wife got home last night and assumed Beth was in her room asleep, so she went to bed. I got home this morning at seven, went to peek in on Beth and found she was gone. Beth has been known to slip over to the Durhams' place to help out with chores. She has never left without telling us, but this morning I figured she might not have wanted to wake her mom. She wasn't at the Durhams."

Stopping briefly to over-come his emotions, Stuart continued, "The Durham boy, Andy, said that he and his friends have ridden their bikes all over town looking for her with no results. What do I do?"

"Stuart, let me meet you and your wife at your place in 20 minutes. I'm going to alert the County, and a couple other departments of bordering towns in the meantime. Can you give a me description of Beth?"

"Uh, sure. She's four feet, eight inches tall, seventy or eighty pounds, has reddish brown hair, she usually wears it in a ponytail in the summer, dark blue eyes . . ." his voice began to crack.

John said, "That's good enough Stuart. Any guess what she would be wearing?"

Composed again, Stuart said, "Blue jeans, she doesn't have anything else, and probably a sleeveless blouse, but I don't know for sure."

"Go on home and I'll meet you in a few minutes" said John.

CHAPTER 15

It was after noon, the sun was hot and the smell of fresh tar used to resurface the side streets of Montgomery the previous week added to the peculiarity of the day. The smell of the tar gave a sense of renewal to the entire town. The tar was covered with pea gravel. For a couple of weeks following the facelift of side streets, all cars would pick up the pea gravel with the tires causing the small stones to ping and bounce around the wheel wells creating a strangely musical addition to Montgomery as the cars rolled down the street.

Nick, Stan and Butch rode up Railroad Street and were amazed at the growing crowd. Cars were parked alongside the road, scattered without order; people were standing in groups talking, pointing and rubbing their foreheads. Dogs barked incessantly, not accustomed to the sight of that many strangers in their domain.

"People must have come here for their lunchtime entertainment" said Stan.

"Yeah, exciting times in Montgomery" offered Nick.

Riding up from behind, Butch said, "Well, plunk your magic twanger, Froggy! What do we have here?"

"What the hell does Froggy have to do with what's going on here?" asked Nick.

"It's magical my friend; purely magical. People appear out of the mist to learn of a mystery" responded Butch.

"Ok Butch, whatever you say" said Nick

Butch was quick to add, "You bet; you can't ever go wrong with the Butch. Hey, let's go down as close as we can. I'll bet we learn something." He took the lead.

Stan and Butch stayed close behind, close enough to ask Butch to not mention the "murder thing" around the bystanders.

As they approached old man Murphy's property, they dismounted, discarded their bikes in the weeds and began to walk along the rope until they came in front of the house. Not much had changed since they'd observed from the tracks earlier in the morning; however a few changes were obvious. The panel truck, presumably, as Butch would have it, "The Coroner's panel truck," was gone, but was replaced by another County car. Cops were in the house, around the house, on the side of the house, and cops were even in the fields and on the tracks performing a thorough search.

Butch experienced a feeling of awe being this close to an actual investigation. He said enthusiastically, "WOW, this is getting bigger and bigger, you guys gotta believe now!"

"Believe what?" asked Nick.

"Believe that old man Murphy's laid someone out. Caplooy! Dead as a mackerel, stiff as a fence post. I told you guys. WOW."

Looking away from the house and nodding in that direction as he spoke, Stan said, "Hey, isn't that Mr. McVee talking to Rively?"

Butch and Nick turned to see the two men talking. Nick said, "Are you sure that's Mr. McVee?"

Butch responded, "Yeah man, don't you remember seeing him at the school picnic. Hell, you were there!"

With uncharacteristic alarm, Nick muttered, "Oh shit!"

"What?" said Stan, as he and Butch sensed a change in Nick.

Nick remained silent momentarily before responding, "That means she really is missing."

"No shit Sherlock, we've known that since we heard it from Andy, where have you been? Christ, we've only been all over town looking for her." Pausing, Butch asks, "You Ok Nick?"

Nick didn't respond.

Stan looked at Nick, cocked his head like a dog trying to understand, and said, "Wait a minute, there's more to this than you're sharing, Bucko. What's going on? What aren't you sharing with your best friends?"

Now Nick was the center of attention, and Nick was feeling it. The inquisition was at hand and he needed to offer something quickly, or his friends would sit on him until he coughed it up. "Look, I guess I didn't think she was really missing; that's all." He added, "I feel sick."

Stan beginning to see that Nick had more in the pot than any of them thought, said, "OK, we're out of here, we are going to talk, right now!"

They ran back down the rope line to their bikes, mounted them and rode to Webster Street. Stan took the lead.

CHAPTER 16

Bob found it hard to believe that two and a half hours ago Montgomery was just another town, doing what any town does on a sunny Wednesday morning; folks finding their way to work wishing they could have slept in or stayed home, milkmen lugging their dairy treasures from the truck to the house, over and over again, dogs in backyards sniffing to see what invaders had entered their territory during the night, and all the other ordinary things that ordinary towns and ordinary folks do on a sunny Wednesday morning. But this Wednesday morning was proving to be anything but ordinary.

He considered the events, the presence of the State and the County in his town, the implications and the complications of the investigation; all was disconcerting. He thought, "What the hell was going on in his little village. After all these years, Thad Murphy is certainly throwing curve balls."

The cellar was beginning to feel like a tomb to Bob; and smell like one too. He leaned against the doorjamb of the cellar and watched from the doorway as the investigator slowly and methodically worked both sides of the cellar.

Henry asked Bob to take his place in the cellar while he tended to others in the investigation. The tall investigator with the pock marks was in the was taking prints when appropriate, carefully placing items of interest in bags and in the boxes; inspecting the floor with diligence before taking a step.

Working on the left side, he pulled the string for the light over the bench, granting him additional lighting while he examined the bench and the electronics.

Retreating to the entrance, he began nearest the furnace and the coal hopper taking photos on the right side of the cellar. He said, "Hey, I'm going to try to approach the back wall."

"Avoid the *bllloood*." An ineffective imitation of Bela Lugosi was offered by Bob.

"Thank you, Charlie Chan."

"That wasn't Charlie Chan, it was Dracula."

"It wasn't Dracula either."

As he inched closer to the back wall, and though he was trying to avoid stepping on the blood-soaked tarp or in the blood itself, he could feel stickiness on the sole of his shoe; each time he picked it up, it wanted to stay put momentarily. Each step took him closer; he was gaining on the view of the corpse. The blow flies were gaining in number with their monotonous buzz, and the smell of decomposition was becoming more apparent.

"So what do you see?" asked Bob, trying to suppress his impatience.

"Well, it is a corpse . . ., but . . . I'm going to slip this metal cabinet out an inch or two to get a better look. You don't see any reason not to from your vantage point, do you, Bob?"

Giving the area a scrutinizing appraisal, Bob responded, "No, I can't see anything that it would hurt."

Half bending, half reaching, trying not to disturb the tarp, the investigator attempted to push the front edge of the cabinet to the left. It was stuck to the floor at first, but it then gave way and slid four inches. This revealed more of the corpse. With his flashlight held high for maximum illumination, the investigator leaned forward. What they were seeing was the upper back and side, with the rump aimed toward the door. Gaining a more complete view, the investigator exclaimed, "Son-of-bitch!"

Immediately, Bob retorts, "What do you have?"

"Let me move this damn box a little farther."

He gently slid the box out another six inches. The investigator flinched as this released more odor of decay. He shined his flashlight at the corpse and shook his head slowly.

"Come on! You're killing me here" expressed Bob.

"My best guess is that Murphy got mad at a dog, killed it, and skinned it. Jesus, this is ugly. What the hell is wrong with that guy?"

"Are you sure it is a dog?" asked Bob.

"Yeah, I can tell by the nails, the snout and the tail. I don't know what else it could be" answered the investigator. "It's a good-sized dog too. We weren't seeing much of it from the doorway. When we get our hands on your Mr. Murphy character, I want three minutes alone with him. I'm a dog lover, and no dog deserves this!"

Not knowing why he was asking, Bob asked, "Can you see the skin too?"

The investigator held his flashlight higher and looked beyond the dog. "I think so; at least I hope so, because there's a pile of something back in the corner." He leaned farther, bracing himself on the wall and confirmed that it was the dog's skin. "Do you know if your Mr. Murphy was a taxidermist?" asked the investigator.

"Beats me. Why do you ask?" responded Bob.

"The cut lines are straight and all appear to be on the underside as if to preserve the rest without damage; looks pretty damn professional to me. You'll see what I'm talking about when we get it out. One thing is for sure, though."

"What's that?"

"All the blood didn't come from the dog. I can't see any incision wounds on the dog; and skinning it doesn't generate that much blood."

"Hey do you need some fresh air?" asked Bob, asking primarily for his own need.

"Yeah, let's take a break. At least now we know what it is."

They emerged with Bob in the lead. Bob was aware of the arrival of the additional car with more County guys for the grid search; Pete Morantz had left the house and was heading up that part of the investigation. Bob was anxious to talk with Henry about the progress inside the house and to have further discussion on the bathroom and bedroom theories.

A five-gallon container of coffee was brought from the diner, which Bob and the investigator found as a welcomed sight. Standing around the coffee container, they held their steaming paper cups close to their noses to allow the fruitful aroma of the coffee to flush the smell of the cellar from their being.

Henry came out of the house and walked to them. "Tell me some good news."

Bob took a quick sip of the coffee and said, "Henry, you aren't going to believe it."

"Try me" responded Henry.

"The corpse is a skinned dog; skin and all."

"A skinned dog." Henry repeated what he heard and shook his head. "What in God's name does that have to do with all this? Have you brought it out yet?"

"No, but we will" answered Bob.

Turning toward the investigator, Henry asked, "What else did you find?"

"I collected items for examination, printed what I could, but nothing really substantial. I'll get back in there and remove that tarp and the dog. The tarp should reveal something, but I'm not sure what at this point" responded the investigator.

"A dog? Are you shitting me?" Henry shook his head trying to make sense of it all.

"Yep, a dog – and no we're not shitting you" answered Bob.

"Any idea whose dog it is?" Henry asked. "Based on the house, I don't see any evidence suggesting he had a dog."

"I'm clueless Henry; and getting more so every minute" responded Bob.

Walking back toward the front of the house, Henry offered, "Okey dokey. I'm heading back into the house, yell if you need anything."

"Sure will" Bob answered.

Finishing their coffee, they headed back to the tomb. The tarp was made of a thick canvas and weighed more than any of them expected.

The sickening metallic smell of decomposing blood increased as they moved the tarp from its resting place. They folded it in half inward, then in half again. Bending it in the middle with Bob on one end and the investigator on the other, it looked like a canoe as they hoisted it up the cellar stairs. Once outside, they proceeded directly to the van. This gave new and exciting hope to the onlookers. Surely it appeared as if the investigators were purposely hiding something inside the tarp. A stir of creative conversations erupted.

They returned to the cellar entrance to discuss how best to remove the dog and the skin without creating a frenzy among the onlookers.

Fingering his temples, Bob said, as much to himself as to the others, "Christ, we've got to get that dog out to the van, but it will cause too much of a scene to do it openly."

Pete Morantz walked back to the house from the grid search.

"Any luck?" asked Bob.

"Not so far. We've checked the field by the garage, and that includes the railroad property, the backyard, and they're now working their way along the tracks and into the field. A few candy wrappers, too old to be considered relevant, an old shoe without a sole, again, likely to have been in the field a long time, grass and weeds were entangled in the eyelets. The area is relatively clean."

Having already been updated on the findings in the cellar, Pete asked while nodding toward the cellar opening, "What's the progress?"

Bob glanced toward the street and the groups of residents. "We have the tarp in the County van, but we have to get the dog out without causing undue unrest with our observers."

Pete responded quickly, "Well hell Bob, back the van close to the cellar and put the dog in a box. That shouldn't create too much alarm, it will freshen their suspicions without revealing anything."

The answer was so simple that it embarrassed Bob. Gazing down, Bob simply said, "Damn. I'm not thinking right."

Pete knew what Bob was thinking and said, "Hey that's why we're working this together. You know the old saying, "Two minds are . . ."

"Yep" said Bob. Walking toward the County guys by the coffee container he declared, "Get a box and back the van up to the cellar."

One of the County guys asked, "What's the box for?"

Speaking in low tones, Bob answered, "The dog; and a separate box for the skin."

The County guys nodded approval; one of them said, "That's a big dog."

"Then get a big box" responded Bob.

CHAPTER 17

The boys rode Webster, but instead of turning north on River Street, as they did earlier to head toward the park, they continued down a slight hill on Webster, which brought them to the river; no guard rails, no signs of warning, just the end of pavement, a brief muddy shoreline, and the murky water of the mighty Fox.

The Fox River is formed in Menomonee Falls, Wisconsin, runs through the Chain O'Lakes in northern Illinois and continues south until its confluence with the Illinois River near Ottawa, Il; a total of 202 miles.

Originally the home for Potawatomi, Sac, and Fox Indian tribes, it would have been picturesque during the early days; lush with vegetation, sloping banks and wildlife abounding, gorgeous rock cliffs. But those pesky settlers arrived; Wisconsin paper mills, Illinois factories producing everything under the sun, and from all of this lots and lots of industrial waste, most of it conveniently dumped into the Fox. Municipalities regarded the Fox as an equally convenient way to rid their communities of sewage by sending it downstream to their neighbors. Montgomery is in the lower third of the river, thus is the recipient of many gifts from their northerly neighbors. All in all, it is a beautiful river gone bad, all in the name of progress.

As they walked from their bikes, they found the remains of a stone wall. It was crumbling from age, but it had served well as a barrier for high water in its prime. They perched on the wall facing the river with their legs dangling.

Stan, looked across the ambling waters and without turning toward Nick, said, "OK Nick, time to spill the beans. What's going on in that nimble brain of yours?"

"Man . . . it's really nothing."

"Bullshit Nick. You know you can't bullshit a bullshitter, cough it up" Stan responded sternly.

Nick was fearful and reluctant to reveal his brief relationship with Beth, knowing that revealing it, even to his best friends, would be the same as renting a billboard. He coughed lightly and said, "Well, a few weeks before the end of school I happened to be walking home and so was Beth and we . . . well, we walked together."

"And . . .?" Stan urged, motioning with his hands.

"And nothing" Nick offered, unconvincingly.

Stan turned toward Nick with a serious tone, "Nick, do we have to dunk your ugly ass in the river to get you to come clean?"

"No. We walked together a few other times too. But that's it."

Still trying get the whole picture, Stan asks, "Nick, I'm not big on geography, but she lives a half a mile beyond your house, so did she walk you home, or did you walk her home?"

"I walked her home."

Butch jumped in, "So, though you might think it's none my business, when were you going to tell your best friends? Or maybe the pact we made to never keep anything from each other doesn't pertain to love affairs?"

"It isn't a love affair!" snapped Nick.

Stan, sensing the tension, offered, "OK Nick, it is not a 'love affair', but frankly, I can't remember the last time you walked me home and I live a lot closer than she does, so that leads me to believe it is something."

"Yeah it's something. I like her. I think she likes me. We talk, but that's it. I'm not holding out anything from you guys" replied Nick.

"Except the romantic strolls from school" Butch added sarcastically.

Stan paused and said, "Nick this brings a new light to her being missing." Pausing again, he added, "You don't know where she is, do you?"

"Hell no! You dipshit, if I knew, do you think I would be this upset? Shit – holy sucking shit! I was anxious to search for her with Andy thinking I could find her and be the hero . . . but, now with the cops involved I guess I realize that it isn't a game and I'm getting a really bad feeling." Nick looked down to his Converse gym shoes for help, "It's like I should be searching for her and not sitting here gazing at a river. Do you know what I mean?"

"Kind of" said Stan.

Butch jumped down from the wall, walked to the river, returning with a used rubber he fished out of the muck with a stick, "Guys, we own this river; we are around it, in it, or on it more often than not, night and day. Used rubbers are everywhere; I'd like to know when people are down here using these rubbers. I have never seen them. Man, I don't get it." Of course, it would be years before Butch came to the realization that used rubbers from the northerly neighbors were only a part of the sewage he and his friends swam in for their enjoyment. The rest of it was really yucky.

"Butch, will you throw that damn thing down and focus. We've got some figuring to do here" said Stan.

As he slung the rubber into the river, Butch offered, "Man, this town isn't that big, she has to be here somewhere."

Exasperated, Nick exclaimed, "Damn it, double damn, son of a bitch . . . I feel like I'm screwing the pooch!"

"Hey, settle down. One over-excited, ill-directed Butch is enough in any crowd" Stan exclaimed.

Butch, realizing he might be under attack, asks "What? What are you talking about?"

"Butch, it was a compliment to your uniqueness" replied Stan.

With his head slightly down and thinking deeply, Nick asked, "Where haven't we looked?"

Suddenly, and with excitement, Butch pronounces, "I've got it!"

Nick and Stan looked at Butch expectantly.

"How about out on Aucutt Road, you know the deserted house on the corner of Albright? And that gun club; it's empty, except on the weekends. Man, she could be there. And how about the gravel pit farther out?"

"Ok" said Stan. "Where else?"

With hope peeking through the curtains, the boys continued to mentally search for possibilities.

Nick broke the thoughtful silence with, "Why would she be out on Aucutt Road?"

"Why is she missing?" Stan replied. "It's not a matter or 'why' but 'where,' isn't it?"

Nick said, "Yeah, I guess so. How about those woods on the other side of the park by the river?"

"Man, are you kidding me? That area is so thick with trees I doubt that even Beth could wiggle her way through; we've only seen that area from a rowboat; but what about the old Mill?" offered Butch.

"Good one, Butch," stated Stan as he punched Butch in the arm. "We'll have to check it out."

Moving toward the bikes, Butch asks, "Where to first, Kimo-sabe?"

Beginning to feel better and more confident, Nick answered, "Let's start with Aucutt Road."

CHAPTER 18

The summer of 1944 was unsettling for the Thomases of Mystic Iowa. In late July, Sally asked for permission to attend the Illinois State Teachers College in DeKalb, Illinois. This request was a surprise to Betty and Grover. Sally never expressed an interest in teaching; in fact, she never expressed interest in attending college at all. Sally's conversations involving education always completed themselves with High School.

Much to Betty's surprise, Sally submitted her application and school records to the college, and her acceptance letter was in hand when she approached them with her request. Dumbfounded and disappointed, Grover and Betty asked if they could sleep on it.

That night, Betty and Grover, Betty in tears, discussed how they should respond to Sally's request. "Why would she want to go to DeKalb, Illinois? She could have chosen Grinnel College in Des Moines, that's only ninety miles away, or Iowa State in Ames, that's only a hundred and twenty miles away, but DeKalb, Illinois? That's three hundred miles - a day trip away!" exclaimed Grover.

Betty, sniffling with a kerchief in hand, said, "It doesn't really matter how far it is, why is she going? She could work with you in the hardware business and take it over; she could stay here and build a family. I am so confused."

Their night was long with little sleep. When they approached Sally the next morning, they gave, with heavy hearts, their blessing to her decision.

In mid-August, Grover, Betty and Sally Thomas headed for DeKalb, Illinois and Illinois State Teachers College. Other than their brief stop for lunch in Davenport, their trip was engulfed by cornfields and a few small agricultural communities.

Normally, their conversations during a drive were lively and covered subjects of various originations, the war, always a big topic, the crop yield for Mystic farmers, the social events, the rumors, etc., but today, the conversations were sparse and forced. Sally feigned her excitement about her new teaching future and the experiences she imagined associated with a new school.

The time went slowly, but in the afternoon they approached DeKalb. DeKalb was surrounded by rolling hills covered with bright green corn stalks. The city stuck up out of the sea of corn like an oasis. West of the downtown area, they found the College. Betty read that DeKalb was widely recognized for the development of "barbed wire," a fitting recognition as far as Betty was concerned.

They met with the college's Registrar, Grover paid the appropriate fees for tuition, books, room and board and they helped Sally get settled into her girls' dormitory. Betty could not understand how Sally could find any of this appealing, but she held her tongue and her feelings in check; that is, until she and Grover were in the car and heading back to Mystic.

They originally planned to stay in a motel for the night and start their return trip early the next morning, but Betty explained to Sally that she would sleep so much better in her own bed that night; they headed out, knowing it would be late when they made it to Mystic.

As they drove west on Route 38, Betty cried like she hadn't cried in years. Grover pulled off twice to console her, but with little constructive impact. The entire trip home provided bouts of tears and conversations seeking the answer "why?" The tears came freely, but the answers remained in the cornfields.

CHAPTER 19

Following his conversation with Stuart McVee, John returned to the station and made the calls to the County, the city of Aurora, and the village of Oswego, giving Beth's description and a brief run-down on the circumstances of her disappearance and the timing. He drove the Village car south on River Street to avoid the congestion on Railroad Street. At Watkins, he turned right, crossed Main and turned left on Railroad, and a quick right put him on Case and the railroad crossing.

John knew this town well; he spent many hours in the Village car checking the properties, the businesses, and the homes as a routine part of his patrol, but John distinctly remembered Stuart saying that he lived east of Baseline, across the tracks. John's mind was not pulling up any homes east of Baseline. Baseline began Route 31and angled west away from the tracks. The space between Route 31 and the railroad tracks was empty, void of any development, wooded and not that hospitable. He considered the possibility that he had heard wrong, or that Stuart, in his confused state, had given the wrong reference.

After crossing the tracks on Case, John turned left on Route 31 and began looking to his left for housing of any kind, but nothing. He continued past Baseline Road, Killian's Auto Parts on the right and was almost to the Caterpillar factory, when he decided to turn around and try again.

The change of direction did give him a different perspective, but it yielded the same frustrating results, until he noticed a disturbance in the symmetry of the shoulder to the right. It appeared so quickly, he drove past it and backed up. What he saw was not a road, not even a driveway, but rather, two rows of compressed grass and occasional mud pockets where a car had driven over it a number of times.

John pulled the Village car on to the trail and proceeded slowly. He could hear the tall weeds scraping the undercarriage of the car. Being jostled about by the uneven terrain, he slowed even more.

Fifty yards from the hard road, he encountered a small creek, not more than three feet across. Stuart, or someone, had placed thick planks across the creek, aligned with the tire tracks. John got out of the car to appraise that the planks would likely support the Village car's weight. Muddy tire tracks appeared on the planks, so John, with trepidation, proceeded on.

Though feeling a slight sagging as he crossed the planks, they held and he continued on the tracks. Within another twenty yards the path led into the wooded area. The trees created a canopy, almost tunnel-like, turning what was bright daylight to dusk. He noticed an opening that revealed a shack with a 1950 green Studebaker parked near it.

John realized that the railroad tracks were not more than a stone's throw away. As he parked the Village car, he thought the clattering trains would make sleeping tough.

John guessed that the shack was built to manage livestock, or for hunting; additions were added later. He could see the sloped tin roof, two windows, with no stoop or steps leading to the door. The parking area revealed only hard-packed dirt and clay; John suspected that rainy weather would be a problem.

Stuart opened the windowless door and walked out offering John his hand. "Not the easiest place to find, hey John?"

"That's ok Stuart, I made it" responded John.

Gesturing with his hand, Stuart said, "Let's go inside, my wife is making coffee."

It was not hard for John to estimate the entire layout of the floor plan. The main room was an all-in-one, kitchen, living room and dining area with a wood cook stove. The cook stove was likely used for heating as well. Doorways on either side of the main room likely lead to bedrooms, which were the add-ons after the initial construction. The doorways were absent of doors, full length curtains strung from the top of the door jamb to the floor provided the limited privacy. No other doorways were evident; this led John to believe an outhouse existed behind the shack.

John was pleased to see that everything was neat and clean; even a few pictures and cheap artwork dressed up the walls. Mrs. McVee was standing near a sink; more curtains hid the plumbing beneath the sink. As she turned to greet them, John was surprised; Mrs. McVee appeared younger than he expected. She was petite. It was obvious that waitressing was taking a toll on her, but she was strikingly beautiful in a natural way.

Stuart McVee, while not a bad looking man, was no match for his partner; his short cropped hair, big nose and pale skin with the remnants of acne was a far cry from the beauty displayed by his wife. They didn't match, and John thought she was no match for this shack.

John could see her eyes were red and cheeks puffy from crying. John offered his hand saying, "Mrs. McVee, I'm John Rively; I'm sorry to hear about Beth, but with your help we'll find her and bring her home." John wasn't sure why he offered such a bold claim, but he saw a noticeable improvement in her eyes.

She squeaked, "Thank you," then added, "Please sit down, have some coffee." She poured coffee from a percolator coffee pot that didn't require an electrical cord.

John sat at the table, took out his note pad and said, "Stuart told me Beth was missing at seven when he got home, and that she might have been missing when you got home last night."

This brought on the tears, but she said, "I get dropped off and walk from the highway around 11:00 at night. I'm always quiet when I get home because Beth is a light sleeper. She usually wakes if I pull back the curtain to her room to check on her." She nodded to a set of the curtains. "She is so reliable, I guess I trusted she was in her room and I didn't want to disturb her. Stuart came home, and . . . excuse my reference, the gates of hell opened."

"I understand" said John. "Has this ever happened before?"

"Never" answered Stuart, quickly. "She obeys, she is considerate, and we never have a problem with her of any kind."

"Ok, can you tell me where you've looked so far?"

Stuart listed all the places they'd looked, including the Durhams, and tried to recall all the places Andy Durham said he and his friends had checked out.

"Does Beth have a group of friends?"

"No; kids Beth's age don't live around here, and Beth is ashamed of this place; we're trying really hard to get out of here and get a place in town" said Stuart.

"What about school friends, did she attend Montgomery elementary last year?" asked John.

"Yes, she attended the elementary school, but she'll be going to Junior High in Aurora next year. Like I said, she doesn't have many friends, she is embarrassed" added Stuart.

Mrs. McVee interjected, "Beth talks about one boy. He walks with her and she likes him as a friend."

Stuart was surprised by this disclosure; he didn't recall hearing Beth talk about him. He asked his wife, "Who is he?"

She said, "Nick something or other."

John offered, "Nick Corrie?"

"Yes, that's it. Do you know him?"

"Yeah, Nick's ok, he's one of the kids that keeps us hopping, but never in serious trouble of any kind. I'll check with him, but my guess is he was one of those helping Andy search," said John. "Can you think of anyone else, child or adult, other than the Durhams that she might go visit?"

The McVees looked at each other shaking their heads.

"How about the clothing she might be wearing, Mrs. McVee?"

"I checked, she doesn't have much, so I'm pretty sure she is wearing blue jeans, white sneakers and a light blue blouse."

"Sleeveless?" asked John

"Yes. How did you know?" asked Mrs. McVee quickly.

"Stuart suggested she was likely wearing a sleeveless blouse during our earlier conversation."

Switching his gaze from one to the other, John asked, "Can you think of anything that might help us with the search?"

Both shook their heads, as in defeat.

"I've notified the Aurora and Oswego departments, and the County. I will update them with this information, tapping his notepad. Now if you learn where she is, please drive over to inform us; it's doubtful that any of us will be in the station; we're working an investigation, but you can call the County and they can reach us by radio."

Stuart answered, "Oh, we will John. By the way, what's the investigation about on Railroad Street, if you don't mind me asking?"

"We aren't really sure. We're hoping to locate Mr. Murphy; he'll shed light on it" responded John, hoping to end the conversation.

With that, Mrs. McVee asked, "Mr. Murphy? Thaddeus Murphy?"

"Yeah, I guess, I mean I guess his first name is Thaddeus. Do you know him?"

"I've never met him, but I know who he is" responded Mrs. McVee.

This conversation was going a lot further than John preferred; he was glad when no more questions were asked. John stood to leave, anxious to get off the hot seat.

Stuart stood to walk out with John. "Thanks John, please find her. She is all we have."

"I promise we will do our best. You come get me if you locate her. Agreed?"

"Agreed."

John precariously turned the Village car around in the cramped area in front of the McVees' home and headed for Route 31.

CHAPTER 20

A ucutt Road is the continuation of Webster Street going west. Once one crossed Route 31 on the west side of the tracks, Webster ceases to exist and Aucutt begins. Not that it matters, but it is the same town, the same street – why the name change? Why, if coming out of the country, couldn't Aucutt Road continue on to the river for an extra three blocks? Or, why couldn't Webster continue on into the countryside? Founders - you gotta love 'em.

Leaving Webster and proceeding on Aucutt (no turn required) was more than just a change of names; it was a change of environment. Webster hosts traffic and activities and people – Aucutt hosts farmers, farm equipment and an occasional car of non-farming, but lost, travelers trying to get anywhere other than Aucutt Road. On the southwest corner of Aucutt and Route 31 sits Schaefer's Greenhouse, purveyors of fine greenery and flowers.

Beyond Schaefers, one becomes rather lonely until Albright Road three-quarters of a mile west; Albright dead-ends into Aucutt. On this corner, the remnants of what was once a family farm; a house, out buildings, trees once planted with love, and bushes once trimmed now sprawl and sag.

The life this farm once produced, and provided to others, was drained away. Most of the windows were broken; the wooden front porch was listing to the side. The steps leading to the front porch were no longer steps at all, but rather, a pile of wood strewn about in front of the porch. The exterior surrendered to the sun and the elements and now sported a weathered gray surface with only patches of the paint still present. The out buildings were partially collapsed and heavily weeded.

Nick, Stan and Butch pulled into the area that resembled a driveway and rolled to the side of the house. Looking around with disappointment, Stan said, "Damn. It doesn't look like anyone has been here for years." The sparse weeds around Stan's bike were nearly as tall as his tires.

Butch, who was originally proud of his idea to check this place, was having second thoughts. This place was almost as spooky as the mausoleum.

Nick pedaled to the back of the house, looked around, rode back to join the others. "Guys, I saw a skunk run under the foundation in the back of the house. If someone was here, and if that skunk is nesting, we could smell the skunk's reaction. I don't think anyone is here, and I really don't want to get sprayed."

"Me either" announced Butch, pleased to see his courage would not be tested today.

Nick continued. "I'm going to climb onto the front porch and yell for Beth, you guys ride to the out buildings and do the same. If we don't hear anything, we head for the gun club."

Having heard nothing, they continued on Aucutt to the gun club. They left their bikes on the side of the road. The gate was secured by a chain and padlock. They climbed the fence and walked down the dirt road to the club.

None of them had been to the club before, but on a day with the wind blowing from the west, the sounds of pop, pop, pop could be heard on the weekends, as the sporty outdoorsmen successfully annihilated those helpless clay pigeons. The clubhouse turned out to be a small wooden structure not much bigger than a shed. Trees were cleared in the direction of the shooting range, but that was it. All three stood facing the shed and feeling stupid, but not saying so. Without a word, they turned to retrace their steps to the bikes.

They agreed that proceeding to the gravel pit would be a long-shot, so headed back to town and the old mill.

They left their bikes in the park and walked under the bridge toward the mill. The bridge was constructed of concrete arches that spanned the river; the arch they walked under was another of their favorite places to hide from the watchful eyes of adults.

Nick remembered Andy saying that they could avoid entering the river by finding a loose plank this side of the hole he normally entered. He looked, and sure enough, he could see the loose plank. He pulled it back and slithered into the darkened building. Stan followed; Butch wedged more than slithered.

This level of the building was cool, damp, musty, and littered with trash from other explorers. Nick called out, "Hey Beth, you in here?" Nothing.

They climbed the makeshift ladder an industrious explorer had made from scrap lumber. The main floor was lit from ambient light coming through windows darkened by years of grime. This was the floor where the asshole brothers locked Phil in the room. They recognized the room from Andy's story as they walked back to it. Peering in to the darkness of the room, Butch shuddered inwardly and said, "Those bastards!" The piece of two-by-four Kurt used to wedge on the door handle was still on the floor next to the opened door.

Nick looked toward the front of the building and called out again, "Beth, hey it's Nick, are you in here?" His elevated voice clanged against the stone walls with a sharp and eerie tone. "How do you get to the upper floors?" he asked the others.

They shrugged.

They walked in different directions in search of the access route to the upper levels. Stan yelled out, "Hey, it's over here." And it was; in the back of the building was a stone staircase against the stone wall, reminiscent of a staircase one might encounter in a medieval castle. No handrail, just stone stairs against a stone wall leading to a hole in the floor above.

They gathered at the foot of the staircase looking up. Butch asked, "Do you think it will hold us?"

Stan answered, "It's made of stone Butch, do you really think it's going to crumble under your big bones?"

Nick, feeling responsible for bringing them here, said, "Hey you guys wait here, I'll go up, look around and be back in a minute."

"Bullshit" responded Stan. "I'm with you."

The two of them climbed up the stairs using their hands to ensure balance. Arriving at the top, Nick turned and extended his hand to Stan as Stan reached the top. The entire upper level was completely visible and totally empty. Knowing the effort was futile, Nick halfheartedly voiced, "Beth?" Nothing.

Stan said, "I think there might be one more level."

Nick responded, "I don't think she's here, do you?"

"Naw."

The trip down the stairs proved to be more of a challenge. Stan started down as one would descend a normal set of stairs. One look over the side and he stopped, turned around and backed down, the same way he climbed up, on all fours. Nick realizing the wisdom in Stan's adjustment, descended in the same fashion.

They made their way out of the old building and back to their bikes.

Flopping on the grass, Stan offered a weary, "Sorry Nick."

Looking at Stan, Nick replied "It's ok."

Time passed before Butch said, "I'm getting hungry."

Nick replied, "Not me, man."

Stan shook his head.

Butch got up and walked toward his bike, "I'm headin' home to see if my mom has started supper yet. I hope my old man isn't home."

Calling him back, Nick asked, "Are you guys up for an all-nighter?"

"Shit yes." Butch walked back toward them. "What do you have in mind?"

"Well, we can get a better eyeball on old man Murphy's place in the dark" said Nick, knowing this would fire up Butch.

"Man, you know I can dig it!" Butch's enthusiasm was remarkably restored. "How about it, Stan?"

"I'm in." Turning toward Nick Stan said, "But gee Wally, won't this get us in dutch with Mom and Dad?"

"Relax Beav; even if we do get in trouble, we can blame it on Eddy" responded Nick.

They all laughed.

"Hey, I'm not Eddy, right?" asked Butch.

Stan put his hand on Butch's shoulder, "Naw, you're not Eddy. You, and only you, will always be Butch."

"Hot shit, this is going to be a blast" said Butch. "I'm going home to eat and sack in."

Nick said, "Ok, how about 11:30, in the alley behind the grocery store. Everybody nab your old man's flashlight, bring candy bars."

"Got it!" Butch said as he headed for his house.

Nick and Stan stayed on the grass for a while. Stan broke the silence and asked, "What are you going to do?"

"I don't know, maybe go home and ask Ma to call the Durhams."

Stan, staring at the ground, said, "Look, I know what you're feeling, but we've done all that we can do."

"I know, but it's a bitch, man. I have to keep trying, for Beth, for me and for her parents. "

Stan rose to his feet, "I got to be careful sneaking out tonight, I almost got caught last time."

"Yeah, me too. See you at 11:30."

CHAPTER 21

Stan left the park and headed for home. Nick remained lying on the grass for a few moments before departing. River Street was jammed with bumper to bumper cars as the factory-induced traffic jam was underway; it was that time of day. Northbound cars lined River Street, while the southbound was open and free of all traffic; a complete reversal from the traffic pattern in the morning. Cars lined up to cross the concrete, four-arched bridge that spanned the Fox; the only bridge that spanned the Fox in Montgomery.

Nick negotiated his way between two cars in line. He was glad to see Charlie sitting on the steps of Shannon's. Nick leaned his Monarch against the front of the building and sat down next to Charlie.

Feeling Nick's disappointment, Charlie waited for time to settle in before he said, "Nicky-boy, something tells me you need to talk."

Nick, with his elbows on his knees and his head resting on his hands, said, "Yeah, but I don't think even you can solve this one Charlie."

"Maybe not, but I can listen. What's troubling you?"

"Ah Charlie, I can't figure it all out. At this point you probably know more about old man Murphy's place than I do, but that's not what's getting to me."

"Ok, what is it?"

"Charlie, do you remember that girl I talked to you about, Beth McVee?"

Playfully, Charlie responded, "Are you kidding me? Beth; the angel without wings, the written words of a scholar, and the eyes of a goddess with lashes that can change weather patterns? Do I remember her, how could I forget her?"

This brought a smile to Nick's face that disappeared quickly. "Charlie, she's missing."

"Missing . . . from?"

"Charlie, we met Andy Durham after we left you this morning and he said Beth's parents were at his place looking for her this morning. Andy's mom asked him to go searching. We helped him; we rode all over the place, including the mausoleum and the cemetery, and with no results." Pausing momentarily he continued, "But when I saw her dad talking with the cops at Murphy's place around noon, that scared me. I think she's in trouble or has been taken or . . . Charlie, I don't know what to think. After seeing her old man, we headed out on Aucutt Road to check that old farm house and the gun club, and we checked inside the old mill." Nick motioned in the direction of the old mill.

"You were in the old mill?" Charlie asked with genuine surprise.

"Yeah, but she wasn't there."

Realizing this wasn't the best time to learn about their entry into the old building, Charlie said, "Someday I want to hear about that old mill, but right now we have bigger fish to fry; how long has she been gone?"

"At least all day and maybe since last night" responded Nick.

"Nick, I am sorry. You didn't need this."

The thoughts of the two friends were not interrupted for a long time.

Charlie asked, "What more have you learned about the investigation at Thad Murphy's place?"

"Not that much, like I said, we were at Murphy's a little after noon and saw even more cops, but that's about it; how about you?"

Charlie stood and motioned to Nick to grab his bike and follow him. They walked along the side of the tavern and found a small patch of grass in the back. Once seated, Charlie said, "Folks don't think I should be talking with you as much as I do, especially about serious subjects, but that's because they don't know you like I do."

He pulled out a pack of Camels and lit one with the Zippo with the wobbling top. Holding up the pack of Camels he said, "Shannon felt generous today. Some days he's a good guy." Following one of his famously deep drags, he said as he exhaled, "Murphy has been the talk here all day long. No one really tells me anything, but I listen. Chuck Morgan was back in this afternoon and attracted an audience; seems that Willy supplies Chuck with information, Chuck runs down here to inform his friends. Chuck has become popular; I think he likes it.

Here's the weird part, it seems as if Thad Murphy killed and skinned a dog in his cellar."

"Skinned, as in removed the skin?"

"Yep, you have the picture."

"Holy shit! Why would he do that?" asked Nick

"No idea, Nicky-boy. But I'm not through; they found a lot of blood in the cellar, more than would have come from the dog. The County tested it and confirmed the majority of the blood is human. Willy heard the discussion when the County returned."

"Human blood? So, whose is it?"

"No one knows for sure, but a lot of possibilities are being discussed; the one getting the most attention in there . . ." nodding toward the tavern, ". . . is that Thad Murphy cracked up, killed someone, and took off with the body."

"Charlie, what do you think?"

"I don't have a clue, but I heard Chuck say that Willy heard the investigators talking about drag marks on the steps indicating something was dragged out of the cellar. All in all, the amount of blood indicates someone is dead and Thad is gone. It's a strange set of circumstances. None of them look good for Thad."

"Did you hear anything else, Charlie?"

"Not really, but you can only imagine how the theories are running wild" nodding toward the tavern again. "Willy did tell Chuck that the County has delivered a stack of photos to the investigators, Willy didn't get to see them. He heard Chief Woodyard say that most of the investigators were going to meet in the police station to lay out reports and evidence. He also heard the County guys say they have a dragnet out for Thad. Nicky, if you were looking for excitement when you woke up this morning, you found it."

"Yeah, and if it didn't involve Beth, I would be enjoying it. Did you hear anything about her Charlie?"

Hesitating and considering not sharing all that he heard from Chuck, Charlie chose to disregard his own caution, "Nicky, Willy said that when the County guys concluded their grid search they laid out a collection of things they gathered; one of the items was a white sneaker. Willy heard the investigators say the sneaker didn't appear to have been exposed to any weather."

"A girl's white sneaker?"

"Don't know, but Chuck's story from Willy stated it was small. It wasn't around Murphy's place, but down around the crossing. Now don't go putting rotten eggs in your basket, Nick. It doesn't mean anything; it simply means they found a sneaker." Charlie watched as Nick studied the ground.

"So what are your plans, Nick?"

Nick continued to look down and said, "We're doing an all-nighter tonight."

"Who's doing an all-nighter?"

"Stan, Butch and me."

"What's Mom and Dad got to say about that?"

"They won't know; we're all sneaking out."

"Nick, I never tell you what to do and I'm not starting now, but strange goings on are occurring in our little village; how strange no one really knows. You boys might want to rethink your decision."

"Charlie, I have to do something; and hell, this is our town, we do all-nighters all the time."

Charlie reached over and lightly hit Nick on the shoulder. "Ok Nicky-boy, sure would hate to lose a mayor. You boys be careful."

CHAPTER 22

College life was a new experience for Sally; new geographically, new emotionally, and new independently. She started her classes, met new friends and became settled in her new environment. Settled to the extent that she accepted it, but unsettled as to why she left the warm and comfortable home that she so loved.

She wrote to Betty and Grover twice a week and received reciprocal letters in return. She masked her homesickness as much as she could, but it leaked into her letters. Betty offered to come to DeKalb for a while if that would help, but Sally rejected the idea and said she would be home for Thanksgiving, though she had no idea how she would find the transportation.

She struggled to find an answer to why it was so important that she live in Illinois. Though she fought it with logical rationale, she knew it was to find her real father; to find out if he was still alive, and if he cared if she was alive. She felt driven by curiosity, disappointment and even anger.

She was able to travel the thirty miles to Aurora in October. The parents of one of the girls she met at school lived in Aurora. They invited Sally to join them for the weekend. Sally jumped at the opportunity. She asked if it would be possible to get a tour of the city. They obliged. She saw the Leland Hotel, the site of her parents wedding reception, but made no reference to it in conversation. She was particularly interested as they followed the river south on Route 25 and looked with interest for a "stately house," as Betty described it, but did not see one that stood out.

While in the hosts' home, she borrowed their telephone directory and looked for a Thaddeus Murphy, but found none. In passing, she asked if her hosts had ever heard of Thaddeus Murphy, but both said they had not. The weekend trip to Aurora helped Sally's emotional state temporarily, but unfortunately created a stronger desire to return to Aurora and search for the man named Thaddeus Murphy.

Betty and Grover were the ones to travel on Thanksgiving; they drove to DeKalb for a long weekend. The reunion was medicinal for all three. They hugged and kissed a lot, toured the campus and the lecture rooms and halls that Sally attended, became far more familiar with the history of barbed wire and the families that forged the way, the Ellwoods and the Gliddens, and they toured the agricultural town from top to bottom. They enjoyed a Thanksgiving dinner with the family of one of Sally's friends who lived in DeKalb. Their parting at the end of the weekend was easier than in August.

One of the things that Sally did not reveal to Betty and Grover is that she had met a boy on campus that she liked. He was not a student, but rather a member of the maintenance crew that took care of the campus grounds. He was a few years older than Sally, but didn't act that way. He was from a poor farming family in Sandwich, Illinois, south of DeKalb. Sally found the name of the town humorous. She would kid him about escaping from between the slices.

He was thoughtful and considerate; often expressing sincere interest in what Sally was learning. Their relationship began as friends, but became more romantic with time. The advancement of their romance was always initiated by Sally. Sally was the first to reach for his hand while strolling, the first to suggest that he put his arm around her while sitting on a park bench, the first to kiss him, and so on. Sally asked him why he was so reluctant to engage in romantic interlude. His response was both simple and touching, "Because you're the best thing that has ever happened to me and I don't want to mess it up by being too bold." She laughed and said playfully, "You could mess it up by not being bold at all, you know."

From that moment on, he took charge and their relationship grew as did their exploration of each other's bodies. Sally did not feel the restraints as she had with Tom Shrader; maybe it was the absence from Betty, Grover and Mystic, or maybe it was because she felt safe and secure with him; whatever she felt, she liked it.

As in the beginning with Tom, Sally allowed him to touch and feel, first through clothing and then under the clothing. Sally enjoyed his touch; not only on her breasts but when he would play between her legs. Sally found herself anxiously awaiting each of the opportunities to be alone in his 1936 Plymouth. The back seat was large, the heater was good and DeKalb provided an endless supply of places to park without being bothered.

During one of the explorations in the backseat, Sally took her turn at exploring. She felt his bump many times as he lay on her or beside her, but she wanted to feel it with her hand. She positioned herself on her side facing him and allowed her hand to slide slowly down his stomach. She had caressed his chest and stomach before, but this time she did not stop at the belt line. He tensed as her hand touched his bump. She was nervous as she unzipped his pants and inserted her hand. She tried to contain her surprise at the hardness and size of a penis. Now they were both tense. Sally became more relaxed and confident and brought it out of his pants. She did not want to embarrass him by looking down, though she really wanted to see it. So she just held it, exploring each inch with her fingertips. Sally noticed that he was immobilized; whatever she was doing, she knew he liked it, and she knew she liked doing it.

Their physical relationship rapidly escalated to the fullest extent. The first time Sally removed all of her clothing, he was stunned. This alarmed Sally, "What's wrong?" He remained silent for a moment and said, "You are the most incredibly beautiful thing in the world. I am not worthy." Sally thrust her arms around his neck and hugged the air out of him. The session that followed can only be imagined.

Sally took a train to Mystic for the three-week Christmas break. So much had changed, not in Mystic, but in her. Her new relationship added a dimension to her life that she couldn't explain, but could only treasure.

Her time with Betty and Grover over the Christmas break was wonderful, she told them about her new boyfriend, however she did not tell them about the seriousness of the relationship. By the end of the three weeks she was anxious to return to school; no, she was anxious to return to him.

Her train ride back to DeKalb was filled with anxious anticipation. He met her at the train station, and their lives together re-fired where they left off. Over the months that followed, Sally shared her entire life with him, her entire present life. She could not bring herself to reveal the truth about Thaddeus Murphy; it was a private place, a special secret place, a place that could not be shared with others, not even with him. Sally felt as if she should feel guilty about withholding from him, but she could not feel any guilt at all. In her heart, they belonged together, but Thaddeus Murphy belonged only to her.

They made two trips to Aurora in the early months of 1945 under false pretenses. Sally said she loved the river and the big city attractions. Always aiming to please, he was more than happy to drive to Aurora to assist in seeking her unidentified fascination, all in the name of love. They rode up and down the Fox River Valley; Sally couldn't get enough.

Sally was to complete her school year in May and return to Mystic for the summer. When she wrote home to say that she was going to stay in DeKalb to work, Betty and Grover wrote back that they were planning to pay her to work the hardware store for the summer. Sally held her ground and agreed to come home the last week in May, but she would return to the job she arranged in DeKalb. The truth was Sally was pregnant. They consciously took precautions; however, those precautions had failed.

When Sally noticed that she was late, she crossed her fingers, but as time went by and she remained late, she was forced to tell him. His response was that of a nobleman; his first concern was for Sally and her emotional state. This calmed Sally who feared that he would be upset and leave her. In classic style he dropped to one knee, swore his everlasting dedication to her and asked her to marry him when she was ready. Sally cried. She cried with joy and appreciation, not lamenting the pregnancy at all. The difficult part would be telling Betty and Grover; but that wouldn't be necessary for a while.

In the second week of May 1945, they went before a local judge and Sally Thomas became Mrs. Stuart McVee.

Stuart drove Sally to Mystic in the last week of May. To say that the announcement that they were married was a shock to Betty and Grover is to suggest that the Mississippi River is but a stream. Betty fought the conflicting emotions of disbelief and confirmed disappointment. She had envisioned the wedding of her daughter for all of the seventeen years Sally had been theirs. More tears flowed, especially when Betty was alone with Grover. Grover felt the disappointment, but accepted the fact that Sally was making her own life now, and he and Betty were but spectators with an interest.

At the end of the week-long visit, Betty and Grover kissed their daughter and new son-in-law goodbye and more tears flowed.

Once back in DeKalb, Sally convinced Stuart that she would not be able to continue with her education, and persuaded him to leave his job at the College. Most importantly to her, she convinced him that they should relocate to Aurora, Illinois to raise their child; besides, the jobs were more plentiful for both of them.

CHAPTER 23

The investigation progressed sharply once they were able to get the evidence off to the County for further examination and testing. It was 1:30 in the afternoon. Two county cops stayed at Murphy's to provide security. Bob, Pete and Henry left for lunch, but agreed to meet at the village station at three o'clock that afternoon to review County findings.

The grid search revealed little, with the exception of a small white sneaker found near the tracks well south of Murphy's property. This appeared to be coincidental until John reported back to Bob and Henry with his notes taken during the McVee interview.

John briefed Bob and Henry on what he learned from the McVees. He described their living conditions. He reported that he felt their heartbreak appeared sincere.

"Bob, do you want me to take the sneaker over the McVees' to see if they can confirm that it may be their girl's?" asked John.

"Not yet, but we will. Keeping the dramatic aspect out of the mix for now is important. If it is hers, we'll know soon enough. Any response from Oswego, Aurora or Yorkville?" replied Bob.

"Not a thing. I called Oswego again to make sure the word was delivered to the next shift. They said they were paying special attention to Routes 25 and 31, and they checked out the hangout areas down by the river. Nothing."

Henry chimed in, "Look, I don't intend to stick my nose where it doesn't belong, but both you guys know that the odds are her old man is involved. Have you verified that he was at work all night and never left?"

"No, but I will, he works at Miller's Tool & Die up Route 31 this side of Jericho Road" responded John.

Bob turned toward John, "John, check with the Durhams to support what you heard from the McVees and see if they feel that anything out of the ordinary could be going on. Check out Miller's, and did you check out his hands and arms for scratches or scrapes?"

"I looked him over real good, both when he showed up at Murphy's and at his house; I could see no recent injuries. If you don't need me right now, I'll head across the tracks to the Durhams and on to Miller's Tool & Die."

CHAPTER 24

At three o'clock Wednesday afternoon, Bob was preparing for the investigators' meeting. Bob asked the Village Clerk to stay at the station to answer the phone while the meeting was going on and gave strict instructions, "No interruptions for those attending the meeting, unless the call is directly related to the investigation." The clerk was excited to be involved. "Chief, before you go in, Stafford's junk yard reported a stolen car from their used car lot. I've made out the report."

"Good job, I'll get to it later." Much later is what he really meant.

Going through his mental check list, Bob confirmed with the County that an all-points-bulletin on Thaddeus Murphy was submitted to the State and all cities and towns within 50 miles. A missing report for the McVee girl was being submitted to all neighboring towns. The evidence from Murphy's cellar was delivered to the County; a few of the reports and all the photos were back. The scene was secured. He shook his head, "I hope that's enough for now."

Bob converted the "court room" portion of the small police building into a crime investigation center. He used cardboard to block out the lower half of the windows to prevent gawkers from seeing the items from the investigation he displayed on two tables in the center of the room. Among the items were the crime scene photos from County. Chairs were positioned about for the investigators when they arrived. A portable blackboard on wheels was positioned with the back of the blackboard toward the windows to prevent visual access to anything that was written.

Bob reviewed every photo provided by the County and the notes he and John had taken, as well as the formal reports on fingerprints and blood analysis. The discoveries from the County complicated the circumstances more than they provided answers. He thought, "What the hell was going on? Murphy's cellar was a real mystery. The McVee girl was another matter altogether. He was still hoping she would show up at a friend's house, but the Murphy situation would not end that conveniently."

Murphy's place became Bob's personal nightmare; the town was on fire with at least a hundred theories as to the events that created the scene.

Bob could not go anywhere without hearing others' ideas of what happened. One lady even suggested that they would find more bodies in the backyard if they dug for them. Imaginations were running wild. Stories that Murphy was responsible for killings in Aurora, Murphy was an escapee from the hospital for the mentally ill in Elgin, Murphy is planning a killing spree; on and on they went.

Bob was convinced that none of them were right, including his own theories. Murphy, after all these years of being the reclusive eccentric, has turned Bob's village upside down. Bob wondered if that was part of Murphy's plan, to gain revenge, or pay back; but for what? Murphy wasn't at odds with anyone, he didn't really create any enemies; what would the revenge angle prove?

It didn't really matter, because now it was Bob's problem. Of course, it was Murphy's problem too, but Murphy was gone and not in the belly of the beast. Where is Murphy? Better yet, what had he done? Bob's head ached. Twenty-seven years of being a civil servant to the village of Montgomery, not far from walking away in retirement, and now this.

The door to the police station opened; Bob could see through the connecting door that it was John followed by Pete Morantz and Henry Conner. Bob said loudly, "Hey boys, I'm in here." The three entered the makeshift lab and looked around. Henry was the first to speak, "Damn Bob, not bad, looks like you do this all the time. Nice set up. You ought to think about being a cop."

"Yeah, that's what I was thinking" retorted Bob.

"More of my guys are coming Bob, they're on their way" offered Pete.

"Ours too" added Henry.

John plopped into one of the courtroom chairs.

Pete asked, "Long day, John?"

"Actually, a long night," John looked at his watch and calculated "It started twenty hours ago."

"Whew, you need to get some sleep."

"Yeah John, why don't you head for home and I'll brief you when you come in – let's say 10:00. Will that work for you?" asked Bob.

"It sure will. I cleared the McVees' story with the Durhams. They said they know Mrs. McVee better than they know her husband, however, they would be shocked if anything out of the ordinary was taking place; they describe McVee as 'adoring' toward his daughter. Millers Tool & Die said McVee was definitely at work all night. The day foreman showed me a timecard that requires McVee to punch in every hour at different stations as he does his rounds." John stood to leave.

Henry stopped him and asked, "John, any chance you know anything about Murphy that we don't? Maybe strange things you may have observed at night that didn't really register at the time?"

"Not really, Henry. I don't recall anything other than the obvious. I would see him briefly from time to time, but nothing sticks out. Bob knows him a lot better than I do."

"Ok thanks, go get some rest" said Henry.

Additional investigators arrived from the County and the State. After they all viewed the items of the investigation, and briefly scanned the photos, Bob said to Henry, "I'm going to ask you to run the show; I've reviewed everything and feel hopelessly inadequate."

"Don't get down on yourself now Bob, this thing is like looking at a jigsaw puzzle right out of the box" replied Henry.

Henry walked to the chalkboard and said, "Let's start by recording what we think we know and discuss each item."

Henry drew a timeline at the top of the chalkboard. All the way to the left, he placed an "X" on the line; to the right of the "X" he entered a short perpendicular line. Above the line he wrote 6:45am 'Rively notified'.

One of the investigators asked, "What's the "X represent? "

"That is the time the cellar became a killing room. I think we're going to be able to estimate that time from the County findings, but right now we will leave it an X." He added another entry for 7:30 with the notation "County," another at 8:05 for "State," another at 8:30 "initial photos," another at 8:55 "clean rooms discovered in the house," another at 9:45 for "dog discovered – photos complete – all sent to County," another at 10:10 "dog and tarp removed," another at 12:45 for "McVee girl reported missing," another at 1:10 for "grid search complete." With that Henry turned toward the others, "Have I missed anything?" asked Henry.

"Nope, I don't think so" responded one the investigators.

The tall County investigator asked, "What's the reference to "clean rooms" mean?"

"You never made it into the house?" asked Henry.

"No, I was in the killing room having fun."

"My guess is you haven't seen all the photos either." Henry addressed all of them and continued. "You have all heard about, or seen, the enormous amount of junk throughout Murphy's house; piles of junk stacked to the ceiling, right?"

The County investigator nodded.

Henry continued, "We found two rooms that were as neat as a pin. No junk, no stacks - kind of two normal rooms in a sea of trash."

Looking shocked, the investigator said, "What'd you make of that?"

"Great question, because we need to talk about it – but let's get to that later."

"If the timeline is acceptable, let's go back to "X." When did the killing of the dog, and the other activities take place in the cellar?" asked Henry.

"According to the lab report, they're estimating midnight, give or take a couple of hours" responded one of the investigators.

"For those of you that have not reviewed the lab reports, they are on the table." Henry pointed in the direction of the brown folders. He continued, "Ok, the lab estimates midnight, but for those of you who worked the cellar, how does that sit with your timetable?"

No one spoke; all that had been in the cellar processed the question, one of them said, "It fits mine, a lot of the blood was dried and the smell of metallic decomposing blood was getting heavy. That takes a while, so yeah, midnight or earlier is my vote."

"Anyone disagree?" Henry asked as he glanced to each person. Each gave a subtle shake of their head.

He erased the "X" and replaced it with "10 to 12pm, Tuesday."

"What was the result of the blood testing?" asked Henry. Henry had read copies of the reports before he arrived at the meeting, but he wanted to stimulate discussion.

Bob said, "What I read was that they found three types of blood; one animal, confirmed as the dog's, and two human samples, one Type A and one Type O, which means two people bled in the killing room, and one bled in the bedroom upstairs."

"Bingo" said Henry. "One of those will likely match up with Murphy, but we're having a hard time finding any medical records on him. Bob told us that Murphy was in the hospital back in the twenties, but our department is not finding any results for that visit. We have people calling doctors' offices right now to see if they have seen a Thaddeus Murphy for medical care. If we find one that has seen him, they may, or may not, have his blood type.

Locating the right doctor's office could take a while, but they are working on it."

"What else did you find interesting in the blood report, Bob?" asked Henry.

"The lab boys couldn't tell how much blood came from the different bleeders, but they did suggest from the amount of blood found on the tarp, and as reflected in the photos, that one of the two bleeders did not survive. Small bone fragments found on the tarp suggest that as well; they are being analyzed. Their estimate is five quarts, including what came from the dog. The dog did not reveal any wounds resulting in a massive loss of blood. They suggest that a blow to the dog's head was the cause of death. However, they think the dog got its revenge, human blood was found in its mouth."

"OK, we have two bleeders. That's new, but the rest we figured out before we sent it off" said Henry. "Anybody review the print file?"

"Yeah" said one of the State investigators holding the print file open, having just reviewed it. "Various prints in and around the bench area, one dominant set, likely Murphy's, it matches most of the prints taken in the house. One print in blood did not match Murphy's."

"Two bleeders, two sets of prints" reflected Henry. "Is it my imagination, or is this not getting any easier?"

Pete asked, "What about footprints?"

"According to our guys, they couldn't pull footprints from that tarp, but the print guys studied the photos and said the patterns on the tarp and on the floor were so smudged that they could not come to a conclusion, lots of slipping and sliding around. One print suggested that it was possibly a size ten or eleven, but the notation suggests that could be from a smaller size sliding in the blood" responded Bob. "Lotta help, huh Pete?"

"Yeah, lotta help."

"So gentlemen, we are down to the photos. If an answer does exist, I think the photos are where we will find it" said Henry. "By the way," he looked toward the two County investigators that took the photos, "You guys did a good job. How good we won't know until we solve this, but good job anyway."

Henry walked over to the tables holding the photos. "We've all done this before, but let's try a new approach." He took pads of paper he brought with him and distributed them to everyone in the room. "Let's break the photos into groups so everyone has a group in front of them. I asked the photo guys to number each photo; the number is in the lower left corner. After you've studied the photo, record your thoughts relating to that photo. When you've finished with your group, exchange with someone else that has finished, but don't share your notes or discuss the photos until everyone has seen them all."

"As you view each photo, look for the obvious clues captured by the camera." Henry began to write on the chalkboard. "Out of place, peculiar, changed, missing, and _____." As he drew the line for the last item he said, "You fill in the blank, look for anything that might help us."

Pete said, "Henry, I forgot my sleeping bag, did you bring an extra?"

Henry chuckled, "No, but I have arranged to have burgers and fries sent over from the diner later."

CHAPTER 25

John Rively headed home following his merciful release from the three o'clock meeting. He wanted to stay because he was learning as he observed the County and State investigators, but he was tired when Willy Smith bounced into his office eight hours ago. He thought as he glanced at his watch, "Eight hours? Was it only eight hours?" It felt like days to him.

His employment with the Montgomery police department began two years and six months ago. He was twenty-six years old, with no police training when he hired on. Bob Woodyard trained him on the particular needs of Montgomery, he received firearms training and medical training at the County and voila, he was a cop.

He took the Montgomery job to gain police experience and hopefully would move on to the State Police, or maybe even the F.B.I. Earlier in his life he had had some brushes with the law, but so far he'd successfully concealed them. Eventually, he would have to come clean, but he hoped that a successful history of being on the right side of the law would offset his previous indiscretions.

Serving Montgomery was a snap; roam the empty night-filled streets, settle a squabble here and there, mind the fender benders, keep peace at the taverns and go home. Yep, it was a snap alright, until Willy came bouncing in; the world changed color. Willy's arrival threw him into a three ring circus of a homicide investigation, a missing person's case and a possible child kidnapping, all in Montgomery.

He found the events surrounding Murphy and his cellar, disturbing, but interesting. The circumstance involving the little girl he could do without. He had a bad feeling about Beth's disappearance, and the possibility of a good ending was evaporating with each hour.

He wanted to believe that everything he was told by the McVees was on the up-and-up, but it was bothering him; it didn't feel right. He couldn't put his finger on it; he had an itch he couldn't scratch. The McVees' alibis panned out, but something needed explanation.

John and his wife, Connie, lived in one of the new starter homes north of the cemetery. The small sub-division, like the cemetery, occupied all of the space between Main Street and River Street. Because of the limited multi-housing projects in Montgomery, the sub-division was unofficially graced with the name "The New Addition." The name would stick for decades.

John pulled into his driveway on James Street and was greeted by Connie. "Hi stranger; looking for a place to bed down? The beds are lumpy, the food is barely edible, but the girls will leave you with a smile" she said.

"Actually, I was looking for one particular girl, is she available?" he said, as he played along.

"No, she's off with a high-payer, but I'm available."

"How long will she be gone?" John asked.

Connie, realizing she had been bested, punched him in the arm and hugged him. "You have to be hungry; would you like breakfast, leftover meatloaf, soup, or something else?"

"The something else is tempting, but I need to grab food, sleep and head back to the station at 10:00 tonight."

"Tonight; I thought you'd have the night off?" she said with disappointment.

"Honey, with all that's going on, we have to have a presence. Bob's been at it since early morning and will continue beyond my arrival at ten o'clock. We're a small department," John offered apologetically.

"I've been hearing all kinds of rumors from neighbors, is it true a murder has taken place?" she asked as they entered the back door of the house.

John slumped into one of the kitchen chairs, "Yeah, it looks like it, but we don't know for sure yet; it looks like a guy named Murphy down on Railroad Street went crazy and did something to someone. The only thing we know for sure is that he killed and skinned a dog and took off."

"What?"

"Honey, believe it or not, I don't have a lot to tell right now. Have you heard about the little girl that is missing?" John asked.

"Well, yes, but is that connected to all of this, is she the one who was murdered?" She stopped what she was doing and sat across from him.

"No - no I don't think so."

"You don't think so what?" she pressed.

"I don't think they are connected and I don't think she was the one murdered. Honey, I'm not sure what I think, if you want to know the truth. It's all up in the air right now" he responded. "I'll know more when I've seen all the results from the County. Bob and the other investigators are going over the lab results and photos right now. They sent me home to get rest. Bob will brief me when I get in tonight. By chance, have you ever crossed paths with the McVees?" He asked.

"No, I don't think so. Where do they live?"

"You aren't going to believe this, but in a shack on the side of the railroad tracks by Baseline" said John. "Back in that wooded area."

"What do they have to do with that Murphy guy?" she asked.

"They have nothing to do with Murphy, they're the parents of the missing girl" said John.

"Oh – those poor people" Connie corrected herself, "or maybe I should say unfortunate people."

"No, you're right on both counts, regardless of your intended meaning. They are poor and they are unfortunate; and their little girl is missing. And ..." he paused, "I don't want you to repeat this to anyone, but something is fishy."

"Fishy how, John? Do you think they . . . kidnapped, or hurt their own daughter?" asked Connie.

"I don't know, but I get the feeling I'm missing a key ingredient. I interviewed both of them at their home. I've confirmed that the dad was at work all night, but it doesn't feel right. Honey, if I promise to tell you as much as I can tomorrow, would you mind if I sleep for a while?"

"Of course not, but at least eat a sandwich before you go down." She turned to the refrigerator to get the lunch meat.

"Do you know what I've been thinking about throughout this day?" asked John.

"No."

"I've been thinking about Sunday's sermon; God protecting the Israelites as they fought battles against enemies bigger than they were, but the Israelites won because God protected them. I kept thinking, 'Where is God today,' why isn't He protecting the people of Montgomery. Granted, they aren't Israelites, but they are good hard-working people. How does that sermon apply to this?"

"I don't know, John. But the pastor did conclude by saying that God's promise to us is that whatever we face, God is there for us, and we won't face it alone."

John finished his sandwich, kissed Connie as he headed for the bedroom saying, "That may be so, but I felt pretty alone today."

Connie stood in the kitchen looking at the chromed tubular kitchenette set and prayed that God would guide John to answers, but most of all that God would protect that little girl.

CHAPTER 26

All-nighters were a regular thing in the summertime. Those officially authorized by parents were "camp outs" when tents were pitched in someone's backyard; long after the parents were asleep the tents were vacated and the explorers began exploring the things that only the darkness of night could make exciting; fishing on the river, or roaming the alleys, hanging out on the railroad tracks, or sitting under the bridge smoking fags and telling stories; all being done while escaping the notice of the local cops. That was the typical all-nighter.

The unauthorized all-nighter required each of the participants to sneak out of their respective homes with the provisions for the evening, without being detected. Most of the houses in Montgomery were small, old and quaint, and each had television antennas sprouting from their roof tops. The old structures found a way of talking with creaks and groans; thus, sneaking out required time and patience. Groaning steps and squeaking door hinges became the enemy. Family pets needed to be bribed to cooperate. Getting out was the main objective, but sneaking back in was equally as challenging. So far, all of them were successful, with only a couple of close calls.

Tonight's all-nighter was especially nerve-racking because of the purpose at hand. Tonight it wasn't about the cigarettes, or the fish, or the stories, or the occasional glimpse of a woman undressing in an upstairs bedroom; no, tonight was about something else. It was about figuring out a mystery. It was about sneaking into a world that was turned upside down. Old Man Murphy was missing, Beth McVee was missing, bad things occurred in a cellar and no one knew anything. Tonight's all-nighter was purposeful – they had to find answers that could bring sense to confusion.

Nick waited until he heard his dad snoring for at least a half-hour. He knew that his mom fell asleep immediately upon hitting the pillow, but his dad was another story. If Nick's timing was off, the all-nighter would be off.

Feeling confident, he crept downstairs being careful with the third step from the top; that one screeched rather that squeaked. He grabbed cookies and a flashlight and slipped out the backdoor. Once outside he breathed in the night air and exhaled with a sense of accomplishment. The night air was fresh and clean, a slight breeze stirred the leaved trees, the quiet was both peaceful and frightening at the same time.

He walked toward the tracks on Clinton Street, staying close to the bushes with a wary eye for any movements ahead. If a neighbor happened to be out, Nick wanted to see them before they saw him. If he detected any movement he would dash into a bush or behind a tree to wait for them to finish what they were doing and proceed when the coast was clear. He saw no movement tonight so he walked up the hill to the alley.

The alley was a cindered one-lane passage that ran parallel to River Street and Main Street. The businesses and homes on Main and River Streets used the alley to access the small garages or storage sheds on the alley. From the alley, one could view the backside of life.

They agreed to meet behind Michaels Brothers Grocery Store. The store was operated by two second-generation Michaels brothers. It was a main artery of life for Montgomery, providing everything a family needed for survival; fresh vegetables, packaged and canned goods, cleaning materials, soda pop, and cut-to-order meats wrapped in brown paper and tied with string. The boxed and canned foods were stacked high on shelves, ice cream was scooped from cardboard cylindrical containers kept deep in a horizontal freezer, the scoop being dipped in water after each scoop of ice cream was deposited.

Most significant to an explorer was the candy displayed in large glass display cases and glass jars on the wooden counter top. To an explorer, the walk on those old wooden floors was a mouth-watering, ever enticing, eye-opening experience. Choosing which, and how many, candies could be purchased with the money in hand was a major undertaking, but a delightful one.

Aside from supplying Montgomery residents with the usual fare, Michaels treated their customers like family; always greeting customers by name and inquiring as to the welfare of family members. Families could run an account with Michaels paying once a week, once a month or when they could.

Nick was amazed by the contrast of the front of the grocery store to the back. Two large plate-glass windows on both sides of the concrete steps entering the store displayed posters welcoming visitors with weekly and daily specials; the back of the store was like the ugly step-child that no one should see. Stacked wooden crates from produce deliveries - flattened cardboard boxes - cases of empty pop bottles, sorted by brand – the smell of discarded vegetables and meat cuts rotting in garbage cans. Nick thought that the store sales would likely drop off dramatically if the patrons entered through the back.

Approaching the back of the store quietly, Nick found Butch back in the shadows sitting on the flattened cardboard boxes listening to his prized transistor radio. The radio was the size of a pack of cigarettes. The tinny sound of Buddy Holly and the Crickets' *"That'll Be the Day"* squeaked out of the small speaker. Nick joined him to stay out of the glow being cast from the street light on Webster Street.

"Hey Butch."

"Hey Nick, you made it."

"Of course I made it. You expected less?"

"No, but your house makes a lot of noise."

"Tell me! I've learned to walk like a cat. I'm getting pretty good at it."

"How about you, did you have any problems, Butch?"

"Naw, my old man is usually so drunk he doesn't know which end is up. He's probably at Shannon's right now anyway. Maybe he won't find his way home tonight. My mom is so exhausted that she goes out like a light."

"Did you bring a flashlight?"

"You bet."

"What did you bring to eat, Butch?"

"Candy bars, and get this, brownies!"

"Brownies?"

"Yeah, Mom made a bunch for her Canasta Club tomorrow night. If she notices some are missing I'll blame it on my older brother. He left to go camping with friends earlier tonight. He'll be gone for a few days."

"Nice move, Butch."

"Thanks. Where's Stan?"

"He'll be here."

Stan arrived to hear about Butch's commandeering the brownies.

"When it comes to food Butch, you are the man in charge" said Stan. "I snagged bread and lunch meat, but that doesn't hold a candle to brownies."

Nick updated the others on the info from Charlie, and said, "Here's what I'm thinking. Everything revolves around Murphy's place, so let's use that as the starting point."

"Man, they will be guarding Murphy's tonight. They have the yard lit up with lights; I could see them from my place" exclaimed Butch.

"All the better for us to see" answered Nick.

"What are we looking for?" asked Stan.

"Anything that will help us understand what's going on. I figure we go down the west side of the tracks and climb up like we did this morning. The darkness will give us plenty of cover to slip in closer. If the guards are talking, we'll be able to hear them."

"Man, we'll interfere with official police work; that could get us in big trouble" exclaims Butch.

144

"I'm not saying we do anything or touch anything, I'm saying we look and listen, Butch."

"Man, I don't know . . ."

"Butch, you can wait for us at the tracks if you want to."

"No, I'll go; I just don't want to end up in jail."

Stan asks "What do we do after we look and listen?"

"We discuss what we heard and try to fit it into the puzzle" responded Nick. "Getting across the tracks could be tricky. We can't be seen. If we try to cross at Webster we might be seen by the guards; Murphy's place is down a ways, but they might have binoculars, and Rively is cruising around. It's too wide open."

"How do you plan to get over the tracks?" asked Stan.

"If we go up Main Street to that area where the big trucks load and unload for Lyon Metal, we can scale the outside fence, go through the lot and scale the fence to the tracks."

"Lyon has night watchmen" said Butch.

"Yeah, but if we scale the fence by the junkyard, and stay behind the parked trucks, I doubt they'll be able to see us; we'll be like shadows in the night. We can walk on the tracks until we get beyond the factory; from that point we'll have to stay low. Even doing it this way, crossing Webster will be tricky. We'll have to do it one at a time with the other two watching for approaching cars."

Standing, Stan declares, "Ok Nick - sounds like you've got this worked out. Let's get rolling."

The boys walked in the darkened alley as far as they could, watching carefully for car headlights. They crossed through the cindered parking lot; near the school ball field, they were required to cross a hundred yards of open land. The plan was to go one at a time and stay low to the ground. Nick went first, followed by Stan. When they were crouching in the bush near the fence of the factory, they looked back to see Butch running upright without grace or speed. Nick said with a chuckle, "He must have missed the 'stay low' part."

Stan added, "If this was WWII, we would be writing a letter to Butch's parents. He might as well have a target on his back."

"Yeah, nimble he ain't" said Nick. They were both laughing when Butch joined them in the bush.

"What? What's so funny?" Butch blurted with limited breath.

"Butch, do remember any reference to staying low?" asked Nick.

"I did, I stayed low and my legs are aching."

"If we'd been under machine gun fire, more than your legs would be aching" said Stan.

"Machine gun fire? What are you guys talking about?"

"Nothing Butch, we were relating you to Audie Murphy in the movie *"To Hell and Back"* said Nick.

"Aw man, do you think Old Man Murphy is related to Audie Murphy? That would be so cool" said Butch.

"Butch, I really doubt it. Now can you focus on getting over the fence?" asked Nick.

Butch looked up at the fence, not having noticed it before. His face revealed ultimate defeat. "Are you kidding me? How are we going to get over it?"

"Butch, it's an eight foot hurricane fence. We use the toes of our shoes to climb up one side, cross over without ripping our nuts off, and climb down the other side. Not that big of a deal," said Stan. "Look, I'll go first to show you how, then you go, Nick will stay behind in case you need help."

"Man, I don't know . . ." said Butch.

"You don't have to know, you just have to do. Are you ready?"

Stan positioned himself at the base of the fence near an upright, reaching high with both hands to get a grip in the diamond shapes; he inserted the toes of his right shoe into the fence, and lifted off. At the top, he used the upright for the crossover, and went down the other side.

Stan, showing no worse for the wear, said, "Ok Butch, do what I did."

Butch did well on the way up. The crossover was another story. Slinging large overweight legs over the fence required Nick to climb up behind Butch and use his back to help Butch negotiate to the other side.

Once on the other side of the fence, Butch lost focus and fell into Stan who had positioned himself to help Butch climb down. Butch's weight sent them sprawling onto the concrete with a thud. Stan took most of the impact when Butch landed on top. Nick scrambled down to see if they were hurt. Stan laid still with the wind knocked out of him and couldn't speak. Butch rolled over gasping. Nick recalled getting his wind knocked out during a baseball game and knew they needed to wait for Stan to relax and get air into his lungs. Nick pulled up on Stan's belt buckle to take pressure off his mid-section. Stan recovered, sat up wearily. Sucking in air he said "Nick, you go first next time."

Following their plan, they stayed behind the large trucks as they worked their way to the fence near the tracks. Stan was dreading getting Butch over the next fence, but upon arrival they all noticed that the fence was loose from the upright at the corner of the fence. With two of them pulling the fencing out and up, the other could slide beneath the fence. Stan said, "There is a God in heaven." He began pulling on the fence to get Butch under it and on the other side.

Their next challenge was the swampy drainage area between the fence and elevated tracks. Unlike the area near Phil's house, the swampy area was only eight to ten feet wide, but it was knee-deep mud, stinky and crawling with critters and bugs. The weeds and the cattails made it even more foreboding. A cacophony was created by the night dwellers; frogs, crickets and things unseen, all making their own form of music. Combined with the darkness, even the most experienced explorer felt a shiver run up his spine.

Nick wandered toward the factory in search of a way to get across. Stan and Butch headed toward the junkyard. Nick gave out a short whistle. He found where someone had created a walkway from old crates and planks. Once across, they climbed the hill of track ballast and began walking the tracks toward Murphy's.

The old factory with its high grime-covered windows was to the left, the beginning of the hump yard was to the right. The combined smells of oil, steel, heat, paint and human labor from the factory collided with the natural smell of animal waste from the hump yard creating a putrid aroma that could not be ignored.

Butch broke out a handkerchief with six Kool cigarettes rolled inside. "I couldn't help myself, if my mom catches on I'm in for it, but what would an all-nighter be without a drag off a fag?" He handed each of them a Kool and they lit up.

Fifteen minutes later, as they neared the end of the factory, Nick stopped and held up his hand for the others to stop. Two blocks ahead he could see movement near the abandoned Railroad Tower. Nick stooped low and motioned for the others to do the same. They crab-crawled to the edge of the tracks and eased down the ballast to get out of sight.

"What is it?" whispered an excited Butch.

"Someone is walking this way" answered Nick

With eyes straining, Butch asks, "Where?"

"Up by the old tower; on the right side."

Stan saw it and said, "Yep. Damn!"

They watched as the walker approached and appeared to be careful crossing Webster without being noticed. Once across Webster, the walker continued on the tracks. The boys crawled to a hand switching station close to the top of the hill. It was not big, but in the darkness it would break up the shape of the terrain and provide them cover.

The walker came toward them and appeared jumpy; glancing around in all directions as he walked. The boys stayed low and silent as he approached. Their hearts were pumping and the adrenalin was flowing. Could this be the answer to the mystery? Nick motioned for everyone to keep down. A familiar image began to emerge from the shape walking toward them. Nick stared and tried to place the familiarity. It came to him, it was Phil! What the hell was Phil doing out here on the tracks at 1:30 in the morning?

Nick whispered, "It's Phil." He motioned them to stay in place. "On three, charge him." As Phil grew closer, Nick counted, "One – two - three."

On cue, they jumped out at Phil. Phil was so startled, that he let out a screech that one would expect from a schoolgirl, he stumbled backward tripping over one of the rails and fell to his knees. This caused the three to howl with laughter. Butch was on one knee gasping for air, Stan was bent at the waist holding his stomach and Nick sat on his butt when his legs lost strength.

Phil, attempting to regain his strength and dignity, remained on his knees. Stunned, he bellowed, "What the hell are you guys doing out here?"

Down on one knee, Butch trying to catch his breath, said, "An all-nighter (gasp), what are you doing here, Phil?"

"You guys are peckerheads, you know it?" Phil seemed to struggle getting to his feet.

"Ok, we're peckerheads all right; payback is a bitch, ain't it Phil!" said Stan.

With the laughter beginning to wane, Nick asked, "Phil, what are you doing out here?"

Phil was at a loss for words, but stammered "It's none of your business."

The serious note of his exclamation bought an end to joviality. The three looked at one another with questioning facial expressions. Stan said "Phil, are you in some kind of trouble?"

"Get bent peckerhead; I can be anywhere I want to be and when I want to be. Get it! Like I said, it's none of your business."

This aroused even more interest and they were not going to let it go.

Breaking the silence, Nick said, "Look Phil, like Butch said, we're pulling an all-nighter, which kind of explains why we're on the tracks, but it doesn't explain why you are on the tracks at 1:30 in the morning. So, how about squaring up with us?"

Phil realized that he needed to offer an explanation. "I was down at my cousins' place in Oswego and I was supposed to get a ride home, but I didn't, so I'm walking home."

"From Oswego?" reaffirmed Butch.

"Yeah, from Oswego, dumbshit. You know that little town south of here?" offered Phil with heavy sarcasm.

"That's a long hike in the middle of the night" said Butch with a sense of wonder.

"Maybe for you girls, but I do it all the time" added Phil, recapturing his swagger. "Let's sit down and have a cigarette."

They sat on the ballast and Phil supplied everyone with a Lucky Strike.

Nick thought Phil must have hit the ballast hard with his knees because he grimaced as he sat.

"Sorry if we caused damage Phil."

"Naw, just stiff I guess. Ok, you guys are doing an all-nighter, but for what? Don't you usually head for the river?" asked Phil.

"Yeah, but we're more interested in what's happening at Murphy's place tonight" answered Nick. "Did you see anything when you came by?"

"Nope, I stayed low on this side. The place is lit up like a circus. You can see the light from here" Phil nodded in the direction of Murphy's.

They all looked and could see the illumination among the trees around Murphy's.

"So what do you think you'll see when you get to the house?" asked Phil.

"Hell, we don't know, but come on and go with us Phil" interjected Butch.

"Bullshit, I'm tired, I'm gonna head for home and get some shuteye."

"We went to your place earlier today," said Nick.

"You did? When?"

"Around noon. Your brother was working on his Ford. He said he hadn't seen you since the day before" answered Stan.

"He's full of shit. He wouldn't know what he's seen if it bit him in the ass" said Phil.

This brought on laughter, as the boys envisioned Phil's brother lovingly lamenting over his ailing car.

Standing, Phil said, "Ok girls; party time is over for me, I'm heading home. Let me know what you sleuths learn. We'll hook up tomorrow." Phil started walking.

"See you Phil" said Butch.

"Not if I see you first" retorted Phil.

The boys gathered up their packs.

CHAPTER 27

In July 1945, Sally and Stuart McVee relocated to Aurora on Spring Street. Stuart was not accustomed to the urban lifestyle; traffic congestion, traffic signals and lots of people, but he felt that the move made Sally happy. Making Sally happy continued to be his sole intent in life.

Though Sally was corresponding with Betty and Grover regularly, she continued to use the DeKalb return address. She had a friend in the administration office that would forward her mail. She did not want to tell them of her motherly state, nor reveal their move to Aurora. She dreaded composing that letter, but now the time had come; it was early August, her friend in administration at the College was good about forwarding mail to her, but she didn't know how long that would last.

She took her time composing the letter, revising every sentence multiple times, restructuring the content to deliver the news in the best light possible. She explained that Stuart was offered a better position in Aurora and now that she was pregnant, not revealing how pregnant, they needed to be concerned about living on one paycheck, at least for a while.

She gushed as she expressed her love for them and the gratefulness she felt for their love for her and thankfulness for their understanding. She even did something she had never done before; she sealed the envelope with a lipstick kiss. She thought that was kind of corny, but she felt like sending them a kiss. She knew this news was going to be troublesome and heart-breaking for them, but didn't know any other way of delivering it. She mailed the letter.

Of course Stuart was not offered a better job, but he was able to find work right away as a grounds keeper for an estate in North

Aurora. The money was comparable to his College job in DeKalb and they watched every dime closely. Sally found part-time work at St. Charles Hospital assisting with the laundry and delivering meals. The hospital was two blocks from their upstairs apartment on Spring Street enabling her to walk to and from work.

Sally enjoyed learning about the inner workings of the hospital. She also took the opportunity to observe the pregnant women when they came in as well as the nursery to see what she and her baby would be going through in January. She was excited about the baby, and she was excited to be in Aurora; if Thaddeus Murphy existed, she would find him.

CHAPTER 28

After encountering Phil, the boys continued walking on the tracks approaching Webster Street, Nick stopped well before the road. "We gotta do this right or we may be seen. I'm going up to the road; you guys watch both ways on Webster. Any sign of headlights means a no go."

Nick crouching low ran to the crossing; getting the sign that the coast was clear, darted across Webster and stood in the shadows of the old railroad tower. He could see everything on Webster and most of Route 31. He signaled for the next to cross.

Stan beat feet across and stood next to Nick. Butch waited for them to signal him over. Both Stan and Nick did a final search for headlights, and gave the signal for Butch to come over. Butch ran, but maybe too fast. His flailing arms and legs resembled a mix-master without a sense of direction. Nick and Stan found this humorous until Butch stumbled and fell in the middle of the road. Sensing that he may have been hurt, they ran out to him. Butch was complaining about squishing the brownies when headlights enveloped them in a ring of light. They froze. The gig was up. The light was from two sources; headlights and a side light as well. It must be Rively.

"Shit!" exclaimed Nick.

"What do we do?" asked a panicked Butch.

"I think we're going to be answering questions for Rively and our parents" said Stan.

"Peachy, downright peachy" said Nick.

The Village car crossed the tracks and pulled to a stop. John Rively stepped out and walked to the boys. "Evening gentlemen. Out for a stroll?"

"No sir" said Nick.

Glancing at his wristwatch, John asked, "Then why are you in the middle of the road at 1:52am?"

"Well sir, Butch fell and we were helping him up" said Nick.

"I can see that, Nick" said John.

"I think you boys need to redirect your Boy Scout hike in the direction of the police station. I'll follow behind - in case Butch falls again."

Butch nervously stated, "Sir, we weren't doing anything wrong, we were just . . ."

John cut him off and asked, "Did I say you were doing anything wrong?"

"Uh, no sir."

"I think we should talk before I call you parents, don't you?"

"Yes sir" said Nick.

They walked toward the station on Webster, crossing the tracks as John turned the Village car around. John followed them the two blocks to the police station.

"What do we tell him?" implored Butch.

Neither Stan nor Nick produced an answer. Eventually, Nick said, "We tell him the truth. We tell him about Beth, and that we're concerned. We're trying to find answers."

John parked the Village car and walked to the police station where the boys were waiting at the door. He unlocked the door and led them into the small station. He retrieved two chairs from the other room so all could have a place to sit.

The police station consisted of a twelve-foot by fourteen-foot room with a wooden desk in the left-hand corner against the back wall, one wooden swivel chair and one wooden side chair. What really dominated the room was a barred cage, six-feet wide, six-feet deep and six-and-a-half feet high. A five-sided barred cage was bolted to a concrete floor; the Montgomery jail. Wedging in two more chairs took creativity. John sat in the swivel chair facing the three boys, wrapped his fingers behind his head and said, "Ok, you were on your way to church and . . ."

The boys looked down, but Nick said, "Mr. Rively . . ."

"Call me John."

"Ok, John, we have a friend that is missing and we're worried. We thought we might observe things and maybe learn about her whereabouts."

"At 2 . . .," glancing at his wristwatch, ". . . 2:00am?"

"Yes sir."

"And if I call your parents they are going to say that you all have their permission to be traipsing about the village in the dark?"

"No sir" responded Nick.

"Well, what are they going to say?"

"That we snuck out, and that we were not supposed to."

"Ok, I'm going to come clean with you boys, but with one condition; that condition is when I am done coming clean with you, you come clean - squeaky clean with me. Do we have a deal?" asked John.

The boys looked at one another and all nodded approval.

"Do you think I'm blind, stupid or completely inept at my job?"

"What do you mean?" asked Stan.

"What I mean is I know you guys roam the streets of our little village, hang out under the bridge and fish on the river late at night. Frankly, and don't tell your parents this, but I don't care. To the best of my knowledge you have never stolen anything or done any damage or caused a problem, so I have ignored it. By the way, a lit cigarette under that bridge can be seen from a long way on the other side of the river. However, tonight is a different story. We have activities going on that require special attention. We don't need to add to the present problems. You boys should not be out on the streets tonight. Are we communicating?"

"Yes sir" said Stan

"Now, is Beth McVee one of your friends? Is she the one you referred to as missing?"

"Yes sir" responded Nick, "We go to school with her."

"Anything else?"

"What do you mean?"

"Besides going to school with her, do any of you have any kind of relationship with Beth?"

The room closed in on Nick. He wasn't expecting this kind of questioning. He was glad that he had squared himself with his best friends concerning Beth, but he was not prepared to square himself with the world concerning Beth.

Reluctantly and sheepishly Nick said, "Yes sir, I walk her home from school once in a while."

"When was the last time you saw her Nick?"

"A couple of weeks ago at the Little League game at the school."

"You haven't seen her since?"

"No sir."

"How did you learn about Beth being missing?"

Stan jumped in and said, "We were in the diner yesterday" he pointed across the street "Andy Durham came in and asked if we'd seen Beth. We said no and he asked where he could look. We all pitched in and rode to different parts of town to look for her, but didn't find her."

All of this information matched what John learned from Stuart McVee. "Ok boys, what's your take on Mr. McVee?"

They looked at one another and shook their heads and shrugged their shoulders. "We don't have a take" said Nick.

"Did you ever see Mr. McVee and Beth together in public, at the school or in any other situation?"

"We saw the McVees at the school picnic" stated Stan.

"How did they seem to get along?" asked John.

"Great. It was a good time for everyone. Beth hung around her friends, Mr. and Mrs. McVee talked to other parents and teachers. That's about it" answered Stan.

"Have you ever seen Mr. McVee get mad at Beth for any reason?"

Again, the boys looked at one another, and shrugged their shoulders and shook their heads.

"Nick, have you ever been to Beth's house?"

"No sir. I don't know where she lives."

"Then how could you walk her home from school?"

"I would walk her to Main and Watkins, and we would part. I don't think she wanted me to know where she lives. It is kind of puzzling" said Nick.

John understood why Beth was hesitant to reveal her living arrangements and asked, "How many times did you walk her home, I mean to Main and Watkins?"

"Maybe six or seven times, always after school."

Butch smiled and nudged Stan, "Six or seven?"

John noticed the exchange, but didn't know what to make of it.

Positioning his chair directly in front of Nick, John looked at Nick and asked, "Nick, do you know where Beth is right now?"

"No sir, I swear. I've been looking for her and I get sick to my stomach when I think about her being missing."

John studied Nick's face carefully, looking for any sign that would suggest that he was lying. Convinced that he was not, John said, "I believe you, Nick. And I am proud that you boys took the time to help Andy, but that is where it ends. You don't belong on the streets late at night, especially with the activities going on that can't be explained."

Butch saw the opening and asked, "What can you tell us about Mr. Murphy?"

"You know I can't discuss an ongoing criminal investigation with you boys, besides I'm hungry, and you boys need to get home" answered John.

"We have food" offered Butch.

Stan chimed in, "Yeah, I can make sandwiches, Butch has brownies, what do you have Nick?"

"Cookies" answered Nick.

"No wonder you boys can stay out all night. I have Cokes in the back." John rose to grab the Cokes.

They spread the food out on the corner of the desk. The brownies were compressed from Butch's sprawl on Webster, but they were still good. The sandwiches consisted of bread and palmetto loaf. Nick's cookies were homemade chocolate chip. All in all, it was a good middle-of-the-night snack.

Nick finished first and said, "Sir, we learned a little about the Murphy situation. Would it be alright if I tell you what we think we know?"

"Sure, but you know I can't divulge anything beyond what you already know."

"Yes sir."

Nick, Stan and Butch walked John through their entire day including the conversations with Charlie.

When they were done recalling their entire day, John leaned back and shook his head, "You boys had a busy day and gathered a lot of information. I'd guess you know more than the majority of the town. Are any of you planning on entering police work after school?"

Butch jumped on this one, "You bet, I read the Police Gazette magazine and watch Highway Patrol with Broderick Crawford, and Dragnet; can you believe that Sgt. Joe Friday? Is anyone that straight?"

John smiled, "Well Butch, I don't think I am." He turned toward Nick, "How about you Nick?"

Nick said, "Maybe."

"I think you should, you have a good head start."

"Count me out" offered Stan. "Too many late hours for me. How long have you been at it today, John?"

"I got a few hours of sleep late this afternoon, but was back at it at 10:00."

Butch couldn't contain his excitement any longer, "You have to tell us what you think happened in Old Man Murphy's cellar. We know he skinned a dog, but what else happened in the cellar? We heard about a lot of blood."

Taken aback by the brashness of Butch's approach, John held up his hands and said, "Whoa boys, I told you that I can't reveal official findings on an ongoing criminal case."

Sensing John's discomfort, Nick jumped in and said, "Butch isn't, and we aren't asking you to risk your job, but we are so confused by all the talk and all the rumors that it would be good to hear from you; you know what's going on."

John sat back, thought for a moment and said, "You boys have the story fairly correct. We removed a skinned dog, and the blood at the scene is likely more than that dog would have produced, in fact, we know that some of the blood came from a human, but truly that is as far as it goes. I am being straight with you. At this point it's a mystery. We don't know where Murphy has gone. Finding him will clear up a lot of the questions, but until we do, I think the questions, the speculations, the rumors and the mystery will continue. More concerning to me is the fact that we have a twelve year old girl missing."

"Yeah, what about that sneaker? Is it hers?" asked Nick.

"We don't know that it is hers, Nick." John wondered how Nick knew about the sneaker.

"Do you know that it's not hers? Feeling a hint of guilt, John responded, "No, but we will confirm today."

"Confirm that it is, or that it isn't?"

"Nick, I don't know, nor will I know until it is confirmed."

Nick asked, "Do you think Beth is connected to the Murphy situation?"

"I don't see how, I see no connection between the two. I was hoping that the missing person bulletin I put out on Beth to neighboring towns would have turned up results, but nothing has come in. We have a statewide bulletin on Murphy and that hasn't turned up anything either.

"Boys, it's three-thirty, the County and State guys could be pulling in here in a while. How would I explain the presence of three junior G-men sitting in my office? Will you guys give me your word that you will head for home right now?"

They all nodded.

John added, "Ok, this never happened, and though I don't feel good about it, I will not mention this to anyone including your parents, if you swear to me the all-nighters end until these situations are resolved. Agreed?"

They all agreed. What they didn't know was that all the photos and investigation items, including the white sneaker were beyond the closed adjoining door to the court room.

The boys went about sneaking back into their homes without any complications.

CHAPTER 29

The investigation room was getting stuffy; more than three hours had elapsed since the meeting began at 3:00. The village clerk brought in Cokes and Seven-up, but the air was stale, heavy and laced with cigarette smoke. One of the investigators said, "Bob, you may think I have to pee a lot, but when I leave I'm really going out to grab air; can we crack a window or get a fan?"

Bob found the comment humorous, but wasn't sure what to do about the ventilation. He went to one of the windows facing River Street. The cardboard he placed on the lower half of the window was intended to prevent the gawkers from seeing in, but he agreed that fresh was air was needed.

Throughout their meeting, he heard foot traffic in the police station and knew they could not leave the adjoining door open without unwanted visitors. He climbed on a chair to examine the window closely.

Unlocking the window, Bob realized that they were double-hung windows allowing the top to come down as well as the bottom to go up. All of the windows required encouragement from the palm of Bob's hand, but all of them eventually opened.

The windows were replaced a few years ago, and though Bob sat in this building for court sessions with the magistrate, for village meetings and the monthly trustee sittings, he'd never seen these windows opened from the top. As the last of all three windows opened, a slight breeze wafted in to the delight of everyone in the room. Bob was heralded a hero. The fresh air cleared away most of the cigarette smoke and some of the mental cobwebs.

Henry stood up and said, "I know some of you have not seen all the photos, but let's start a dialog and compare notes. Who has the first group of photos?" The investigator to his right handed over group #1.

"Ok, who hasn't seen group #1?" asked Henry.

A State investigator raised his hand; Henry handed group #1 to him. "While he has a chance to look them over, review your notes on this group and we'll move on."

Group #1 consisted of the original photos of the stairs leading to the cellar.

"So who would like to start?" asked Henry.

Bob offered, "In photo # 3 the marks on the top two stairs are clear, but I can't figure out what would cause this type of drag mark."

The County investigator took the photo and said, "I know what you mean, the concrete is not damaged, it is . . . marred or smudged with drag marks."

"Must have been cushioned but heavy" said another investigator.

"Other comments?" asked Henry.

"Yeah, no bloody footprints are coming out of the cellar; considering the mess that would be impossible. Either Murphy flew out of that cellar, or he changed shoes before coming up. Were any shoes found in the cellar?"

"Nope" answered Henry. "Anyone see any in the photos?"

All shook their heads with a negative response.

Henry went to the chalkboard and wrote, "Questions" underlined, under that "Cellar exit – how?"

The investigators continued through the groups of photos, discussing and analyzing each photo. The chalkboard began to fill with notes. Items on the left represented what they felt were facts, items on the right represented the questions. The right side of the chalkboard was getting heavy, and the left side was comparatively sparse.

When they were discussing Group #4, photos of the bench area, one of the State investigators identified a discoloration on the cellar wall. "You know, it is subtle, but you can see the outline where coal dust is around it, but not on the spot itself." As they passed the photo around, unanimous agreement took place.

A nail stuck out from the wall above the area protected from the coal dust. When the photo came to Henry, he studied it and said, "Great observation." Looking harder he said, "Look closely at the top portion of the clean area; it appears to be a variation." The photo was passed around again.

As the two County guys studied the photo together, one of them asked, "Bob, do you have a magnifying glass?"

"Sure, you'll find two of them behind you on the shelf; I figured we'd need them."

Now with the magnifying glass, one investigator said to the other, "Does it look to you like a strap or a rope?"

"Yep, it does."

"Ok, so fill in the rest of it" stated Henry.

"It looks to me as if whatever was hanging from that nail was hanging from a strap or a rope."

Henry moved to the blackboard and wrote under "Questions," 'What was hanging on the wall and what happened to it?'

The diner delivered the burgers as Henry promised and the discussion of the photos continued until 8:30. The chalkboard was getting crowded on the right side. Henry said, "Let's give it a rest. We have things to work on. I'm going to stick around to record what's on the blackboard. Let's hook up again at 10:00am tomorrow morning."

CHAPTER 30

Nick was up at 8:00 on Thursday morning; his mom had not left for her factory job yet; her Thursday shift started at 10:00 and ended at 6:30.

"Nick, did you sleep ok last night?" she asked, looking at him closely.

"Yeah Ma, I slept great."

"You look tired and not rested."

"Naw, I'm fine. Would you call Mrs. Durham to see if they've found Beth?"

"Margie called me last night to tell me that Beth was still missing. She mentioned that you and others helped Andy search for her. That was nice of you. What do you think is going on, Nick? Montgomery has never seen this much excitement before. And Mr. Murphy . . . he has always been a strange duck, but . . . oh my."

"I know Ma; it is kind of a drag."

"I don't want you hanging around the Murphy place today."

"Ma, they have it roped off; I couldn't if I wanted to; cops are everywhere, more than I've ever seen before."

"Still, you stay away. And, I want you in before dark tonight."

"Ma, I can take care of myself."

"I don't care, you be in before dark, young man."

"Ok Ma."

Nick kissed his mom and headed for Stan's.

Stanley Michael Baker was Nick's best friend since kindergarten. Their chemistries didn't necessarily match; they were more complimentary than alike. Stan was bright, but not forward, while Nick was bright, but would not hesitate to launch into anything that he felt worthwhile. Stan enjoyed Nick's leadership, Nick enjoyed Stan's stability. They became a team early. Butch came along and added the flavor to the trio.

Gerald Walter Miller, aka "Butch," came up with off the wall comments and observations that often took people by surprise. His thinking and motivations were influenced heavily by the action around him. In school, he was always the one that left both fellow students and teachers with jaws agape.

Butch was the butt of fat jokes, but he took it in stride. His home life was difficult. Butch adored his mom, but his dad drank too much, too often and provided more than his share of family embarrassment.

Nick knew Butch resented his dad and would go to great lengths to avoid having contact with him. What a contrast to how Nick felt about his dad. Nick wished he could spend more time with his dad, but his dad was always working. When he wasn't working, he was resting so he could work more.

At Stan's house, Nick knocked on the screen door. No answer. He knocked again. No answer. Figuring that both parents were off to work and Stan was sacking in, Nick opened the door and proceeded to Stan's bedroom. Sure enough, Stan lay with his mouth open, apparently dreaming wonderful dreams. Nick slipped in and slowly pinched Stan's nose shut. Stan's body realized that his oxygen supply wasn't working properly and he bolted upward looking for the cause of the problem. When his eyes fixed on Nick, he said, "Damn you, Nick!"

"What did I interrupt, a love scene with Annette Funicello?"

"I wish. You interrupted needed shuteye, but . . . if you could arrange something with Annette, I will be your slave for two months, three if you want to press the bargain."

"Come on sleepy head, we have work to do."

"Work? What are you talking about?"

Nick sat on the edge of Stan's bed and said, "Maybe work is the wrong word, but we need to find Beth. She has to be here somewhere. I'm hoping she's with friends, or . . ." The futility of his thoughts became painfully present as his voice trailed off.

Stan became uncomfortable; his best friend was struggling, and too deeply involved in matters neither of them had encountered before. Stan wanted to say anything to help the situation, but found no such words in his vocabulary, so he fell back staring at the ceiling. After a few moments he said, "Let's go talk to Charlie – he may have learned more by now." Stan jumped out of bed with false enthusiasm and began to dress hastily.

Nick and Stan approached Shannon's on their bikes. They could see Charlie on the front steps, reliable as a sentinel, elbows on his knees and watching a world that ignored him, but he watched it with interest anyway.

As they placed their bikes against the wall of Shannon's, the saucy guitar licks of Duane Eddy's *"Rebel Rouser"* leaked from the bar's open screen door. Charlie greeted the boys with a genuine smile, "Aren't you missing a member of the court?" he said with a raspy chuckle deepened by years of smoking cigarettes.

"Yeah, he's sawing logs; we were up late last night" responded Nick.

"Up late? - oh yes, the all-nighter. You know, I'll bet that picnic table in the park is not taken at this early hour. Shall we reserve a seat?" Charlie said while motioning toward the park.

It was the same table that hosted their meeting the day before. Charlie settled on the bench, extracted the pack of Camels given to him the day before by Shannon. Out came the Zippo with the wobbly top. Exhaling his first deep drag, he said, "I didn't mean to be rude, would you boys like to partake?" offering the pack toward them. Both refused.

"Ok, tell me the good news derived from staying up all night."

"Good news? I wish" said Nick, as he proceeded, with Stan's help, to recount the entire night, including their being caught and having a talk with Rively. Good laughs erupted as Stan and Nick recounted Butch's fence crossing and how they paid Phil back with a good scare on the tracks.

As they covered their conversation with Rively, Charlie seemed to be concentrating especially hard. Nick said, "Charlie, are you fixed on to something?"

"No, but I sure have been thinking a lot about you boys and what is going on. I've been listening a lot too."

"What have you heard?" asked Nick with excitement.

"Well, not that much, but a little here and a little there. Willy Smith relaying to Chuck Morgan was the main source for a while, but now Willy's out of it, so I am not sure how reliable my information is."

"Charlie, it doesn't matter – divvy up," said Stan showing impatience.

"One of our illustrious patrons was in late last night; he knows one of the County cops. According to him, they found blood from two people in the cellar – and that one of the two people was likely killed."

"How would they know that? Body parts?" asked Nick

"No, they determined it by the amount of blood in the cellar."

"But why two people bleeding?" asked Stan.

"Don't know, my boy. I am simply repeating what I heard."

"Holy shit," said Nick. "This is too damn real."

"Real it is, my friend. So real, it is making my skin crawl, and I wasn't the one sneaking through the dark last night like you boys" said Charlie.

"Charlie, you know all we know, can you make any sense of it all?"

Charlie leaned forward with his elbows on the table, "We have complications that seem to be complicating themselves. Two mysteries, two people missing; I think we need to separate them first and then try to combine them."

"You think they're connected?" asked Stan.

"Not necessarily, but common sense suggests they might be. Before we go headlong into the mysteries, I have been thinking about Thad Murphy. I told you boys about him yesterday, but the more I think about him, the more I realize how much time has passed. Thad has been stuck in his house a long time, and that can do things to a person's mind."

"What do you mean?"

"Being alone isn't necessarily a bad thing, but it could be if the person was wallowing in the wrong kind of thinking. I can't even pretend to know what Thad Murphy thinks about, but I do know the facts. He was a hotshot, and that ended with the death of his wife and the loss of a child; Thad may be carrying a lot of guilt, or he may not be carrying the guilt at all. He might think it is all somebody else's fault. Either way, thoughts like that can take a heavy toll, especially over time."

Stan interjected, "How could he blame anyone but himself for his wife's death, based on the story you told us yesterday?"

"That doesn't sound logical does it? But that is what some people do. They fail to take responsibility for their own actions, and fail to accept the results created by their actions. When that happens, they want to blame others. Maybe they blame circumstances, or society, or the cosmos; it just wasn't their fault, so it must be someone else's fault. They might feel that revenge is necessary."

"That doesn't make sense, Charlie" said Nick.

"No, I agree, it doesn't, but I have lived long enough to know it happens. Left to our own thinking, we can create any world, any excuses, any reasons we want to create. Without input from others, we have no check and balance device to say we are wrong.

Now the reason I have brought this up is to say, one part of our mystery is Thad Murphy. One distinct possibility is that Thad popped a cork and we are learning about the aftermath. What I shared with you concerning the lack of accepting responsibility supports that possibility. Thad is somewhere, probably not here in town, but on the run, and the cops are going to have to catch him to find the answers to the rest of the questions."

Charlie leaned back and continued, "But the other mystery is the one that I have thought about most. That little girl . . ." Charlie quickly personalized his reference, ". . . I meant to say Beth, has me baffled. The talk is crazy, some say it is her blood in the cellar and Murphy killed her, others say her old man did her in and she is buried, yet others say it could be a coincidence and a stranger made off with her and she may, or may not be found in the days to come. Did Rively say anything about that shoe?"

"Yeah, they're going to confirm if it is Beth's today. But I don't know how" answered Nick.

"Probably with her parents" offered Charlie. "Besides the shoe, what do we have other than she is missing? Nothing; no one saw anything, knows anything, and yet both of our mysteries take place within a short distance of the other. Do you see why common sense suggests that they might be connected?"

Both boys nodded in agreement.

"Now if I told you boys to leave it to the cops to solve the mystery, I know I would just as soon wish this table to turn to gold, so I am not going to be so foolish, however, you need to be smart. Stay out of the cops' way, and do what you are going to do during daylight hours. You were lucky last night."

"We know we were, Charlie. Rively could have caused us big problems with our parents" said Nick.

"Ok, think in another direction. The cops are trying to find Murphy and Beth with their methods, you think differently. Think like boys. Where would you go, what would you do to solve the mystery, but don't go where the cops are going. You have a head start on that kind of thinking; you've checked the mausoleum, the old mill, that old house on Aucutt Road; how long do you think it would take for the cops to check places like that?" asked Charlie.

The boys shrugged their shoulders.

"It could be weeks, or maybe not at all. You boys keep doing what you are doing, but again, do it during the daylight and stay out of the cops' way. Think like boys," stated Charlie.

"But Charlie, where do we look?" asked Stan.

"You look where your minds send you." Charlie smiled. "I best get back over, but let's talk later today."

With that, Charlie stood slowly and waited for the boys to gather up their bikes.

"Thanks Charlie" said Nick

Charlie gently squeezed Nick shoulder, "Today, I wish I was a part of the Mayor's court. Actually, I wish that most days. Good luck, boys."

CHAPTER 31

On January 5th, Sally, who continued to work throughout her pregnancy, felt the first of the contractions that would lead to the birth of Elizabeth Christine McVee on January 6, 1946. Stuart was by her side for everything except the birth itself. He held her hand, wiped her brow, and appeared to suffer every pain Sally endured. He was excited to have a child, but didn't like seeing his beloved Sally having to suffer. Waiting for news from the delivery room was agony.

The news arrived; Stuart and Sally had a little girl. One of the nuns directed Stuart to a phone. His first call was to inform Betty and Grover. As was expected, Betty cried. Grover told of their plans to drive to Aurora to greet their new granddaughter.

His next call was to his family. They, too, were coming to Aurora. Stuart beamed and walked on air as he headed to Sally's room.

Life for the McVees settled after Beth's birth. Stuart's job as an estate keeper worked out well, though the owner of the estate was experiencing mounting health problems. Sally returned to her hospital job in March. A couple with two young children lived on the ground floor beneath the McVees. The mother of the children agreed to care for Beth while Sally was at work.

Sally often wondered if Beth was ever confused as to who was her mother. Most of Beth's waking hours were spent with the babysitter, but Sally rushed home each day and made over Beth in every way possible.

Stuart spent every available moment after work and on the weekends with his family. While the guys in the neighborhood would walk two blocks to a favorite tavern, Stuart rarely accepted their invitation. His idea of a well-spent moment was enjoying his little girl and her gorgeous mother.

He feared that the birth of a child was going to change the physical relationship he and Sally mutually enjoyed, but it didn't. They used each other as a primary source for enjoyment and entertainment. It wasn't only the love-making that made them happy; it was the act of being so familiar with each other that they were content and comfortable. What tavern could offset that?

Sally's intelligence and get-it-done attitude was genuinely appreciated in the hospital. She didn't remain in the laundry department after Beth was born. Upon her return, she was asked to work in the records section and administration. Sally was thrilled; she was good with numbers and was rapidly learning the hospital jargon and written correspondence. Though still struggling with doctors' handwriting, or inexcusable cat-scratching, as some referred to it, she was recognized as a person to go to if a tough job needed to be handled.

Over the next nine years, Sally became an administrative expert in the eyes of her superiors. In 1955 the hospital asked her to personally review files stored in a dust-laden room on the top floor of the building. All of these files were at least twenty years old. Normally, activities such as this would have been relegated to a lesser-valued employee; however the hospital management felt that every effort should be made to ensure that the files being destroyed were not likely to be needed by the hospital or the patient. Once cleared for disposal, the files were to be carried to the boiler room where maintenance personnel would incinerate them.

The first two weeks of Sally's temporary assignment proved to be terribly boring; visually scanning file after file after file, revealing little that could justify her time. She set aside two files that she would forward to her supervisor for further review. The rest she directed to the boiler room for their fiery finale.

One afternoon, when her toughest job was to avoid glancing at the clock more than twice an hour, a particular file caught her rapt attention. The name on the file was Thaddeus Artimus Murphy. It was a thick file, much thicker than most, indicative of the patient having spent a long time under the care of the hospital.

Sally felt guilty about spending the rest of the day enveloped in this file. It was all recorded. Details of him being brought in to the hospital in 1927, his injuries, his treatments, the names of the doctors that treated him, his medications, his progress and even an entry relaying the fact that his wife died from injuries resulting from the same car crash that put him in the hospital.

This file would not make its way to the incinerator, nor would it need to be reviewed by her supervisor. She knew that removing this file from the hospital could result in her losing her job, but only if she got caught.

She was successful in extracting the file from the hospital, but where would she store it? Stuart wouldn't know anything about Thaddeus Murphy, but why would she have a file that large outside the hospital?

For the first few days, she kept it buried beneath her shoes and shoe boxes in the closet she shared with Stuart, but she did not want to risk him accidentally finding it. Eventually, she was able to reduce the size of the file substantially by removing the items that were of no interest to her. She stored the thinner file in a box of old sweaters in the closet. She smuggled the discarded parts of the file back into the hospital and they made their way to the big burn.

Sally arrived home an hour before Stuart made his drive home from North Aurora. She wouldn't dilute the time she spent with Beth and Stuart. Beth was in third grade and brought home drawings, paintings or school work she wanted to discuss with Sally.

Sally found time to study the file when Stuart was on a walk with Beth. The first thing she acted on was the address in the file. During the first weekend following her discovery, she convinced Stuart to take her and Beth for a ride along the river. The address in the file fit Betty's description of what once was Thaddeus' parents' home, the one he inherited. She located it as they were on their drive; the name, Anderson, was professionally painted on the mail box and children were playing in the yard. It was a dead end.

For weeks she continued to devour the file, re-reading notes and comments, but found nothing that helped. Frustration was her enemy until she saw it. One doctor visited often, but did not treat him, and was not associated with the hospital; Dr. Robert Deuel Larsen. His office was on Broadway in Aurora; only four blocks from the hospital.

The next day during lunch, Sally walked to Dr. Larsen's office, located on the second floor of an office building. She climbed the steps and entered the waiting room. The lunchtime arrival worked to her benefit; the doctor was out to lunch and so were the patients. The full-time nurse and part-time receptionist sat behind her desk. Sally put on her most charming smile and said good afternoon. The nurse returned the greeting and said, "May I help you?"

"I hope so. I work at St. Charles hospital in administration. We have a file we want to close out, but the patient has moved. I believe Dr. Larsen sees the patient. The patient's name is Thaddeus Murphy. Do you happen to recognize the name?"

The nurse rummaged in a file drawer, "I do recognize the name; it is unusual enough . . . here it is. What were you looking for?"

Sally was almost unable to withhold her elation, "Just an address, nothing more."

"The only address I have is Railroad Street in Montgomery, no street address at all. Oh yes, I remember, Mr. Murphy walks to and from Montgomery and always pays in cash. We never need to bill him. He told me that he walks to our office and to his bank. I don't know why I mentioned his walking; most of our patients drive a car or take the bus. Mr. Murphy is getting up in age, I don't know if all that walking is good for him" stated the nurse.

Writing down Railroad Street in Montgomery on a pad of paper she kept in her purse, Sally said, "This should help a great deal. Thank you."

"Did you make a special trip here for an address?" asked the nurse.

"Heavens no, my next stop is Sensenbaugh's across the street" said Sally smiling.

"I get it" replied the nurse, returning the smile. "Have fun shopping."

The trip back to the hospital and the rest of the day was a day of walking on clouds for Sally. She had him.

CHAPTER 32

With Charlie headed back to Shannon's, Nick and Stan rode their bikes up the hill to the diner; they were both hungry and they needed to talk about their plans. Plans? What plans? That's what they needed to talk about – what do they do next, where do they go, what do they expect to find? A plan would be nice.

The counter in the diner was nearly filled; two of the three booths were occupied, however, the booth farthest from the door, the one the boys occupied yesterday was empty. The greasy smell of bacon and sausage was surprisingly appetizing. It was early, but the Wurlitzer thrummed to the beat of the Everly Brothers' "*Claudette, pretty little pet Claudette, never make me fret Claudette.*"

As they made their way to the booth, they could see it was scattered with the dishes of previous customers. Mr. Durham, Andy's dad, was seated at the counter with a cup of coffee in front of him. He was talking with one of the investigators the boys observed at Murphy's.

They slid across the booth's red Naugahyde seats opposite each other. Stan looked at all the dishes on the table and said, "Looks like we missed a party." The table top was covered with dirty dishes, used paper napkins, syrup that didn't make it on pancakes and used coffee cups, one with red lipstick smeared on one side.

"Yeah, wish I could have attended" responded Nick.

Miss Personality sauntered up to the booth with her white pocketed apron and white waitress-hat pinned in her hair, "You boys could have waited for me to clear this before you sat down!"

What Nick wanted to say was, "Yes, and based on your mood, a rat couldn't have climbed up your ass and chewed on your intes-

181

tines," but he didn't, he said, "Sorry, we didn't see the dishes when we walked in. Can we help you in any way?"

This mannerly response disarmed Miss Personality momentarily, "No – but thank you. Please keep your arms off the table and I'll get the mess out of here."

Both boys exaggerated their willingness to comply by placing the palms of their hands on the cool Naugahyde and smiled at one another.

Hauling off her first arm load of dishes, Stan said, "Isn't she a peach? If only I was older, maybe I would have a chance."

Squinting at Stan, Nick said, "I am worried about you."

"Worried? What's to worry, she's employed, full-bodied, personable, charming and will teach me things I have been thinking about lately. Mom will love her."

Squinting even more, Nick cocked his head and said, "You either convince me that you have a very sick sense of humor, or I am calling the Fire Department."

"Cool your jets. I thought we needed to lighten the mood" responded Stan.

Miss Personality continued to clear the table until it was empty; with a wet rag, dingy and soiled, she removed the particles of food and spilt syrup, leaving a shiny coat of slimy dampness. "I'll be right back" she said over her shoulder.

"Do you think it's safe to touch?" Stan asked looking at the table.

"Not yet. Let the bacteria drown first" said Nick.

"Good idea."

Miss Personality returned with order pad in hand, "What'll it be boys?"

Nick looked at the 'daily specials' blackboard, "Early morning breakfast, eggs scrambled, please."

Without looking up she turned slightly toward Stan. Stan said, "Oatmeal, toast and a glass of milk, please."

Turning away she stopped and looked back at Nick, "Milk for you too?"

"No thank you, I'll have coffee" said Nick.

She paused assuming this was a joke, but when no laughter led her to believe that the order was sincere, she moved on to the other side of the counter.

They sat in silence for a while. Nick said, "Charlie says we need to continue to think like boys and not like cops."

"Yep" responded Stan.

"Ok genius, what's our plan?" asked Nick.

"The plan is to hire a whirlybird and fly over everything until we locate Murphy and Beth. We bring them back and look like heroes. Get our names in the papers and all that stuff. What'd you think?" asked Stan.

"I think you're into your old man's homemade wine."

"Could be, but that's the best I can do. What's your plan, Cisco?" Stan replied, pronouncing it 'Ceezco' as Poncho would have referred to his companion, The Cisco Kid.

"I don't have a plan; you know that; but we need to come up with one. Let's eat, gather up Butch, and maybe Phil, then go to think."

CHAPTER 33

It was a sunny mid-April day when Beth was walking down Railroad Street, she was on her way to the store. Her mom left for work before she arrived home from school and her dad was preparing to go to work. Beth looked at a small list of items needed from the store; she needed to go, but to comply with her parents' wishes she wanted to get it all done before dark.

Another reason she wanted to get it done was a book she was reading. It was entitled "Hot Rod" written by Henry Felson; it was really a boy's book, but she'd borrowed it from the school library and was enjoying it immensely. It was about boys and their hot rod cars, their girlfriends and racing. She hoped to finish it tonight.

As she approached the only house on the west side of Railroad, she noticed an old man looking her way. She wanted to be cordial, but her parents warned her to avoid people she did not know. She continued walking, looking straight ahead. As she neared the house she glanced up to offer a pleasant "Hello" to the old man. To her surprise, he had ventured closer to the street. Her "Hello" was already out. Momentarily frightened, she prepared herself to run. But the old man smiled sweetly and said, "Hello, my name is Mr. Murphy, may I ask you a question?"

Beth stopped. Ten feet separated them which gave her enough room to run like crazy if necessary. She responded warily, "Yes."

"I am sorry if I am making you uncomfortable, you have absolutely no reason to be alarmed. I am curious about your family. I think I saw you and your mother in the store a couple of weeks back. Would you mind telling me your mother's name?" asked Murphy.

Still wary and not sure if she should engage with this stranger, she appraised her flight strategy and concluded that an answer could do no harm. "My mother's name is Sally McVee, my dad's name is Stuart and I am Beth McVee."

A disarming smile spread across his face, "Well Beth McVee, it is my distinct pleasure to make your acquaintance. As I said, my name is Murphy, Thaddeus Murphy. I think your folks would prefer that you call me Mr. Murphy. I have lived here a very long time, much longer than you have been alive. Most folks don't walk Railroad Street much, so I don't get to talk a lot. Maybe I wouldn't talk even if they did, but I consider this a special day to have made your acquaintance."

"Thank you, Mr. Murphy, uh, it was nice meeting you too." Sally departed with a swell of confusion. It was nice that he spoke to her, and what a smile, but why was he asking about her family? She hurried to the store, gathered the items on her list and decided to walk Main Street to Watkins, instead of Railroad Street.

That night she did finish her book, she thought it was great. She decided to experiment with more books written for boys. They delivered more excitement than the books written for girls.

Before she turned off the light she thought about Mr. Murphy. She replayed their meeting in detail. She pictured his face and his expressions. She recalled every word he said. She wasn't experienced at reading people, but she was pretty sure his greeting was genuine. But why was he asking about her family? Her family didn't get out much because of her parents' conflicting work schedules.

That Saturday Beth was helping her mother clean their house, as was usual for most Saturdays. Her mother believed that a dirty house was not an option.

Beth loved her mom and thought she was the prettiest woman in the world. In addition to cleaning the house together, they would take time combing each other's hair, applying nail polish to each other's fingernails and talk about fashions. Sometimes, her mom would apply a hint of lipstick to Beth's lips.

They enjoyed being together on the Saturdays; working around the house while listening to the radio. Beth's favorite station was Chicago's WIND, playing the latest in Rock n' Roll; Frankie Avalon, Bobby Darin, Connie Francis and of course, Elvis Presley. The music often caused Beth and her mom to clean while doing dance moves or swaying to the beat. Her dad was able to sleep through it all, though they purposely kept the volume low.

In between songs, Beth turned to her mom and said, "One afternoon last week I was walking to the store and a man asked me for your name."

Her mom froze and said, "What man?"

"Mr. Murphy; on Railroad Street." Beth noticed the change in her mom and regretted bringing it up. "He said 'Hello' and asked for your name. He was polite, Mom."

"Beth, I do not want you talking to him under any circumstances. He might seem nice, but that doesn't matter. Please do not talk to him. He is a strange man" instructed Sally.

"Ok Mom, I won't even walk down Railroad Street anymore. Do you know something bad about him?" asked Beth.

"No sweetie, strange people do strange things - that's all" responded Sally while putting her arm around Beth's shoulder.

"Ok," said Beth. She turned up the radio to regain the mood squelched by the inquiry.

In the days to come, Beth kept thinking about her mom's reaction to Mr. Murphy. Surely her mom would have told her if Mr. Murphy was a bad man, or if he did something to another girl. Why had she reacted with alarm; and why the strong insistence to stay away? If he is a strange man, does that make him a bad person? It is like he said, "People don't walk his way much"; that alone could make a person a little strange. Beth tried to put it out of her mind, but it kept coming back.

A week later, Beth was on her way from school walking toward the tracks on Watkins. Mr. Murphy was on the corner of Watkins and Railroad Street. Keeping his distance he said "Hello Beth."

"Mr. Murphy, I am sorry, my mother has asked me not to talk to strangers" stated Beth.

"Or did she say not to speak to me, specifically?" responded Murphy.

Beth blanched at his bluntness, but responded, "Mr. Murphy, I am sorry." She began walking toward the crossing.

"It was my fault, not yours" blurted Murphy.

Beth stopped and turned toward him, "What was your fault?"

"I should have asked you not to mention anything to your mom that we talked."

Completely baffled by this exchange, Beth wanted to walk on home, but some sadness in Mr. Murphy made her stay, though she kept her distance. "Why don't you tell me what's going on?" she asked.

"It's not your mom's fault either, it's my fault. I should have never approached you and if I could undo it I would. I knew I caused a problem when you stopped walking down Railroad Street; that's why I walked here to try to make things right. To let you know you didn't do anything wrong" said Murphy.

"Mr. Murphy, I am totally confused, but I promised my mother I wouldn't talk with you" said Beth.

"Totally understandable, Beth, and please obey your mother. But please also understand that you have not done anything wrong. Can you do that?" asked Murphy.

"Yes, I think so. Goodbye Mr. Murphy."

"Goodbye, Beth."

Beth continued her walk home. "This is a mess!" she thought.

At the same time Murphy sauntered toward his home. Any observer could have concluded that his thoughts were more important than his destination.

CHAPTER 34

Nick and Stan found Butch riding away from his house. They waived him over. They stood facing each other straddling their bikes.

"Hey guys, you aren't going to believe what I read this morning. Man-o-man! You know I have all those back issues of Police Gazette magazine?"

Nick and Stan nodded.

"Well, I got up this morning and was leafing through issues from last year and *BLAM*, guess what I ran into?" asked Butch.

"Two cockroaches humping between the pages" said Stan.

"No. Get serious here, this could be helpful" responded Butch.

Nick interjected, "I have a sneaking suspicion this is going to take a while, let's ride over to the hump yard to the old caboose. We can sit in it and talk."

"Ok, but you guys gotta hear this" said Butch.

They rode west on Webster; prior to crossing the tracks they looked toward Murphy's. The police activity was less than the day before, but the ropes were still up and they could see at least one cop car. A single group of gawkers were talking across from Murphy's.

They crossed the tracks and immediately turned right on the gravel, left their bikes between the concrete works company and the tracks and walked to the old caboose. They climbed up into the caboose and sat on the wooden benches with the cracked leather cushioning.

Stan pulled a handkerchief from his shirt pocket, he held up three Chesterfield cigarettes. "My old man left his opened pack on the table while he was in the john this morning; I figured he wouldn't miss three – and I figured we'd enjoy them more than him anyway." He handed them out.

Butch lit his hurriedly, but could hardly wait to tell them about his find. Once all three were settled back with their cigarettes, Butch said, "Ok, last year in Wisconsin, a guy named Ed Gien was caught red-handed with a woman's body hanging and, get this, gutted in a shed behind his house. She was missing her head! The head was found in his house with the head of another woman. They found all kinds of other body parts throughout his house."

Enthralled, Stan asked "Body parts from the same woman?"

"No man, the guy was a *body snatcher* and a murderer!" exclaimed Butch.

With this, Nick jumped in, "A body snatcher?"

"Yeah, the guy would dig up recently buried bodies of women in the cemeteries and take them home. He made things with their body parts."

"Like what?" asked Stan

"Like lampshades from their skin, and cushions, and bowls from their skulls, and a skin suit and . . ."

"Ok Butch, you are over the edge. Are you making this up?" Stan asked.

"No man, I swear on my mother's life it's true. I read it, man" responded Butch.

"All right, all right, we got it Butch, a really bad man did really bad things in Wisconsin last year, but what's that got to do with us and how is it supposed to help us?" asked Nick.

"Man, I don't know, but I was thinking, maybe there's a connection between this Murphy thing and Ed Gien" said Butch.

Stan said, "Butch, great story, you snagged me, but where do you see a connection? They caught the guy in Wisconsin, right; he's in jail, right?"

"Oh yeah, but maybe there's a connection between him and Murphy . . . pen pals, or . . ."

"Thanks for brightening our day with your beautiful story of the dead beauties and the beast, but let us bring you up to date on our talk with Charlie this morning" said Nick.

Nick and Stan did their best to relay what they discussed with Charlie that morning; Charlie's explanation of what Murphy may have been going through mentally and that Murphy probably snapped; and that Charlie thinks they should continue to think like boys and not like cops. Go places the cops wouldn't think to go, like the mausoleum, the old mill and places like that.

"Think like boys and not cops? What's the difference?" asked Butch.

"What I think he means is the cops use the sophisticated approach, fingerprints, interviews, tests and that sort of stuff, and we use our . . . . .help me out here Nick," said Stan.

"You've got it, we use the street knowledge and our noses to lead us to places and things they overlook" said Nick.

Quizzically Butch looks at Nick and asks, "And what places would that be? We've looked everywhere we know of."

"Well, according to Charlie, we haven't" responded Nick.

"Did Charlie recommend any places?" asked Butch.

"No. But, I think he feels we have other places to look, we just haven't thought of them yet" said Stan.

They sat in silence, thinking. Breaking the silence, Butch said, "You know, Phil is a stiff pain in the ass, but he isn't as wrapped up in this crap as we are, he has a fresh mind. If we have to go through mental exercises, wouldn't a fresh mind be helpful?"

"You know Butch, every now and again you make sense" said Nick.

They headed out of the caboose to their bikes and on to Phil's house.

CHAPTER 35

Sally obtained the general address for Thaddeus Murphy in Montgomery, but she needed to come up with a reason to go. Two weeks later she found her reason in the Aurora Beacon News, the local newspaper; the DeSenza Brothers carnival was in Montgomery through the weekend, sponsored by the VFW.

The carnival would be an opportunity for the three of them to engage in the festivities, and possibly find the abode of her long lost daddy. Not that she would want to approach him, but that nagging desire to find him was burning within her for a long time now.

Saturday afternoon arrived, and none too soon. Conversations concerning the carnival dominated their lives since Sally brought it up earlier in the week. Everyone was excited. Beth had never experienced a real carnival with rides, games and booths. This was truly going to be a special day for the whole family.

They arrived in Montgomery to find cars parked up and down both sides of River Street, cars parked on the side streets as well; cars and families filled Montgomery to the brim. Families walked hand-in-hand toward the parking lot of the small VFW building with the look of anticipation. An air of excitement swirled all around them.

The majesty of the Ferris wheel was positioned close to River Street and served as a welcoming symbol that could be seen for blocks. The lower-slung Tilt-a-Whirl ride was in front of the VFW building. The tented carousel with undulating painted horses and calliope music rotated in between. Lines of people snaked away from each ride as the "carnies" enjoyed their moment of power.

The smaller tents ringed the lot on the river side, with hawkers offering encouragements to try their game, and even demonstrating how easy it was to win. Kewpie dolls, those big-eyed, out of proportioned figurines styled so that might look like a cowboy, a fireman, a dancer or your Aunt Dorothy was on at the lower end of the prize selections. "Just knock those three milk bottles down, sonny, and you can win a Kewpie Doll. Knock 'em all off the table and you can choose from the upper shelf. Couldn't be easier; this could be your lucky day! Come on, you can't win unless you play." The hawking grew monotonous, but it added to the experience. The real value of the Kewpie Doll was when it was used as chalk on sidewalk chalk after it was broken.

In the center of the lot sat the largest of all the tents, the bingo tent; prizes were displayed and hung from the tent supports as enticements to sit down and play. Stuffed animals, Mix-master blenders, electric fans, toys, and other desirables were as easy to obtain as simply as getting your numbers to line up in one row. Just under the outer edges of the rectangular tent a narrow table, with stationary stools on the outside, ringed the tent area leaving the center protecting the yet-to-be-won wonderful prizes, volunteers checking the winning cards, and of course the bingo caller. "Under the G – G58, under the B – B5", and so on, until the unwanted squawk of "Bingo" filled the air. It was unwanted as long as it was you doing the squawking.

The food tents were closest to the VFW building, spilling out the delicious smells of popcorn, cotton candy, taffy, burgers, and barbequed beef; all intended to tantalize the taste buds. Members of the VFW volunteered to work many of the food stalls; however, the barbequed beef topped with cole slaw and served on a hamburger bun was their show stopper.

Beth's senses had difficulty taking in the combination of the sounds, smells and sights. Sally and Stuart marveled as they watched their little girl spin from one attraction to the other. They rode rides, played games, and ate more often that afternoon than they normally would have in two days. When it was over, they wearily walked back to their car parked three blocks away on Main Street.

Once seated in the car, Sally said, "Stuart, this is a special little town."

Stuart responded, "Sally, I think they refer to themselves as a village."

"Town or village, let's ride through it before we go home. I would like to see more of it."

"Sally, I think we already have" said Stuart, starting the car.

"No. There has to be more, Stuart." Pointing down Main, she said, "Look, I can see more houses down that street. Let's ride for a couple of minutes" implored Sally.

So, that's where they headed; down Main past the grocery store and the church. After six or seven blocks they were out of roadway forcing them to turn left for one block, forced to turn left again which put them on River Street. All the time, Sally was commenting on the small quaint houses and lovely neighborhoods she saw: reading every street sign as it passed by. She said, "Stuart, this is fun, would you turn left again, I think we missed part of the town?"

Stuart obediently turned left on Jefferson and crossed over Main. Sally saw the street sign for Railroad Street as they approached the "T" in the road. Stuart said, ""Which way do you want to go?"

"Let's ride it all, it's such a pretty community, it won't take us long" responded Sally.

Stuart, not having received clear directions, turned left. In two blocks they were confronted with the back entrance to Western Electric. As Stuart was turning the car around, Sally continued to extoll the virtues of this wonderful little village.

A few houses were on the east side of Railroad Street, but only one house on the west between the street and the tracks. She was looking for telltale indications that might reveal which of these houses belonged to Thaddeus Murphy, but no indications appeared. The house on the west did not look cared for, or for that matter, lived in. They proceeded across Webster and ran out of roadway again at Mill Street.

"Thank you Stuart that was so much fun. This is the kind of town that I would like to make our town."

"Don't you mean village?" reminded Stuart.

"Yes, village, I like that."

Sally knew how to drive a car and obtained an Illinois driver's license, but preferred to let Stuart do all the driving; however, she needed to get back to Montgomery. She couldn't create another guise as an excuse to go to Montgomery, so she came up with an idea. Beth was in school most of the day; Stuart was at work, so she asked for a day off from the hospital.

She took a bus from Aurora to Montgomery and became familiar with the bus schedule for a return ride that would get her home at about the time she would normally get off from work. The ride to Montgomery was exciting; she didn't do much alone any more, other than work; this she wanted to do alone.

She got off the bus near Michaels Brothers Grocery Store and looked around. It really was a pretty little town . . . or village. She thought she should familiarize herself with the amenities so she walked up the concrete steps to the store.

The store was reminiscent of Mystic. When she opened the door, she felt the recollections of Mystic flood over her. Wooden and glass display cases greeted her and the creaks in the floor made her think of her dad's hardware store. She walked around the glass cases to the wooden counter. A voice from the back of the store said, "Be right with you."

A man about Sally's age, wearing a white apron looped over his neck and tied about the waist, came from the right. "Yes ma'am, what may I get for you?"

Sally realized she needed to make a purchase, but more importantly she needed to inquire without appearing to inquire. She said, "I didn't mean to bother you, but I'm considering moving to

Montgomery and I wanted to see all that I could see, before I make my decision."

"Well ma'am, we don't have a lot to see, we're not what you might call a metropolis, but I think you'll find the people pretty friendly and hospitable. Do you have children?" asked the grocer.

"Yes, a nine year old girl."

"Our elementary school is just up Main Street. We have a bunch of good kids around here" declared the grocer.

"I've heard good things about the people. My mother has a relative in Montgomery, but it's been a while since she heard from him. I think she said his name is Murphy."

"Thaddeus Murphy or Robert Murphy?" offered the grocer.

"You know, I'm not sure, but Thaddeus sounds familiar."

Pointing to the southwest, the grocer said, "If it's Thaddeus, he lives on the west side of Railroad Street, a few blocks away. If it's Robert, he lives up in the New Addition on Martin Avenue."

"I'm not sure, but thank you" Sally responded.

"Where would you being moving from?" inquired the grocer.

"We live in Aurora; we like it there, but we visited here during your carnival and I fell in love with the quaintness."

"Well, I think you'll find it comfortable."

"I am sure I will. I think I might visit your elementary school later. You have been helpful." Sally purchased a *Chunky* candy bar and a pack of *Teaberry* gum from cardboard displays on the counter.

"That'll be a dime, Ma'am."

Sally paid, turned and walked out. "Goodbye for now."

"Good luck" said the grocer. Having appreciated the beauty of the lady, he thought, "Now that would be a nice addition to our community" and headed to the back of the store.

Sally walked down Main Street glancing toward Railroad Street at each cross street she approached. A breeze wafted through the trees bringing with it the faint smell of creosote from the railroad ties. She remembered that Jefferson Street led her and Stuart close to the only house that fit the grocer's description. The side streets and Railroad Street were void of sidewalks; only River and Main Streets gave strollers the comfort and safety of concrete walking paths.

Sally wanted to look as inconspicuous as possible so she stayed on the east side of Railroad as she walked south from Jefferson. The house was as unattended today as it was the day when she, Stuart and Beth drove by after the carnival. What should have been lawn was wild grass and weeds. The windows of the house were dark; it seemed vacant of human inhabitation. She wondered if something may have happened to Thaddeus Murphy; maybe the grocer wasn't aware. No chance, grocers knew everything that was happening in a small town; Sally remembered that from Mystic. Grocers, barbers and hair dressers served as the unwritten social link upon which everyone relied for current and valid news.

Sally took another chance; she walked over to Main Street looking for anyone working in their yard or garden, or hanging clothes in their backyard. A few houses ahead Sally saw her, an older women bent over a flower bed. While still thirty feet away, Sally offered, "Hello. I'm sorry to interrupt your gardening. Your flowers are beautiful".

The woman leaned back, smiled and used the back of her hand to flick away hair that fell on her forehead. She responded, "Oh, Hello. Thank you. Sometimes I wonder if it's worth it, but I do enjoy seeing them grow."

"I am visiting your village." Sally was hoping that using 'village' would help to endear the woman to her quickly. "I've not been in this part of the village before, it's charming."

"Charming? Well, that's a new one. But . . . Harold and I have been here so long, maybe it is charming and we've taken it for granted" responded the woman.

"If you don't mind me asking, how long have you and Harold lived in Montgomery?" asked Sally.

"Oh honey, we've been here all of our lives. He grew up in a house on River Street that has long been torn down, and I grew up a few blocks down Main. We're as much Montgomery as Montgomery is us. There isn't much about Montgomery we don't know." The woman stood up stretching her back, "I'm stopping for iced tea, could I interest you in joining me?"

"Sure, I'd love to" replied Sally.

They walked down a narrow sidewalk along the house. Bushes made it necessary for Sally to duck as they entered the backyard. The air was heavy with the aroma of cultivated plants, gardening and flowers. Though she could not see through the bushes surrounding the backyard, she was certain that all the neighbors gardened or had flower beds. The woman pointed at a round table under a large oak tree and said, "Sit right at the table, the tea is already made, I'll be out in a minute."

Sally couldn't believe her luck, this lady knew everything Sally wanted to know, but she was prepared to be careful; she didn't want to tip her hand or cause suspicion.

The woman returned, "My name is Norma Tinker, now I wouldn't have chosen that last name, I just happened to fall in love with a man with the last name Tinker." She laughed; Sally laughed with her.

Sally said, "My name is Sally McVee."

"Good to meet you, Sally McVee," Norma said as she poured tall glasses of iced tea from a pitcher.

"Who are you visiting?" Norma asked.

"No one in particular. My mother used to know people here and often suggested that I consider raising my daughter in Montgomery. I've come to take a look. I rode the bus from Aurora; my husband has our car at work." That sounded shallow and empty to Sally, so she quickly added, "We currently live in Aurora, but mom always said I should visit Montgomery. So, here I am." She smiled and raised her palms as a sign of surrender.

Norma said, "Honey, I couldn't agree more with your mother. Aurora is a nice place to shop, but when the shopping is over I am beating feet back home to little Montgomery. Did your mother live here; maybe I knew her?"

"No, but she said her cousin lived here, but she hasn't seen or talked with him in years," responded Sally.

"Do you know his name?" asked Norma.

"Yes, it is Thaddeus Murphy" Sally said while swallowing hard. She wasn't expecting the conversation to progress as quickly, or as deeply, as it was going. She hoped it was going in the right direction.

"Thad Murphy," Norma said as she smiled and sighed.

"Do you know him?"

"I guess as well as anyone can know Thad Murphy. He keeps to himself in that house on Railroad Street. Rarely ever see him and when you do, a curt "Hello" is about all you'll get. Your mother is his cousin?" asked Norma.

"Yes."

"What's her name?"

"Betty Thomas." Sally really wanted this questioning to go the other way, so she redirected it away from her family, "Mr. Murphy still lives here?"

"Oh yes, but like I said, he hibernates in his house and doesn't come out much" responded Norma.

"Does Mr. Murphy live with his family?"

"Family? He doesn't have any family that I know of. He doesn't have any friends that I know of either. He's a strange one, indeed" responded Norma.

Realizing she needed to cut off the obvious interest in Mr. Murphy, she probed, "Enough about him. Please tell me if you know of any houses or apartments for rent in this neighborhood."

"My gosh . . . " she took her time thinking as if she was going street to street, ". . . you know, I can't think of a single one. We don't see a lot of people come and go here in Montgomery. I guess you could say that once it grabs you it doesn't let go." Norma snickered as she said this.

"That's a pity; I like what I see" said Sally.

"How long are you going to be here?"

Sally glanced at her watch, "I need to catch a bus at 2:45, so I still have a few hours."

"Well, Harold will be here at 11:30 sharp for lunch; he's knows everything about Montgomery. If anyone knows about available housing, it will be him" offered Norma.

"Would he mind if I stopped by during his lunch to ask him?" asked Sally.

"He'd be thrilled" replied Norma.

Standing, Sally said, "Then I will be back. Thank you so much for your hospitality and kindness."

"Honey, I like company. I'm glad you stopped by."

Sally walked north on Main Street, continually casting an eye toward Railroad Street.

CHAPTER 36

Nick, Stan and Butch rode their bikes past the junkyard and on to Sard Avenue. Nick could not stop thinking about Butch's story on Ed Gien. "What would drive a person to dig up bodies? Or hang them in a shed? Or make things out of their body parts? Why am I even thinking about this? This is sick and perverted stuff!"

They pulled into the Glastons' driveway; the boys could see one of the asshole brothers working on the '49 Ford. The front left wheel was removed. As they approached, without being asked, the asshole brother said "He's in the house."

Nick said, "Thanks."

He, Stan and Butch rode closer to the house, dismounted and were laying their bikes down, when the door to the house opened. The other asshole brother emerged with sandwich in one hand and a Royal Crown cola in the other. Seeing the three approaching the porch, he yelled back into the house, "Hey cracker-ass, you have callers." He walked by the boys without acknowledging them.

Phil appeared in the doorway and came out on the porch. "Hey, what are you guys doing here?"

Nick answered, "We're trying to think through a process and we thought you might have a fresh approach; you want to hang out for a little while?"

"Naw man, I can't, I got other stuff to do, but thanks" replied Phil.

"Could we stay around here to talk; will that work?" asked Nick.

Phil glanced toward his brothers and said, "Ride across the street to the cemetery, I'll see you in ten."

As the boys descended the steps, one of the brothers yelled at Phil. "What's the matter, won't they play with you either, dumbass!"

Phil retreated into the house as the boys rode to the cemetery.

Within ten minutes Phil rode his bike to meet them. The boys stopped on the graveled road so Phil could see them when he came. Phil pulled up and said, "Let's ride deeper, I don't want my brothers causing us problems."

The boys looked quizzically at one another, "Cause us problems? What problems?" All three looked over their shoulders toward Sard Avenue as they rode deeper into the cemetery.

They stopped near an upright spigot sticking out of the ground; it was a source of water for flowers brought by visitors. It was also a source of water to drown out the gophers from their gopher holes. The boys spent their share of time capturing gophers in a bucket as the gophers raced to escape the flood of water.

Phil dismounted and let his bike drop to the ground; the others did the same. They sat on the grass.

Nick hesitantly asked, "What's with your brothers?"

"They think their shit doesn't stink, and everybody else's does. Their problem is they are morons in giant proportions. But, we didn't come here to talk about them. If we did, I'm leaving" stated Phil.

"No man, sorry, I didn't mean to . . ." said Nick before being cut off.

"Hey, no sweat, what did you girls want to talk about?"

They told Phil about being caught last night by Rively.

"Are you shitting me? Rively caught you after you saw me?" asked Phil with genuine surprise.

"Yep," responded Stan.

"How'd he see you guys and not see me?"

"Timing, I guess" said Stan.

"So – you're on the street today – what'd your parents say?" Phil inquired.

"They don't know" Butch said proudly, as if he'd pulled it off single-handedly.

"We talked to Rively at the station and he agreed not to tell our parents if we stayed off the streets at night until this Murphy thing is done" said Nick

"No shit!" exclaimed Phil. Pausing, he asked, "What did you guys talk to Rively about?"

"We talked about Murphy's place, but mostly about Beth being missing. I think he thought we might know something that would help. He asked us when we saw her last and that kind of stuff. That's about it" said Nick

"Well, you girls certainly got lucky last night."

"Yeah, that's what Charlie says, 'We got lucky', Charlie also said we should continue to think about places to look for Murphy and Beth; places the cops wouldn't think of. That's where you come in; we've looked everywhere that comes to mind, but if we put our noggins together, maybe we can come up with more areas to look. Butch here . . ." Nick nodded toward Butch ". . . thinks your fresh mind would be a good addition to our thought process. How about it, Phil, can you think of any places to look?"

Phil immediately and emphatically shook his head, "They aren't going to find old man Murphy. He's long gone."

"How do you know?" asked Butch

"Why would you stay around if you did that?" Phil nodded in the direction of Murphy's house.

"He doesn't drive, how would he vamoose?" asked Butch.

"Come on, he could hop a freighter – look at all the bums riding the rails, he could become one of them and no one would know the difference; or he could just walk off, I've seen him walking to Aurora on the tracks behind my house. Or he could thumb it on the highway, but you can bet he's not here." Phil said this with such conviction that it caused the boys to agree with him.

Recalling that Charlie was challenging them to think about new possibilities, Nick asked Phil, "Phil, if you were Murphy where would you go?"

"I don't know, but I'd get the hell out of here. I wouldn't stick around to answer questions from the cops. That kook is so kooky he might have even stashed a boat on the river and used that to get away" stated Phil with animation and conviction.

Nick realized that Phil was focusing only on Murphy, so he asked, "What about Beth?"

"What about her?" snapped Phil.

"What do you think happened to her?" asked Nick.

"How would I know? Do you think I have a crystal ball?"

Sensing a change, Nick said apologetically, "No man, you seem to have thought it through and I thought you might have some thoughts on her too."

"Naw, I don't have any thoughts on her, all I know is that Murphy's at the center of it, and you ain't gonna find him. This is going to be one of those stories that goes on forever without an end. You guys aren't going to solve it, any more than the cops are, but good luck. Count me in if I can help."

Phil stood, but winced as he applied pressure to his left leg. Nick looked at Phil's leg and said, "Sorry if that's from last night."

"Yeah, you guys got me good, I have to give you credit; that is, until I get you back" Phil said with a laugh.

Phil rode the graveled road out of the cemetery to Main Street.

"He thinks he's got it figured out. And we sit here with hands as empty as when he came; where to now, Kimosabe?" asked Butch.

Nick said, "We'll have time to think about it, because I have to help my dad in the garage this afternoon. He left me a note asking for my help. He has a big overhaul job and needs me to wash parts and answer the phone. I'll show up around noon and will be done by four o'clock. But in the meantime we need to think – like Charlie said – like boys, not cops."

"Ok, but haven't we been doing that all along?" Stan asked with sarcasm.

"Yeah, but Charlie thinks we need to think more" responded Nick.

"Well, we can check on Route 31, toward Caterpiller, down by the river" offered Butch.

"That's a start; and how about the other side of the river?" added Stan.

"Yeah, and they're building that new bridge across the river by Western Electric, man, that is going to be a big bridge! Have you seen it lately?" Butch asked.

"Wow, you guys got the juices flowing. Keep it up" Nick said in an encouraging fashion.

Feeling energized by Nick's encouragement, Butch threw out, "What about the abandoned grain elevator up north of the hump yards?"

"Yeah, we should have thought about that sooner" said Nick, and with reluctance he added, "What about the junk yard?"

"Whoa Cisco, pull back on the reins. I am not going anywhere near that place. Those dogs would eat us for lunch and chew on our bones for days! No way Jose!" exclaimed Stan.

The mention of the junk yard produced the effect of a bucket of cold water being thrown on the conversation. They sat in silence for a moment when Nick said, "You're right, if we can't imagine getting in and out alive without a dog hanging on our ass, how could anyone else? Scrap it."

Butch let out a big sigh and said, "Whew, I was working on an excuse - any excuse, not to join you guys on that one."

They laughed.

"Ok, I'm going to go to my old man's place. If I show up early, he'll let me leave early. What are you guys going to do?" asked Nick.

"Butch and I will continue to think about places to look; hell, we might even reconsider the junk yard and get that done before you get off" offered Stan.

Butch eyed Stan with contempt, no words were necessary to communicate the adamant refusal written across his face.

"Cool it Jasper, I was just joking" Stan said, "We'll do more exploring before swinging by your old man's garage this afternoon."

They mounted their bikes and rode to Main Street. At Clinton, Nick peeled off to the left toward his dad's garage as Stan and Butch continued on Main.

CHAPTER 37

The Montgomery police station was filling up again at 10:00 Thursday morning. John was still around. Other than his visit with the boys, it was a fairly typical night of riding the streets.

Twice during the night he stopped by Murphy's to talk with the new County guys dispatched to secure the scene. They were about the same age as John. The second time, John brought them fresh coffee and sweet rolls from the diner. The rolls were nearing 24 hours old, but at five in the morning who's going to complain?

The County guys asked a lot of questions, they were briefed, but their assignment was to make sure the place was secured, but not to enter the house or the cellar. John filled them in the best he could.

Bob showed up at the station looking a little worse-for-the-wear; he'd left the station at 11:30 last night. John, as ordered, returned to the station at 10:00pm. Bob and John spent an hour and a half going over the pertinent observations and conclusions resulting from the three o'clock meeting.

Henry and his investigators showed up, as did Pete Morantz, but he was alone, "My guys will be here at noon, they're coordinating with all the other departments. Yorkville brought in a guy, convinced he was Murphy, but it turned out he was a farmhand out of Plano."

"Thanks Pete" said Henry. Pointing toward the room designated the investigation room, he continued, "Let's retire to our favorite room and strategize our day."

"For what it's worth, I thought last night's meeting was productive, not that we have a clue on solving it yet, but we are getting closer. Any epiphanies overnight?" Henry asked.

"Any 'what' overnight?" asked Pete.

"Any thoughts or ideas on this case that came to you overnight that you would care to share with the rest of us?" Henry smiled as he clarified. Something told him that Pete knew what an epiphany was, but asked for the benefit of the others.

If their heads were filled with marbles, a resounding rattle would have reverberated off the walls as each shook their head in response.

"All right, no epiphanies. I guess we resort to old fashion gumshoe techniques; cold canvassing, the heart and soul of good police work." Pointing at a map, he said "We need to grid this entire area, including the few residences and businesses on the other side of Route 31, each of us taking an assigned area; ask every adult, every child, every worker, and any talking animals what they saw that might have the slightest bearing on our two cases. By the way, this morning John confirmed with the McVees that the sneaker found belonged to the missing girl. We definitely have two crimes; fortunately both are in close proximity to each other.

I don't have to remind you guys that prodding always gets us a little more information. The average guy may not think the blood-splashed car was unusual until you prod him a little. We have a lot of people to talk to and not a lot of time, so don't engage in fanciful speculation with the citizenry. We want to know about anyone they saw around Railroad Street; anyone walking, anyone in cars, motorcycles, low flying blimps or bicycles.

If you hit something hot, cut off your canvass and report. Bob, do you know anyone in Western Electric that could get us in to interview employees who would have arrived early Wednesday or gone home late Tuesday?"

"I can get us in, and I'll get a map of the town for the grid" answered Bob, rising to go to the other room.

The grid was laid out; more County and State investigators were called in to assist. John headed home with the agreement to be back at 6:00. Bob volunteered to handle the interviewing of the Western Electric employees. The search was on for information, any information that could give them a much-needed break in the case.

CHAPTER 38

Sally walked around Montgomery biding time until Harold came home for lunch. At 11:35 she walked past Norma's flower beds, approached the Tinkers' front door and rang the doorbell. Norma answered and greeted Sally as if she had been there on many occasions, "Sally, come on back, Harold is in the kitchen."

Sally followed Norma through the small living room and down a hall to the kitchen. Harold was at the table with a sandwich and a bowl of soup in front of him. "Harold, I want you to meet Sally McVee" Norma exclaimed.

Harold stood, nodded in a gentlemanly fashion, "Sally, good to meet you."

"I don't mean to interrupt your lunch . . ." Sally began.

Cutting her off, Harold said smiling, "Don't give it no mind, I can chew and talk at the same time."

"No you can't Harold Tinker!" Norma offered sternly.

Looking at Sally and nodding toward Norma, Harold laughingly said, "She thinks she's my mother. Hell, she's tougher than my mother was any day. What can I do to help with your cause?"

"Mr. Tinker . . ."

Harold, still smiling, cut in again, "Sally, Mr. Tinker was my father, he's buried up in Riverside Cemetery; my name is Harold."

"I'm sorry Harold, I mentioned to Norma that I'm looking to move to Montgomery and would like to rent a place in this part of town. Norma couldn't think of any, but assured me that if anyone knew of a place it would be you" answered Sally.

"She did, huh? She leads me to believe I don't know my . . ."

Norma cut him off this time, "Harold! Would you please help this young lady and let your humor have a holiday?"

213

"Yes dear. Sorry Sally, now, let me think." This reminded Sally of watching Norma earlier in the day, Harold's mind began envisioning the streets of Montgomery and all available housing. He took a bite of his sandwich, chewed it, swallowed and said, "There's a place down on Mill Street, the Johnson's moved out; her folks in Peoria are doing poorly, so they moved to be closer."

"I'm not sure where Mill Street is located?" Sally queried.

"Where the bridge crosses the river; it's about a block and a half this side of the bridge" Harold explained.

"I really wanted to find a place close to here" offered Sally apologetically.

Harold went into his mental real estate exploration again. Another bite, and he said, "I have to agree with Norma on this one, I'm not aware of any available houses or apartments in this part of town. Even the small brick units down by Western Electric are all filled right now."

Sally was becoming disappointed, but said, "I'm sure you've thought about it, but what about Railroad Street or Jefferson, or Scott Street? I've walked around town and really would like to be in that area."

Shaking his head and chewing more of his sandwich, Harold said, "No, I know that area really well; I can tell you who lives in every house, and can name their kids too. Nothing comes to mind." Harold could see the disappointment coming over Sally. "You might think about taking a place on a temporary basis until a house is available."

"That might work; do you have a place in mind?" Sally asked hopefully.

"Well, Jake Andrews has a place, it's not much to look at, but it might serve your purposes on a temporary basis" responded Harold.

"Where is that?" Norma stopped putting lunch away to ask.

"It's over the tracks by Baseline Road" answered Harold.

"Mr. Tink . . . I mean Harold, is it possible for me to see it?" asked Sally.

"I'd have to get a hold of Jake, but I think we can pull that off. I can call you once I know" responded Harold.

"That would be wonderful Harold. I'm home most evenings." Sally wrote her phone number on a pad that Norma handed her. "You have been so helpful, both of you. I'm not sure how to thank you."

"Move to town and make our scenery a little prettier" responded Harold.

Norma said playfully, "Harold, you need to go back to work."

Sally left the Tinkers offering her thanks numerous times.

That night Sally approached Stuart about the possibility of moving to Montgomery. As always, Stuart was supportive of anything Sally felt she needed. He mentioned that the owner of the estate he served was not likely to need his services much longer, the owner's health was such that he would be moving to New York State to live with his daughter. If they moved to Montgomery, Stuart felt that it would be necessary for him to find work near Montgomery. Sally told him that she'd heard about a place that might be available and that a man was calling to arrange a time for them to look at the property.

Harold called Sally and made an appointment for the McVees to meet Jake Andrews on Saturday afternoon at 1:30 at the diner in Montgomery. Sally made arrangements to allow Beth to stay with the family that lived below them.

Jake Andrews was farm-grown; tall, wide and thick all over. He wore bib overalls, a flannel shirt and laced boots that were covered with something that looked like mud, but smelled much worse. He was waiting in his Ford pick-up truck and waived Sally and Stuart over before they entered the diner.

After the introductions, Jake suggested they all pile into his truck to go see the house. The only seat in the pick-up was barely enough; Jake's bulk took up half of the seat. It might have been their imaginations, but the truck seemed to lean toward Jake's side.

Jake said, "If you like it, we can do work on the road getting in." This caused Sally and Stuart to wonder what could be wrong with the road. All the roads they encountered were reasonable, but neither said a word.

Jake crossed the tracks at Case Street and turned left on Route 31. Sally began to think it was not going to meet her needs when Jake slowed and turned left where no sign of a road existed. Jake said, "It's been a while since anyone has been back here, so the weeds have taken over. Bumping along in what seemed like a field, Jake said, "This place was originally a one-room shack for hunting, but we've added on twice; the town allowed us to tie in for electricity and water. The big drawback is the lack of indoor plumbing, if you know what I mean. We built a new outhouse out back." He quickly added, "With an electrical light."

They crossed a tiny stream and drove through a stand of trees. When Sally first saw the shack, she was repulsed. It was a shack! Stuart looked at the shack, glancing at Sally for her appraisal. Realizing what Stuart was doing, Sally began making comments about what needed to be done to make it more attractive, and that it was meant to be a temporary residence until they could find what they wanted in town.

Jake walked them through the shack and around the property. "You've already guessed the other drawback is the trains. They clatter through here night and day. People say they get used to it and block it out, but I don't know that to be true personally. I live a long ways from the tracks."

Jake agreed to improvement and repairs before the McVees moved in. The McVees agreed to stay on the property for at least six months, after that the rental agreement would be month to month allowing the McVees to move if they found their permanent housing.

Sally asked Jake how she and Beth would get to town if Stuart drove the car to work.

"Not a problem, you can follow the trail down the tracks, not more than two or three hundred yards; you can cross at Case

Street. It's safe, you won't run into anyone back here" replied Jake.

This wasn't perfect by any stretch of her imagination, but it would get her closer; certainly in walking distance of that house on Railroad Street.

The McVees moved to Montgomery a month later.

CHAPTER 39

Stan and Butch rode past Murphy's place to take another look. Only a handful of gawkers remained. Two County cops occupied the cop car parked in front of the house, the ropes still encased the yard like a shrine. The cellar doors were closed. The trampled weeds in the yard were a testament to the heavy foot traffic it faced the day before.

Butch stopped, straddled his bike and surveyed the scene like a highly-paid private investigator taking another look to find what others missed; eyes narrowed and with his head slightly cocked to one side. He imagined himself coming up with the critical observation that would break the case wide open. He looked for the clue that would jump out and grab him. When it did, he and Stan would ride to the station and inform the investigators.

Stan interrupted the mood when he said, "Seen enough, Charlie Chan?"

Thoughtfully, Butch replied, "You know the answer is right in front of us, but we haven't recognized it yet."

Stan took another look at the house and the old garage and said, "You might be right Butch, but I don't see it, so let's get productive and do what we can." With that, Stan mounted and began riding. Butch followed.

When they came to Watkins, Stan pulled off to the side; he motioned for Butch to do the same. "This is as good of a place to start as any" said Stan.

"Start what?" asked Butch.

"The search, numbskull; we are looking for Beth, remember?" answered Stan.

"Without Nick? I thought we were going to meet up with him and start the search?"

"Come on, we can cover some of the ground now; when we hook up with Nick we'll have something to report" stated Stan.

Shrugging his shoulders, Butch said, "Ok."

They crossed Railroad Street, hiding their bikes behind the tall pine trees by the brush factory. Stan said, "Why don't I work my way to the river and you work your way along Western Electric, we'll meet up here and head to the next site."

"We're splitting up? Why?" quizzed Butch.

"Because we can cover more ground, and it's broad daylight. Come on, this won't take us more than a half hour." Stan headed into the pines.

Butch headed around the National Brush Company and toward the back gate of Western Electric thinking, "Splittin' up doesn't make any sense at all; we're a team, like the Three Musketeers, 'All for one, and one for all.' This isn't a team, this is a one-man hike." He involuntarily scuffed at the ground with his sneaker.

Stan made it through the pines without being seen; this was important because the owner of the brush company forbids kids on his property. More than once the owner had come running out of the building like a lunatic screaming that kids were not allowed to play on company property. He said this with a heavy foreign accent which meant every other word was unintelligible. Everyone would scatter and regroup across his property line returning a barrage of vulgarities that would have made any parent proud, "Stick it up your ass, old man - Your mother wears combat boots and rolls you in shit to improve your smell - If your dick was any shorter, you'd have a bump on your ass," etc., etc. Stan smiled recalling those encounters. He could smile now that he was through the pines.

He continued toward the river and walked through back yards and stayed close to the high fence that separated Western Electric from the rest of the world. He kept reminding himself to keep an eagle-eye out for . . . for what? What the hell was he looking for? Beth wasn't going to be strolling along and be surprised to see him and say, "Hi Stan. I've been out for a long walk. Think my parents are going to be mad?" Come on, he was too wrapped up in Nick's romantic interests. No, he is not looking for Beth, but anything that might . . . be helpful? "I don't know what to look for; I am just going to look for whatever I need to look for" he said to himself and kept walking and looking.

He crossed River Street staying close to the Western Electric fence. As he approached the river, he saw that construction barriers had been placed to prevent anyone from going any farther. The construction of the Route 30 by-pass bridge across the Fox was underway. Stan slipped around the barriers and continued toward the river.

It had been a while since he was down here and was excited to see the progress - huge concrete walls and supports on both sides of the river, as well as concrete supports at mid-way points in the middle of the river. Looking up he thought, "Now that is impressive!" The sight was those gigantic burnt-red girders that spanned from one support to the other; crossing the entire river, like a highway in the sky. He imagined walking those girders to the other side with Nick, Butch and other friends – well, maybe not Butch. They would have to do it on the weekend when the construction workers weren't present.

He could see Boulder Hill, a new housing development on the other side. This bridge was going to expose a whole new world to them, and new girls too.

Shaking his head to refocus on his task, Stan looked up and down the river. The murky water and the muddy river bank looked the same as always, the aquatic smell of fish and river life hadn't changed either. He walked the bank to Case Street and began his trek back to meet Butch.

He was walking up the hill on Case Street when the wail of the volunteer fire department siren sounded. The siren was mounted high on a tall pole and rotated back and forth to send its beckoning to all corners of Montgomery.

Everyone had a member in their family that served as a volunteer fireman. The siren would sound, men would scramble from their homes and businesses to their cars, place the little blue flashing light on the dashboard, and drive like maniacs to the fire station, kicking up dust as they went. It was a moment of urgency and excitement. The whole town took notice when that siren sounded.

Stan's uncle worked at one of the local factories and was released from work when the siren went off. Stan heard his uncle say on some days he prayed that siren would sound.

The siren was a call for volunteer firemen to come to an emergency, but more than that, it was a call to every explorer to drop everything and race to the fire department on his bike. Once the volunteers were assembled and the fire truck or ambulance pulled out of the garage, bicycled explorers would trail behind at a safe distance.

Stan was a long way from the fire department and a long way from his bike, and the siren was beckoning. Timing was lousy.

He walked briskly up the hill and toward his meeting place with Butch. If they hurried, they might get to the site of the emergency in time to have one of the more timely explorers fill them in.

Butch made his way around the brush company and was looking at the manned guard shack at the rear entrance to Western Electric fifty yards to the south. He figured the guard would not be particularly fond of a kid hanging around W.E. property, so he gave the guard a wave and walked as if crossing the tracks on Case.

Once to the tracks, the guard's view was obstructed by foliage. Butch turned left and began walking the tracks. He too began to wonder what he should be looking for, but decided he'd know it when he saw it.

Still out of sight of the guard and parallel to the guard shack, Butch drifted down the ballast; because of the crossing, the tracks were not elevated as high. He looked in the bushes to his left.

While walking and looking to the right at the ballast he heard a noise behind him. Before he could turn, Butch saw a flash of light, everything went black.

Stan heard the cyclical screams of the fire truck and other emergency vehicles coming as he was making his way to the bikes. He said to himself, "Yes! Luck was coming their way." He began to run. When he reached the bikes expecting to find Butch waiting for him, he found the bikes, but no Butch. The fire truck, the meat wagon and the Village Car were now in sight. He grabbed both bikes bringing them out in the open; when Butch arrived, they'd be ready to go.

As the vehicles, with lights flashing and sirens screaming, passed Watkin, Stan's patience ran out; he laid Butch's bike down and rode to the corner to see the direction they were going. Butch was probably right around the corner and he could catch up.

CHAPTER 40

As Stan made his way around the brush factory and on to Railroad, he could see a fire truck, the meat wagon, and a Village car parked at varying angles near the tracks. Other cars accumulated from onlookers. He recognized the uniform of the guard from Western Electric as he walked toward the tracks.

Stan put his bike down on the grass, looked around for Butch, and walked closer to the site. It appeared that the firemen were tending to a person lying on the ballast off the roadway. He was totally engrossed in the excitement and continued to edge closer, conscious to avoid getting in the way. He could see a person laying on their back and not moving. Then he saw them! Those are slip-on sneakers! Those are Butch's slip-on sneakers! But why would someone be wearing Butch's . . . NO! It can't be Butch! I was just with him. He moved closer not caring about getting in the way. Air left Stan's lungs and he felt faint. He stopped in place, but could not unscrew his eyes from Butch's legs. Move – damn it!

The firemen were grouped around Butch, checking his pulse and the other things Stan had seen them do for others during emergency calls – but that's Butch. Come on Butch, move. Stan was within ten feet of Butch's prone body and he could see Butch's face. Butch's normally puffy cheeks were pallid and gray, his eyes were closed and Stan could see that Butch was not responding to the firemen's efforts. He jumped as a hand was placed on his shoulder. Turning he saw Bob Woodyard, "What happened, son?"

"I . . . I don't know. I wasn't with him – I was . . . over that way and coming to meet him." Stan tipped his head in the direction of the brush company, but couldn't take his eyes off his friend. Stan

225

was amazed; the body he was looking at looked like Butch, but not really. "Chief Woodyard, do you know what happened to him?"

"Mr. Killian saw him lying here and called it in from the brush company. I'd say he was struck by a car that didn't stop. Killian said there was no car was in the area when he found him" responded Bob.

The firemen collapsed the portable gurney to the ground next to Butch. They were discussing the process of lifting him onto the gurney.

John Rively walked up and stood beside Bob. "What's the lowdown, Bob?"

Bob was surprised to see John, "I thought you headed for home?"

"I did; I heard the siren and figured you might need help" said John. Touching Stan's elbow, he said, "Stan, you ok?"

"I guess so, but Butch is my friend. I wish I would have been with him." Stan was stunned.

"Hey, you've seen these guys work before, they're good. Don't be worrying about it, he'll be back terrorizing the town soon enough." John said this strictly for Stan's sake; based on his observation things did not look good at all. Turning back to Bob, "So what happened?"

"Don't know for sure, Killian found him lying there. My guess is a car hit him and left" said Bob.

"Stan, how come you weren't with him?" John directed the question to Stan.

"We split up and were going to meet by the brush company" responded Stan.

"What was he doing over here?" asked John.

"We were just looking – for anything that might help." Stan said it sheepishly, not sure if this was a breach of their agreement with John.

John put his arm around Stan and said, "Son, it's going to be ok."

"Where do you think they'll take him?" asked Stan.

"They'll take him to St. Joe's on Lake Street; that's where they normally go" answered John; he walked closer to the firemen as they were putting Butch on the gurney.

Stan watched as they lifted Butch's limp body onto the gurney, it was like they were lifting a ragdoll, and when they laid his head down they put it to the side. Stan could see blood at the base of his skull. Stan felt like crying, but held back the tears; he wasn't going to let that happen. Butch was his friend and Stan would stand strong – he'd be strong when Butch couldn't. Stan continued to stare at Butch on the gurney; this is his friend, he didn't like what he saw, but sometimes you just can't look away.

Butch was loaded into the '54 Chevy panel truck converted into an ambulance. John walked to Bob, "How was he laying when you got here, Bob?"

"Pretty much the same way he was laying when you got here" answered Bob.

"No one moved him?" John queried.

"Not that I know of; I doubt that Killian moved him. Why?"

"Did you see the wound on the back of his head when they were lifting him onto the gurney?" asked John.

"Yeah, that doesn't look so good. I hope the kid's going to be ok."

"Bob, it looked to me as if the blood ran down the back of his neck and forward toward his chest. It couldn't have done that if he was lying on his back; it would have run into the ballast. I think he was moved" stated John.

"Well, shitcakes and buttercups!" exclaimed Bob. "We'll seal the place off. Let's get Henry and Pete up here pronto – good God Almighty, what more can happen!"

John headed for the Village car, radioed the station. John gave a brief description of the situation. Henry and Pete were on their way.

The ambulance left for the hospital; Bob rousted everyone away from the tracks to preserve the scene as much as he could.

Henry and Pete walked up to Bob; Pete said, "John said a kid got hit by a car and we should look at the scene; something special that you picked up on, Bob?"

"I didn't pick up on it at all; John did." Bob walked them through the limited facts as they knew them. "I was convinced that he'd been hit by a car and left lying here, until John noticed dried blood that flowed the wrong way."

"Good call on his part; so how does that change your take on what happened?" Henry asked.

"Well, the guy that found him said he didn't move him, nor touch him in any way. This is a busy crossing this time of the day; I doubt he was lying here very long. He would have been noticed. The kid was visible from various directions; the crossing, Railroad Street and the office entrance to the factory. So I'm considering the possibility he was dumped here from a car or the bed of a truck. What do you guys, think?" replied Bob.

John rejoined them, "I spoke with the guard at Western Electric. He said they received numerous deliveries this morning, most having come across the tracks from Route 31. The last wasn't more than fifteen minutes before he heard the siren."

Pete offered, "Which means the kid wasn't here more than five minutes, ten at most." He pinched his chin with his forefinger and thumb, "Let's run with the theory that he was dumped. You said he was twelve years old; so why dump a 12 year old? Was he a trouble maker? Did he have trouble at home?"

John responded, "I know the kids of this town, and no he isn't a trouble maker, and I don't think he has problems at home. His old man is in Shannon's often, drinks too much, but I have never heard of any kind of problems that would lead to this. He's a good kid."

"Ok, he's a good kid that got walloped on the head and dumped by the railroad tracks during daylight hours. Or, he got hit by a car, the driver got out, rolled him over to check on him, got scared and high-footed it out of here" offered Henry.

"The blood on his neck suggests he was lying face down longer than a few minutes," said John. "He had to be lying face down long enough to allow the blood to flow down and to the sides, some of it dried. The wound looked significant enough, but it takes time for blood to flow and dry."

"Let's do a cursory scan of the area" said Henry as he looked around. "We have a Chinaman's chance in hell of getting any tire tracks off this crossing, and footprints aren't likely either. Let's spread out."

CHAPTER 41

B eth kept her promise to her mom, it was hard. She wanted to know why she was caught between two forces; one force she loved very much, her mother, the other force was a strange old man that knew something that he said wasn't her fault, wasn't her mother's fault, but rather, was his fault. Fault for what?

Beth did not want to upset her mom again by asking her about it, she wanted to ask the old man to explain himself – no, she wanted to demand the old man explain himself, but to do so would require her to break her promise to her mom. Every day she thought about the old man when she walked to and from school. She would look at his house on Railroad Street as she walked on Watkins. She would think to herself, "That old devil owes me an explanation!" but that's as far as it would go - until the day school let out an hour early.

Beth walked Watkins, looked toward the house on Railroad Street; the old devil was out in his yard. Beth fumed as she walked; at the last moment she turned north on Railroad. Her pace increased, as did her heart rate. She was going to get an answer. Shortly after she turned he was no longer visible. This made Beth even more determined - she walked faster; he wasn't getting away.

Approaching his property, her determination began to wane, replaced with reluctance and trepidation. She had made her mind up; she was going to talk to him today and get it over with. She marched up the three steps of the front porch and was about to rap on the door with her knuckles when the door opened. Surrounded by his junk and darkness stood the old devil himself. Beth was startled. She took a step back holding her right hand to her mouth. Murphy felt guilty having caused her to be frightened;

he said, "Beth, what are you doing here? I didn't mean to frighten you." He stepped out and closed the door behind him.

"Uh – I was coming to ask you to – uh – explain yourself" Beth said, still unsettled.

"Beth, does your mother know you're here?" Murphy inquired.

Casting her eyes downward, she said, "No she doesn't. But, I would really like to know what is going on, and you seem to be the one to tell me."

"No Beth, your mom should be the one."

"She won't, or can't, or doesn't want to, anyway, it upsets her. But it doesn't seem to upset you, so I've come to you for the explanation." Beth was beginning to recover and felt her determination returning.

"Beth, your mother does not want you speaking to me, yet here we are standing in the open where the world can see, does that make sense? Don't you think your mother will find out?" asked Murphy.

Beth glanced around considering what Murphy said and began to agree that anyone could clearly see them on his front porch. She was about to respond when Murphy said, "If you think we must talk, let's go to the backyard, the trees will provide a little privacy."

Beth hesitated, "You go first Mr. Murphy."

Murphy smiled, understanding Beth's concerns about him being behind her, so he stepped around her and walked down the steps and turned left. Beth followed behind at a safe distance. Her mind focused on what she would do if Mr. Murphy attempted anything out of the ordinary; her eyes were focused on him. If he tried anything, she would bolt and run like crazy.

Murphy walked around the side of the house to a stump still in the ground and a three foot piece of the fallen tree trunk not far away. Motioning toward them, he said, "Would you prefer the stump or log?"

Beth considered this and said, "The stump, please." She quickly determined the log was lower than the stump, which would make it more difficult for the person on the log to rise and move quickly if needed.

"Fair enough." He walked over to the log and sat down facing the stump.

Beth sat on the stump, but faced slightly toward the road.

"Ok Beth, what may I do for you today?"

"You know what you can do for me; you can tell me what's going on? What is it that is not my fault, and not my mother's fault? What is your interest in me and my family? What is the big mystery?" responded Beth.

Murphy looked at Beth, at the ground, then toward a space that wasn't in Montgomery at all. After an uncomfortable period of silence, Beth said, "Well, are you going to tell me or not?"

Murphy's simple answer was, "I don't know."

"You don't know what the mystery is, or you don't know if you are going to tell me?"

"I don't know that I should tell you, Beth."

"Of course you should, you were the one to bring it up, not me. You are not being fair, Mr. Murphy!" snapped Beth.

"Yes, you are right; I should have never brought it up. I . . ." Murphy's voice trailed off as he looked at the ground.

"Mr. Murphy, you are interested in my family, and it must be important, why can't you talk about it?"

"Beth, it's not that easy. I will consider your request, but you must provide me time to consider it" responded Murphy.

"You have had time, Mr. Murphy. What did you expect me to do with your 'It's not your fault' statement? Just twiddle my thumbs and say, "He's a crazy old man and doesn't know what he is saying?" Realizing her words came out stronger and more spontaneous that she intended, she immediately said, "Mr. Murphy, I am sorry, I . . . I don't think you are a crazy old man, but you have to agree that you aren't being fair."

Murphy liked the grit this young girl was displaying, but withheld a smile and said, "Beth, your parents must be proud of you."

Not expecting this response, Beth said, "Yes, I hope they are - but what's that got to do with you telling me why you're interested in my family?"

"Beth, will you give me a couple of days to think about it?"

Realizing that she had said all she could to secure an answer, she relented, "Will you promise to tell me in a couple of days?"

"No Beth, but I will promise to give it serious consideration."

As Beth stood up from the stump she asked, "Mr. Murphy, what do you do with all that stuff in your house?"

"You saw it?" Murphy asked.

"Yes, when you opened the door. It's all stacked up. Is your whole house that way?"

Feeling unexpectedly exposed, Murphy said, "I have lived alone a long time. I see people discard things that don't necessarily deserve to be discarded, so I bring them here. Sometimes I use the things, sometimes I don't. And, I have gathered a lot of things, haven't I?"

"It looks that way, Mr. Murphy. Do you ever sell any of it?" quizzed Beth.

"Not really. I don't have anyone to sell it to; besides, I get attached to it over time. You may want to reconsider whether or not I am a crazy old man" Murphy said with a smile.

Beth returned his smile and began to walk toward Railroad Street as she said, "Mr. Murphy, I will be back in a couple of days."

"See you then, Beth." Murphy stood and began walking to the back door of his house.

With Beth on her way home, Murphy entered his house, exhaled and looked around. Many years had passed since he observed the interior of his house like he was doing at this moment. To the best he could recollect, no one, other than himself, had ventured across his thresholds for decades. He was viewing a lifetime of collecting. At the moment, he couldn't remember why he began collecting, but whatever the reason may have been, it caught on.

If he was to invite Beth into his home, he was going to have to provide space that she would find comfortable. He started in the back bedroom, a bedroom estranged from human existence for a very long time.

CHAPTER 42

Stan rode away from the Case Street crossing feeling as if he was riding through mud. He would take Butch's bike to his house; he would walk back to get his own bike.

When on his own bike, every turn of the bicycle sprocket was forced as he pedaled toward Nick's dad's garage. Back at the tracks, other explorers peppered Stan when they learned it was Butch, "Man, do think he was dead? What was he doing on the railroad tracks? Do think a train hit him?" Stan understood the questioning, it was a part of exploring, but he needed to get away. What was he going to say to Nick? Their best friend is being hauled off to the hospital in a meat wagon and Stan wasn't there when Butch needed him.

Stan was confused as to what had happened to Butch; first they were saying he was hit by a car. Knowing Butch, that wasn't hard to accept. Butch often became focused on one thing, forgetting to pay attention to anything else, inviting a minor disaster to occur. Like the time a group of them were behind the school at night. When someone saw headlights coming and yelled 'cops!', everyone turned to run into bushes in the cemetery. Butch began running, but forgot to turn, still looking behind him for the headlights. He ran into the steel post holding the basketball net and backboard. Nick and the other guys dragged Butch to the bushes before the cops arrived. He was knocked cold. That was Butch, so maybe he did get hit by a car because he wasn't paying attention. But he heard Chief Woodyard say he was likely dumped in that spot. That one blew Stan's mind. Dumped? He was just with Butch; how could someone 'dump' him. This is all about as crazy as it can get.

He pulled onto the graveled driveway of Paul's Auto Repair; a two and half car, concrete block building with two bays. The bright sunshine made it impossible to see in the garage, other than to see both bays were occupied by ailing cars requiring mending.

The car on the left, a '55 Chevy, was elevated off the ground and supported by jack-stands; the car on the right, a 1954 Pontiac Chieftain, was on its wheels but with the hood up. Stan could hear Bobby Darin, *"Bing, bang, I saw the whole gang, dancin' on my living room rug, yeah! Flip, flop they was doing the bop . . ."* coming from a box radio. Stan wondered how long that would last, Mr. Corrie hated rock and roll music and could only take so much before he would climb out from under the car, not say a word, walk over and turn the radio off. Nick would complain, but to no avail.

Approaching the left bay, Stan could see two gray uniform pants legs stained with oil and grease protruding from under the driver's side of the Chevy. Nick's dad was on a creeper beneath that car. "Hey Mr. Corrie, its Stan."

"Hey Stan. Heard you crunching the gravel; you're not here to steal my help are you?"

Stan changed direction and entered the garage between the Chevy and the Pontiac.

"Uh, no sir, but I have news to tell Nick that you might want to hear" said Stan.

Stan could now see Nick back in the corner, elbow deep in cleaning solvent as he cleaned the caked grease and grime from parts removed from the dismantled engine. He was wearing a pair of oversized coveralls with the sleeves rolled up. "What's cookin, good lookin" said Nick, in hopes Stan could steal him away.

Stan walked to the front of the cars and toward the work bench, "Can you come over here for a minute, and you might want to turn that radio down?"

Nick cocked his head realizing that Stan would not normally address him this way, wiped his hands and arms on a red shop rag, turned off the radio and began walking toward the bench. Mr.

Corrie pushed out from beneath the Chevy and was sitting on the creeper wiping his hands on another red shop rag. He stood, walked toward the bench, nodding toward the Chevy. "This better be good, son, that baby has to be done tomorrow." He sat on the rolling stool. Nick perched on a stack of tires. Stan remained standing.

"Did you hear the fire whistle?" Stan began.

Nick and his dad nodded.

"It was for Butch." A slight catch in Stan's voice revealed his emotion; he tried to mask it with a cough.

"What happened?" asked Nick.

"Nick, I don't know, man. He got hit by car or hurt in another way. When I got to him the firemen were already working on him; he was out and the back of head was bashed in."

"By the time you got to him? Where were you? Where'd this take place?" Nick asked excitedly without pause.

"Boys, let's slow it down" encouraged Mr. Corrie. "Stan, take a couple deep breaths and start from the beginning."

This proved to have a calming effect on Stan, "Ok, we left you this morning . . ." Stan walked them step by step through the entire event, splitting up to cover more territory, hearing the sirens, seeing Butch, including relaying what he heard the cops say about the possibility of Butch being dumped. When he was done, he stood looking down.

Mr. Corrie gave Stan a moment, "Do you have any idea how badly Butch is hurt?"

"Mr. Corrie, I have never seen Butch look like that. He was sunken in and didn't look good at all. It was all kind of scary."

"Yeah, I can only imagine, son. But, like everything else in life, it all comes out in the wash. Butch is young and a lot tougher than we give him credit for. The hospital will take care of him. Trust me." Mr. Corrie continued looking toward the solvent tub. "Nick, you finish up the manifold, water pump and valve covers; when you're done, you two can take off. After I get the oil pan off, I'll take a break and make a couple of calls to see what I can find out."

"Thanks, Dad" said Nick.

"That's ok, but don't scrimp on getting them clean. They need to be ready to go back on" responded Mr. Corrie.

Stan helped Nick finish washing the parts. They worked fast, but thoroughly examined each part before declaring them clean. Stan followed Nick as he went into the house to wash up and change clothes.

While they were in the house, Mr. Corrie made a call to one of his friends at the fire department; this friend worked in close proximity to the fire station, so was likely to have been at the scene.

CHAPTER 43

John headed for home to get reSt. Bob, Henry and Pete were back at the station. The rest of the investigators were on the canvass with additional inquiries about any vehicle seen in the vicinity of the Case Street crossing. The village clerk was asked to remain at the station all day until the crisis passed; she was thrilled. Montgomery was popping.

Pete playfully said, "Damn it to hell, Bob, did you really think we didn't have enough to do. You're stacking up these cases like cordwood?"

"Pete, if I knew what was going on, I would be thrilled to get everything solved and go fishing" responded Bob, he continued. "In twenty-seven years, I have never seen this much activity in my little village. And I don't mean at the same time, I mean in total. Christ, I am worried about that kid. Any report on his condition?"

"None so far, but from what I heard from the firemen when they got back, it doesn't look good, Bob. Sorry" said Henry, as if offering condolences.

"Thanks." Bob appeared disheartened, "Two of our kids . . . I'd have bet a dollar to a donut that girl was going to show up at a friend's house. The reports from the different departments have produced squat. Not a sign. Then we have Murphy and his cellar of horrors. I see new reports have come in from your boys, Henry; anything revealing?"

Henry picked up the reports, "Yes, they confirmed that the bone fragments on the tarp are human and they've determined through microscopic evaluation that they are the result of bones being sawn."

"Sawn?" repeated Pete.

"Sawn, as in to take one's saw and saw bones" clarified Henry.

"So Murphy sawed someone to pieces" stated Bob with pursed lips. "Aren't we going to be messengers of madness when this gets out?"

"If we can get it figured out before the details get out, it's going to be a lot easier to handle." offered Henry.

"Agreed," said Pete, "But in case we need a reminder, we don't have anything to lead us to believe we are going to figure it out."

The phone in the other room rang. The village clerk stuck her head around the corner, "Chief Woodyard, it sounds like one of the other departments." Bob went to answer it. While he was gone, Pete said to Henry, "This is taking a toll on Bob. What do you think we should do?"

"What can we do? Get him to step down? Hell, he's a good man. For a small town cop, he's one of the beSt. We need to stand with him and figure this out. Maybe we need to focus on one aspect of our three-ring circus and not try to solve everything at once" said Henry.

"If they are connected, solving one will lead to solving them all" offered Pete.

Bob walked back in. "Oswego is holding a vagrant they stopped on the tracks. He's acting strangely and not talking. They think we may want to talk with him. I told them we would be down."

Pete said, "That's only a couple of miles from here, and on the tracks. It sure couldn't hurt."

"Before we leave, let's share with Bob what we were discussing" said Henry.

"What's that?" asked Bob.

Pete jumped in, "Let's do it on the way down. We're going to have time in the car, let's make it productive."

During their short ride to Oswego, they tried to focus on which of the three cases would provide the most likely results. They concluded that none of the three presented any obvious opportunities, but the results of the canvass could change all of that.

CHAPTER 44

After Nick cleaned up and changed clothes, he and Stan walked back to the garage. Nick said, "Thanks, Dad. We're taking off."

"Hang on a second." He slid his creeper from under the Chevy. Standing, he said, "I talked to Ted Blankenship; he was one of the firemen that took Butch to the hospital." He paused. "Boys, your friend is seriously hurt." He paused again, "He might not make it; you boys should be prepared for that."

Stunned by what they were hearing, Nick said, "Dad, did Mr. Blankenship say that?"

"In so many words, he did. He said the doctor at the emergency entrance examined Butch while he was still on the gurney. He ordered that the back of Butch's head be packed in ice immediately. Ted said that is not a good sign; it usually means that they think the brain is swelling. The ice is to reduce the swelling. Ted thought the position of Butch's injury might even involve the base of the skull and the spinal cord. He said swelling in that area doesn't usually end up good. Now I am telling you this because I think you boys deserve to know, but you are not at liberty to share that with anyone else. Ted trusted me with this information. Butch's parents arrived at the hospital when Ted was leaving, but Butch has other relatives that may not know anything yet. Do I have your word that this conversation stays in this garage?"

They both nodded as Nick asked, "Dad, can we go see Butch?"

"Son, the only people that are going to get to see Butch for a while will be his mom and dad. But if we get good news on Butch, I'll take you two to the hospital."

"Thanks, Dad."

Nick and Stan found no words for the occasion. They headed for the river in silence.

With their bikes on the grass in the park, they slipped beneath the bridge. Large boulders provided a place to sit. The slope of the arched bridge created a quaint, almost secret, environment. This spot wasn't secret; most of their friends knew about this place, it just felt secret. A place to go when the rest of the world was too busy - too screwed up - or too dangerous.

Nick said, "Stan, I might cry, but if I do, and if you tell anyone, I will kick your ass up between your two front teeth. Agreed?"

Stan nodded slowly and said, "The same goes for you."

They sat in silence as the traffic overhead thumped across the bridge. Stan said, "What the hell are we going to do without Butch? He's like the Abbott & Costello of our lives. There is no other Butch. Do you know anyone like Butch?"

"Nope." Nick did not trust his ability to say more.

"Nick, if I hadn't sent him out on his own, he'd be sitting here with us" said Stan.

"Oh bullshit! We've done this sort of thing all our lives. This one didn't work out, that's all" said Nick.

"No man, you don't get it, Butch didn't want to split up; in fact he wanted to wait for you so we could all search together. But I wanted to show you we could get stuff done while you were working. I think I have shit for brains" said Stan.

"Hey! You got to cut the crap. You didn't do anything I wouldn't have done. Neither of us would do anything to put Butch in trouble. Come on, think about it, how many times have we bailed his ass out, or willingly carried his load because he's our friend?" asked Nick.

"Plenty" responded Stan

"Exactly; and you know what?"

"What?"

"I don't care what the stupid doctors say; I'm going to choose to believe we'll be bailing him out of his messes for the rest of our lives. The doctors can kiss my rosy ass. Butch is tough. He's going to make it; and when he does, I'm going to be standing next to you, giving him a ration of shit that will rattle his rafters!" stated Nick with conviction.

"Me too; that's what I'm going to believe. Butch is going to make it. But when he does, I'm still going to apologize for sending him out on his own. When I'm done apologizing, I'm going to rattle his rafters too!" said Stan.

They laughed as the mood magically changed.

"Hey, do you remember the last time we walked the tracks to Aurora to see a movie?" asked Stan.

"Yeah, *The Attack of the 50 Foot Woman*," that was a drag; about as believable as wings on a frog's pecker" said Nick.

"I agree, but do you remember going into Stout & Newman's Drug Store in the Leland after the show?" asked Stan.

"Oh yeah, we went back to sit at the soda fountain counter, and Butch walked to the other side and laid a silent green bomb that almost made that guy eating a burger throw up. Oh God, that was so boss. The guy didn't know where it came from; I don't even know that he knew Butch walked behind him. He started gagging on his mouthful of burger." Nick laughed so hard, it was difficult to get the story out. "Butch made it all the way up to the big glass ball with colored liquid in it near the front of the store. The waitress, in the cute little uniform, walked over to check on the guy who she thinks might be choking; the smell hits her and stops her dead in her tracks. She thinks the guy laid the bomb, so she retreats. The guy spit his mouthful of burger onto his plate, looks around, but who can he blame? He's embarrassed because Miss Cutie thinks he farted, so, he lays down money and leaves like an elm tree."

Both have tears running down their cheeks, but not tears of grief. Stan said, "Butch generated atomic gas that day. Even at the show he cleared all the seats around him, including us. That girl went up to complain to management and Butch convinced the manager that it was her, not him that cleared the seats."

"That's our Butch; we have to have him back!" Nick's laughing was beginning to hurt.

The laughter helped a lot. Stan reached into his pocket. Wrapped in thin cardboard, Stan pulled out three cigarettes; bent but smokable. "I'm saving Butch's for him." He wrapped the last cigarette in the cardboard and put it back in his pocket. They lit up. Nick had to admit the cigarette sure tasted good. He felt the smoke go down in his lungs, but didn't cough.

Finishing by flicking the last of their cigarettes into the river, Nick said, "We still have work to do, but let's go find Charlie first."

CHAPTER 45

The McVees moved into their new home. Sally worked hard to make the shack as attractive and comfortable as she could. She scrubbed every nook and cranny to remove what years of neglected cleaning left behind. She bought cheap throw rugs, curtains, and minor decorations to cover up the ugliness. Everything was organized and cleaned.

Not all the furniture they brought from their apartment on Spring Street fit in the little shack. Stuart stored the surplus in a rickety lean-to not far from the outhouse. The lean-to was anything but a sealed structure. Rain seeped in from the roof; rodents found a new home for their families and that which was intended as storage became that which became trash.

Beth was not impressed when Sally and Stuart took her to their new home for the first time. In the beginning, it was a novelty to have woods to play in and no traffic to worry about, but she hated the outhouse; it stunk, she could see spiders while sitting on the bench, she could only imagine what was crawling around beneath her with her bottom totally exposed.

She would wait until absolutely necessary, run in to the outhouse, strain to finish her business and run out. She absolutely refused to use the outhouse after dark.

One night after going to the drive-in theatre on Montgomery Road with her mom and dad, she lay in her bed agonizing with a bursting bladder; certain she could no longer hold it, she snuck out and peed in the weeds beyond the front door, then snuck back in. Her mother would have had a cow if she knew what Beth did in those weeds, but that outhouse would never see Beth if the sun wasn't shining. She accepted the shack, the conditions, the clattering, whistle blowing, vibrating existence of the trains because her parents promised that it was only temporary; they would find a nice house in town soon.

Sally tried to keep her job at St. Charles hospital, but the travel to and from work proved a challenge. The walk, in good weather, from the shack to the bus stop at Main and Webster was long. As winter approached, she couldn't imagine what it would be like; the path along the railroad track would never be shoveled and she wouldn't find sidewalks, shoveled or not, until she reached Main Street. The bus schedules were such that if you missed your intended bus, the wait for the next bus was at least forty-five minutes.

Stuart did not find work right away and was able to provide transportation to and from the bus stop for Sally, but was hired as a night watchman by Miller's Tool & Die located on Route 31 toward Aurora. This made it more cumbersome for him to provide routine transportation in the morning and the afternoon.

Sally resigned her position in the hospital with great reluctance. The hospital made numerous attractive offers for her to stay, but Sally refused them.

A small restaurant needed a waitress in Oswego on Route 34, four miles from the shack. Stuart took her to apply. She was hired. The best news was that one of the waitresses that worked the same shift as Sally lived close by and agreed to provide transportation if Sally would share in the cost of the gasoline. Sally was picked up and dropped off on Route 31 by the shack. Of course, this too was only temporary; once they lived in town she would be close to the bus stop and could secure employment in Aurora again.

Sally was feeling guilty about what she was putting her family through to satisfy her quest to be close to the man that she longed to know, but loathed at the same time. She couldn't explain it to herself, let alone explain it to another person.

Her life was based on the love Betty and Grover lavishly heaped upon her. Murphy was nonexistent until Betty and Grover dropped the bomb. Was she out for revenge? Was it morbid curiosity? Why couldn't she accept the good life she had and let the rest of this obsession go? Answers evaded her; her only burning desire to see the man that she imagined as evil itself. She couldn't explain why this meant more to her than her family.

Sally looked for reasons to go the store, or to take letters to the post office requiring her to walk to the center of Montgomery. Stuart always drove them to the store for serious shopping because of the long walk and multiple paper bags of items to be carried, but Sally invariably found convenient reasons to walk to town. She avoided walking directly in front of Murphy's house. She would walk on Railroad, but turn on Jefferson before approaching his house; all the time watching his house, looking for anything that would reveal the man.

They lived in Montgomery for a month before Sally caught her first glimpse of the infamous Thaddeus Murphy. She was on one of her contrived walks to town. As she approached Jefferson Street she saw the cellar doors on the side of the house were opened, they were always closed. She slowed, her heart beat quickened; was he in the cellar? She wanted to stop, sit down and wait, but she couldn't. It would be far too obvious. She couldn't wait on a street without sidewalks. She didn't know any of the residents in the neighborhood. The police might even be called if she acted too suspiciously.

Her mind raced, but her eyes never left those cellar doors. Even at a slow pace she was now at Jefferson, she didn't want to turn right. She didn't know what to do. If she walked to Main Street, to Watkins and back to Railroad, he would surely come out of the cellar and return to his cocoon.

She had no choice; she walked as fast as she could to circle back to Railroad Street. As she was rounding the corner from Watkins to Railroad she was out of breath. She thought, "Please let those cellar doors be open." Breathing hard and straining, she walked, slowing her pace to a leisurely stroll when her eyes fixed on the open cellar doors.

She stopped twice to look for imaginary items in her purse. Once she stopped to retie her shoes. "Come on you old goat, show yourself! You can't avoid me forever. Take a look at what you threw away. Take a look at your garbage." Her mind was in overdrive.

Without any warning, he appeared. He exited the cellar walking to each side of the staircase to close the doors. She was disappointed. This monster was an old, frail-looking man that appeared more pathetic than menacing; much smaller than she expected. Sally kept her head down, but her eyes fixed on the man named Thaddeus Murphy. Having closed the cellar doors he walked to the back of the house.

Sally approached Jefferson and defiantly continued on Railroad. "You aren't the boogeyman I was expecting; as a matter of fact, you're a disappointment. But, we'll see. I am your daughter, you nasty man. I won't let you forget that. You will pay."

CHAPTER 46

Bob, Henry and Pete were greeted by the department chief for Oswego, Ken Bellows. After shaking hands, Ken faced Bob and said, "Bob, seems like you have attracted a swarm of bees up river. I hope they don't drift downstream."

"It's worse than a swarm of bees, Ken; more like an evil tornado" said Bob.

Thoughtfully, Ken said, "You know, our quiet hamlet has been dealing with the "Black Shirt Gang," but that's child-play compared to what you have going on."

Pete asked, "The Black Shirt Gang?"

"Yeah, just a bunch of punks and hoodlums that think the color of their shirts makes them tough. They cause a ruckus and try to intimidate anyone that will buy into their bullshit. Last Sunday they showed up at the drag strip out on Route 34 in full uniform and tried to bully their way around. Those guys that race out at the dragway didn't buy in. When we pulled up, the boys in Black Shirts were encircled by racers with wrenches in hand. We got their asses out the gate and told them not to come back. They aren't smart enough to figure it out, but we saved them from eating some Snap-on steel. That's about the height of our excitement" stated Ken.

"Are you up to date on the latest with our developments?" asked Bob.

"I think so; we're looking for a guy in his late fifties or early sixties and a young girl age 12" responded Ken.

"We have more." Bob recounted the event at the Case Street crossing in detail as Henry and Pete listened.

When Bob was done, Ken said, "All three are in the same area. Right?"

"You got it" said Henry. Oswego was in Kendall County, not Kane County, so Henry was out of his jurisdiction. "That's why we're so interested in meeting your gueSt. According to what we heard, you picked him up on the tracks a couple miles from our triangle of mystery. What can you tell us about him?"

"Well, in light of our rowdy neighbors to the up-river . . ." Ken looked at Bob and smiled, ". . . we've asked our guys to heighten their observation skills for anything that might be helpful. One of our guys was heading north on Route 25 and saw movement up on the trestle where the tracks cross the river. He wasn't sure what he saw, so he turned the squad around, waited a minute, drove back and parked. He climbed the ballast to get to the tracks. When he got to the top, a guy was walking away from him on the tracks about twenty-five yards down the line. My guy figures it to be your guy Murphy. He pulls his gun, orders the guy to stop. The guy turned around, saw my guy and the drawn gun and decided to run. My guy caught him and hauled him in. In the process, the guy got busted up a little; the story I get is that when my guy took him down, he hit the ties and the ballast face firSt. I hope that is all true.

We have treated him medically, no serious injuries. The guy is not Murphy, he's taller than the description you gave us and he's younger, probably in his forties, he isn't talking. He won't tell us his name, where he was coming from, where he's going or what he's doing in this area. We all know from experience that silence indicates a problem. That's why I called you."

"Thanks, Ken" said Bob.

"Yeah, thanks, we need a break" said Pete.

Ken walked them to the cell area. The cell had four walls, unlike the cage in Montgomery. Ken opened the door. On the bench sat, as Ken described, a man in his forties, five feet ten inches tall, one hundred seventy pounds, wearing clothes that looked and smelled like they hadn't been laundered since they were retrieved from a pig sty, heavily scuffed shoes, and a face that likely hurt a lot. The cell reeked of a disgusting odor, likely not present before the arrival of the guy on the bench. The prisoner didn't bother looking at any of his new-found friends.

"Any chance we can talk to him in an area with more ventilation?" asked Bob.

"Yeah, I'll put cuffs on him and we can talk with him out back at the picnic table" said Ken.

The prisoner sat at one end of the picnic table staring at the table top; Bob sat opposite him at the other end; Henry, Pete and Ken stood around the table.

Bob began, "Look, I don't know what your story is, and if it doesn't involve me, well, frankly I don't give a damn. But, unless you can convince me that you aren't the guy I'm looking for, your ass is grass and I have the lawnmower. And buddy, we're not talking vagrancy or stealing chickens here; if I were you, I would clear my name off my list as quickly as I could – that is, of course, if you can. All I'm asking for is a little cooperation and a little communication and I will be gone. Now, how about it? Can we communicate?"

The prisoner defiantly stared at the table top.

Bob rose and walked to his side of the table and stood directly across from the prisoner. He put one foot up on the table, leaned so his face was level with the prisoner and said, "Ok, let's consider what you're facing; kidnapping of a 12 year old girl and the possible murder of another child, all that occurring in an area that you just left. We have footprints . . ." Bob was lying, ". . . and a witness . . ." lying again, ". . . that gives a description fitting your height and build. We have either solved the crime, or you need to prove to us that we have the wrong guy. Now you can play the tough guy role and not talk, or you can answer a few questions. The tough guy route might appear attractive from your vantage point, but from my vantage point it is plain stupid. You aren't walking away from here unless you clear yourself. "

As Bob delivered this, the prisoner looked up. Bob figured it was in response to the possible charges. After a moment, the prisoner said, "I ain't done none of that stuff."

"Fair enough; I want to believe you, but I need lots more to get me there. What were you doing on the tracks?"

"Walking; waiting for a slow freighter to hop. I should have grabbed one in Aurora . . ." he paused ". . . but I got crosswise with a couple of guys and needed to get out."

"When did you leave Aurora?"

"Last night."

"What time?"

"Probably around eleven to eleven-thirty."

"Strange time to head out from anywhere, wouldn't you say?"

"Like I said, things happened, I got crosswise with a couple of guys, I left."

"You guys travel light, but you always have personal items with you, where's yours?"

"I told you I had to get out– in a hurry; get it, my stuff got left behind."

"So what kind of scrape did you get into with these other guys?"

"Man, what's that got to do with this?"

"With what?" asked Bob.

"With . . . what you were talking about – the girl and the murder thing . . ." responded the prisoner. ". . . I didn't have nothin' to do with that at all."

"Ok" said Bob. "You leave Aurora and head out; you should have been way beyond Oswego when you were stopped."

The prisoner responded, "I stopped to sleep for a while."

"When and where?"

"Man, off the tracks, I don't know – same side as the factory, I guess."

"The 'I guess' is not an answer that will set you free, what factory, what time?" said Bob.

"It's a big factory on the eastside, back a few miles; I passed that and bedded down under bushes on the same side as the factory. I walked pretty fast coming out of Aurora, I wasn't sure if they were coming after me, so I bedded down."

"So what did you see during your trip from Aurora?"

"Nothing man, just railroad tracks, oh yeah, one train going into Aurora, and that's it. It's just railroad tracks."

"Anything unusual along the tracks?" asked Bob.

The prisoner looked at Bob like he was nuts, but said, "Yeah, a house was lit up with lights before I got to the factory, I couldn't figure that one out, so I kept going" responded the prisoner.

"Look, we're almost friends now, so what's your name?" asked Bob.

The prisoner paused, but answered, "Jesper, Aubrey Jesper."

"Where do you call home, Aubrey?"

"Originally; Mankato, Minnesota. But that was a long time ago."

"Aubrey thanks for talking, but I need you to think really hard about anything you saw or heard as you walked from Aurora. Will you do that for me?"

"Man, I done told you everything."

"I know you have, but I want you to take a moment to rethink your entire walk to see if you might have missed anything. I'm going to ask Ken to get you coffee. Would you like coffee, Aubrey?" asked Bob.

"Yeah, I would; any chance for food?"

Ken walked into the station; Bob followed him while Henry and Pete sat with the prisoner in silence.

As they walked through the station Bob asked, "What'd you think, Ken?"

"First of all, he smells a lot better at that picnic table than he did in that cell; secondly, I hate to say it, but, I don't think he's involved in your mess" answered Ken.

"I don't either, his answers seem in order, however, I want to get him to think about what he saw. You never know" said Bob.

"Yeah, you never know."

When Bob and Ken returned with coffee and left over donuts, they removed the hand-cuffs. Aubrey went after the donuts with vengeance.

"Been a while since you ate, Aubrey?" asked Ken.

Aubrey needed to chew and swallow before he could to talk. He said, "Yeah, I guess I am pretty hungry."

"Have you thought about your walk from Aurora like I asked?" asked Bob.

"Yeah, but you have to understand that I was walking fast and keeping an eye on my behind. I didn't know if those guys were coming after me."

"Sounds like you made a couple of enemies; you never did say what the problem was" interjected Pete.

"It was a card game, that's all."

"In light of the fact that you didn't have any money on you when we picked you up, suggests to me that those guys thought you might have been cheating and took all of your money as pay back" said Ken.

"Yeah, but I wasn't."

"Ok, you were coming down the tracks, walking fast, looking backward occasionally; did you see anything on or around the tracks that looked out of place?" asked Bob.

Aubrey gazed on something beyond the horizon and shook his head slowly, as if he was replaying the journey in his mind. "Nope. But that cattle pen sure has an aroma; I couldn't walk fast enough to get past it. I told you about the house that was lit up."

Bob cut in, "What about the house that was lit up? Do you remember anything leading up to or after that house that was strange?"

Aubrey continued to shake his head slowly. "That's it, except for the noise after I was in the bushes."

"Tell us about the noise" said Henry.

"I slid back in the bushes and was conking out, when I heard talking, or at least I think I heard talking, you know what I mean, when you're not sure if you're asleep?"

"Yes, we understand" said Henry.

Aubrey continued. "Well, it kind of jolted me because I thought the guys from Aurora were coming after me, so I slid deeper into the bushes. I heard a metal clang, crunching on stones, then silence. I figured they might have bedded down too, so I stayed where I was and kept quiet. I must have slept quite a while; the heavy bushes kept the sun out of my eyes. When I woke up I stayed under the bushes for a long time to make sure those guys weren't around. I got up, looked around for any signs of anybody else; I was alone, and I headed this way. I tried to cross that trestle when no cars were coming, but I guess I was seen."

Bob asked, "You said you thought you heard talking and you heard a clang. Can you tell us about that?"

"Nuttin' more to tell."

"Think about it. Did you make out any words?" asked Bob

Aubrey appeared to be really trying, "Naw. It was a man's voice though. Like I said, I thought it was those boys from Aurora, so I laid low."

Bob continued to pursue, "All right, tell us about the clang. Have you ever heard it before? Can you give us an idea of what it might sound like?"

"You know, it was definitely metal; it was a clang. That's the best I can do."

"Was it a clang like a bell?"

"No, it was like . . . like heavy metal hitting something."

Bob handed Aubrey a card and said, "Aubrey, I don't know what plans Ken has for you, but I need you to promise me that you will notify me if you think of anything that you think I might need to know. Can you promise me that?"

"Sure; you been square with me. Did a kid really get killed?"

"Not yet, but it might end up that way. Thank you Aubrey" responded Bob.

As they were leaving, Bob, Henry and Pete thanked Ken for his ongoing assistance and headed back to the Montgomery station.

CHAPTER 47

Nick and Stan were surprised when Charlie was not on the steps of Shannon's. Nick motioned to Stan to ride Mill Street to the back of the tavern. Charlie was sweeping off the landing to the back entrance. Nick gave a sigh of relief as he said, "Hey Charlie."

Charlie leaned his broom against the building and walked to them. "I've been waiting for you boys; I was keeping busy to keep my mind occupied. I heard about Butch. How's he doing?"

Nick responded, "Not good, according to Mr. Blankenship. My dad talked with him on the phone after Mr. Blankenship returned from the hospital; but Stan and I believe Butch is tough and he's going to pull through." Hesitating, he continued, "How about you, Charlie?"

Charlie had heard various reports on Butch that filtered into Shannon's over the past couple of hours; none were good. He also felt the need to encourage these boys. He responded, "You know what, if I was to place a bet on a racehorse, I'd place my bet on any one of you three if you were in the running. I believe in character and the power of positive thinking. According to Norman Vincent Peale, we all have the ability to influence ourselves and those around us with the way we think about things. You boys are good thinkers."

"Who's Norman . . .?" asked Stan, not able to remember the rest of the name.

"Aw – it doesn't matter, what matters is that you boys keep thinking that Butch will pull through. Not to get all religious on you, but a prayer can't hurt either."

"Thanks Charlie" said Nick.

"So, I bet you boys want to compare notes" said Charlie.

"Yeah; if you have the time" said Nick.

"Time? That's all I have. Time, time and more time." Charlie laughed as he led the boys to a grassy area at the back of the lot.

Seated on the grass, Charlie reached in his shirt pocket, but realized he'd smoked his last Camel earlier. Seeing this, Nick glanced at Stan's jeans pocket and said to Stan, "Butch would offer it to Charlie." Stan unrolled the cardboard and handed the slightly bent Chesterfield to Charlie.

Charlie said, "What about you boys?"

Stan replied, "Charlie, we smoked one under the bridge. That one was Butch's, but I agree with Nick, he'd want you to have it under the circumstances."

"Well boys, I am touched. Thank you and we will all thank Butch later" responded Charlie as he produced the wobbly top Zippo.

Charlie took his famously deep inhale and as he blew smoke to the sky, he said, "All I heard from the patrons are stories that are more made up than real, so I don't really have anything to add to our collections of facts, but I have been giving this whole thing a lot of thought. And, I am beginning to see it differently since Butch got hurt. The first reports suggested that he was hit by a car, but now the feeling is that it wasn't a car."

Stan chimed in, "Yeah, I heard the cops talking about Butch being dumped on the tracks."

"Be that what it is, we need to really think this thing through. Now take Butch; there was no reason to hurt Butch – so we think; but someone thought there was a reason. What could that reason be?" Charlie paused, "First, we have the dealings in Murphy's cellar; at about the same time Beth goes missing, and Butch ends up on the tracks unconscious. I am beginning to see less and less coincidence, and possibly more and more of a pattern. How about you boys?"

Nick responded, "Don't know Charlie."

"Well, the possibility of two strange happenings in this tiny town is, - well, it could be a coincidence – unlikely, but possible; but three? Doesn't seem right, does it?" asked Charlie.

The boys shook their heads.

Charlie continued, "Now this is where it gets tricky – we could let our minds go wild, like the majority of those in Shannon's and create stories that sound good but have no foundation. Or, we can think. What are the commonalities in the three events? What does Murphy have to do with Beth, if anything? And how does Butch fit into the mix? That last one is probably the easiest."

Caught up in Charlie's line of thinking, Stan asks, "Really? How?"

"This is just an old man thinking out loud, but you boys are nosing about and making it pretty obvious that you are serious. Maybe Butch got too close and someone felt threatened. Or maybe he tripped upon something, or saw something that someone didn't want him to see. Are you tracking with me?" asked Charlie.

Nick replied immediately, "Yeah!"

"That takes me back to the first two mysteries. If Murphy killed in his cellar and took off, he wouldn't be a threat to you boys or Butch. He'd be gone, right?"

Both nodded.

"Ok, if Beth was snatched, I doubt they did it for the ransom, her folks don't have anything – so, whoever took Beth probably hauled her off." Charlie noticed that Nick was affected by his bluntness concerning Beth. "Sorry, Nick, I am not being diplomatic, I'm sharing thoughts here, not absolutes."

Nick said, "I understand Charlie, keep going."

"So it seems to me that the mystery remains in our midst."

Attempting to clarify, Stan asks, "So you're saying that whoever is doing all this stuff is still here in Montgomery?"

"It doesn't really matter what I think, what do you think?" replied Charlie.

Stan and Nick, glanced at each other, Nick said, "But who Charlie?"

Charlie laid back, shook his head and said, "I surely don't know, Nick, I surely don't know." After pausing, he continued, "What concerns me most is if it's as I think it might be, you boys need to lay low for a while and let the cops do the searching. Too many people are getting hurt; I hope you are hearing what I am trying to say."

"We hear you, Charlie, but who can it be? Everything points at old man Murphy" offered Stan.

"Maybe; maybe not, but I think the person is close by and seems to be playing for keeps. You both know I enjoy hearing about your explorations, you make me feel young again, but now I fear for you and your safety. You boys are brave, courageous and bold, like Wyatt Earp on T.V., but you are also smart. Now is the time to be smart. Whatever is going on, isn't good" said Charlie.

"But Charlie . . . we have to do . . . ." implored Nick.

Charlie knew what Nick was feeling, "Yes, yes you do. You need to contribute because you owe it to your friends, Beth and Butch. What I am suggesting is that you do something, but not what you normally would do; I'm asking you to think. Think about the questions I asked you earlier. Think about all three mysteries as one, break them apart and think about them individually. Think about everything you know, or think you might know, about the circumstances that have developed in the last couple of days."

"Ok, then what?" asked Stan.

"You go talk with your buddy, John. Tell him everything you can think of. Let the cops take the risk, that's why they get paid. From what I can determine from the stories that wander in off the streets, they are doing a pretty good job" answered Charlie.

"What about Butch?" asked Nick.

"Like you said, Butch is going to make it, when he does he's going to want to come home to his sidekicks. If you go get yourselves hurt, he might not come home to anyone. Boys, I am not one to give advice often, but I am giving you advice to use your brains to think. Stay off the streets for a while. Help the cops do their job and stay safe. Does that make sense?" asked Charlie.

Reluctantly, they both nodded in agreement.

"Charlie, you are a smart man, you must have an opinion of who's at the bottom of this; who do you think it is?" asked Nick.

"Nick, you are making me blush; if I was a smart man would I be cleaning the toilets in Shannon's? Come on, the difference is I have acquired the experience your few years haven't afforded you. But thank you for the compliment, it makes me feel good" responded Charlie.

"Charlie, who do you think it is?" asked Stan with persistence.

"Thad Murphy is in it one way or another; that's for sure. Maybe he's the only one, but maybe not. But like I said earlier, whoever it is, is close by. Whether it's Thad, or not, whoever it is knows what's going on and is observing."

Charlie stood up. "I am proud of you boys. If you get to see Butch you tell him old Charlie is thinking of him."

"We will" said Nick.

"You do that. The word for the day is 'think.' Will you do that for an old friend?" asked Charlie.

"Yep" responded Stan.

"Yep" responded Nick.

"I'm headed back over; it's that time of day; more patrons, more work" stated Charlie.

"Thanks Charlie" said Nick. The two boys headed for their bikes.

CHAPTER 48

Beth waited the allotted two days before returning to Mr. Murphy's house. To ensure enough time to talk with him, she told her dad she was working on a project after school. She walked Railroad from Webster eyeing the old house. She imagined all sorts of things that Murphy might tell her, if he told her anything at all. She was still uncertain about Mr. Murphy; he was nice enough, but like her mom said, he was strange.

As she left the street to walk across the over-grown weeds, she crossed her fingers. One stride on the front porch and the door opened; Mr. Murphy smiling slightly said, "I figured you'd be here today, Beth."

"Yes, Mr. Murphy. We agreed" responded Beth.

"Well, if we are going to talk, let's do it out back" said Murphy. He, remembering Beth's cautionary attitude, stepped in front of Beth and began around the side of the house. Beth followed.

When she got to the backyard she was surprised to see two wooden chairs, a pitcher of liquid with two empty glasses on a small table near the stump. She said, "Mr. Murphy, what if I didn't come today?"

"I never considered it, Beth. You have proven to be a person of your word, you said two days, this is the second day, so here you are" answered Murphy.

"Well . . . uh, Mr. Murphy, thank you." Beth was beginning to feel that this arrangement was a peace offering before he told her that he was not going to tell her anything. She sat down.

Murphy began to pour from the pitcher into the glass closest to Beth. "I'm sorry, but I don't entertain." He put the pitcher down, "It's only water, but it is cold."

Before reaching for her glass, she asked, "Aren't you going to have a drink, Mr. Murphy?"

Understanding the meaning of her inquiry, he filled his glass and took a long drink.

Beth followed suit with a long drink of her own. She asked, "Mr. Murphy, thank you for the hospitality . . ." Smiling, she added, ". . . and the chairs, but we both know why I am here today. Have you decided to talk with me or not?"

Murphy was tickled with her spunk. He wiped his brow, hesitated and responded, "Beth, I will talk with you today, though I'm not sure this is the right thing to do. I will have to do this at my speed and if I determine I need to stop I will appeal to your compassion to allow me to do so. Will you agree to that?"

Beth was encouraged, but skeptical; she agreed.

He began again, "I need one more commitment from you. Regardless of what I tell you, can you promise me that you will not reveal our conversation to your mother or father?"

Beth thought about this for a moment. Being dishonest with her parents was troubling. It never occurred prior to her walking to Mr. Murphy's two days ago. It bothered her greatly to know that she disobeyed her mother's wishes, but this mystery was a barrier between her and her mother. If the mystery was solved, things could return to where they once were. She looked at Murphy and said, "Yes."

Murphy's eyes became serious, sending their own warning and said, "Beth, you are a young girl, but I can tell you are older than your years, so I am going to hold you to that commitment."

Beth felt the strength of his statement, and a slight chill down her spine; she nodded.

"I have not rehearsed this so you must understand that I am merely speaking out loud. What I must say, I am not sure I can; what I can say, I am not sure I will be able to get out, but I will try. It might help me if I tell it as a parable.

Many years ago a young man considered himself charmed. He was educated, respectably employed, owned a home, and enjoyed a family. Things were going along as nicely as anything could go along.

His beautiful wife brought him the sunshine in the morning and pleasant dreams every night. He worshiped the ground she walked on. He regarded her as the greatest gift he'd ever received.

He worked hard for his employer and worked hard to be a good husband and father. But, like so many young men, his interests were many and varied. He enjoyed socializing, he enjoyed drink and he enjoyed automobiles. He knew of nothing in this world that he would have allowed to come between him and his beautiful wife; however, when things are left untended they can grow lives of their own." Murphy paused to take a drink. "On a warm Saturday night following a social gathering . . ." Murphy stopped again, stared off into the field, collected himself, and continued, ". . . the young man became foolish and did a stupid thing; he became reckless and foolhardy. It was a night filled with enchantment, the stars shone like diamonds in the sky. The warm breeze made his wife's hair flutter like gold ribbons in the air as his automobile raced along the countryside. He was going too fast, lost control and crashed the car into a field. He killed his wife." Everything about Murphy sagged.

Beth was dismayed by his disclosure. She didn't know what to say, so she said nothing. Silence existed between them for a long time.

Murphy started again, "The young man lost everything that meant anything to him. Prior to finding the love of his life, he longed to be loved and desired to love another. When he found her, his life became full and he knew she was a gift from heaven. He was such a fool, such an idiot, such an irresponsible nincompoop; he deserved to be jailed for his stupidity, but the court deemed the death of his wife the result of an accident. Accidents are things that happen when no one is at fault. He knew who was at fault; he was." Murphy's delivery quickened with passion. "His desire for the thrill became more important than his love for his wife. His desire for the thrill took away his life. If the young man was not such a coward, he would have taken his own life and put an end to the story. But he was a coward. So, he spent the rest of his life alone with only his memories."

Two streams of tears trailed down Beth's cheeks. She felt the pain of the story, but abruptly asked, "What about his family; his children?"

Murphy sat with his eyes cast on his lap. Slowly he raised his head to look at Beth. He was tempted to say that they were dead, but knew that would require an explanation all of its own. He said, "The young man remained stupid for many years, Beth."

Not at all satisfied with that answer, she asked, "What does that mean? What happened to his children?"

"It wasn't children, Beth; it was one beautiful little girl. She was young."

"What happened to her?"

"She went off to live with his cousin in another state" responded Murphy.

Beth tried to grasp all that he shared in this sad story. She was pretty sure the young man was Mr. Murphy, but did not want to put him on the spot yet. She understood the pain he must feel for being responsible for the death of his wife, but she did not understand the shallowness of the answers concerning his daughter. She asked, "Didn't the young man continue to see his daughter; you know, visits, holidays and Christmas?"

Murphy straightened his back, looked over Beth's head and said, "No."

"Why not?"

"Beth, I think I have gone as far as I can go today, so I am appealing to your compassion to allow me to continue again later" said Murphy.

Reluctantly, Beth relented by saying, "Mr. Murphy, thank you for the parable, but you haven't finished it. I will be back tomorrow after school. Would that be alright?"

"Yes, Beth, that will be fine. Why don't you walk to the back-yard and avoid the front porch. You can even walk down the field to the backyard. I really don't want you to get in trouble with your mom" answered Murphy.

As Beth walked away, she stopped, turned to Murphy, "Thank you again Mr. Murphy, but I want to know about his daughter. Ok?"

Murphy nodded and started for the house. Inside, he sat on one of the kitchen chairs; there used to be only one, now there were two. How was he going to do this? He'd cleaned out the two rooms. In the process, he'd made the stacks in the center of the house even higher and more crammed. He hoped that she could accept the narrow pathways to rooms he prepared because of her; he was proud of the rooms. He wondered if she would be willing to go past the stacks. He hoped she would.

CHAPTER 49

At 5:15 Thursday afternoon, the investigators' canvassing reports were in. Bob, Henry and Pete were going over the reports and talking with the investigators that stuck around.

Leaning back in one of the chairs in the investigation room, Pete said, "So, what do we have so far?"

Bob responded, "Before we get into the reports, I received a call from the hospital; the kid is in bad shape. He suffered. . .", now reading from notes, ". . . a basilar skull fracture involving the temporal bone and possible hemorrhaging."

"Ok, so what does that mean to those of us that can barely read a newspaper?" asked Pete.

"That's what I asked them, only in a different way." Bob was smiling and continued, "The kid received a severe blow to the lower portion of the back of the skull. They cannot appraise the actual damage until the swelling goes down. The back of his head is still packed in ice. Their fear is that the hemorrhaging will block the blood flow to the brain and . . . that's not good. The guy said that if an injury like this does not kill you, it leaves what's left in bad shape. For what it is worth, the guy said it was this type of injury that killed Bill Vukovich during the 1955 Indianapolis 500."

Pete interjected, "No kidding! Vukie, the mad Russian, was going for his third Indy 500 win in a row; he got caught up trying to avoid an accident in front of him. He was a hell of a racecar driver." No one responded.

Bob continued, "The reason they called was to inform us that the doctors that examined the kid thought we should know that they found rust at the point of injury. They couldn't identify the source, but they thought that whatever hit him had not used for a while. It was flaky with rust."

"Well, for the most part, that supports it was not likely a car. Cars have a lot of chrome up front" said Pete.

"It also eliminates the possibility that he fell on the tracks and cracked his head on the rail. I considered that possibility. Rails don't have time to accumulate rust" said Henry.

"Did they give you any idea as to size or shape of the object? Did it have edges of any kind?" asked Henry.

"No, but the guy said the doctors described the injury as a "blunt injury." That leads me to believe that they mean no edges; how about you?" responded Bob.

"Yeah, probably so" answered Pete.

Reading a report, Henry announced, "It looks like we might have found the owners of the dog. An older couple on Jefferson, down by the river, said that their dog has not been home for a couple of days."

"What kind of dog?" asked Bob.

"The report said that the owners considered it a mutt, but they were told that it was likely a Shepherd, Mastiff mix; which would explain the size of the corpse. The color of the dog given in the report matches what we found as skin - or pelt" responded Henry.

"Does the report say that the investigator made any reference to the connection between their dog and the Murphy investigation?"

"The investigator specifically states that he did not mention it, but got the sense that the old couple heard rumors about a dog being skinned" responded Henry.

"Did the owners suggest that the dog left their property often?" asked Bob

"According to them, the dog often left for hours but always returned. They never knew for sure where the dog went, because it was a roamer" said Henry.

"Looks like it roamed in the wrong direction this time. My guess is that Murphy didn't like dogs. What about a connection between the dog's owners and Murphy?" asked Pete.

Bob jumped in saying, "I know the Aigner's; they have to be in their late 70's and I doubt that we'll find a connection. He drives an old '46 Chevrolet to the store and back, but not often. They keep to themselves."

"We're going to have to inform them about their dog, but I hope you all agree that we should do it later" responded Henry.

Everyone agreed.

Henry said, "The investigators that searched the tracks at Case Street report nothing more than what we found at the scene. However, they found the area described by the vagrant being held in Oswego. They found the bushes he slept under; recent scuff marks were present and it matches the area the vagrant described. The report states that the investigators stayed on the tracks to be able to observe both sides, but when they thought that they identified the bushes, they dropped down to inspect closer. I'm guessing that this part of the report is for our amusement, but the report said that the vagrant must have taken a crap, because the smell of human feces was strong."

"Hey, vagrants have to crap too" said Pete.

"The report goes on to say the investigators drove to Aurora, walked down to the large hobo camp and confirmed with a few of the hobos that a problem occurred the night before, resulting in the unscheduled departure of a card-cheating bum before midnight. Their description fits the vagrant. They said he was in a hurry" said Henry.

Henry continued, "According to this one, the Western Electric guard does not recall any cars or trucks crossing the tracks after his last delivery about fifteen minutes before he heard the fire department siren. He is pretty confident no cars crossed from either direction."

"What about employees of the brush factory? Did any of them have a view of the crossing from a window?" asked Bob.

Henry shuffled through the reports, found the one labeled "National Brush Company"; he read it and responded, "Seems that the owner has all desks positioned away from the windows to make sure employees remain focused on their work. This report offers nothing."

Continuing to scan the reports, Henry said, "Mrs. Ava Carter lives on Railroad and seems to have drilled the investigator on how she feels too many kids regard the railroad tracks as a playground; that it is dangerous and the kids should be kept off them."

"Ok, but did she see anything?" asked Bob.

"The investigator asked her if the increase of kids playing on tracks was recent. She said she thought it was, but couldn't describe the kids, or the times she saw them. She said she would recognize the one boy and one girl, because they were the most frequent violators. The investigator asked if the boy and girl were always together, but she said, "No, she didn't think so" responded Henry.

"So, she can't describe the boy or the girl, or the times she saw them, but she would recognize them? Our kids are around those tracks all the time. Yes, they regard it as a playground, but that has been going on as long as I've been here. I don't see much to follow up on" said Bob.

"Me either" said Henry.

Henry pulled a file with black diagonal stripes on it; these files indicated official County investigation material. He opened it and said, "We checked on the McVees. Three years ago, Mrs. McVee abruptly resigned her administration position with St. Charles hospital to accept the position as a waitress in a greasy spoon down on Route 34. Mr. McVee resigned his position as an estate caretaker to become a night watchman. They moved from an apartment up on Spring Street in Aurora to inhabit a shack next to the railroad tracks. That seems strange to me, does it seem strange to any of you?"

"Yeah, it does to me" said Pete, "Any reasons for their actions?"

"None so far; I think we need to have more conversation with them. Something doesn't seem right. I have no idea how that influences any of this, but we need answers" said Henry.

"Anything else show up that raised your eyebrows?" asked Pete.

"Nope; she's originally from Iowa, attended Illinois State Teachers College up in DeKalb, moved to Aurora, went to work for the hospital, was liked a lot, promoted and left. His family is down in Sandwich, he worked at the College in DeKalb, met her, moved to Aurora, worked as caretaker of an estate in North Aurora, left that job to work at Miller's Tool & Die out on Route 31. Everything is clean on the surface, but something is wrong."

Bob said, "I'll go over to their place tomorrow morning and nail it down."

"Anything else worthy of conversation?" asked Bob.

"Yes," said Henry. "Since the Western Electric guard was the only human being in reasonable proximity to the scene with the kid, I ran a criminal record check on him; seems he has a few brushes with the law that could make him a suspect."

"What kind of brushes with the law are we talking about?" asked Pete.

"Funny you should ask. His name is Solomon Burgmeyer, also known as "Solly." Seems that Solly has a violent side. Cleveland 1952 – Assault and Battery; Chicago 1953 – assault, armed robbery; did a year in Cook County jail for that; but here's the one that worries me, St. Louis, Missouri 1950 – child kidnapping, charges dropped, lack of evidence."

"Holy mackerel, Andy!" stated Pete.

Energy flowed into Bob and the rest of the investigators. A sense of excitement filled the room.

"How'd you get this info so quickly?" asked Bob.

"After our initial investigation at the tracks, John brought me his interview report. He interviewed him and figured I'd want it for the file. On a hunch, I called in a rush request for his criminal history when we got back here and asked that the results be driven down to us when received. It was delivered about fifteen minutes ago" responded Henry. "Thought you guys might find it interesting."

Pete's voice was almost squeaky with excitement, "Interesting? Holy Mother of Christ! He is at the epicenter of all three situations we're working on. Have you picked him up yet?"

"Pete, I just received this, remember?" responded Henry.

"Yeah, yeah, I'm sorry. So what's the plan?"

"The plan is for our departments to go over to Western Electric; Solly Burgmeyer has likely gone home by now, but we need to get personnel in Western Electric to provide us with information, like his home address and why a guy with a record like this would be hired as a security guard" responded Henry.

"Management is gone by now" offered Bob.

"Too bad; we call them back in" responded Henry.

"So you save the best for last, Henry. Nice touch!" said Pete while smiling.

"We're going to move on this right away, but I think we should read each of the canvass reports for subtleties, look for what is hiding in the details" responded Henry.

"Yeah; like the devil himself" added Pete.

"Look guys, John was supposed to be in at 6:00, but since he stuck around to help with the Case crossing situation, I told him to come in at 7:00; that's about forty-five minutes from now. I'll stick around to bring him up to date, but I will hook up with you guys" stated Bob.

CHAPTER 50

Nick and Stan rode their bikes up the hill on Mill Street away from Shannon's turning left on Main. Nick rode up along Stan and said, "Let's ride down to the Case Street crossing and call it a day."

Stan nodded agreement. He understood what Nick was feeling because he felt the same way. They needed to see where Butch got hurt one more time; they owed it to Butch. They pedaled on without further communication.

They laid their bikes down in the weeds prior to the tracks. Ropes were strung to prevent anyone from walking down the trail between the tracks and Western Electric. They stood looking at the area where Butch was found. Since this was the first time Nick viewed the actual spot where their friend went down, Stan was giving an exact description. Nick asked a few questions to clarify his understanding of the scene. When the conversation was over, they stood and looked at the spot where Butch had laid. Stan reflected on how limp Butch looked as they loaded him on to the gurney. Becoming uncomfortable, he turned away. Nick turned as well; he thought Stan had heard a noise. "What is it?" asked Nick.

"Nothing; I don't like what I saw, I guess" answered Stan.

"Let's get out of here" said Nick.

Stan stopped and said, "Wait a minute. Someone's coming from Webster. See 'em? They're this side of the tower."

Nick squinted and said, "Yeah, they're staying pretty low on that side. Let's get closer to see who it is."

The boys decided to stay on the tracks as they walked. Attempting to heed Charlie's advice, they knew they would have multiple escape options high on the tracks if the situation made it necessary.

Their vision was obstructed occasionally by bushes, but they recognized the familiar stride of, none other than Phil Glaston. Phil was gliding down the tracks with a sack slung over his shoulder.

As they grew closer, Nick and Stan negotiated off of the ballast to the path Phil was walking. Nick said, "Phil, are you living on the tracks these days?"

"Naw, heading down to my cousins' place for a party tonight. You guys want to come?" responded Phil.

"You're going to Oswego again?" asked Stan.

"Yeah, man, they live down by the river. We can party and make all the noise we want; it's a blast. It's not that far" responded Phil.

"Phil, did you hear about Butch?" asked Nick.

"No, did he find a surprise between his legs without the use of a mirror?" responded Phil sarcastically.

"You might want to sit down for this one, Phil" said Stan.

They all sat on the weeds at the base of the hill leading to the tracks. Nick started, with Stan filling in with the details of Butch being carted off to the hospital in the meat wagon, and the comments by the cops.

Phil did not respond at first, but asked, "How bad is he hurt?"

"Well, my dad's friend told him that Butch has a brain injury. Stan and I feel that we know Butch better than anybody and while Butch may have his quirks, he is tough. He's gonna make it" said Nick.

"Are the doctors saying that, or are you guys saying that?" asked Phil.

"Screw the doctors!" said Stan.

Phil sat, dumbfounded. "Man, a brain injury? Are you sure?"

"That's what they're saying. Dad said they packed his head in ice when they got him to the emergency room" said Nick.

"Packed his head in ice? What the hell for?" asked Phil.

"I guess to keep the swelling down in his brain" answered Nick.

"Holy shit!" said Phil.

"Yeah, holy shit" said Stan.

Phil appeared stunned, gathered himself, and asked, "What was Butch doing by the tracks?"

"Man, we were looking for anything that might help figure out what the hell is going on. It was midday; I didn't think anything like this could happen" answered Stan.

"Why weren't you guys with him?" asked Phil.

"Nick was working for his old man, Butch and I split up to cover more territory" said Stan.

"So, where were you?" asked Phil.

"I was way down Case by the river" answered Stan.

Phil nodded, "Well, this is a shocker. I hope you guys are right about Butch. I hope he makes it." Phil paused, and continued, "I have to make it to the party, girls. Sure you don't want to come? You never know, might even be girls ugly enough for you two."

"Look Phil, Charlie thinks that whoever is doing all this shit is still in town and that we should stay off the streets and let the cops do their work. I don't know if you should be walking to Oswego on the tracks. Can't one of your brothers give you a lift?" said Nick.

"Man, it's no big deal, and no my brothers can't give me lift. I wouldn't take it if they offered. Besides, I don't want them at the party" responded Phil.

"Man, you gotta use your head. Bad things are happening all around us. Why don't you walk down Route 25 on the other side of the river instead of the tracks?" offered Stan.

"Look girls, I think it's cute that you're so concerned about me, but I know what I am doing. Besides, I will keep my eyes wide open and my trouble antenna extra high, but I'm going to Oswego to have fun, and that's that" Phil said with conviction.

"Ok Phil, but when you get down around Case Street you'll have to stay on the tracks because the cops have it roped off" said Nick.

They all stood. Nick asked, "What do you have in the pillow-case, Phil?"

"Snacks for the party, dumbass. Stole 'em from my parents. I'll blame it on my stupid brothers" responded Phil as he began walking.

"Keep your trouble antenna up, Phil" said Stan.

"Always" responded Phil.

Phil remained low on the side of the tracks; Stan and Nick climbed the ballast and walked the tracks back to their bikes. Because of the slip and slide ascent up the hill of ballast, Phil was ahead of them as they walked back to their bikes. Stan said, "Hey is Phil still limping?"

"Yeah, it looks like it. We must have gotten him real good last night." replied Nick

"I don't know if he's smart walking the tracks. Charlie is right. Bad juju is coming down on us. I wish we could have talked Phil out of it."

"Talk him out of it? Give me a break. We don't have a prayer at talking Phil out of anything. Phil does what Phil wants, when Phil wants to. I actually think he might have felt bad about Butch; didn't you?" asked Nick.

"Yeah, that's the biggest show of compassion I think I have ever seen him display. You don't think our Phil could be growing a heart, do you?" Stan feigned surprise.

"Not a chance" responded Nick.

CHAPTER 51

It was Friday, May 9th and Beth was walking to Mr. Murphy's house. Recently, a boy in Beth's class walked her home from school a few times, or at least part of the way to her house. If she could have her way, no one would ever see the place where she lived. She never understood why her mom wanted to leave Aurora for this ramshackle dwelling in the middle of nowhere. It was supposed to be temporary, but three years isn't temporary. What were they waiting for?

She loved her mom and dad and knew they loved her. They provided her with everything she needed; they helped her with her homework; they found entertaining things to do on the weekends, but why didn't they move away from that God awful shack?

She really liked Nick, the boy that walked her home. He was funny and didn't act as screwy as other boys in her class. He was even interested in her writing projects. She smiled as she thought how timid he was with her. She didn't know she was going to do it, but the last time they parted, she kissed him on the cheek when they said goodbye. She watched as he melted before her eyes. She loved it. She was going to kiss him again, but on the lips this time. What in the world would he do when she did that? She didn't know, but she would know, because she wanted to kiss Nick Corrie. Nick offered to walk her home again today, but not today, today she needed answers.

Today she hoped to learn the rest of story, or parable, as Mr. Murphy called it. She thought a lot about the young man that lost everything after an accident. She thought that the young man was being too tough on himself. People make mistakes, do stupid things, but where does forgiveness come in? Shouldn't we be able to forgive ourselves for being stupid? She wanted Mr. Murphy to answer questions, like what happened to his daughter? But the biggest one was what does this have to do with her family.

Taking Mr. Murphy's suggestion, she cut through the field and walked to his backyard. Mr. Murphy appeared in the back door at the precise moment that she approached the small table with a pitcher of water and two glasses. "Hello Beth. Did you have a good day at school?"

"Yes Mr. Murphy, and how was your day?" answered Beth.

Murphy smiled and said, "My days run together Beth, I guess they are all good. However, I must say that knowing I would be facing interrogation added more value to this day."

Beth immediately felt bad and responded quickly, "Mr. Murphy, I don't want to interrogate you. I am merely interested. You've said things that I find confusing. I deserve to know what is behind them. But I don't want you to think I'm interrogating you."

"Beth, I used the wrong word; you don't interrogate me, but I feel the necessity to answer your questions the best I can. I hope I have not started on the wrong foot with my poor choice of words" responded Murphy.

"Mr. Murphy, I'm here to understand what your connection is to my family, and I'm interested to learn the rest of the parable. Is that fair?"

"Yes, that is fair. And, I am prepared to do what I can to help you understand. Once again, I am going to ask for two promises: First, if I determine I can't continue, you agree to defer the conversation to another time. Secondly, that our conversations remain between us. I feel that I am violating the relationship between you and your parents. This does not make me feel good. I can't even explain why I am going against my own common sense, but I am, and I accept it. Will you agree to my conditions once again?"

"Yes Mr. Murphy" answered Beth.

"Beth, does anyone know that you are talking with me?" asked Murphy.

"No. Not a soul" responded Beth.

"It is best to keep it that way. Now, where did we leave off?" asked Murphy.

"Mr. Murphy, I asked you what happened to your daughter, and you said she went off to your cousin in another state."

"Actually, the parable was about an unnamed young man, but you have made me that young man, is that correct?" asked Murphy.

Beth flushed. How could she have been so stupid? Of course the parable was about an unnamed young man, but she blundered badly. "Mr. Murphy, I am sorry – I assumed that the young man was you. I didn't mean to invade your privacy. I . . ."

Murphy cut her off, "Beth, it is ok. I am not a good storyteller. Your assumption is correct; I am the young man." He looked down at the table searching for more words, but none came.

Beth felt horrible, how could she have messed this up so badly? "Mr. Murphy, I feel that I've made a big mistake. Would you like me to come back another time?"

Murphy continued to look down. Shaking his head he said, "No Beth, you were being honest and I am proud of you for doing so, but it has been many years since I have spoken of these events. It was easier to hide them in the parable, but that is foolishness. I knew who I was speaking of, and you knew who I was speaking of, so who's fooling whom?"

"Mr. Murphy, if you are mad at me, it's ok. I deserve it. But . . ."

Murphy look up at her, smiled again as he cut her off, "Miss McVee, I could never be mad at you. I can be mad at myself, but not at you. You are a ray of sunshine that brightens my world and I thank you. I need to get myself together. Are you ready?"

"Yes"

"We have to go back to that night . . ." Murphy's demeanor darkened as he continued, "Beth, as God is my witness, I never meant to bring harm to my Sara. I would have died for her, but I wasn't thinking of her safety, but of my car, the speed, the excitement, the enjoyment. I drove on that road so many times; I thought I knew it like the back of my hand. Maybe it was the drink, but that curve appeared out of nowhere. I braked hard, but once that front wheel hit the ditch I knew it was going over. I don't remember anything after that.

I awoke in the hospital and was eventually told that my Sara was dead. I couldn't even go to her funeral." Murphy appeared to shrink in size and spirit.

Beth remained silent. Murphy sat silent for a few more moments, before continuing, "I didn't want to leave the hospital, I didn't want to face anyone, I didn't want to go on living. The world that seemed so good became dark and foreboding. I wanted to leave it all, not for another location, but leave it all permanently. I considered ending my own life many times, but being of a cowardly nature, I could never bring myself to take action. So, I shut out the world that I tainted. I am what people would call a recluse, a hermit, possibly even an ogre. I understand why they feel that way because I have chosen to give them that impression."

"Mr. Murphy, I'm sorry that things worked out the way they did, but you haven't said anything about your daughter."

Murphy sighed, "I know. That is the part that has haunted me the most. At first, I justified my actions by thinking that it was best for her to have people that she deserved; people that were reliable and responsible, people that would always put her first. At that time I couldn't think of myself as being worthy to have someone as special as my daughter. I couldn't imagine facing her knowing I was responsible for what happened to her mother. I buried myself deep into self-pity." Murphy paused to extract a handkerchief from his pocket. He wiped his eyes. "Beth, this is excruciatingly hard, because I am revealing to you how shallow I am. My life has been one regret after another. And here I sit baring my soul to a wonderful young lady who probably can't make head nor hair of what I am saying."

"Mr. Murphy, I think I understand what you are saying, but I believe the past is the paSt. Why don't you look forward and put the past at rest?"

Murphy smiled, "She is wise as well as smart."

"I don't know if I am wise, but it sure seems to me that you have paid whatever price was necessary for whatever happened a long time ago, Mr. Murphy."

"Maybe so, Beth, but it has been a long time in the making."

"Mr. Murphy, can you contact your daughter?"

"Yes. In a way, I think she has contacted me, but doesn't want me to know."

"What?"

"Well, now we are at the heart of the matter. Beth what do you think my Sara looked like?"

"I have no idea. You have never described her to me."

"I guess I haven't. She was so beautiful. Men would gawk at her, heck, I would gawk at her. She was a little bit of a thing, short, but not too short. Pretty blond hair, fine facial features with creamy skin that invited a touch. Her eyes were soft and lovely." Murphy was no longer in 1958, but where he longed to be; with his Sara. "I met her at a party and knew from the first moment that I would never be the same again. She was magnificent. I was introduced to her and preceded to trip over my tongue repeatedly trying to be cordial. She laughed, but not in a way that made me feel uncomfortable, but to let me know it was alright. I didn't let her out of my sight. No matter where we were or what we were doing, Sara was my princess and I wanted to make her a queen." Murphy stopped, snapped back to 1958. "Does my Sara remind you of anyone?"

Beth was not expecting the question, she instinctively shook her head and began saying, "No, I don't . . ." Like the flash of a lightning bolt, the thought came to her. "My mom! I think you have described my mom! Mr. Murphy, why did you describe my . . ." Beth was dumbstruck. Everything in her mind went topsy-turvy. What is he saying? Thoughts were flashing in her mind with thunderous impact. She couldn't arrange them in any order.

"Beth? Are you alright?" asked Murphy.

It was Beth's turn to become speechless, she slowly nodded her head. She wanted to ask questions, but there were so many that she couldn't formulate any one in particular to ask.

"Beth, I am of the suspicion that I have made a huge mistake. Please talk to me" implored Murphy.

"I . . . well . . . I'm trying to figure out what you're saying. Is my mother your daughter?"

"Is your mother Sally Thomas?"

"She used to be" responded Beth.

"Are Betty and Grover Thomas your grandparents?"

"Yes."

"Then your mother is my daughter, Beth. And, though I don't expect you to accept me as such, I am your grandfather" stated Murphy. "For years I accepted the circumstances of my doings until I began seeing your mother walking around town. The first time I saw her I thought for sure that I was going crazy. It was like seeing my Sara walk again. Her looks, the gait, her mannerisms, her beauty; everything reminded me of the love I lost. It was like my Sara had come back again, only she was young and I was old. At first, I thought it was another cruel trick that life was throwing my way, but the fact that she made it a point to walk up Railroad, then turn on Jefferson led me to believe that she was interested in me. I determined that she found out who I was and wanted to venture close, but not too close. One day I was in Michaels Brothers when she walked in with you. I was so elated that I could hardly contain myself. I almost approached the two of you, but thought better of it. Your mother obviously doesn't want anything to do with me and her feelings are justified, so I left the store. I saw you on the street that day and was overcome with my need to confirm what I thought was true. In retrospect, that was a foolish thing to do. That has brought us to this uncomfortable moment. But, another reason I stopped you that day was because I wanted to talk with the beautiful little girl I thought was my granddaughter. I wanted to hear her voice, to look into her eyes, to share a moment with her that I didn't deserve. For that reason I have no regrets. You are an exceptional girl, Beth."

Unsteady, both emotionally and physically, Beth responded, "Thank you Mr. . . ."

Murphy jumped in, "Beth, Mr. Murphy is acceptable considering the circumstances."

Beth continued, "Well, thank you. I need to think about this for a while. So you think my mother knows you are her father?"

"I believe so," answered Murphy.

"Why wouldn't she tell you . . . or me?"

"Beth only your mother can answer that. But remember, your mother has her reasons. You may not agree with them, but she has been forced to live with them a long time" responded Murphy.

"Mr., uh, Murphy, I think I need to go home now" stated Beth.

"Beth, would you drink some water first?" asked Murphy. "You don't look stable at the moment. I am concerned about you."

Beth filled the glass closest to her and drank water and took a long inhale of air. "Mr. Murphy, I'm not sure what to do."

"Beth, I must remind you that you have made a commitment to me to keep our conversations confidential. My request is not only for me, but for your mother too. She did not want you or me to know about this, and I doubt that her feelings have changed, simply because you and I have talked. Will you uphold your commitment?" asked Murphy.

"I will try, Mr. Murphy, but I'm really confused right now" responded Beth.

"I would like to show you something in my house that I have done for you. We can do that now or another time if you wish."

"I think another time if you don't mind. I need to think" responded Beth.

"Fair enough. Beth, I know you have a lot to think about. Your mom loves you very much, so as far as she is concerned, let this be for now. I see no value in springing this on her at this time. Do you?"

Beth gave thought to this, "No, but it should be talked about. This is a mess!"

"Well stated, as I would have expected. Do you now understand why I accept sole responsibility for this mess, as you call it?" asked Murphy.

"Yes." Beth stood to leave.

Murphy stood at the same time. "Beth, I must say that I am sorry for involving you in all of this, but I must also say that I do not regret getting the opportunity to know you. You make me proud."

"Goodbye Mr. Murphy."

CHAPTER 52

A t seven o'clock sharp, Bob was reading the canvassing reports when John came into the station. "Hey chief."

Bob looked from the reports to his watch and responded, "Always on time, I like that about you John; I can count on you."

John said, "That's why I'm here."

"Grab a chair, we have developments, it's a mixed bag, some I think you are going to like, others you won't" said Bob.

John slid a chair closer to the table, but with the back of the chair toward the table; he sat in it with his forearms draped over the back of the chair. "Let's get the bad news out of the way first" requested John.

"The hospital called, Butch is in bad shape. He took a blow to the back of the head with a rusty object causing a fracture and possible hemorrhaging. They won't know exactly what they're dealing with until the swelling goes down. They weren't encouraging."

"A rusty object? Like what?" John asked.

"Rusty enough to be flaky" said Bob.

John sat thinking and nodding his head.

"You have ideas?" asked Bob.

"No, I but I'm going to think on it" responded John.

"Ok, here are the reports from the canvassing effort. We have all agreed to read them, you should as well, but the upshot so far is we know the dog belongs to the Aigners down on Jefferson; we haven't told them that it is their dog, but everything matches. Investigations confirmed the story from the guy being held by Oswego. The County investigated the McVees and raised red flags. I'm going over to their place tomorrow morning to get further details about their move here.

Here's that part I think you'll like the best; Henry, on a hunch, came back here from Case Street and ordered a criminal history on the guard at Western Electric."

"The one I interviewed?" asked John.

"Yep, as you know, his name is Solomon Burgmeyer, goes by Solly. Has a history of violence: Cleveland, Chicago, did time in Cook County, and was charged with child kidnapping in St. Louis, but charges were dropped for lack of evidence" offered Bob.

"Well, well" said John with a big smile, "Maybe we got our break."

"Yeah, maybe, and Henry is giving you the credit for thinking to pass on the report with Burgmeyer's name" said Bob.

"So, what does this guy have to say?" asked John.

"Henry, Pete and the other guys are tracking him down right now. When we're done here, I'll join them."

"Man, I hope he can shed light on this mess" said John. "Before you go, I have two things I want to bounce off of you."

"Fire away" said Bob.

"I'm glad you're going to the McVees. They have been bugging me since I interviewed them," said John.

"Bugging you how?" asked Bob.

"I can't explain it. It's like an itch I can't scratch. Like leaving the house and you know you've forgotten something, but have no idea what it is. That's where I am. They seem like good people, concerned about their daughter; they say the right things, but . . . I wish I could put my finger on it; there's more to the story than they're willing to tell" said John.

"Are you getting that feeling from the father or the mother?" asked John.

"I don't know. Stuart, the father, seems like a straight-shooter; Sally, the mother, is a looker, so be prepared; she seems to be really broken up over her missing daughter. All this seems right, but I'm thinking there's a rat in the woodpile. When you talk with them tomorrow, watch for it. If anyone will see it, you will" said John.

"Ok, what's the second thing?" asked Bob.

"I want to go down to the Corries when we're done here. Nick Corrie and Stan Baker are Butch's buddies. They're good kids, but nosier than what is good for them. I want to confront Nick to see if he knows anything that might be helpful. Nick and Beth McVee were getting to be friends before her disappearance. I don't think he's involved in any way, but I think it's worth the time" responded John.

"I think that's a good idea. Find out what you can, and take good notes." Bob stood and stretched out his back with a groan.

"You thinking about fishing with grubs out on Blackberry Creek when this is over, Bob?" asked John.

"No, I'm thinking about retiring with the grubs out on Blackberry Creek when this over" answered Bob.

CHAPTER 53

Sally McVee became a sideline attraction for the diner in Oswego. Men enjoyed being served by her and watching her as she hustled food to the tables from the shelf between the kitchen and the counter.

Being served and watching her was as far as it would go. Sally never flirted, never encouraged flirting or any other advances that men would extend to other waitresses. She was friendly, cordial and quick with the orders and the food, but everyone knew that Sally McVee offered nothing more; and would stand for nothing more.

The owner of the diner once said to Sally in a joking manner, "If you throw out your charm you'll increase your tips." Sally's response was immediate and emphatic, "If I throw out my charm, you better watch out because that cast iron skillet will be right behind." That set the tone. The regular customers enjoyed being served by Sally. The men, regular or not, enjoyed the view when Sally was serving, but the view was always from a distance.

Sally worked in the diner for almost three years. She made friends among the customers and staff. She learned about their families and openly shared about her family. The only thing that she guarded was where she lived. She was embarrassed by the shack.

She became more confused as to why she ever thought it was a good idea to occupy a hunting shack. She and Stuart agreed that it was time to move into the town, but wanted to wait to buy a home rather than rent an apartment. They were getting close to having a down payment.

Sally's discovery and physical sighting of her long lost daddy did not reduce her loathing of the man, Thaddeus Murphy, but reduced her need to know him. She realized that time and her imagination allowed her to believe that he was a monster, a sadistic, conniving architect of hate and deceit. When confronted by reality, she realized he was just an old man who chose to live in his grave before he died.

Sally grew more content with living her life rather than living her life for a man that did not know her, and did not love her. She reflected on her years of fantasy. Tracking down Thaddeus Murphy was an obsession. She could not understand how she became so driven to find who he was, where he was and what he was. All she really understood was that she still hated him for abandoning her, but the rest of it was not as important as it once was.

Her walking trips to the center of Montgomery were now limited to genuine needs, rather than those that she used to make up. When walking, she would still look in the direction of his old house, but never walked down Railroad Street. A few times she saw him in his yard from Watkins. Once she ran into him in Michaels Brothers store when she was with Stuart and Beth. She and Beth entered the store while Stuart was parking. Sally saw him and knew he saw her. Sally guided Beth toward the opposite side of the store. By the time Stuart entered the store, Thaddeus Murphy was gone. That was good.

CHAPTER 54

John left the station after meeting with Bob. He was pleased to hear progress was being made; the investigations were becoming a heavy load for all concerned. If anyone could ferret out what it was about the McVees that was off kilter, Bob could. He decided to stick around the next morning to hear the results of Bob's interview with them.

The news on Butch sounded bad. Connie asked him to pray with her as she prayed for Butch that afternoon. He felt good about that. He believed in God, but wasn't exactly sure what to do with that belief, but Connie had the answers. She approached God as if asking a friend for intervention; and she did it convincingly.

John was thankful that he passed on his hand-written report to Henry on his interview with the Western Electric guard. He did not suspect the guard in any way, but it is the little things that make the big things develop. He felt he was lucky. He might hear more about the guard before the night was over.

He pulled the Village car in front of the Corries' home. The small boxy structure was rumored to have been one of the earliest houses in Montgomery, erected in the 1840's. Two steps of concrete separated the sidewalk from the front door. John rapped on the rickety wooden screen door. He could see Mrs. Corrie come from the kitchen area. With alarm, she began asking before she was at the door, "John, is everything alright?"

"Yes, nothing to worry about; is Nick around?"

"Yes, he's upstairs. He's not in trouble, is he?"

"No Mary Hilda, he's not in trouble. I would like to talk with him - and the two of you, if you have time" responded John.

Raising her voice she called for Nick and Paul. Both responded immediately. Paul appeared first, he must have been in the kitchen. As Paul entered the living room, John could hear the creaking of the wooden stairs as Nick descended them. John realized he had created an awkward moment. "Please relax. I only stopped by to talk."

"About what?" Paul asked.

"Well . . ." John looked toward the kitchen table. "Do you mind if we sit down, this could take a few minutes?"

Mary Hilda realized she was not being hospitable, "Of course not. Please. Would you like lemonade or coffee?"

"Coffee sounds good" said John.

"Is Butch ok?" asked Nick, daring John to say he wasn't.

"As far as I know, Nick. That's not why I'm here, but I will bring you up to date on what I know."

They all settled in around the small Formica table with chrome legs. Mary Hilda prepared two coffees for John and Paul and placed them on the table along with sugar and a half-pint waxed cardboard container of cream.

John continued, "I'm here to talk with Nick about everything that's going on. He and his friends seem to have more information about certain aspects of our investigation than we do. I want to make sure that I'm getting it all. As you might expect, these are not routine times for Bob and me. The County and State are dedicating men and services, but we don't have much to wrap our arms around. Nick and his friends might be helpful; they have been in the past."

Paul asked, "Really? How have they been helpful?"

By the tone of his dad's voice, Nick wasn't sure if he was headed for rough waters or not.

John continued, "Well Paul, these guys . . ." nodding toward Nick, ". . . see our little village from angles that you and I wouldn't dare. They ride around on the bikes, go to places we don't go, aren't afraid to ask questions, and stick their noses where you and I would never think to. Don't take me wrong, they're good kids and I envy them for their youth. I think we all need to talk. Are you ok with that Paul?"

"Sure."

"Ok. Nick, let's talk about Beth. You told me that you walked her home from school a few times."

"Part way home" said Nick.

"Right; you said down to Main and Watkins. I want you to think about your conversations with Beth, any observations about her home life, anything that might help me understand her family."

"Like I told you, she's just a friend and we talked about all kinds of things, but never about her family" responded Nick.

"Nick, did you get the impression that Beth liked her mom and her dad?"

"Oh yeah, she said that she did fun stuff with them. She told me that she loved working with her mom around the house. She said her dad worked nights, but on the weekends, and before he would go to work, he would talk to her about her writings. That's about it."

"Ok, but you never detected any problems, or areas when you felt Beth became uncomfortable?"

"No . . . other than where she lives. I found out today from all that is going on that she lives on the other side of the tracks. So big deal; I mean who cares? I don't know why she was so secretive about that" responded Nick.

"Thanks Nick, but if you think of anything, no matter how small, you come see me. Agreed?"

"Sure."

John continued, "Now, I'm going to reveal a few things that must remain in this room. I think the more Nick knows about the situation, the more he may prove to be helpful."

Paul interrupted, "Before you go any further, do you think the McVees are responsible for the daughter's . . . being missing?"

"Paul, it's anybody's guess, but we can't eliminate anyone until we find her. Now this next part definitely stays here. We found out that the security guard at the back gate of Western Electric has a criminal history that has raised him as a suspect. Bob and the rest of the investigators are tracking him down right now. So, we're looking in every direction for anyone that might shed light on what's going on."

"Why is the guard a suspect; and for what?" asked Nick.

"Look, three events have occurred in a small geographical area. That guard is right in the middle of that area. His criminal history requires us to interview him" responded John.

"What kind of criminal history?" asked Nick.

"Nick, I can't go into details, but he has done things that most people don't do. We need him to convince us that he's not involved. That's all I can say for now."

Mary Hilda asked, "What about Butch? Have you heard anything?"

"Yes, Bob talked with the hospital. Butch has a blunt injury at the back of his head. They confirmed that he has a fracture and possible hemorrhaging, but they won't know anything until the swelling goes down. Based on what Bob heard, Butch is seriously injured."

"Have they eliminated the possibility that he was struck by a car?" asked Paul.

"Pretty much. But we don't know for sure what caused the injury" responded John.

"Stan said he heard the cops say that he was dumped" added Nick.

John paused, "Maybe, but nothing is for sure, Nick. We need answers before we will know."

"Who, in their right mind, would do that to a child? If you hit them with your car, why wouldn't you stop? Or if you didn't hit them with your car, why would you hurt a twelve year old boy?" asked Mary Hilda.

"I don't know, Mary Hilda, but we will. We need to figure it out" responded John. "Nick, do you know the Aigners down on Jefferson?"

"Yeah, the older couple; she bakes chocolate chip cookies with walnuts. She always has some for us. We call her Grandma Aigner. Why?"

Looking toward Mary Hilda, John said, "I'm sure that the rumor mill has informed you that a dog was found in Mr. Murphy's cellar – that dog belonged to the Aigners. We have not told them yet, but the description is a match with the findings. Nick, can you think of any reason that dog would be over near Murphy's? Did you ever see it in that part of town?" asked John.

Nick thought for a minute, "It's a big dog – brownish and kind of lumbers along. Yeah, I've seen it. He's skittish and won't let any of us pet him, but I have seen him in that area. Holy smokes, he's the dead dog?"

"'Fraid so; did you see the dog at Murphy's?"

"No – not at Murphy's, but I remember seeing him in the field by Murphy's house. He was hanging out, or maybe looking for rabbits" answered Nick.

"What can you tell us about what happened in Mr. Murphy's cellar?" asked Paul.

"Not that much; it's not that I can't tell you, it's that we aren't sure what happened. We found a skinned dog, a tarp on the floor with a lot of blood, and we know Mr. Murphy is gone. The lab tests suggest that two people bled in that cellar and in all likelihood only one survived" responded John.

Nick knew this information from his conversation with Charlie, "So, if it was Mr. Murphy, he killed someone, hurt himself in the process, and left with whoever he killed?"

"That's a possibility," answered John. John chose not to mention the bone fragments on the tarp. The gruesome thought of cutting up a human body did not seem to have any value to the conversation.

"Nick, I want you to tell me about all the places you, Stan and Butch went, what you did, and who you talked to since yesterday morning," stated John.

"Everything?" Nick asked with a touch of exasperation.

"Yes. Your friend, Butch, is in a hospital right now and probably because of events relating to your activities. I can't promise that, but it is a probability that we have to explore."

Nick began to replay their travels beginning with his meeting with Stan and Butch at nine o'clock Wednesday morning, viewing Murphy's house from the tracks, Phil scaring the crap out of them, riding to the park, talking with Charlie, learning about Thaddeus Murphy, seeing Andy Durham in the diner and searching for Beth. He conveniently left out the mausoleum and the all-nighter. He wondered if John was going to insist, but John did not let on that he knew any more than Nick was willing to share. Nick did comment on the numerous conversations that they shared with Charlie and the advice offered by Charlie over the past two days.

John stopped Nick, "Let me get this straight, your friend Charlie was getting information from Shannon's and comparing what he knew with what you boys could find. He advised you to think like boys, but to continue to search, but when Butch is injured, he suggests the person involved is close at hand and you should stop searching. Is that right?"

"Yes; with a lot of conversation in between" responded Nick.

"Did he say who he suspected is the person involved?"

"No, he said that whoever the person is seems to know what's going on and is watching."

"How does he know that?" asked John.

"Charlie is a really smart man. I know he isn't respected, but he thinks a lot and gets us to think. That's what he wants us to do right now – think. He said we need to stop doing what we normally do and think" responded Nick.

"I'm not disagreeing with him, but he seems to know more than we do, wouldn't you say?" asked John.

"You should go talk with him, John. He'll talk with you, especially if I'm with you" offered Nick.

"Maybe I should, Nick. Nick, think hard on this one –any chance that Charlie may know more than he's telling you?"

Nick responded vehemently, "No way! Charlie squares up with us. He wouldn't hold back anything."

John held his eyes on Nick for a minute, "Ok Nick."

Nick rubbed the side of his face and asked, "John, this is off the subject, but are you aware of Phil Glaston's brothers?"

"Are you talking about Kurtis, Benjamin or Frank Glaston?" asked John.

"I think it's the first two" answered Nick.

"Probably so, Frank is a guest of the State of Illinois, and has been so for the last year and a half. Kurt and Benjy have caused their share of problems. Why do you ask?"

"I don't know, they seem strange and pretty mean to Phil, that's all" responded Nick.

"Do you have reason to believe they're involved in any of this?" asked John.

"No. I was asking for your opinion of them. I think Phil is afraid of them."

"Speaking of Phil, you didn't mention him much in your recap of activities. Where's he been?" asked John.

"Phil's been around, but he has cousins that live on the river in Oswego. He's been visiting them a lot lately. We saw him late today on the tracks. He was walking down to his cousins. Stan and I warned him not to, because of all the crap that is happening. But, Phil is the man, and wouldn't listen to us" said Nick.

"What time did you see him?" asked John.

"Around five o'clock."

"Exactly where?" asked John.

"Stan and I rode down to see where Butch was found. We felt we owed it to Butch. Phil was coming down the other side of the tracks from Webster" answered Nick.

"Was he going to continue on the tracks after you talked with him?"

301

"Yeah. We told him about the ropes. We told him we thought he ought to walk down Route 25, but Phil is a jerk. He said he knew what he was doing."

"Have you heard from him since?" asked John.

"No. No reason to."

"Do you know his cousins' name?" asked John.

"I have no idea, I've never met them" answered Nick.

"I'll see if I can check on him" stated John.

"You don't think anything has happened to him, do you?" asked Nick.

"No. I'm following up" answered John. "Can you think of anything else we should talk about Nick?"

Nick shook his head.

"Thanks for your time, Paul and Mary Hilda. You have a fine boy. Please remember that this conversation involves sensitive matters. Eventually it will all be on the table, but for the time being please keep it under wraps." John stood, extended his hand to Paul.

"Nick, I might take you up on your offer to go see Charlie" said John as he was walking the few steps to the front door.

"No problem" answered Nick.

After John left, Nick's Dad said, "Nick, I think I can get you and Stan up to see Butch tomorrow morning, do you want to go?"

Nick jumped at the offer, "Yes, but I thought you said that only his parents are allowed?"

"That's true, but I called Ted Blankenship and he's agreed to take us. He can get us in through the emergency area; what happens after that, he can't promise."

CHAPTER 55

On Tuesday, May 13th, four days after learning the secret that billowed with significance, Beth was walking home from school. Once again she avoided Nick at the end of the day to keep from having to tell him that she could not walk with him. She wasn't sure why she did it, but at Webster she was pulled to the weSt. Going west meant only one thing; Railroad Street. She wanted to talk with Mr. Murphy again. If it was all true, he was her grandfather.

Grover was her grandfather, but she didn't have much contact with him. Beth and her parents visited them once in Iowa for a few days when Beth was six. Her grandparents visited them in Aurora each year, especially around holidays. They would meet at the hotel where they stayed and ate in restaurants. She really liked her grandfather from Iowa, but didn't really know him. Her father's father died before Beth was born. Now, according to Mr. Murphy she was the owner of two grandfathers, both claiming to be her mother's father. It was all so confusing.

Throughout the weekend, Beth wanted to face her mother and ask for an explanation, but knew in her heart that, based on her mother's initial reaction to her talking with Mr. Murphy, things would not turn out good. So much was at play. The only person willing to talk about it was Mr. Murphy.

She was walking through the field approaching Murphy's house. She could see the two chairs and the small table with a pitcher of water and two glasses. Did he put them out every day thinking I would be here? She continued toward the table. As if she hit an imaginary trip wire, Mr. Murphy exited the back door. "Hello Beth. I am thrilled that you returned."

"I am . . . surprised that I did. I mean I wanted to, but it is all strange. I think you know what I mean."

"I do. You are a courageous young lady."

"Mr. Murphy, do you put this water out every day?"

"No, just today."

"But how did you know? I didn't know until ten minutes ago. Could you see me coming?"

"No. I guess living alone causes one to develop senses that one didn't know existed. I just get feelings; there are times when they are compelling" offered Murphy.

"Are you ever wrong?"

"Probably – but, who's keeping score?" Murphy said with a smile.

"Mr. Murphy, do have any other surprises for me? I'm not sure I can take much more."

"I hope not, Beth. I am simply a strange old man who has put himself in a fix. I don't want to hurt you, cause you discomfort or alarm you. We can go as slowly as you wish."

"You aren't going to send more wallops my way, are you?"

"I don't think so" said Murphy.

"Ok, so . . . you are my mother's father, you are my grandfather, my mother refuses to acknowledge you, I can't reveal that I know all of this, and here we are. That sums it up, doesn't it?"

"As succinctly as possible, Beth."

"So where do we go from here?"

"We could get to know one another. I'll tell you about me; you tell me about you, and we become friends. How's that for a start?"

Nodding her head she responded, "I'd like to get to know you, I mean beyond the accident. You may have lived alone, but you have had time to think about things; I'd like to know what you think about. I'd like to know more about my grandmother and your family."

Murphy responded, "And I would like to know what you think about, and about your family. I think we will be able to fill enjoyable hours becoming friends."

"You said you wanted to show me something in your house. Is this a good time?"

"As good as any."

Murphy was suddenly filled with concern, short of fear. His house knew no visitors for as long as he could remember. He wondered if Beth would be frightened or repulsed. Could this undo the progress he'd made with her? It didn't matter; they were walking toward the back door now. He stopped before entering. "Beth, I have lived a strange life. I have collected too much stuff. My home is messy. If you get uncomfortable, walk out. What I want to show you is on the other side of the house. We have to pass the mess to get to it. Can you do that?"

"I don't know, Mr. Murphy, I haven't seen the mess yet."

Murphy smiled and said, "Good answer, Miss McVee, good answer."

He started up the back steps with Beth trailing behind. As he entered the kitchen, he waited to hear a gasp of horror, but none came. Without saying a word, he proceeded through the kitchen to the main room. "This gets rather tight for a moment but it will open up." He did not turn around, but continued walking, and holding his breath at the same time. When he entered the bathroom, he immediately turned to the right through the small doorway to the bedroom. He walked to the far end of the room. Slowly he turned around expecting to be standing alone, but she was facing him. Her eyes reflected amazement and wonder. "Mr. Murphy, is this your bedroom?"

"No Beth, it is your room."

"Mine?"

"Yes, I cleaned it for you. I knew from the beginning that we would need a place to talk if we encountered bad weather. So I cleaned this room and the bathroom, so you would feel comfortable. Is it ok?"

Beth looked at the beautiful quilt on the bed, felt the lace curtains, leaned to look out the window and looked back at Murphy. "You did this for me?"

"Yes."

"It's beautiful . . . it's my room . . . but, how did you know to prepare it?"

"Neither magic nor wonder is involved in this; I knew you would be uncomfortable anywhere else in the house, so I simply imagined what might make you comfortable. This is what I imagined."

"It is ideal. I do feel comfortable. Thank you Mr. Murphy."

"Please sit down so we can talk."

That was the beginning of many opportunities for Beth to stop off on her way home from school to talk with her new grandfather. They traded stories, shared thoughts, examined Beth's writings, and recalled past events that were significant to their current lives. Beth's visits were short for the remainder of the school year because she needed to be home after school. However, summer vacation allowed them to lengthen.

Beth learned about Thaddeus Murphy and his family. She never said anything, but she sensed that his parents were cold and did not seem to share their emotions openly. When Mr. Murphy spoke of them, it was veiled and superficial, but when he spoke of his Sara, he became vivid in his recollections and vibrant with emotion.

She learned that Mr. Murphy's only friend since moving into this house was an old dog that would join him when he worked in the cellar. He told her that he noticed the dog outside the opened cellar doors at first. Without invitation, the dog joined him in the cellar while he was working. He didn't know the name of the dog, so he called him "Dog." Dog was comfortable with the name. Mr. Murphy never fed him because he did not want to interrupt the feeding schedule the dog's owner established. Dog would saunter down the steps in the beginning and lay near the door to watch Murphy work; when Murphy turned off the light, Dog would bound up the steps and be gone.

His visits grew more frequent. Instead of entering quietly and laying by the door, Dog would enter, wag his tail until Murphy scratched his head acknowledging his existence, Dog would lie down and watch Murphy work.

Beth could tell that Murphy appreciated Dog's friendship. On one occasion, she met Dog. Dog wasn't sure about her at first, but when Murphy took her by the hand and led her to Dog, he warmed to her quickly.

She concluded that her grandfather, Mr. Murphy, was an intelligent man and liked to talk. She liked talking to him. She wished she could bridge the difficulties that existed between him and her mom. She knew them both and believed, if given a chance, they would enjoy each other's company. But she was clueless as to how to build that bridge. It might as well be the Golden Gate Bridge in San Francisco. But she would work on building it. If only she knew how.

CHAPTER 56

At seven o'clock Friday morning, John was feeling the effects of a twelve hour workday. He'd received a call from Bob at eleven o'clock the night before. They found Solly Burgmeyer, not at the home address provided by Western Electric, but rather, at Chick'n Jacks, a restaurant/bar across the river on Route 25.

Solly was in the bar section of the joint, and had been there since he'd gotten off from work. He was cooperative though thick-tongued.

According to Bob, they escorted him to Geneva, the County's headquarters for criminal investigations. Solly, in his inebriated state, confirmed his criminal history, but absolutely denied any involvement in the three-ring circus occurring in Montgomery.

To his good fortune, Solly returned to work Thursday morning from a week-long vacation in Wisconsin and wasn't in Illinois during the timeframe beginning with Tuesday night and ending Wednesday morning. Further investigation would be done to confirm his whereabouts, but a call to the night manager of a resort in Tomahawk, Wisconsin confirmed the registration of a Solly Burgmeyer through 30th of July. The night manager said that he recalled seeing Mr. Burgmeyer's Dodge in the parking area every night, and definitely the night of the 29th.

The six hour travel time to Tomahawk appeared to have cleared Mr. Burgmeyer of everything except the assault on Gerald "Butch" Miller. The evidence did not suggest that he was involved with that offense either.

When they were finished with the interview, they drove Mr. Burgmeyer to his apartment, not allowing him to get his Dodge parked at Chick'n Jacks. His biggest challenge would face him in the morning; detailing how his employment application failed to reflect the time spent in Cook County jail, as well as the convictions that should have been disclosed at the time of application. Sorry Solly, better luck next time.

John was as disappointed as the rest, but facts tell the story. Bob told him to never get discouraged if facts didn't lead in the direction you wanted them to go. He told John, "Without facts, we would all be walking in circles." John recalled that conversation and decided it was good to get an unwarranted suspect off the table early. Unfortunately, Solly was the only immediate suspect, unwarranted or not, on the table.

Following up on Nick's concern for Phil, John called Oswego asking them to locate Phil at his cousins' house. John felt stupid not being able to provide the name of the cousins, but you can't provide what you don't have.

Oswego reported back that they couldn't locate Phil Glaston. They reported that they had checked the few houses along the river with no results. This gave John concern, but he would deal with it before he came in for his next shift. He would mention it to Bob in case he wanted to follow up during the day.

At 7:00, Bob came into the station revealing all that the lack of sleep can reveal; stooped shoulders, bags under his eyes, and patches of whiskers that a halfhearted attempt at shaving left behind.

John said, "Bob, I can stick around if you want to stretch out on a comfortable hunk of wood in the cell."

"I'd rather swallow a razor blade, but thanks. Things to do, people to see and crimes to solve; too many damned crimes, for my liking" responded Bob.

"Mine too, Bob, but we need sleep too" said John.

"What are you saying? That I look like shit?" asked Bob.

"No, but I've seen you look better."

"Well, let's go over to the diner and I'll take the coffee intravenously and you'll see a new man. Besides, we need to lay out the plan for the day. And I want to hear what you learned from Nick Corrie last night" responded Bob.

"You're the boss. Lead the way."

They walked over to the diner. A person at the Phillips 66 station, diagonal from the police station and across from the diner, waived to them. Not wanting to engage in needless conversation at this point, they both waived back, but kept their eyes on the door of the diner. They slid into the booth closest to the door. Neither made an effort to look up or down the counter to identify who was in attendance this early.

They each ordered the breakfast special of the day and coffee from the waitress the boys referred to as "Miss Personality."

Bob said, "What did you learn at the Corries last night?"

John pulled out his note pad. "I really quizzed Nick about anything he might have learned about Beth's relationship with her parents. He swears she paints a Saturday Evening Post setting of their home life. Nick said he can recall seeing the Aigners' dog in the general area of Murphy's place. I asked Nick to review everything he, Stan and Butch did since Wednesday morning." John fanned four or five pages of notes at Bob.

"So?" Bob gestured with his hands, "Do you want me to beg for a summation?"

"No, sorry. Nothing so far, but I'm going over the notes again when I get home. What do you know about this Charlie character at Shannon's?"

"Charlie? Charlie's been around a long time. I like him. I don't know what happened to bring him to where he is; he's quick-minded. People refer to him as the town drunk, but find one person that can honestly say that they have seen him drunk. I haven't. Old man Shannon told me that Charlie might drink a beer or two during the day and maybe another two at night, but that's the minor leagues compared to the majority of our upstanding patrons of Shannon's. He does his job and stays out of the way. Why do you ask?" inquired Bob.

"Nick and his friends have been parlaying with Charlie since this all began Wednesday morning. He'd gather what he could in Shannon's, they'd gather what they could out riding around town, then put the pieces together. He gave them a pretty thorough run down on Murphy. Told them things I didn't know."

"Like what?" asked Bob?

"Like Murphy's accident way back when that took his wife's life, and that Murphy swore to never ride in a car again."

"Yeah, the accident was tragic. What else?"

"He advised them to think the ways boys think and look places we wouldn't think to look. That is until this thing with Butch occurred; now he tells them they need to stop looking and start thinking. He thinks the one responsible for these problems is close at hand and is watching. They need to protect themselves. He thinks Butch got too close to something." John stopped to sip coffee.

"Sounds to me as if he's giving the boys good advice; what's your concern?" asked Bob.

"Well, maybe his reputation as a town drunk caused me to underestimate his ability to think rationally. I got the sense he was figuring things out too quickly for a person with a liquor soaked brain."

"Have you ever talked with Charlie?"

"Maybe a cordial greeting, but no, I don't think I have" replied John.

"Make it a point to. He may have good advice for us too; who knows."

Bob finished his breakfast while inhaling three cups of coffee.

"You do look better, Bob" said John, and continued, "A couple of other items; both have to do with the Glastons."

"The Glastons; again? And the week was going so well. What now?" asked Bob.

"Late yesterday afternoon, Nick Corrie and Stan Baker rode down to the Case Street crossing; kind of a respect sort of thing for their buddy. They ran into Phil Glaston heading south to his cousins' place by the river in Oswego. Nick said they tried to talk him out of continuing on the tracks, but he refused their advice. I told them that I would find out if he made it alright. I called Oswego for help. Oswego couldn't find him. I'll check with his parents later this afternoon before I come in, unless you want to check it out."

"Any reason to believe it's a problem?" asked Bob.

"None."

"Check on it when you can" instructed Bob. "What's the other Glaston thing? I am on the edge of my chair" asked Bob.

"Nick asked me what I know about Phil's brothers. I didn't say much. Nick said he thought Phil was afraid of them. If you don't mind, I'll check in on those two when I go over to see the parents" stated John.

"Your call."

Bob threw enough money on the table to cover both breakfasts and a tip.

"Thanks Bob. Are you heading over to the McVees?" asked John.

"Yeah, want to come along?"

John thought about it a minute, "You know, I would, but you might get a different look if I'm not present. I'll wait at the station to compare notes with you."

"I'll keep it short. Any tips on what I'm looking for?" asked Bob.

"I get the feeling that the picture is not complete. Try not to get wrapped up in Mrs. McVee's eyes, they are captivating."

Feigning surprise, Bob said, "I might be longer than I originally thought."

Bob was back at the station in forty-five minutes. He entered the station, sat on the wooden chair at the desk, held his chin in his hand and stared at John lying on the planked bench in the cell.

John wasn't sure what to make of this strange behavior. "Ok Bob, if this is a test of my patience, I failed. What are you thinking?"

Bob removed his hand from his chin and said, "You are absolutely right. Something needs to be brought to surface, but I didn't get it done. I am not their favorite police chief right now."

"What happened?" asked John.

"I started asking about why they moved to Montgomery and resigned from promising jobs in Aurora. They talked about how much they like Montgomery, and the people, and the neighborhoods, etc., etc. Stuart explained that the owner of the estate he was caring for announced he was moving away and Stuart's job was to be eliminated. I found that acceptable, but when I pressed for Sally's explanation, the air came out of their balloon. Sally was convincing herself more than she was attempting to convince me that it was a good move for them. I asked her, 'A solid administration job in a hospital for a waitressing job in a diner?' Sally unraveled a bit and asked what this had to do with finding their daughter? Why were their life choices taking a front seat, while finding their daughter was in the back seat? She almost had me feeling I was making a mistake, but she took it too far. She laid it on too thick. She's hiding something, John. She was deflecting my attention away from the something by getting me on the defensive. What is she hiding John?"

"I wish I knew. I'm glad you picked up on it, because I've been fussing with it since Wednesday" said John.

"You didn't get the feeling that she's involved with Beth being missing, did you?"

"No, but I left with the feeling that whatever I was missing was important. I think it will help our cause, if we can find it" responded John.

"I'm going to run this by Henry and Pete. If they feel the way I do, we're bringing in the McVees for formal questioning; while separated" stated Bob.

"Happy Friday, Bob. See you this afternoon" John said as he started for the door.

CHAPTER 57

Nick was up early Friday morning. He rode over to Stan's house; rapped on the front door; rapped again. Nick entered, made his way to Stan's room. Stan was stretched out with a blanket pulled around his midsection. His legs were bare. Nick kneeled down at the head of the bed. In a high squeaky voice he said, "Stan, it's Annette. Would you like me to slide in next to you?"

In an explosion of motion, Stan catapulted out of the bed knocking Nick to the floor, and sat on Nick's chest. "Yeah, you fish-mongering hunk of crap; slide right in and I'll cut your dick off."

Nick was shocked by the sudden eruption and found himself pinned to the floor. "Well, I guess it's safe to say you heard me coming."

Stan began to laugh as he rolled off of Nick. "Man, I am so good, I heard you when you left your front door."

"Maybe I didn't leave by the front door."

"And maybe your nose is growing, you fool." Stan continued to laugh. "I love it when you get that "Holy shit, where'd that come from!" look on your face." Stan remained on the floor and leaned his back against his bed.

Nick sat up. Trying to recover his dignity, he said, "Good morning Stanley, your breakfast is in the parlor."

"You crack me up. Man that was good. You didn't see it coming, and you almost peed your pants."

"Ok, ok. You got me. Now get up, Dad's taking us to see Butch."

"When?" asked Stan.

"Now asshole!" Nick stood to prompt Stan to urgency. "Get going. Dad's waiting on us."

"Is Butch better?"

"We'll find out for ourselves, if you get off your ass and motivate."

They raced their bikes back to the Corries' house sliding the bikes sideward as they slid into the driveway to the garage. Mr. Corrie walked out of the garage, locked it and headed for the car; the boys followed. Mr. Corrie said, "We'll pick up Ted. Now we can't stay long because Ted has to work today."

Stan replied, "No problem Mr. Corrie. We appreciate you doing this for us . . . and Butch."

As Ted promised, he was able to use his contacts in the emergency entrance to locate Butch's room. "You guys go on up, I'll wait for you here. You won't be allowed in the room, but you can see Butch from the hallway. If you are asked to leave, just retreat. Ok?"

"You got it" answered Mr. Corrie.

The sterile hallways of the hospital set the mood; the white walls and the white tile floors were void of color. The smell of disinfectant partially masked the unpleasant smells that the boys could not identify. The nurses paraded in white shoes, white stockings, white dresses and white silly hats. A brown metal waste basket in the corner of the hall appeared colorful in this sea of whiteness. Sounds were accentuated and rippled off the white walls. Everything seemed to clang.

Mr. Corrie coached the boys as they walked, "I don't know how this is going to go. We don't know who's with Butch, so follow my lead."

The boys nodded in agreement.

The door to room 316 was open. Mr. Corrie motioned for the boys to wait as he approached the room. Mr. and Mrs. Miller saw Paul, rose and came to the doorway to greet him. Mrs. Miller said, "Paul, thank you for coming."

"How are you folks holding up?"

Mr. Miller responded, "Never in my life would I have imagined what this could be like. Our boys are our lives. Butch is trying hard." He looked down and shook his head.

"I know. Butch's buddies wanted to see him if that is ok?"

Mrs. Miller leaned out of the door, saw the boys and nodded approval; her eyes registered pain and defeat. They approached slowly.

Mrs. Miller stepped aside revealing the room, the equipment, and the bed that held their friend. The room was as uninviting as the hallways; sterile, white, cold and barren of color. The stainless steel equipment around the bed added to the sense that it was about equipment and machinery more than it was about things that were alive. Even the metal night stand was painted a hard white. A muted small picture of a haloed Jesus hung above the bed.

The boys gazed upon their friend in the high bed. He was covered by a white sheet, but his head appeared to be mired in clouds of white; the clouds were actually pillows holding the ice packs to the back of his head. His flattop that always spiked straight up was lying flat. He looked uncharacteristically thin and frail; only his knee caps broke the flow of the white sheet.

A tube snaked its way up Butch's nose, held in place with adhesive tape, and other wires and tubes that trailed off the bed were connected to Butch's body. Nick noticed that Butch's eyes were not completely shut which gave him momentary hope, but he concluded that his friend with partially opened eyes wasn't seeing anything at all.

Mr. Corrie put his arms on both boys' shoulders and gave them a gentle squeeze. It was then that they noticed Butch's prized possession; his transistor radio was sitting on the white night stand. The thin melodious tones of Tony Williams and The Platters emitted from the small speaker. How ironic, Nick thought as the lyrics to "Twilight Time" drifted toward them. "*Heavenly shades of night are falling, it's twilight time, Out of the mist your voice is calling, 'tis twilight time, When purple-colored curtains mark the end of day, I'll hear you, my dear, at twilight time.*"

Mrs. Miller noticed the boys looking at Butch's radio. "The doctor wants us to talk with him and keep things as normal as possible. He loves that radio. We gave it to him for his birthday."

Stan said, "We know, Mrs. Miller. That radio is important to Butch."

The boys saw enough; they turned toward the sterile hallway. Butch's mom came to them with puffy eyes well lubricated with tears. Nick spontaneously embraced her and said with a cracking voice, "Stan and I have talked about this; Butch is going to make it. Don't listen to the doctors, we know Butch and he's going to pull through. He's tough, and we're in his corner."

Mrs. Miller leaned back to look into Nick's eyes. "You are good boys – and I believe you."

Stan, standing close by, said, "Mrs. Miller, when he wakes up, you tell him we're waiting for him and we have things to do."

Mrs. Miller wrapped her arms around them and held them.

Mr. Corrie stepped aside to talk with Mr. Miller. "Have the doctors given any indication of what's going on?"

Mr. Miller shook his head, "Nothing has changed; the doctors are waiting for the swelling to go down to determine what procedure they are going to perform next."

"Everyone in the village is pulling for your family, you need to know that."

"Thank you." Mr. Miller continued, "And thanks for bringing the boys up. Butch thinks the world of them and will appreciate knowing that they care about him."

Mr. Corrie responded. "They more than care about him, he's their buddy. You can remember what that was like."

Mr. Miller nodded his agreement and smiled, offered his hand and said thanks again.

CHAPTER 58

On July 29th, Sally prepared for work. In was a beautiful after-noon. Having forgotten to purchase a small present for a co-worker celebrating a birthday; she decided to walk to Michaels Brothers. She loved walking in the sun-soaked days. Walking east on Watkins to Main Street, she looked, as she always did, toward that house on Railroad. Would the old goat be out today? She saw movement at the back of the house. Continuing to walk she looked intently to identify the source of the movement. Oh my God! No! She spun around and began retracing the path she just walked. Arriving at Railroad Street she waited as Beth walked from Murphy's house. "WHERE HAVE YOU BEEN?" she barked at Beth with a coarseness that Beth rarely heard.

"I was visiting Mr. Murphy, Mom." Beth's mind was wild with anticipation and fear. How was she going to be able to explain this? Her mom looked madder than she ever remembered.

"I thought we agreed that you would avoid that old man! What happened to that agreement?"

"Mom, I was only talking to him. He's a nice man and . . ."

"He's NOT a nice man, Beth; you don't know what you are talking about. We're going home right now!" She grabbed Beth's hand roughly and stomped, more than walked the entire trip to the shack.

Beth attempted conversation as she was being pulled, but her mom told her to be quiet and they would talk about it when they got home.

Sitting in a kitchen chair, Beth waited for her mother to speak. Beth knew she'd really kicked the hornet's nest this time, but this reaction by her mother was beyond anything she imagined. She hoped her dad would wake up. He was always cool-headed with an understanding nature; he could help her.

In a low controlled voice, her mother said, "Beth, I have never been more disappointed in you than I am right now. I don't want to wake your father, so we will delay our discussion until tomorrow morning. You are not to leave here. Do you understand me?"

"Yes, Mom."

Sally dressed for work. She was overwhelmed with anger toward her daughter for disobeying, anger toward herself for being so trusting that her daughter would always do the right thing, anger toward the old goat for violating her life, again!

She tried to calm herself by thinking the storm was over and she only needed to deal with the cleanup, but she found no solace. The storm was only beginning. Why would her daughter want to talk to that old goat?! Why?

She continued to do things mindlessly as she waited until it was time to walk to Route 31 for her ride. She needed to find a solution; this was not going to pass without a plan.

CHAPTER 59

B ob, Henry and Pete were sitting in the makeshift investigation room; the notes were still on the blackboard, stacks of photos were piled haphazardly on the tables, and reports and files added to the disarray.

Pete said, "Gentlemen, could one of you describe a good night's sleep please? Not that I am deserving of one, but I'd hate to lose my recollection of waking rested."

Henry responded, "Ok, prima donna, here you go; following your favorite meal and two glasses of succulent wine, you slip between a set of clean, crisp sheets; the pillow under your head is cool to the touch, a pool of peaceful thoughts wrap around you as you drift weightlessly, serenity streams through you. Nine hours later, you awake to sounds of song birds and a cool breeze, you stretch your muscles feeling strength and vitality, and bounce out of bed ready for any challenge. How'd I do?"

Pete didn't say anything. Bob said, "Henry, any idea where I could find those clean, crisp sheets?"

"Yeah, in your dreams, big boy; let's get it going. Did you have a chance to get over to the McVees?" responded Henry.

Pete shook his head, "The Lord giveth, and the Lord taketh away. You couldn't let me savor that for two minutes, could you?"

Henry responded, "Nope, crimes are in our midst; we are paid by the good citizens to find them. How about it, Bob, did the McVees give you anything helpful?"

Bob leaned back, looked at the ceiling and said, "Yeah, a bad feeling. John got it right on Wednesday. I got it again this morning."

This caused Henry and Pete to sit forward on their chairs. Pete said, "What kind of bad feelings?"

Bob looked at them, shook his head and said, "Feelings that tell me we are not getting the whole story."

Henry asked, "From the father or the mother?"

"The mother."

This surprised them both. "The mother?" asked Pete.

"Yep, the mother."

Bob proceeded to review his entire interview with the McVees; stressing the mother's discomfort while explaining why she left a respectable job in a hospital to wait tables in a greasy spoon.

"So what do you think is in play, Bob?" asked Henry.

"I don't know, but we need to find out. John has good instincts, he picked it up first; I got a dose of it this morning. I think we need to get them in here to be interviewed separately. Mrs. McVee doesn't go to work until early afternoon; he goes at six o'clock, so we can gather them up if you guys agree."

"Absolutely" responded Pete.

Henry added, "I agree, but what are we looking for? Answers to why they moved here and possibly used bad judgment in leaving their jobs?"

Bob answered, "I know it sounds crazy; something is hanging, but I can't nail it, and neither can John. I guess the important part is that we're not getting the whole story; something is being left out that may have significance on that girl's disappearance. I couldn't care less why they moved here, or what they left behind, but why they are holding out concerns me."

"Yeah, me too" responded Henry.

"It's agreed. Let's go get them" stated Pete.

They took Bob's Village car and Henry's County car over to the barely visible car trail off of Route 31.

Bob didn't need to knock at the door; Mrs. McVee greeted them with, "What's going on? Have you found Beth?"

Bob responded, "No Mrs. McVee, not yet, is Stuart available?"

"He's sleeping, he . . ."

"No, no I'm not." A voice came from inside the shack. Stuart appeared bare-chested and sleepy-eyed. "What's going on? Have you found Beth?"

"No Mr. McVee. We hate to inconvenience you, but it is necessary that the two of you come with us for formal interviews," stated Bob. "This is Lieutenant Henry Conner, from Kane County, and this is Sergeant Pete Morantz, from the State of Illinois. We need to fill in the blanks."

"But why; are we suspects?" asked Stuart.

"Frankly, Mr. McVee, everyone is a suspect until we find the person who is responsible for this. You and Mrs. McVee need to help us find the right person. Would you like to throw on a shirt, please?" Bob nodded toward the door of the shack.

They transported the McVees to the station in separate cars.

When they arrived at the station, Bob asked if he could have a couple of minutes to make sure the town hall portion of the station was prepared to receive guests. He stacked the photos and files upside down and away from where the conversations would take place, and erased the blackboard; Henry had reduced the notes to writing for the file. Glancing around he did a final check to make sure everything was out of viewing.

Returning to the cars, he invited them in. Entering the station and seeing the five-sided cage bolted to the floor jolted the McVees. Bob said jokingly, "Don't worry about that; it's intended for wayward animals until we find their owners."

Neither of the McVees believed him, joke or not.

While pointing to the town hall section of the station, Bob said, "Mr. McVee, would you be kind enough to join me in this room?"

"But I thought you wanted to question both of us?" questioned Stuart.

"We do. Mrs. McVee will be talking with Henry and Pete while I'm talking with you. Do you object?" answered Bob.

"Well, no, but I thought we should be together." Stuart offered in a juvenile fashion.

"Mrs. McVee, do you object to talking with Henry and Pete?" asked Bob.

"No, not if it will help bring Beth home" answered Sally.

They were standing in the small area next to the cage, Bob could tell that everyone was getting uncomfortable in the cramped quarters. "Stuart, join me, this shouldn't take long."

Stuart went through the doorway to the town hall. Bob shut the door. "Please have a seat."

Henry and Pete offered the desk chair to Mrs. McVee; it was the most comfortable chair in that section of the station.

The interviews began.

CHAPTER 60

Nick and Stan thanked Mr. Blankenship before Nick's dad dropped him off. Standing in front of the garage, they thanked Nick's dad. Once on the street, Nick said, "Let's head for the bridge."

Both boys looked for Charlie as they rode past the tavern. Charlie was absent. They rode to the side of the bridge, squeezed through the parking logs, deposited their bikes and walked to their sanctum.

Nick sat on one of the boulders and said, "We have a lot to talk about Poncho."

"Well, let 'er rip, Cisco."

"I didn't have a chance to tell you that Rively showed up at my place last night" stated Nick.

"What? And you just thought to tell me now?" Stan stated with disappointment.

"Well, you were too interested in attacking me half naked this morning, then we were with my dad. John asked us not to talk about our conversation with him, so I couldn't tell you in front of my dad."

"Your dad's not here now, so divvy up."

"Ok, he peppered me again on what I know about Beth. He wanted to know more about her family, like I know anything about her family. He confirmed that two people left blood in Murphy's cellar."

"Is one of them Murphy?" asked Stan.

"He didn't say so, but I got the drift. Murphy's the guy they are after."

"What else?"

"Well, Rively asked me to tell him everything us guys have done since Wednesday morning. I laid it out."

"Not the all-nighter!" exclaimed Stan.

"No, no, and Rively was cool about it. I didn't tell about the all-nighter or about the mausoleum. Rively didn't say a word."

"Whew – your mom would have told my mom and that would have ruined the rest of the summer."

"No shit, Sherlock. Do you think I'm that stupid?"

"No, but I didn't like the way it was going there for a minute. Bring it on."

"I told him about our conversations with Charlie and what Charlie thought. I think that made him consider Charlie as a suspect."

"Charlie? No way, man!" stated Stan sharply.

"I know. I told him I'd go with him to talk with Charlie if he wanted me to. He asked me if I thought Charlie was holding out on us. I told him 'no chance,' that Charlie has always been straight with us."

"Damn right! He's the only adult that is straight with us; maybe Rively to some extent, but Charlie respects us."

"Hey, get this; the dog that was in old man Murphy's cellar belonged to the Aigners down on Jefferson."

"Grandma Aigner?"

"Yeah!"

"I didn't know they owned a dog" stated Stan.

"You remember that big brown dog we've seen around; it kind of lumbers along, but keeps its distance?" asked Nick.

"Oh yeah, that dog is dead?"

"That's what Rively said."

"Holy crap."

"I've saved the best for last" stated Nick with a smile.

"What, man? Come on."

"You know the guard on the back entrance to Western Electric?" asked Nick.

"Yeah, he was at the tracks yesterday when . . . Butch was . . ."

"He's a suspect."

"A suspect? A suspect to what?" asked Stan.

"Rively found out that he has a criminal history that made him a suspect, and he said the guard is right in the area where all this shit is happening."

"What kind of criminal history?"

"He wouldn't tell us, but said that this guy has done things most other people don't do" stated Nick.

"Man, you are full of news today, bucko."

"That must be why Charlie calls me the Mayor."

"Ok Mayor, what else . . . oh wait, I almost forgot."

Stan pulled out a full pack of Chesterfields from his jeans pocket. "My old man bought a carton, so I emptied them out and removed one of the packs on the bottom. I put the other bottom pack on angle and put the rest back in. I don't think he'll notice."

"You are the devious one" said Nick.

Stan removed the cellophane, tore away the foil and tapped out two cigarettes. They lit up and sat back. Nick was really beginning to enjoy smoking.

"Ok, give me more" requested Stan.

"I asked Rively about Phil's brothers."

"Phil's brothers? Why'd you do that?" asked Stan.

"I don't know. It bugs me that they are so mean to Phil. I was wondering if Rively knew anything about them."

"Did he?"

"Yeah, he said Phil's older brother, Frank, is the guest of the State of Illinois, and that the other two have caused problems, but that's it. I told him that I thought Phil was afraid of them."

"You did?"

"Yeah, but I don't think it did any good" responded Nick.

"I also told him that we saw Phil on the tracks and told him we didn't think it was a good idea to walk the tracks to his cousins in Oswego, and that Phil told us to piss up a pole."

"What did Rively say about that?"

"He said he was going to check to see if Phil made it to Oswego ok."

"Hey, what didn't you tell Rively?" asked Stan.

"Nothing that I can think of."

"Damn, so where does that leave us?"

"Right where Charlie told us to be – thinking" answered Nick.

They paused for a while and looked out onto the river. A carp surfaced about twenty feet away to suck scum from the surface.

"So Mayor, are you going to lead us in thinking, or do I have to call for a new election?" asked Stan.

"You know, I've been thinking a lot since Charlie told us to. I've been thinking about Beth mostly. It's difficult to think about what might be happening to her. She's a good person, smart, cute and she cares about things that blow right by the rest of us. I have tried to tie her to Murphy's cellar, but I can't see it. I think Beth is separate from Murphy. What do you think?"

"Well, I don't know her the way you do, but she's not a trouble maker, she's never mean to anyone; she definitely reads more than the rest of us, and I don't see any connection with Murphy either. She . . ." Stan stopped for thought and continued, ". . . maybe her old man is involved. I heard my dad saying that they should be looking at him real hard" answered Stan.

"Charlie said the person who is responsible for all of this is in our midst and watching. Have you ever seen her old man any-where other than the other day at Murphy's?"

"The school picnic."

"Yeah, but where else?" asked Nick.

"Nowhere."

"Well, if he is the one, he sure lays low."

"Agreed" stated Stan.

Nick continued, "Ok, a person in our midst is watching, or at least knows what is going on. That means we know them. That means we should be able to recognize them; an adult that we see around and pay no attention to. Like Charlie said, if Murphy was involved in the Beth case, he would have been seen if he stuck around to whack Butch. That old man was on everyone's watch list since Wednesday morning. And why would he whack Butch? If Butch had seen him, Butch would have been broadcasting his find like a foghorn in a storm. I think we have two people we are looking for. One is Murphy, but the other is tied to Beth's disappearance. The one that got Butch could be associated with either. My head hurts."

Stan used the front of his T-shirt to fan the imaginary steam from Nick's head. "Man, you have been thinking about this."

"Only day and night since Wednesday morning" responded Nick.

Stan picked up at that point, "Ok, you have my juices flowing now. Butch was thought to have been hit by a car, but later the cops thought he was dumped by the tracks. We find out that Beth lives down the tracks from where Butch was found. Maybe we need to tie those two together. By the way, I didn't know of any houses on the west side of the tracks. Did you?"

"No, but it can't be far if Beth walks to school" answered Nick.

"Good point. What if Butch stumbled on something having to do with Beth's being taken; what could he have stumbled onto? What's down by the tracks that could reveal a clue?"

"Nothing. It's wide open around the tracks, you have Western Electric to the east, the grove of trees to the west, the tracks in the middle, Route 31, and that's about it" answered Nick.

"Now my head hurts" said Stan.

Instead of fanning his T-shirt at Stan, Nick leaned across the boulder as if picking something up and returned with a handful of river water that he slung at Stan. "Man, you are overheating, you're on fire!"

"You jerk!" said Stan while wiping his face with his T-shirt.

"Hey, let's ride over to Phil's to see how the party was, and bounce this stuff off of him" suggested Nick.

"Ok. But hang on a minute . . . do you still think Butch is going to be ok?"

"Man, that wasn't our Butch we were looking at this morning. Those doctors have to do some things to get our Butch back. But he's coming back. He damn sure better!"

"Did you see his eyes?" asked Stan.

"Yeah, but that's got to be associated with the brain thing. They get that straightened out and his eyes will be fine. Stay with me on this one, Poncho. Our Butch will ride again."

"Ok, Cisco! Or excuse me, Mayor Cisco!"

CHAPTER 61

Bob found questioning Stuart a straight-forward affair. He did not detect deception or the indications that Stuart was holding back. Stuart admitted that he was puzzled as to why his wife wanted to live in Montgomery, and even more surprised that she was accepting of the shack.

Stuart rambled openly, "Sally has always been a neat person. Nothing remains out of place for long. This has been an adjustment for me, but a good adjustment, I guess. The shack is ugly as hell, but you noticed it's organized and clean. That's because Sally keeps it that way. She has Beth thinking the same way. If I leave anything in the wrong place, one of the two of them will point it out to me. Not that I'm complaining, they are great girls; it's just that I've never felt that the shack is where we belong. We've been saving everything we can, and we are close to having a down-payment on a place here in town."

Bob interrupted, "Stuart, do you ever get mad at the girls for pointing out when they think you are . . . well, being messy?"

Stuart's smile brightened the room, "Aw heck no! I love it. They keep everything so nice. I'm the luckiest man on earth." The smile slid off his face. "Or, at least I will be again when you find my Beth."

Bob looked down at the handwritten reports and notes he and John compiled from the interviews with the McVees. He wasn't really looking for anything, but was overwhelmingly convinced that this guy was telling the truth and all of it. To continue the dialog, Bob asked, "Are you aware of anyone, adult or child, who would have a reason and the opportunity to take Beth?"

Stuart responded immediately, "No sir. Beth didn't have friends hang around. She spent her free time over at the Durhams. Margie said Beth loved the animals and Margie said she liked having her around. The Durhams are as broke up about this as we are. Andy Durham helped search for her; he seems like a great kid, works all the time. The only other young friend is the kid that walked her home from school. I don't know him, but John said he was alright."

Bob looked at John's notes and said, "Nick Corrie?"

"Yeah, that's it. Do you know him?"

"Sure, he lives about a block from here. From what I understand, he's been searching hard to find her too. It was his friend that got hurt down on Case Street yesterday" answered Bob.

Stuart gave a look of confusion, "How'd he get hurt on Case Street?"

"We're not sure, Stuart. Didn't you hear all the sirens; it's not far from your place? It happened right at the crossing" asked Bob.

"Sally says I could sleep through a bomb explosion. It's because of the trains. If you can't block them out, there would be no sleeping in the shack. What happened to the boy?"

"Like I said, we don't know for sure, but we're looking into it. Let's go back to Beth; Stuart, how is your wife's relationship with Beth?"

"They're like two peas in a pod. They're like girl friends at times, doing each other's hair, listening to the radio; it's fun to watch" answered Stuart.

"Have you ever seen your wife strike Beth, or get mad at her?"

"Never. Sally can be stern when Beth needs discipline, but that's all it takes. Beth is a good girl. She does what we ask and rarely complains" answered Stuart.

The interview in the jail section of the station was not as conversational as Bob's and Stuart's exchange. Henry and Pete were feeling the same element of reservation that John and Bob had picked up, but so far, neither of them found a reason for it. Mrs. McVee's answers were direct and concise. Henry tried to trip her up on the reasons why she left her job in Aurora, but Sally's answers were well-thought through and difficult to challenge. Henry had done most of the questioning so far.

Pete began his questioning with Mrs. McVee's relationship with her daughter. "Mrs. McVee, I have kids, I love them, but I can get pretty damn mad at them. Has that ever happened to you?"

"Well, no. Beth doesn't cause us problems. She gets high grades in school and stays out of trouble. She helps with most of the chores around the house. Sergeant Morantz, I don't have a reason to be mad at her. Why are you questioning me about Beth? Do you think I stole my own daughter?"

Pete, rather than jump to the defensive, sat in silence for a moment and stared at Mrs. McVee. "No Mrs. McVee, I don't think you stole your daughter; but I do know your daughter is missing. You and Mr. McVee have asked us to find her. We want to do that, Mrs. McVee, but something seems out of place. I don't know what is out of place, but something doesn't seem to fit. Please help us identify that so we can move on to more important things."

Sally didn't flinch. She stared back at Pete and said, "Something may be out of place, Sergeant Morantz; I believe your reports will give that something the name Beth McVee. She is out of place Sergeant. She is supposed to be in our home, she is not. You feel that the best use of your time is to badger the two people on this earth who love her more than anything else, rather than to spend your time finding her. Is something out of place, Sergeant? Yes, my daughter and your priorities. What other questions do you have for me?"

Henry jumped in to let the steam escape from the dialog, "Look Mrs. McVee, and I speak for Pete, and Bob, and John, and every one of the investigators working on this case, the best present any of us could receive today is to find your daughter. We've come to know her; she has become personal to us. She's not only a little girl to us now, she is Beth McVee with auburn hair, pretty blue eyes, four feet eight inches tall, approximately 80 pounds, likes to write, and enjoys animals. She is real to us. We want to find her. We're picking up on reluctance or reservations that we would like to identify and put aside. Would you please help us do that? If you do, we will have one hundred percent of our focus on the other aspects of the investigation."

This strategy impacted Sally. She began to tear up, looked down at the desktop, and said, "I want to help you. I want Beth back. But I don't know what you're asking. Stuart and I have been honest with you. I have nothing more to tell. My heart is breaking. Please find my daughter."

Henry and Pete looked at one another, Pete said to Sally, "We will find your daughter, but let's go back to Wednesday morning . . ." they retraced the events and the questioning continued.

CHAPTER 62

Nick and Stan rode up Mill Street on their bikes. Charlie was not visible around Shannon's. They pedaled up the hill, turning on Main Street. Once on Main Street they began to race each other, pedaling hard, but straining harder to muster the grit it would take to grab the edge away from the other.

Past the factory on the left, the school ball field on the right, the school; Stan took the lead as Nick began to pressure. Beyond the school, Stan's bike gave way with a loud SNAP and a grind! Stan almost went over the handlebars. Nick braked immediately. Stan regained control of his bike and coasted to the shoulder. With the bikes stopped, they leaned forward over the handlebars, gasping for breath. Their drive to outdo the other was fierce. Nick was the first to speak, "Man (gasp), you broke (gasp) that chain on purpose (gasp), I was taking you to the cleaners."

"Kiss it, Corrie (gasp), I owned you!" responded Stan.

They fell off their bikes and onto the grass laughing. Once their breathing returned to normal, Nick said, "Damn, that was fun!"

"Yeah, I hope I can find enough of the pieces to repair the chain" said Stan.

"Come on, we can find them" offered Nick.

The majority of the chain wound itself around the rear sprocket. The broken link was gone. Stan said, "All I need is a pair of pliers and a screwdriver. I keep a connector link in my handlebars. Help me pull off the grip."

They pulled and twisted the grip. It came off and sure enough, wrapped in white adhesive tape was a connector link. "I have to hand it to you Stanley that was good thinking" said Nick.

"Thanks. Now, do you have pliers and a screwdriver in your bars?" asked Stan.

"No, but I'll bet we can borrow them at Stafford's."

They wheeled the bikes over to the office section of the junk yard. Nick was pretty sure the guys at Stafford's would recognize him from the trips he made with his dad. The owner did recognize him and lent them the tools. Nick said, "Why don't I ride on up to Phil's, grab him and come back here. You'll have it done, and we'll ride somewhere to talk with Phil."

Concentrating on removing what was left of the broken link, Stan said without looking up, "It's a plan."

Nick rode the short distance to Sard Avenue, angled left, and turned left into the Glastons' driveway. The black Ford Hot Rod wassitting alone without its owner. Nick thought to himself, "Hey Asshole, your baby's crying. What a jerk!" He walked up the stairs to the porch, rapped on the screen door. Benjy, the jerk Nick was thinking about, came to the door offering his warm and friendly greeting, "Yeah."

"Is Phil around?" asked Nick.

"He's not with you guys?"

"No. We saw him yesterday before he went to your cousins' party in Oswego" answered Nick.

"You mean Yorkville" said Benjy.

"I mean Yorkville, what?" quizzed Nick.

"Yorkville is where our cousins live."

"Oh yeah, I must have been confused. Sorry. So you haven't seen him yet today?" asked Nick.

"Look I don't care if I ever see the puke, but no I haven't seen him. When you do see him, tell him to get his ass home; he's way behind on his chores. Mom and Dad are going to be plenty pissed at him." Benjy turned, indicating the conversation was finished.

Nick walked off the porch confused. He'd let the cat out of bag about the party at their cousins; he momentarily forgot that Phil didn't want his brothers to know about it. Benjy didn't react to it, so maybe it was harmless. But . . . Yorkville? That's another eight miles down the tracks. No way! He wouldn't walk that far. He gathered his bike and rode away toward Sard Avenue. His thoughts were tumbling over the conversation with Benjy. Yorkville? What the hell? He rode onto Main Street and saw Stan standing next to his repaired bike. "Hey, did you return those tools?" asked Nick.

"Yes, mom" answered Stan smiling. "Where's Phil?"

"Man, we need to talk" said Nick, nodding in the direction of the cemetery.

They rode across the street, laid their bikes down and sat on the grass.

"You look like a bird crapped in your oatmeal. What's wrong?" asked Stan.

Nick hesitated, "I'm not sure . . . I talked with Benjy, the bad ass. He said he hasn't seen Phil and he thought he was with us. I told him we saw him yesterday when Phil was on his way down to their cousins' party in Oswego."

"Oh shit. Phil didn't want his brothers to know" inserted Stan.

"Yeah, I screwed up, but it was out before I remembered. But the surprising part is that Benjy said his cousins live in Yorkville, not Oswego" stated Nick.

"Say what?" Stan said with genuine surprise.

"Yeah, Yorkville" repeated Nick.

"What the hell? Phil didn't walk to Yorkville for a party."

"That's what I was thinking. It smells strangely fishy here, Poncho. Phil is up to something. I don't get it" responded Nick. "Why would he lie to us about where he was going?"

"Oh I don't know, because Phil is a jerk?" responded Stan in a voice heavily layered with sarcasm.

They sat cross-legged in silence until Nick said, "Let's go find our buddy Phil and get answers."

"To Yorkville?"

"No, dodo bird! He didn't go to Yorkville. He has something going on here. We need to find him" said Nick as he picked up his bike.

They hadn't ridden more than one hundred feet when Nick looked across the truck loading lot that the boys crossed the night of the all-nighter. On the tracks walking north was their buddy Phil. Nick slammed on his brakes and pointed in that direction. Stan saw him. They pulled the bikes off and leaned them against the hurricane fence that Butch had struggled over.

During the daylight hours, the gate to the truck loading lot was opened, but they still needed to be careful not to be seen. After doing a thorough scan for unwanted observers, Nick and Stan entered the gate and ran to the fence. Staying behind the trailers as often as they could, they made their way to the northwest corner where the fence could be pulled away at the bottom allowing them to pass under. They passed under, found the makeshift bridge and scrambled up the ballast. Phil was well ahead of them; they yelled for him to hold up. Phil heard them, turned in their direction, began walking back to them and said, "Hey girls, what's cookin'?" asked Phil.

Nick took charge, "Phil, man, we're glad we found you."

"Ok, so you found me."

"So, how was your party in Oswego last night?" asked Nick.

"Out of sight. Beer, girls and music; my kind of a good time" answered Phil with swagger.

"Your cousins, right?" asked Stan.

"Yeah."

"Man, how long did it take you to walk it?" asked Nick.

"Not long, it's only a couple of miles. Why the questions?" inquired Phil.

"Well, we were pretty worried about you, that's all" answered Nick. "But that's not why we ran over here. Man, you gotta come with us. You got see this, Phil."

"What?"

"Look, I can't explain it; I have to show it to you. It won't take long, come on" urged Nick.

"This better be good" exclaimed Phil.

"Oh man, it is" said Nick as they slid down the ballast.

Once they cleared the truck loading lot, Nick and Stan grabbed their bicycles and walked them across to the cemetery. "Where the hell are we going?" asked Phil.

"You gotta see it, Phil. You won't believe it!" said Nick.

"Ok, ok. I'll see it. But where is it?"

"It's in the mausoleum." responded Nick.

"The mausoleum? Bullshit." Phil stopped walking.

"Come on, man. I promise it'll be worth it" implored Nick.

Reluctantly, Phil continued walking. Stan and Nick noticed that he was still limping from the night on the tracks.

They came to the mausoleum. Nick and Stan stashed their bikes and they crawled under the bushes, through the window. Before they crawled in, Stan gave Nick a questioning look with his eyes. Nick replied with an almost unperceivable nod of his head. Stan trusted Nick and crawled without a word.

It took a moment for their eyes to adjust. Phil said while looking around, "Ok girls, I'm here, where is it?"

Nick positioned himself in front of the window. "Phil let's sit down, we need to talk."

"What? You thin brained lollipop, you brought me here to talk? About what?"

"Phil, sit down" said Nick sternly.

"You gonna make me?" asked Phil.

"If necessary" stated Nick.

Stan became uncomfortable with the sudden tension. "Come on Phil, we need to talk. Sit down." Stan removed his pack of Chesterfields and handed one to Phil.

Phil sat down reluctantly and asked, "What the hell do you want to talk about?"

Nick nodded a thanks to Stan and said, "Phil, you have been bullshitting us for the last few days, and frankly you aren't leaving this place until you come clean."

"Oh yeah! So you think you can stop me from leaving?" Phil started to rise.

"No Phil, I can't stop you, but we can" answered Nick.

Phil noticed that Nick was holding a piece of the metal bar that was originally part of the bars on the window. Phil's face reflected confusion and fear. "What are you going to do, beat me with that?"

"Not unless I have to, Phil" said Nick.

Stan was totally shocked. Nick never used force or bullying to get his way. Stan was speechless and wide-eyed with a Chesterfield between his fingers.

Nick looked intently at Phil and began. "Phil, you've been hiding something from us. You don't have cousins that live in Oswego. Your dumbshit brother, Benjy, told me your cousins live in Yorkville. What's the skinny, Phil? What's so damned important that you need to lie to us?"

"Screw you! I don't owe you shit."

Nick swung the bar toward Phil with surprising speed catching Phil unaware. From a seated position, Phil flung himself backward to avoid the blow. "You son of a bitch! You could have hurt me!"

"Phil, either start talking or I will hurt you. I swear I will" responded Nick.

Turning to Stan, Phil said, "Come on Stan, are you going to let him do this to me?"

Stan was still so stunned by what was transpiring he could barely believe it, but he stood up and said, "Phil, not only am I going to let him; I'm going to help him. Now why don't we all sit down and talk. We have questions – you have answers; talk Phil." Stan was proud that he was able to muster the strength to deliver such a convincing response.

Phil looked from Stan to Nick, and sat back, only farther out of reach from Nick and the bar. "Well . . . my cousins' place is kind of between Oswego and Yorkville and . . ."

Nick cut him off, "Phil, I want to beat your brains out. Don't you get it? Give me one more reason and I will fulfill my wish. TELL US THE TRUTH, Phil!!"

Any swagger, bravado or tough guy persona that Phil ever displayed was gone. He slumped with his head down. "Why are you guys doing this to me?"

Nick slid on his butt to get closer to Phil, "Because Phil, you had all the answers to the Murphy situation when we talked in the cemetery yesterday morning; you were convincing. You figured it all out. Murphy wasn't going to be found, the cops are idiots; you even thought through Murphy's escape routes. But when I asked you about Beth, you became defensive and led the conversation back to Murphy. I've been thinking about that Phil. The brainiac spends time to convince us that he knows exactly what happened at Murphy's, but he doesn't even want to talk about Beth. Then Phil, you are mysteriously gone a lot since Wednesday morning. Things to do, places to go; no time to hang out. I found that unusual too Phil."

Phil jumped in, "I can explain that. I feel really bad about Beth . . ."

Nick raised the bar and stared at Phil, "One reason Phil, just one reason and you're going to eat this steel. Got it?"

Phil was frightened now. He believed Nick would do what he threatened. "Ok, what about it. I didn't want to talk about Beth. So what."

"If that was it, Phil, I would be feeling bad about doing this, but it doesn't stop, does it? You weren't in Oswego last night, were you?"

Stan, having sat down again, saw the color drain from Phil's face as Phil slowly shook his head.

"Where were you Phil?" asked Nick.

Silence.

Stan using a softer tone pleaded with Phil, "Phil, tell us where you were and what's going on. You have to admit Nick's points are good."

More silence.

"Ok Phil, while you're thinking, think about explaining the pillowcase of snacks that were for a party that never happened" added Nick.

More silence.

"Ok Phil, I'll fill in the blanks. I think you know where Beth is. I think the food was for her. I think you've been gone a lot lately because you've been spending time with her, you sick bastard! How am I doing Phil? Tell me I'm wrong! Tell me I'm imagining all of this. Tell me Phil!" Nick was screaming at that point.

Phil stared at the concrete floor.

Stan said, again using a softened voice, "Phil is it true? Do you know where Beth is?"

Silence.

Stan continued, "Phil, you have to talk. Nick isn't going to let this go. Square up with us. Is she ok?"

Phil shifted and laid on one side with his hand propping up his head. "I never meant for anything to happen. I only wanted to talk to her. Tuesday night I was coming across the tracks by Railroad Street, she was coming out of that path that leads to her house. I thought she might talk to me, but instead she got real nervous. I walked behind her trying to explain that I just wanted to talk. She turned and began to run down that path to her house and started screaming. I panicked. I wanted her to stop screaming. I tackled her and held my hand over her mouth. I looked around to see if anyone was around. I told her I would let her up if she promised not to scream. I told her I wouldn't hurt her. I never wanted to hurt her. She agreed. We stood up. I knew I'd screwed up real bad and I didn't know what to do. I needed time to think, but she kept trying to pull away from me. She kicked me in the shins and hit me with her free hand. I spun behind her and picked her up so her feet were not on the ground. She started to scream again and I held her with one arm and used my free hand to cover her mouth. I don't know why, but I crossed the tracks and started walking down the path on the east side, I guess to get away from anyone that might see us. I couldn't understand why she screamed. As I walked, I came to that concrete bunker that goes under the Western Electric fence. Do you remember how we broke the padlock on the metal door, but could reposition it so it looked like it was locked?"

Neither Stan nor Nick responded. That bunker was a place they had discovered. It was used for something sometime, but it was an empty concrete bunker now.

"Well, I threw her in the bunker and told her if she heard anyone walking on the ballast it would be me and if she made any noise I would come in and beat her. She started crying. I shut the door."

"Is that where she is?" asked Nick.

"Yeah." Phil muttered.

Without an exchange of words, Nick and Stan broke for the window; scrambling as fast as they could for their bikes. "Go to River Street, it'll be faster" Nick said as he jumped on his bike.

They rode the graveled cemetery road to River Street almost losing control as they turned right on the asphalt of River Street. Their bikes were swaying side to side as they pumped hard on the pedals. As they blew by Shannon's, they saw Charlie sitting on the steps. Neither boy looked his way. They pedaled uphill toward Webster Street, Nick yelled to Stan, "You tell the cops – I'll meet you at the bunker!"

CHAPTER 63

The interview with the McVees ended at noon with no revelations. Henry drove the McVees to their home and returned to the station. He joined Bob and Pete in the investigation room.

"I hope you have good news, Bob" said Henry as he walked in.

"I was hoping the two of you were going to be the good news givers, but Pete has briefed me on your session with the lovely Mrs. McVee. What do you make of it?" responded Bob.

Henry squinched up his face and said, "I'm going to shoot from the hip. Pete, check and see if you got the same impression. First off, Mrs. McVee is quite a lady; she's articulate and she is crafty. She plays the game effectively, but maybe too effectively. That might be what is setting off our 'dig for more' meters. I think – no, better yet, I know she's withholding, but, here is the catch; I don't think it has anything to do with her daughter's disappearance."

Pete whistled, and said, "Zing – that one is going in a direction I didn't expect. How in the world did you conclude that?"

Henry answered, "Well, I haven't concluded anything other than she is withholding, but I am thinking out loud. When it comes to her discussing her daughter and the fact that her daughter is missing, I don't detect any haze or smokescreen, but when she discusses why they came to Montgomery, red lights go off and the haze appears. Now, are the two connected? Who knows – I don't - that's for sure, but I do know that she isn't sharing pertinent information."

"What makes you so sure that her withholding doesn't involve her daughter?" asked Bob.

"It's a gut feeling, Bob. She has convinced me that she's rattled to the core over her daughter being missing. She is genuinely distraught over Beth. If that was all there was to judge, she is innocent. But, I don't think that's all there is to judge."

Bob asked, "Ok, but what could she be withholding that is pertinent, but not to the Beth situation?"

"I don't know, but let's think about criminal activities people get involved in that they don't want others to explore" offered Henry.

Pete asked, "Criminal activities like . . . illegal gambling, prostitution, drug running, moonshining, stolen car rings?"

"That's a start. If we don't buy the reasons she's giving us for moving here, what are the reasons she moved here?" responded Henry.

Pete turned to Bob and asked, "Have you noticed any illegal activities that have escalated lately?"

"Hey guys, this is Montgomery, not Cicero. Other than the run-of-the-mill traffic violations and scuffles at the drinking establishments, about the most illegal thing I can think of is . . . Stafford's, a junk yard up on Main, they reported a stolen car off their used car lot Wednesday morning, but I don't see any patterns. We are not the community of crime. Hell, if she was selling herself as a prostitute, she'd have a better clientele in Aurora, not here. Gambling doesn't fit either. I'm struggling with that theory" responded Bob.

Henry was quick to offer, "I meant it as a thought for us to consider. She's withholding; we have to figure what and why?"

Pete scratched his head, pointed at the stack of files relating to their three investigations and said, "Look, if we're convinced that she's not connected to her daughter's disappearance, let's focus elsewhere and come back to her mysterious ways when we have more time."

Henry nodded his agreement.

Bob was about to speak as the door to the police station opened with such force that all three of them were startled. Stan burst into the investigation room. He was out of breath but blurted, "I know where Beth is! Come on. Nick is already on the way!"

CHAPTER 64

Nick was running out of steam when he rounded the turn from Webster to Railroad. He was breathing hard and his legs burned with fatigue and pain. He was forced to sit on the seat and pedal.

His mind was flip-flopping from the elation that Beth was found to the prospects of what he might find. He was glad he asked Stan to get the cops. In a way, he wished he'd have cracked Phil in the head with that bar. That piece of shit; what was he thinking? Beth never hurt anyone; she wasn't like other girls with the batting of their eye lashes and their foolish flirting. Beth was a good person. He pedaled harder as his anger grew.

Without warning, the thought came to him, "What if Phil was lying? What if this was Phil's way to get everyone on the wrong track? What if Phil lied again to buy time to run away?" Nick stood to pedal again; pedaling harder than he'd ever pedaled before.

He threw his bike down when he came to the ropes that blocked the path on the west side of the tracks and began running. His legs didn't respond to the call for speed. He stumbled and fell. He knew he inflicted injuries to his knees, but scrambled to his feet and continued to the concrete bunker. He yelled, "Beth – it's me, Nick. I'm going to get you out. Beth!"

The broken padlock was on the metal door as Phil said it would be. He grabbed it. "Beth, it's me, Nick!" He threw the padlock to the ground and began opening the door when he heard, "Nick?" from a small voice resonating off the concrete walls inside. The old rusted door could only be opened halfway before it hit the ballast that time had piled up around it. Out of the darkness of this concrete prison emerged the prettiest face in the whole world. It was dirty, tear-stained with strings of hair hanging haphazardly around it, but it was beautiful; it was the face of Beth McVee, his friend. Barefooted, she pushed by him to get out. "Is he here?" she asked with a mixture of apprehension and anger.

Nick was surprised by her strength as she bolted by him, "If you mean Phil, no, he is not here, you're safe, and the police are on the way." They could hear the sound of the Village car siren coming their way.

"How did you know where I was?" she asked shielding her blinking eyes from the brightness.

"I threatened to beat Phil to death if he didn't tell me where you were" answered Nick.

"But, how did you know to ask him?"

"Some thinking, Beth - just some thinking. I'm sorry it took so long" Nick offered.

Beth realized a long story needed to be told to learn how Nick found her, but she knew in her heart that Nick was responsible for her rescue. "Nick, you aren't going to understand this right now, but I want to do this before anyone comes." She walked to Nick, put her palms on his cheeks and kissed him on the lips. It was brief, but oh so effective. Nick felt the softness of her lips and the tenderness of her hands. His knees grew weak. In typical Nick fashion, the best he could offer was, "Thanks."

Beth smiled. "I am so tired, Nick. I haven't slept much and I've been really frightened."

This brought Nick to his senses. "Did he hurt you, Beth?" Nick predetermined that if Phil had hurt her, he was going to find Phil and fulfill his wish of cracking him in the head with the bar and maybe worse.

"No. He didn't hurt me . . . I mean physically. But, I cried. I was alone, it was dark, I was afraid and I didn't understand." She began to cry.

The cyclical scream of the Village car siren ended, now the fire department siren began beckoning a call for the volunteer firemen to race to an emergency; this emergency.

The sound of running on the ballast forecast the arrival of the police. Stan was in front leading them. He yelled, "There she is!"

Bob, Henry and Pete lagged behind Stan. They were not as accustomed to running on the jagged stones. Stan ran up to Beth and Nick, stopping abruptly in front of them. "Holy crap! You're ok! Holy crap!" he said excitedly.

Nick said with a smile that almost closed his eyes, "Stan, you need to work on that vocabulary, but, holy crap, she is ok!"

Bob, Henry and Pete joined them. Bob heard the exchange between Beth and the boys; he tenderly put his hand on Beth's shoulder. "Honey, you have no idea what a happy moment this is for us."

Beth responded as she continued to shield her eyes, "Me too."

"I can only imagine – no, I can't imagine, but it's over now." Bob said as he involuntarily pulled her close to him for a slight hug."

The sirens from the fire truck and ambulance were approaching.

Pete walked over to the bunker for a closer look. He did a quick assessment. Approximately ten feet by ten feet; six slabs of concrete arranged in a cube. Five ventilation tubes allowed air from the top, but the air in the bunker was stale and rank.

He surmised that the bunker was used for electrical equipment by Western Electric, but wondered why the entrance door was on the railroad side and not the Western Electric side of the fence.

An olive drab army sleeping bag was lying against the wall. Near the sleeping bag was a rusted black and chrome Eveready flashlight, discarded wrappers and bags, and empty pop bottles; presumably from the food that he brought to her. An oil lantern sat in the middle of the bunker; next to the lantern was a single white sneaker. In the far corner sat a dented galvanized bucket. Pete was

349

pretty sure it contributed to the rank smell. As he returned to the rest of the group, the only word that fit was "tomb-like."

The firemen arrived. Beth was sitting on the portable gurney they carted over the ballast. The same gurney they used to transport Butch. Nick recognized the fireman that lived near the church; he was kneeling beside Beth asking her questions and checking her over.

Pete motioned for Bob and Henry to step aside so they could talk. Pete said, "He entombed her in that bunker. It looks like he fed her junk and made her use a bucket for a bathroom. Any indication of her being . . . hurt any other way?"

Bob responded, "Not so far, I heard the fireman ask if she was injured anywhere and she said "no." Of course, she may deny it out of embarrassment, but when they get her to the hospital we'll know for sure. The doctors will check her over pretty good. By all accounts, she is one tough little girl. She confirmed that it was Phil Glaston."

Henry asked Pete, "Did he leave anything . . ."

A scream rang out. Sally and Stuart McVee were running down the path; they didn't even slow as they passed the officers. Sally dropped to her knees on the ballast and wrapped her arms around her Beth as she sat on the gurney. Stuart walked to the opposite side of the gurney and hugged his daughter from the backside. Beth and Sally were crying; Stuart wanted to cry, but wouldn't allow himself to show that much emotion. The firemen, allowing the family limited privacy, walked over to the cops. One of the firemen said, "After they have a few minutes, we should get her to St. Joe's."

"Is anything wrong?" asked Bob.

"No. She doesn't show any sign of physical injuries, but we need to get her checked out."

"No problem. Will it be alright if her parents ride with her?" asked Bob.

"One of them can, but we'll have two of our guys in the back. It gets pretty crowded with more than three riders and one patient" answered the fireman.

They strapped Beth to the gurney and carried her to the ambulance. Sally and Stuart each held one of her hands as they walked on either side.

Stan nudged Nick and said, "I've seen two of my friends carted off. I don't like that meat wagon."

Nick put his hand on Stan's shoulder, but could not claim words that were appropriate for the moment.

With the meat wagon gone, Bob, Henry, Pete and Stan climbed into the Village car to head back to the station. Nick rode his Monarch.

Inside the station, the boys replayed the events of the mausoleum for the officers. Bob, who was rarely seen with a gun, strapped on a pistol that he retrieved from a drawer. "Boys, I can't explain how much we appreciate what you did for Beth, and for us. But now, you have to stay clear. We have no idea what might happen. If you see or hear from Phil, call the County immediately, but let us handle the rest. Agreed?"

The boys nodded.

Bob, Henry and Pete went searching for Phil Glaston.

CHAPTER 65

Before riding off from the station, the boys agreed to tell Nick's dad about Beth and to fill him in on the details, however, they also agreed that the conversation with Phil took place in the cemetery, not the mausoleum. They wondered if telling the cops about the mausoleum would end their secret sanctuary forever. Maybe so, but they both agreed not to divulge it to Nick's dad.

They rolled up the graveled driveway, placed their bikes along the side of the house. Nick started talking before he entered the garage, "Dad, dad, we found Beth!" A sudden screech of creeper wheels came from one of the bays. "You what?"

"Yeah, we found her down by Western Electric in a concrete bunker" repeated Nick in rapid fire.

"Wait a minute. You're talking too fast, so slow it down so I can understand." As always, he was wiping his hands on a red shop rag, only this time he walked over to the GOJO hand cleaning dispenser hanging on the wall and began cleaning his hands.

"O K D a d, i s t h i s b e t t e r?" said Nick accentuating his slow talking.

"Not as good as when I hang you on a hook."

"Ok, ok, Dad, got it. We found Beth" stated Nick.

"Who found Beth?"

"Stan and I found her; oh yeah, and the cops" answered Nick.

They walked Nick's dad through the conversation with Phil, the discovery of Beth, and their conversation with the cops.

"Phil? Your Phil?" asked his dad.

"Yeah, Phil Glaston; and he's not our Phil; not ours anymore" responded Nick.

"Yeah, Mr. Corrie, I think he's going to be the cops' Phil for a while. I don't know what he was thinking" stated Stan.

"How did you boys come to the point that you thought Phil was the person that took Beth?" asked Nick's dad.

"Well, it's like I was telling Rively when he was here last night, Charlie told Stan and me to start thinking about the circumstances; 'the facts, ma'am, just the facts' like Joe Friday says on Dragnet, so that's what we've been doing. When I learned from Phil's brothers that Phil was lying about going to Oswego, we began putting the other stuff together. When we met Phil on the tracks and he proved he was lying by lying again, we knew he was involved. The rest speaks for itself" answered Nick.

"Mr. Corrie, I didn't have a clue until your son started acting like the bad guy in a John Wayne movie. I don't know about Phil, but I was scared" offered Stan.

"B.S., Stanley, '. . . we have questions – you have answers . . .' that was pretty strong too, you know" responded Nick smiling.

"Pure fear on my part, I didn't know what to say" said Stan sheepishly.

"I am proud of you guys, but I'm not happy about you taking risks. It could have turned out differently" stated Nick's dad.

Chuckling, Stan added, "Yeah, for sure Mr. Corrie; Nick could have smacked Phil with that bar. I don't think I've ever seen Phil move so fast in his entire life. Cool guy Phil just about dirtied his diaper."

Nick's dad became serious, "Ok, you guys are heroes, and I am proud of you, but let's stop it right here. No more Guadalcanal charges of any kind. And I mean it."

"Dad, we're heading down to tell Charlie" said Nick as he turned to leave the garage.

Charlie was perched on the steps of Shannon's. He saw them coming and started to smile. "Well, well, the Mayor and his court have news, I detect."

Stan and Nick started to prop their bikes against the building, but Nick said, "Got time to go to the park, Charlie?"

"I wouldn't miss it if it was my own funeral" he responded, and rose for the walk across to the park.

The boys fed their bikes between the parking logs and headed for the wooden picnic table. Charlie was right behind. When Charlie arrived, Stan's pack of Chesterfields was on the table. "Come on Charlie, we have to celebrate."

Charlie brought out his wobbling top Zippo to light all three cigarettes. Exhaling his first deep drag, he said, "So?"

"I think you already know, Charlie" said Nick.

"Maybe, but I want to hear all the details from you. Don't make me beg. I get grumpy when I am forced to beg" Charlie said with a sly smile.

So, once again, the boys told the story, detail by detail, as they walked Charlie through their coercing of Phil and the discovery of Beth McVee.

Charlie stroked the stubble on his chin, smiled and said, "You boys are something. I tell you to stop doing and start thinking, and kapowee, you turn up with the missing girl. I have to hand it to you. Have you told your dad yet, Nick?"

Nick smiled proudly, "Yeah, right before we told you, Charlie."

"He must have the face of the Cheshire cat" said Charlie.

"I think he's proud, but he doesn't want us to do anything like that again" said Nick.

"Wisdom; the old acquire it, yet the young need it. Sounds to me like your dad hopes you stick around awhile. You know I agree with him. Right?" asked Charlie.

"Yeah. We aren't planning anything, Charlie, but the Butch thing still needs answers" responded Nick.

"What's the word on Butch?" asked Charlie.

"Oh man, we forgot to tell you. Dad took us up to see Butch this morning before all this other stuff started happening. We didn't get to go into the room, but we saw Butch and his parents. Butch doesn't look like Butch, it's pretty scary, Charlie. But Stan and I know Butch, he's tough" said Nick.

Stan interjected, "Charlie, have you ever known anyone that has been hurt in the head like Butch?"

Clasping his hands behind his head, Charlie looked high into the trees, "Well, let me think."

It appeared to the boys that Charlie was working pretty hard on the question, "You know, I was working a ranch out in Wyoming and a ranch hand got thrown from his horse and landed on his head. It was about a mile from the ranch house, the guys riding with him raced in to tell the owner. The owner took a buckboard wagon to pick him up. I was working around the ranch house that day, so I didn't see him until they brought him in. He didn't look good at all; he was gray, limp as a ragdoll and not breathing like the rest of us. Frankly, I figured him for dead. They unloaded him in the house, rather than the bunkhouse and sent for the town doc. I never knew much more than what we were told, but a couple weeks later he was back in the bunkhouse. He was a little loopy after that, so he returned to his home, wherever that was. Before I left the ranch, we got word that he recovered, and was working again."

Nick turned to Stan, "See. Tough guys can do things others might not be able to."

Stan nodded his head.

Charlie offered as warning, "Now boys, keep in mind that I don't know if it was the same kind of injury that Butch has, but it was a pretty bad head injury that cowpoke suffered. But, Butch is a tough boy."

"Man, I wish we could tell Butch about finding Beth. That could cause him to jump right out of that bed. Can you imagine . . ." Stan imitates Butch to the tee. ". . . oh man, oh man, you gotta tell me the details. Was she all bloody, or was she unconscious? Did she have that faraway look in her eyes? Come on, give me the details!"

The three laughed; Nick patted Stan on the back, "Good to have you back, Butch."

Stan continued in his portrayal of Butch, "Back? I haven't been anywhere. What are you guys talking about? Tell me about Beth, was Ed Gien involved?"

This brought on more laughter. Stan distributed cigarettes again.

When things settled down, Charlie said, "What have you boys been thinking about when it comes to Murphy?"

"Nothing really, Charlie" said Nick.

"Things over at Shannon's have quieted down too. I hope the cops have something going."

"I didn't get that feeling when I ran into the station to tell them about Beth. They were sitting around" added Stan.

"Sitting around doesn't always mean sitting around; they may be putting together a strategy, or discussing how to employ a strategy. That's a possibility" responded Charlie.

"Yeah, maybe" said Stan.

"Boys, unless you're going to tell me how you have solved more crimes, I'll mosey on over to my job" Charlie announced.

"Thanks, Charlie" said Nick

"No. Thank you. You boys are my heroes."

CHAPTER 66

Bob, Henry and Pete decided to go to the Glastons' place. If Phil was home, they would take him in. If not, they would head to the hospital to see if they could question Beth following her exam.

Bob and Pete hopped in the Village car; Henry took the County car. With lights flashing, they headed to the Glastons, Bob was leading. For affect, Bob started his siren as he approached Stafford's junk yard. Henry picked up on the psychological impact and started his. Coming off of Sard Avenue, they whipped into the Glastons' driveway to see a shiny black '49 Ford and other cars, most seemingly in inoperable condition. Bob noted that the grass grew up around the tires on all of them except the Ford.

The sirens in the driveway brought both brothers out of the house before the cops exited their vehicles.

Pete and Henry followed Bob as he approached the porch. Kurt and Benjy displayed looks of astonishment on their faces, they were sure that the cops had come for one of them.

Bob climb the steps to the porch, "Kurt, Benjy, are your folks at home?"

"Nope – at work" responded Kurt.

"How about Phil?"

'Nope; was a while ago, but he left."

"Where'd he go?" continued Bob.

"Don't know – don't care" answered Kurt. Realizing he was off the hook, his cockiness began to emerge.

"Where do your folks work?"

"What's this about, anyway? We're busy" responded Kurt with attitude.

"It's about you answering my questions in a mannerly fashion – or maybe you'd like to do this at the County, Kurt?"

"Dad works at Lyon and Mom works at Processed Plastics down on Rathbone."

"Mind if we come in to look around?" asked Bob.

"What for?" asked Benjy.

"We need to find Phil right now."

"Like Kurt said, he's not here!" stated Benjy.

"Mind if we look?" Bob said pointing toward the open door.

Benjy paused momentarily, before saying, "The place is a mess."

"We are not judges for the Good Housekeeping Seal of Approval, Benjy, we need to look around" responded Bob.

'The place was a mess' was an understatement; dirty dishes stacked on the counters and the sink, clothing strewn about, holes in the fabric covering the furniture and the telltale aroma of a cat box that should have been cleaned last week.

"Where's Phil's room?" asked Bob.

"All the way down and on your right" said Kurt pointing down the hallway.

Without speaking, the three cops searched in different directions; each opening doors to rooms and closets, looking behind furniture and any space large enough for a person to hide. Bob went down the hall to the right.

When Henry and Pete were finished, they drifted down the hall and to the right. Pete's only word was 'damn!'

The cops returned to the front porch where Kurt and Benjy were sitting with their backs to the wall of the house. Kurt's engineer boots rested on an overturned five gallon bucket. Benjy gave them a look of disdain.

"Stand up, boys!" barked Bob.

They purposely took their time rising to their feet; once up, they stood with their shoulders and heads cocked to one side communicating their self-promoted toughness.

"Exactly what time did you see Phil last?" asked Bob.

Benjy responded, "Can't recall."

"Fine" said Bob as he turned toward Henry and Pete. "Cuff 'em. We'll take them where they can have time to sharpen their memories."

Kurt offered quickly, "He was here about an hour ago; he grabbed some stuff and left."

"What did he grab?"

"Shit out of his room. I wasn't paying attention, I don't know what he took" responded Kurt.

"Where'd he go?"

"Out the door" said Kurt.

"Look genius, I assumed he went out the door if he left; where'd he go after he went out the door?" asked Bob.

"I told you I don't know; I was watching TV."

Bob turned to Benjy, questioning without saying a word.

"Man, I don't know either; like Kurt said, he walked out" Benjy offered.

"Ok, where do you think he went?" asked Bob.

Benjy and Kurt looked at one another. Kurt said, "Phil's a dumbshit, we don't know where he goes; and that's the truth. Why don't you ask those screwballs he hangs out with."

"What screwballs would that be?" asked Bob.

"I don't know their names, they ride bicycles; they've been around a lot lately looking for him" answered Kurt.

Bob asked, "Which of those cars still run?"

Benjy responded, "My Ford: the rest need work."

"Do the others run?" Bob persisted.

"No."

"Give me the keys to the Ford" Bob demanded with his hand held out.

"No way! That's mine" responded an agitated Benjy.

"Give me the keys or we call the wrecker, Benjy. Those wrecker guys are known to be a little rough, if you know what I mean. A nice car like yours might not come back looking as pretty as it does right now" Bob said.

"What are you going to do with them?" asked Benjy.

"We're going to hold them until we find Phil. Not that we don't trust you boys, but Phil might return and steal your car. I will return the keys personally once this is over. Now get them" said Bob.

Benjy produced his keys; a small chromed skull with red-jeweled eyes adorned the key chain.

"You boys stay here while we walk the grounds" instructed Bob.

They checked the interiors of all the vehicles, the out buildings and the entire yard out to the swampy area. A smell of decay grew stronger as they approached the cattails and marshy ground. "What the hell? Does that swamp smell that way all the time?" asked Pete.

"I doubt it" replied Bob, as he edged closer without venturing into the muck. "Something has died in that swamp. We can check it out later when we have boots."

They finished the cursory search of the property and returned to the house. Benjy and Kurt were still on the porch.

Henry pulled a card from his pocket, "If you boys hear from Phil, I want you to call 6-2211, it's on the card, that will get you to my office. Tell them that you have been in contact with Phil. They will radio me. I will get here pronto. I know you might think about aiding Phil, but that would be a stupid move on your part. Accessories to a crime go to jail too. Call, alright?"

"Yeah. Do I get my keys back then?" asked Benjy.

"You bet" answered Bob.

When Henry got to the County car, he radioed to have an investigator sent to the Glastons with waders to determine the source of the smell of decay they detected in the swamp. He gave an all-points bulletin for the arrest of Philip Girrard Glaston, age fourteen, six feet tall, approximately one hundred and seventy pounds, with dark hair combed into a pompadour.

Bob asked Henry to have his office call John Rively; Bob wanted John to escort Mrs. Glaston to her home from her work place. Henry asked another investigator go to Lyon Metal to escort Phil's father to their home. When they were done at the hospital, the cops would return to the Glastons to interview the parents.

Bob, Henry and Pete headed for St. Joseph Hospital in two cars, without lights or sirens.

CHAPTER 67

Sally and Stuart waited for the doctors to complete their exam of Beth. Cloaked in a white coat a doctor came out to escort them to a corner of the waiting room for privacy. "Your daughter appears to be fine, physically. She has no signs of injuries, however she needs sleep; considering the ordeal she's been through, that is not surprising. She's getting a bath right now; she asked for one."

"So, she's going to be ok?" asked Stuart.

"Well, it certainly seems so, physically. However, it will be important to monitor her behavior for a while. Events like this may produce any one of various psychological reactions."

"Can you give us an example?" asked Sally.

"Errant behaviors or acting in ways she wouldn't normally act, eating habits may change, anger, fears that weren't present before, nightmares, digestion problems, emotional peaks and valleys, who knows? However, right now she seems reasonably strong. She has questions about the boy that . . . imprisoned her, but they appear to me as healthy questions; like why, what is going to happen to him and things like that. Only time will tell how she chooses to deal with it."

"When do we get to take her home?" asked Stuart.

"It could be tonight, or it might be tomorrow. It's customary for us to have the hospital psychologist spend time with her. He has been called. Once he has done an assessment, we'll let you know about her release. I'd say she is doing remarkably well for what she's been through. As I said, she is getting a bath now, and a good meal will be waiting for her when she's done."

"Thank you, doctor" offered Sally.

Sally and Stuart waited another thirty minutes before being sent to Beth's room. She was sitting up on the hospital bed with a tray of food in front of her. A large glass of chocolate milk was half finished. She wasn't wasting time; the food was being devoured.

Pulling chairs close to the bed so they could touch her, Sally said, "Looks to me like you're pretty hungry, honey." Beth was trying not to talk with her mouth full, but was also trying to satisfy the hunger bug that was gnawing on her stomach, and said, "This food is so good!"

"Take your time, honey, we aren't going anywhere" said Stuart while squeezing her knee. "You are a miracle again."

This time Beth couldn't refrain, with food still in her mouth she asked, "Again?"

Stuart smiled as his eyes grew watery, "You were a miracle when we got you; now you are a miracle when we got you back."

Without warning, Sally said, "We're leaving the shack as soon as we can find a place in town."

This stopped Beth dead in her tracks, she stopped eating, looked to find assurance in their eyes, and asked, "Do you mean it?"

"Yes" answered Sally. "I mean it."

"When?"

"Tomorrow is not soon enough, but we have to find a place first" answered Stuart. "It won't take us long, I promise."

"Oh, WOW!" Beth laid back; the head of the bed was partially elevated. She began imagining living in a neighborhood again and saying goodbye to that spiders' lair of an outhouse.

Sally broke the mood, "Now don't get yourself worked up. You have to eat and get rest. We'll do our part; you have to do your part. Deal?"

"I'll do my part" responded Beth.

Sally turned to see Bob, Henry and Pete standing in the doorway. Bob said, "Sorry to intrude, but if we could talk with Beth for a couple of minutes, it might be helpful."

Stuart asked, "Do we have to leave?"

"By all means, no. In fact, we hope you stay" responded Bob. Bob walked close to Beth's bed, "Beth, you look better already."

"Thank you. I've had a bath and really good food." Beth looked at her parents, "And mom and dad told me we're moving."

"Not far, I hope?" offered Bob as he looked at Stuart.

Stuart responded, "No, somewhere in town. It will be good for all of us."

Looking back to Beth, Bob said, "Now that is really good news." Pausing for a moment he continued, "Beth, would you mind if we ask you a few questions? It will be helpful in our investigation."

"No. But have you caught him yet?"

"No, not yet, but we will Beth. Are you alright answering a few questions?" asked Bob, again.

"Sure."

"Ok, where were you when Phil approached you?"

"I was walking on the path near the crossing."

"What time was it, do you remember?"

"Shortly after Dad went to work; maybe six thirty."

"Where were you going?"

"I was going to walk over to Main Street and back. I had been writing for a long time and needed a break. When I write, I need breaks."

"Ok, you were coming off the path near the crossing. Where was Phil?"

"I don't know. He must have come from the highway because I didn't see him. He was behind me when I heard him say my name. He startled me."

"Ok, then what?" asked Bob. Henry was taking notes on his pad.

"Like I said, I was startled. I didn't expect to meet anyone on the crossing. At first, I didn't say anything. He said he didn't mean to bother me, he only wanted to talk. I turned to go back home. I guess I was really frightened. He followed me. I started to run.

367

He caught me and we fell to the ground. He put his hand over my mouth; I couldn't figure out why he was doing this. He's really big. He told me he would let me up if I stopped screaming. I didn't know I was screaming. We got up and he held on to my arm. I tried to pull away, but couldn't break his hold. He kept saying he wanted to talk. I kept thinking 'about what?', but I didn't say that. I kicked him and hit him, which made him mad. He picked me up with one arm and started carrying me. I think I screamed because he covered my mouth with his free hand; I thought I was going to suffocate, so I stopped struggling. I was so afraid. He carried me to that cement locker and threw me in. It was dark. He stood in the doorway and said that he would bring me things to make me comfortable. I told him I didn't want to be comfortable; I wanted to go home. He said that if I heard footsteps on the ballast it would be him and if I made any noise before that door opened, he would beat me. I started crying." The speed of Beth's delivery quickened considerably.

Bob jumped in, "Beth, please slow down. You're doing a great job of explaining everything, we're not in a hurry; and we don't want to upset you. Do you want to stop for now?"

"No, not if this will help you catch him" answered Beth, now with a calmer delivery.

Pete interjected, "You are a brave girl. The bravest I have ever met. Tell us what you want to tell and do it at your speed. We can do it now, or after you rest."

Beth finished what was left of her chocolate milk. Sally and Stuart sat by her side. Stuart patted her leg, "Are you sure you want to do this now?"

Beth nodded.

Beth took a deep breath and said, "I cried for a long time, but I thought that my crying wasn't helping, so I sat in silence. I was afraid. He came back in an hour or two with a sleeping bag that smelled musty, potato chips and pop, an old flashlight, an oil lantern and a bucket. He said to use the flashlight only in an emergency; the batteries were almost dead. The bucket was my bathroom." This caused her to pause revealing embarrassment. "We only used the lantern when he was present. He would open the door occasionally to allow fresh air in. He said he wouldn't leave any matches with me because if I lit the lantern without fresh air I would die from the fumes."

"How long did he stay with you that night?" asked Bob.

"Not long. I told him that my grandfather was expecting me and when I didn't show up he would come looking for me. That wasn't true, but I was trying to think of a way of scaring him."

"Your grandfather?" asked Bob.

That moment, Beth realized that she spoke words that she would have to explain. She was so intent to tell the whole story she told what she shouldn't have. She looked toward her mother. Sally smiled at her and said, "It's ok honey, go ahead and tell them."

Stuart looked to Sally, "Tell them what?"

Sally ignored Stuart's query and said to Beth, "It doesn't matter honey, please continue."

Everyone in the room had question marks running through their heads; the silence was like a wet blanket until Beth continued, "Mr. Murphy is my grandfather, but my mom . . . doesn't want anyone to know. For a while I would visit with Mr. Murphy at his house. Mom got real upset with me." Beth looked to her mom hoping that her mom was no longer angry with her. Sally gave her an approving nod. "I thought by telling Phil that my grandfather would be looking for me that Phil would let me go. But all he said was, 'Who's your grandfather,' I told him, and he left. I thought maybe he got scared and just left me."

At this point, Bob asked, "To make sure I'm clear, Thaddeus Murphy on Railroad Street is your grandfather?"

Sally answered, "Yes, he is my father, though I have never spoken to him. I was raised in Iowa after he gave me up. I guess he told Beth during one of her visits with him."

Bob's mind was racing with possibilities, as were Henry's and Pete's, but Bob knew to keep the focus on Phil right now, "So Phil left, but he obviously came back. When did he come back?"

"I'm not sure, I fell asleep, but it was quite a while. He returned with more snacks and pop."

"Did he say anything about where he was?"

"No. He lit the lantern and sat on the floor and started to talk. He did have on different clothing."

"What did he talk about?" asked Bob.

"He talked about his family and how much he hated his brothers, and how he wished he could talk to girls, and how he really didn't mean to hurt me, and how he didn't know what to do about me, and all kinds of stuff. He simply talked. He would ask me questions; sometimes we would sit and not talk. Other than threatening me if I made noise, he just wanted to talk. He was really strange."

"Did he stay with you the whole time?" asked Bob.

"No. Sometimes he'd leave for hours, but would return with more food. If I used the bucket, he'd empty it outside." She paused, "Sometimes he'd come during the day and sometimes at night. A little light came through the holes in the ceiling, not enough to really see, but I could tell if it was night or day. One time he fell asleep, but he was by the door. I thought about trying to get by him, but he would hear that door open, it made a lot of noise; I didn't think I could outrun him if I got outside. I did wake him after a while to open the door because I was afraid the fumes might kill us both."

"Beth, did he ever talk about your grandfather, Butch or anyone else?" asked Bob.

"No. He always talked about things about him. I think he is not happy with his home life. He talked about his brothers a lot and how he'd like to see them leave."

They were interrupted by a knock on the opened door. The doctor introduced himself as the hospital psychologist. "Looks like we have a party going on; may I join you?"

He introduced himself to Beth and her parents. Bob, Henry and Pete said they would be back if they needed more. They thanked Beth for her cooperation and headed for the door.

"Mr. and Mrs. McVee, could we plan time together once you have Beth home?" asked Bob.

They both nodded an agreement.

CHAPTER 68

Phil Glaston was on edge. He wasn't sure what to do, but he knew he needed to do something. The hole he dug for himself was a hole that even well-placed lies could not provide him a way of escape.

He saw the past three days as a blur, a blur of excitement, a blur of promise, but also, as a blur of accomplishment. He spent time with a girl; he actually talked with her, and she talked with him. He didn't want to restrict her the way he did, but she was getting used to it. She talked with him. She talked to him for hours. He really liked talking to her. But, those dipshit girls, Butch, Nick and Stan, stuck their noses in his world. What business was it of theirs what he did? He didn't hurt the girl; he never would have hurt the girl. He just wanted to talk to her; to learn how to talk to other girls.

Butch, that fat pig; why was he poking around where he shouldn't have been? He never saw it coming. Phil only meant to knock him out with that piece of iron like they do in the movies, but brain damage? That didn't seem right. And lugging the fat slob back to the crossing was no fun.

And the old man was at the end of his trail anyway; living like a hermit with all the junk. What the hell kind of life was that? If the old man would have accepted what Phil said, he'd still be alive, but no, he got excited and tried to become a hero; some hero. 'Your granddaughter asked me to tell you that she's going out of town for a couple of days with her parents, and she's sorry about not coming over, but she'd like to see you when she got back.' Wasn't that message simple enough? No, he asked questions, and when the answers weren't good enough for him, he ran for something in the bedroom. Well, he didn't find it, now did he? What a fool. It didn't take much to take him out, but carrying him past all that junk to the cellar was another matter. That was when Phil knew he needed transportation.

And that damn dog! It bit him on the leg! Where'd he come from? He wished he could have kept that pelt.

He wished it would have been his brothers that he got rid of and not that old man. His brothers deserved to have their eyes ripped out of their stupid heads, and turned loose to wander through traffic.

His brothers were the biggest jerks in the world. Maybe this would be a good time to get even; maybe he could go back home and hit them in the head with a hammer. Maybe he could skin them the way he skinned his animals. His brothers deserved it. He began to chuckle; if he skinned them, he could mount them in silly positions. The rest of the world would see them as Phil saw them; as complete morons.

They thought they were so hep, so cool, so sure that their younger brother was not capable of anything. Well, when all this comes out, they may think differently. Of course, if they were mounted, they wouldn't be thinking anything at all. They'd be staring off into space with those glass eyes. One them standing on his head, the other bent over with his head between his knees looking backward. That vision caused him to chuckle again.

His brothers didn't give a damn about anyone except themselves. They were worthless. They thought it as their right to belittle him, call him names, play dirty tricks on him and make fun of everything he did. Well, maybe it was time to even the score.

Phil was walking toward the car he stole on Tuesday night. He never intended to steal the car, but he couldn't carry that old man very far; he was forced to steal it. When he was done using it, he parked it in the weeds near the abandoned grain elevator. No one ever went to the grain elevator, it was a wasteland. The only way to access it was from Route 31. It was a safe spot. He could live out of this car for a long time. He'd have to stay out of sight, but that wouldn't be hard.

He sat in the car staring out the windshield toward the elevated tracks. Across the tracks, on the other side, Nick and Stan ran to the cops. Phil heard the sirens. Big deal! They probably released the girl. They found that he did not hurt her. He would stay low for a while. Or maybe he could slip in and out without being seen and finish business.

Phil felt his heart racing, but he wasn't sure if it was fear or excitement. He felt exhilarated by the things that had happened over the past three days, but he wasn't sure where all of this was leading. He could stay in the car, but for how long? He could do the things he wanted to do, but he needed to think it through. He decided to lay back and rest.

CHAPTER 69

Nick and Stan went home for the night. Talk was all over town about Beth being found and the search for Phil Glaston. Of course, talk was also abundant over the fact that Nick and Stan found her.

Telephone calls to the Corries and the Bakers were continual since late afternoon. The moms were proud and more than willing to accept the nice comments about their sons. Generally, the calls were long, involving the details of Beth's discovery, Phil's unexpected behavior, and Murphy's cellar of horrors. Though the news from the hospital concerning Beth was good, the discussion concerning Butch's condition usually dampened the spirits which led to the end of the call. Moments later the phone would ring again.

It was seven-thirty when Nick decided he needed to talk with Stan. He wasn't sure if his 'after dark curfew' was still in place, but it wasn't dark yet. Not taking any chances, he slipped out the back door, walked his bike away from the house and made his way to Stan's house.

Not sure of Stan's 'after dark' status, Nick pitched pebbles at Stan's bedroom window. On the third toss, Stan's smiling face appeared. Nick motioned for him to come out.

Exiting the back door, Stan walked to Nick and whispered, "Hey Cisco, why're you so secretive?"

"Man, I didn't know if your parents wanted you out at night. I even slipped out of my place without an announcement" answered Nick.

"Are you kidding me, I am the toast of the town around here. Mom has been on the phone non-stop. I could press for a new bike and get it."

Nick said, "I've been thinking a lot about the past three days, we need to talk."

"Yeah, me too; let's go" said Stan as he walked to the detached garage to get his bike.

They rode the alley to Mill Street and down the hill to the park. Because of the time of day, they walked their bikes close to the river, so they would be able to keep an eye on them from under the bridge. Once seated on the boulders, Nick said, "So, you said you had been thinking, what have you thinking about?"

"You said it first, what have you been thinking?" responded Stan with a smile.

"Well, I don't know any of this for sure, but Phil is on my mind. I've been replaying the past three days and trying to focus on Phil. Do you remember when he scared us on the tracks on Wednesday morning?"

Sarcastically, Stan answered, "No, it slipped my mind."

Nick continued, "Well, what did Phil say when you asked him if he knew what was going on over at Murphy's?"

Stan thought for a minute, "He said he knew what was going on over there."

"Exactly! But how could he? You and Butch were at Murphy's before I was, did you guys see him?"

"No."

"He lives six or seven blocks north of Murphy's. How would he have known what was going on at Murphy's? We didn't know anything other than an investigation was being conducted, but Phil didn't have any questions or concerns, he was more interested in scaring us. Does that seem right to you?" asked Nick.

"No man, it doesn't."

"And, do you remember when we were talking with Charlie in the park and Phil described Murphy as a 'crazy old man that collects junk'? How did he know he collected junk? I didn't know he collected junk until after the rumors got out. Did you?"

"Nope."

"Well, that has to mean that Phil knew what was going on before the rest of us. Right?"

"Right. And Phil was uncomfortable when we were talking about Murphy with Charlie. He wandered off, came back, and eventually left" answered Stan.

"I think Phil is involved in old man Murphy's cellar. That's what I think" stated Nick.

Stan responded, "I was thinking the same thing about the Butch situation. It took place on the crossing near the concrete bunker. Remember when Charlie said 'maybe Butch got too close to something someone didn't want him to see?"

"Yeah! And maybe that something was the bunker, and maybe Phil was the someone that didn't want Butch to see it" answered Nick.

"We, my friend, are cooking with gas" said Stan proudly.

"Wait a minute. Do you remember meeting Phil on the tracks Thursday night? Did he ever ask us who whacked Butch, or if the guy was caught?"

"Nope. But he was pretty upset" answered Stan.

"Yeah, he was upset that Butch was hurt, but I think he knew who whacked him!" stated Nick.

"And Rively told us that two people bled in that cellar. Phil has been limping a lot. He led us to believe that we caused the limp when we scared him on the tracks, but come on, he didn't go down that hard. Maybe he has an injury that bled . . . in the cellar."

"Ok, Cisco, what do we do now?" asked Stan.

"Well, Poncho, it is time to mount up and find the sheriff."

Darkness was beginning to blanket the village as the boys rode the streets in search of John Rively in the Village car. After twenty minutes of riding, they waived him down as he was crossing the tracks at Webster. Following a brief exchange, they agreed to meet at the station for their discussion.

John, sat in the wooden desk chair, looked at the boys and said, "Well, you did it; you found her; congratulations."

"Thanks, we appreciate it, but we have other stuff to talk to you about" said Nick.

"Ok, let's talk" responded John.

They told John about their recollection of the past three days and all of the indicators that Phil was connected to Murphy's cellar and Butch. John sat forward, "Are you boys getting help with this stuff, besides from Charlie?"

"No. What do you mean?" asked Stan.

"Well, Bob asked the County to call me to come into work this afternoon around 2:30. We interviewed Phil's parents. Afterwards, Bob, Henry, Pete and I discussed everything that came down, and concluded that Phil might be involved in the Murphy case. But we're supposed to be the experts. You boys seem to be upstaging us" said John.

Nick and Stan looked at each other with smiles, then back at John. Nick asked, "What can you tell us about Phil? Have you caught him yet?"

"No, not yet, but we are in pursuit. Bob is still searching; Henry has three of his guys patrolling with him in two cars, and Pete has his guys searching as well. I get to watch over the lonely streets of Montgomery" answered John, sounding disappointed.

"What are they doing?" asked Stan.

"Checking every truck stop, diner or widening in the road within fifty miles of here. Pete has the entire state on alert for him. He's driving a recognizable car; they should get him soon."

"A car? He doesn't have a car, and he's not old enough to have a license" said Stan.

"Well, you're right on one count; he's too young to have a license, but he has a car. Stafford's reported a stolen car on Wednesday morning. With everything else that was going on, we didn't give it a priority. Bob started putting the pieces together and stopped by Stafford's after he left the hospital this afternoon. A 1955 four-door DeSoto was stolen Tuesday night . . ." He pulled his note pad from his shirt pocket. ". . . teal blue body with a white horizontal stripe down the side that dips down over the wheel well, with a dark blue top. We don't know for sure, but we are banking on the fact that he stole it and is running away in it" said John.

"Holy shit . . . oh, sorry" said Nick.

"That's alright, it's one of the moments when anything goes" said John.

"What else can you tell us?" asked Stan.

"Did you know what hobbies Phil enjoyed?" asked John.

"Being a jerk?" answered Stan, quickly.

That brought on laughter. "Besides being a jerk, what were his hobbies?" John asked.

"I don't know of any; maybe combing his hair?" said Stan. More laughter.

"Ok, you guys didn't know that he liked to stuff animals?" asked John.

"Stuffed animals? Like you get at the carnival?" asked Nick.

"No, I mean real animals. It's called taxidermy" answered John.

"Phil?" asked Nick. "So what's that got to do with your investigation?"

"The dog was skinned" stated John.

Like light bulbs flashing, Nick and Stan displayed a look of wonder and understanding on their faces. Nick asked, "How did you know he stuffed animals?"

"They went into his room when they were looking for him, and that's where they found his stuffed animals. His parents confirmed that he liked taxidermy; they weren't too happy about it" answered John. "And investigators found the remains of his handiwork in the swamp near his house."

"WOW!" said Stan. "So, you guys definitely think he's involved with Murphy?"

"Maybe worse, but we'll find out when we get him" said John with a guarded tone, which the boys knew meant not to take it any farther.

John appeared to think to himself for a moment, "Hey, I think we should talk; would your parents mind if you guys ride along with me for a while tonight?"

"No, they wouldn't mind" answered Stan.

"Ok, call them" said John; nodding toward the phone.

CHAPTER 70

Both boys were thrilled when they received permission from their parents to ride with John as he did his rounds. Before they left the station, Stan slyly smiled at Nick and said, 'shotgun', thus was able to sit in the front seat with John. Nick regretted not thinking to do it first, but this was a good night anyway.

Once on the streets, John said, "The reason I thought it was a good idea to have you guys ride along is because I need you to help me think like Phil."

Exercising his smartass side, Nick answered, "So, you want us to teach you to skin animals, kidnap young girls, and what else?"

John turned in the driver's seat to look at Nick. "It seems the late hours have brought out your wit. Let's see if we can put it to good use." Looking out the front windshield again, he said, "Take your time on this one; if you stole a car from Stafford's, where would you stash it without it being seen for three days?"

"I thought you said he was in the car getting away?" asked Stan.

"He probably is, but if we can find where he stashed it, we may find evidence he left behind" answered John.

Stan stared at the lower dashboard to consider the possibilities; Nick responded immediately, "Have you checked his yard, there's a lot of cars parked around?"

"Yep" answered John.

"Have you checked the parking lots for Shannon's and The Mill tavern?" asked Stan.

"Yep, and nope it's not in the parking lots; the owners said they don't recall seeing a car fitting the description during the past week."

Stan said, "There really aren't that many places that you can stash a car in Montgomery without it being seen."

"Bingo, that's why I called in my best thinkers to help me figure it out" said John.

John's intended compliment was regarded by both boys as accelerant and a challenge. How could they not come up with the answer with that hanging over their heads?

Simultaneously, Nick and Stan said, "Route 31."

Stan reached over the seat to offer his palm to Nick for some skin.

"Where on Route 31?" asked John.

"Well, the old grain elevator is across the tracks from Phil's place on the east side; that would be a starting place. It rarely gets visited, and all Phil would have to do is get across the swamp and climb the hill to the tracks" said Nick. Leaning forward and punching Stan's left shoulder, he asked. "When was the last time we went to the grain elevator?"

"Last year, maybe the year before" answered Stan.

"The grain elevator it is" said John, as he headed to Route 31.

The entrance road to the grain elevator was long past maintained. Besides having lost the war to weeds, it was bumpy causing the undercarriage of the car to bottom out and the heads of the occupants to hit the headliner on occasion. In total darkness, the headlights illuminated only that which was directly ahead of the car.

The multi-story elevator was once tall and white, but the sun, time and weather chipped away at the stucco exterior making it appear ominous, like a decaying carcass lurking in the darkness.

John lost the indications of the original trail, so he chose to drive around the building to the right, bumping and bouncing as they went. As they cleared the elevator they could see a teal blue DeSoto parked between the elevator and the elevated tracks. In that space of approximately 200 yards, the DeSoto was parked in the center aimed at the tracks.

"Well, I'll be damned!" said John, as he began radioing the discovery to Bob. Bob was currently between Oswego and Plainfield checking out a truck stop. With this news, Bob was on his way with lights blazing. Bob alerted Henry and Pete who headed back to Montgomery.

The headlights of the Village car were focused squarely on the DeSoto. John put the car in gear and inched forward stopping far enough away so the headlights lit up the area around the DeSoto. John got out and slowly walked to the DeSoto to find it empty and without keys in the ignition. He returned to the Village car; turned off the engine and turned out the lights.

"I take it he's not in the car?" said Nick.

"No he's not." While removing the flashlight from his belt, he said, "I'm going to take a walk around. I shouldn't have brought you boys here, but I thought we were looking for what he left behind; I wasn't expecting to find the car. I want the two of you to stay put and wait for Bob to show up. An extra flashlight is in the glove box if you need it."

John walked past the DeSoto and toward the ballast hill; the light from his flashlight danced from side to side as he scanned the weeds and bushes he was invading. Suddenly the light disappeared.

Nick said, "Where'd John's light go?"

"Man, I don't know. What do you think we should do?" answered Stan with a stressed voice. Both boys leaned forward, eyes straining into the darkness, but without reward.

"Let's wait; he may have gone behind something we can't see because of the darkness" said Nick.

More minutes passed with only the darkness filling the space in the direction John walked.

Nick and Stan got out of the Village car and yelled for John. Silence answered back. They tried again with the same result.

"Get the flashlight!" Nick directed.

Stan retrieved it; four batteries with a three and one half inch lens.

Cautiously, they walked beyond the DeSoto in the direction they last saw John's light. They called for John again, but the stillness was deafening. The flashlight illuminated everything in its field as Nick scanned back and forth while moving forward. Occasionally, Nick would raise the angle of the light to hit the higher bushes.

They were approximately one hundred feet beyond the DeSoto. Had they not been facing away from it, they would have seen the dome light illuminate momentarily. It was then that they heard the roar of the DeSoto's Hemi V-8 engine; a second later they heard the spinning of the rear tires. The DeSoto was being propelled right at them. Stones were hitting the undercarriage, weeds were being mowed down and the engine whined as fuel was being thrust down its throat.

By the time the boys realized they were a target for two tons of shiny chrome and metal, the DeSoto was on them. Nick threw his body to the left; Stan attempted the same to the right. The noise was thunderous as the DeSoto exploded by them, followed by the stones and debris sprayed on them by the spinning tires.

Still on the ground, Stan shouted, "Nick, you ok?"

"Yeah, but I dropped the flashlight. He must have run over it. Let's run for the grain elevator. Stay low!" responded Nick.

They needed to run one hundred and fifty yards to the safety of the grain elevator. Bent at the waist with knees partially flexed, they headed to the only available cover, the decaying carcass of the grain elevator in the darkness. Without warning, they were knocked to the ground by a force coming from their right side. Stunned from surprise, they hit the ground to hear John say, "I thought you were supposed to stay put!"

Panting and still frightened, Nick said, "Your light went out."

John's voice revealed anger, "I turned it out. I heard movement and wanted the darkness on my side, not his. I heard you call, but didn't expect you to come looking for me."

"Sorry" said Stan.

"Are either of you injured?" John said with a calmer voice.

"No."

"Damn it! I should have never brought you boys out here. Let's make for the elevator and wait for Bob" said John.

Still running without lights, the DeSoto turned around and was headed back toward the Village car, which was now south of their position.

The DeSoto was moving slowly as Phil searched for them, or hopefully their bodies.

Employing the crab-crawl technique, the three moved toward the elevator on all fours. As they neared the old structure, the lights of the DeSoto lit up the area. All three instinctively dropped to their bellies. This gave them the lowest possible profile, but it also eliminated their direct view of the DeSoto and its driver.

John whispered, "Crawl to the corner of the elevator, and go to the other side."

They nearly reached the northeast corner of the elevator when the scream of the DeSoto's engine indicated that Phil had located them. "Run!" yelled John.

Scrambling to their feet they ran. John purposely maintained the rear-guard position to protect the boys. John cleared the corner as he heard the scraping of metal on stucco as the DeSoto clipped the edge of the building. "Find a way in and go up, now!"

Nick was leading, but could not find an entrance on that side of the building. With his Converse All-stars almost sliding out from beneath him he turned the next corner. Mid-way down that side of the building was a closed wooden door that consisted of aged vertical planks. Rather than try to open it, Nick swung out and threw his shoulder into it. The door creaked and bent in. Stan and John joined him with the next attempt and the entire door slammed to the floor in a cloud of dust; as did all three of them. Coughing and sputtering from inhaling the dust, they got back on their feet. As John turned on his flashlight, the room lit up, but not only from John's flashlight; the DeSoto's headlights found the doorway precisely at the same moment.

John yelled, "Get away from the door! Go to the other end and find a way up!" John removed his Smith and Wesson .38 Police Special. He had never pulled it before. He didn't want to use it now, but Phil was leaving him no choice. He would use it if the boys' lives were put in any further danger.

Nick and Stan were ten feet ahead of John. The light from John's flashlight and the light from the headlights of the DeSoto gave them adequate light to see the interior of the large room. The wall behind them exploded with sound and impact; the entire structure shuddered dislodging clouds of dust to rain down. The DeSoto hit the doorway with considerable speed, but the size of the old structure required substantial construction to support the weight from above. The crashed DeSoto was stopped with one fender protruding through the doorway with the headlight still burning. Escaping steam hissed from the radiator adding to the eeriness.

John thought the entire structure might come down on them. He continued to run. The dust made it difficult to breathe and see. All three were searching for access to higher levels. As they neared the far end of the structure, their hopes of stairs or a ladder began to sink. The light from the DeSoto's headlight darkened for a moment and then returned. The dust was thick as it entered their lungs and caused them all to cough.

Through the dust, John could see a pile of rubble and lumber to the right. He yelled to the boys to head for it. It was in a corner of the building and would give them protection. As John gathered them in behind the pile and turned off his flashlight, Phil's resonant voice boomed through the empty space. The hollow echoes made it impossible to tell the exact direction of the voice. "Come on girls, don't you like my adventure? You want to stick your noses in my business, well, here we are."

It was Phil's voice, but it sounded like a voice from one of the horror films the boys had seen at the movies. "Come out to play, girls. You think you are so cool, so smart, well, let's see how smart you are now. Hey Nick, Beth thinks you're really smart. Maybe you can impress her by getting out of here." The snickering voice was growing nearer.

John said in a surprisingly calm voice, "Phil, I want you to stop where you are. We can work this out, but you have to stop now. I talked with your mother today. She's worried about you, as is the majority of the village."

Phil cut in yelling, "You are full of shit, Rively! What are you going to do shoot me?"

"Yes" was the singular word that echoed back to Phil.

The dust was beginning to thin. Peering over the rubble they could see Phil Glaston thirty feet away. His face was too dark. It took a moment for them to realize it was covered with blood. He must have hit the steering wheel during impact with the wall.

"Phil, I have my gun pointed at you. I am going to step away from the pile. Raise your hands high over your head and turn away from me. We can walk out of here and get you help."

"What – and spoil our fun? Nick and Stan like this kind of fun, don't you, girls?" said Phil.

"Phil, you're a smart guy. Everyone was off base throughout this whole thing, so be smart now and stop" warned John.

Phil advanced forward to within twenty feet of them.

John projected a calm demeanor on the outside, but his mind was racing and his hands were shaking. His dominant objective was to protect the boys. "Phil, let me see your hands!"

Phil's laugh was deep and sinister. "You won't shoot me, you pussy! You ride around town in your uniform and think you're so tough, but down deep you're nothing but a pussy!"

Phil came at them faster. The blood from his face was soaking the front of his shirt. It was then that John saw a large knife in his right hand.

The sound of the .38 pistol discharging inside the elevator was earsplitting. The muzzle flash resembled lightning. The boys were shocked by the noise; and even more shocked by the thought of what the noise represented. In slow motion they watched as Phil stopped advancing, stood still for a moment and slumped to the ground.

John ran to Phil and kicked the knife from his hand. The kick wasn't necessary, the hand was limp. John rolled Phil to his back and reached for his wrist checking for a pulse. He found himself praying that his fingers would feel the thumping of a heart, but the wrist was silent.

Nick, Stan and John kneeled beside Phil Glaston. The angle of the light from the DeSoto's headlight cast ghoulish shadows on Phil. A large gash over his right eye was the source of the blood. The gash was as long as his eye-brow and split open three quarters of an inch. Blood ran into Phil's half opened eye creating a grotesque sight. The smell of cordite hung in the air; a feeling of dread dropped from above as the dust had earlier. The presence of death was numbing.

John sagged as he holstered the pistol and said, "I'm sorry you boys had to see that."

Neither boy said a thing; they were looking at the corpse of a friend.

Stan, with a quivering voice, almost whispered, "You saved our lives, John."

Nick didn't say anything, silence seemed adequate, but eventually said, "Yeah John, you were something."

They were all experiencing the conflict of shock, emotional pain and the wonder of survival; they stood.

Outside, the faint sound of a cyclical siren could be heard coming closer.

John closed his eyes, sighed and said, "Come on. Bob is on his way." They walked toward the door occupied by the DeSoto.

CHAPTER 71

The County coroner was called to make the official pronounce-
ment. County investigators took reports from John, Nick and
Stan separately. The large field lights brought in by the investigators illuminated the interior of the grain elevator so brightly that
everything that once hid in darkness was now totally revealed.
Phil's body remained lying face up, still and unmoving. The blood
on his face darkened as it dried. Nick and Stan found themselves
avoiding glances in Phil's direction as the investigators' flash bulbs
flashed.

When the interviews were over, Bob told John that he would
take the boys home and explain the circumstances to their parents.
John was relieved. He didn't want to talk about it anymore, he
didn't want to think about it anymore; he wasn't sure he wanted to
be a cop anymore.

Bob took the boys to the station and called the Corries asking them to meet him and the boys at the Bakers. Explaining the
events at the grain elevator horrified both sets of parents. Bob
apologized for inadvertently exposing the boys to the situation.
He explained that John thought highly of the boys and was just
expecting to gain their perspective on the situation. Both boys
were uncharacteristically quiet.

Dreading the task, Bob drove directly to the Glastons to inform
Phil's parents. John requested to go with Bob, but Bob thought
better of it. John had killed their son; not willingly, but a justified
killing or not, it would not be good to put the killer of their son in
front of them at this time.

Throughout his career Bob had informed parents that their
child was taken to the hospital, or was killed in a car accident, a

couple of times he informed parents that their child drowned, but he had never been required to inform parents that their child had been shot dead by a member of his department.

It was 1:30am, the night was damp and the smell of swamp was acrid when the tires of the Village Car crunched to a stop in the Glastons' driveway. The thirty or so steps from his car to the house were agonizing; each step seeming more difficult than the last. The noise of his knuckles rapping on the door seemed explosive. Light came from a window, the door began to creak, and a squinty-eyed Mr. Glaston appeared in the doorway. "You've found him?"

"Yes. Can you ask Mrs. Glaston to join us?" responded Bob.

Mr. Glaston's face revealed what he knew was going to be bad news; he turned to go down the hallway. Moments later he returned with a bathrobe-clad Mrs. Glaston. Her face was pinched, but her eyes were wide, "Let's sit down" said Bob, motioning toward the living area.

"Why?" asked Mrs. Glaston, in a way that exposed her dread.

"Please" asked Bob.

The conversation was the most difficult conversation he'd ever conducted. The hysteria, crying and mournful exchange brought out Benjy and Kurt. Mr. Glaston delivered the news of Phil's death to them.

Bob was disgusted when they showed little emotion. He expected them to say, 'So? Can we go back to bed now?' But they didn't. What emotion they did show was concern for their mother, but none for Phil.

Bob explained that a full investigation was being conducted and a formal report would be complied. Before he left, he handed Benjy the key ring with the chrome skull with red-jeweled eyes.

CHAPTER 72

Saturday morning at seven o'clock, Bob, John, and Henry were in the station next to the cage; Pete had left. All of them worked through the night attempting to arrange the pieces of the puzzle that led to the death of Philip Glaston. The initial investigation was completed, the elevator was secured. The mood was somber and restrained. Their faces reflected the results of carrying a heavy load for a long way; and though they didn't communicate it, they felt regret. Regret that they had not been able to prevent any of it; regret that people do some really stupid things sometimes; and regret that they had chosen a profession that made it their responsibility to clean up the messes.

The ringing phone startled all three of them. Bob answered. Listening, Bob said, "Ok Willy, slow down, where are you? We'll be right down." He hung up.

"Well?" asked Henry.

"Willy Smith and a couple of his cronies are fishing on the river near Case Street; seems that they've come across something in the water that has an unpleasant smell. Willy is pretty shaken up" answered Bob.

John's Village car was the most accessible so they all piled in and drove to Case Street. Willy was in the street waiting for them. Before they could get out of the car, Willy began, "We were working our way down-river when Frank began complaining about the smell, then I smelled it and we started looking for the source of the smell. I thought it would be a dead coon or possum, but when we got to the fence at Western Electric that goes into the water we saw it." Willy was running out of breath.

"You saw what?" asked Bob.

"The bag" answered Willy.

"What bag?" asked Bob, as they began walking toward the river.

"The bag that smells!"

Realizing that Willy's communication skills were hampered at the moment, Bob said, "Willy, take us to it."

Willy walked them to the river and under the monster of a bridge with the burnt red girders. Willy's two friends stood near the construction equipment looking wide-eyed. One of them staring toward the Western Electric fence said, "Willy thinks it's a body!"

Bob, Henry and John walked the thirty feet down the shore and to the fence. The smell of decomposition was oppressive. Partially in the water and wedged against the fence was a dark green army duffle bag. John waded out to retrieve it. Gagging and holding back vomit, he grabbed the strap to pull the bag to shore. Bob began to feel the outside of the bag, as did Henry. Henry said, "Let's not go any further, I'll radio my investigators from the car if you guys will stay here. I'll be back in a minute."

CHAPTER 73

The discovery of Thad Murphy's dismembered body brought Pete back to the station by eleven o'clock. Henry was alone in the station when he arrived. Settling into one of the chairs in the investigation room, Pete playfully stated, "What? You didn't think it was fair that I headed out? So you purposely bring an end to all this fun so I have to come back in? Thanks."

"Yeah Pete, we did it just for you" said Henry.

"Ok, so you found him in the river. Did you find anything else?" asked Pete.

"Yep, when the investigators opened the duffle bag, John lost his breakfast, Bob, though he wouldn't admit it, came close, and I kept a cool exterior while praying that I wouldn't join John. It was pretty horrific. The kid cut him up so he would fit in the duffle bag, hence all the blood in the cellar. That river water didn't freshen up things by the way. Along with the body parts, they found the saw, a hammer, bloody rags and a large knife. The knife was similar to the knife Phil Glaston was brandishing in the grain elevator. It was a skinning knife. My guys are still at the river if you want a gander" answered Henry.

"No thanks. I'll take your word for it. Besides, I grabbed breakfast and I would like to keep it. Are Bob and John with them?" said Pete.

"Naw, we knew word about the discovery would spread like wildfire, so he and John went over to inform the McVees before the rumor mill got to them."

"Who discovered him?" asked Pete.

"Do you remember the little guy that spent most of the time sitting by the garage on the first day?"

"Yeah, he's the one that was with John when they discovered the cellar."

"No! He found the duffle bag?" asked Pete.

"You got it. His name is Willy Smith. He and his friends were fishing and noticed the smell. Willy, still dealing with what he saw in the cellar on Wednesday, chose to call us before attempting to pull the bag out of the water. When our lab guys arrived, they instructed everyone within eyeshot to leave the immediate area. Even though they left before seeing anything, we knew the rumors would be rampant."

"Holy crap" responded Pete.

"Yep, holy crap and then some."

They heard a vehicle stop outside the station. The door to the station opened. Bob and John entered, walked to two empty chairs and plopped down.

"So, how'd it go?" asked Henry.

Bob removed a handkerchief from his pocket, wiped his brow and said, "Pretty damn rough. For a daughter that never met her father, Mrs. McVee was a basket case; that was until she realized how hard her daughter was taking it. The granddaughter feels it's all her fault because she told the Glaston kid that her grandfather would come looking for her; poor kid. John and I did what we could to smooth that one over, but I think we failed. How about you, John? Do you feel the same way?"

"Yeah, I do." John paused and then continued, " The girl is facing rough waters for a while. She's really a neat kid, but to carry that kind of guilt can do bad things if she can't get rid of it. I am going to keep tabs on her."

"Good idea" said Bob.

They sat in silence for a while, "Alright, let's pool our great minds, shall we. I've been trying to piece this all together, so what's your take?" asked Henry.

No one spoke. Hesitantly, John said, "According to the reports, the Glaston kid, whether by coincidence or staged, approached

Beth by the tracks. She reacted differently than he expected, he panicked and tried to stop her from leaving, she fought, his panic escalated and she ended up in the bunker. Her story about the grandfather coming to look for her caused him to feel he had to take out the old man. Because of the blood in the house, I would guess that his encounter with the old man began in the bedroom; they ended up in the cellar. He felt the need to dispose of the body. He couldn't carry the old man around town so he saw the duffle bag hanging on the wall. At that point, things were getting pretty weird" John paused.

"Keep going. We're on the same track" said Pete.

"Well, I don't know if he got handy with the saw at that point and later went to steal the car, or possibly the reverse, but anyway, he loaded Murphy in the duffle bag, which gives me shivers down my spine, and took the bag out to the car. Somewhere along the line he wiped his shoes clean or changed shoes. He either dumped the bag in the river at Jefferson Street or Case Street; it found its way down to the fence at Western Electric. Willy found it this morning. The dog thing has me stumped. That was a big dog, and not that friendly, so I'm pulling a blank on that one" responded John.

"What about the Miller kid?" asked Henry.

"He got too close to Glaston's lair of romance. Glaston took him out. That's the best I can offer" answered John.

"Not bad, John" said Bob. "Anyone have anything to add?"

Henry and Pete shook their heads, Henry said, "Nope, I think that's a pretty fair appraisal."

"Any further word on the Miller kid?" asked Pete.

"Not that I have heard" responded Bob.

"John, how are you doing?" asked Henry.

"I'm doing ok. But, I haven't taken that much time to think about it."

"It's going to hit you sooner or later, but it will hit you" said Henry.

"I figured as much."

"If you need help, call me. We'll do everything we can" offered Henry.

"I will. Thanks."

Pete added, "Yeah, you call him, John. Guys go their entire career and don't go through what you went through."

John nodded his head.

"We'll have more details on the findings in the bag tomorrow, but I'd say we can leave that in the hands of our lab. Bob, you and John need rest. I have asked to have one our guys come down to cover for you boys tonight. He's off at eight tomorrow morning. If you need more help than that, give me a holler" said Henry.

"Much obliged" said Bob.

"Yeah, much obliged" said John.

CHAPTER 74

Two funerals were scheduled for the following week; both to be conducted at Healey Chapel on Downer Place in Aurora.

On Tuesday, August the 5th, the service for Philip Girrard Glaston was conducted, a young man that longed for acceptance, but found it only in a deranged world he created. Attendance, as might be expected, was slight; friends of the parents, close neighbors, and a few others that Nick and Stan did not recognize, likely relatives. Bob Woodyard attended, John did not. The Corries and the Bakers were the only attendees that would have represented friends of Phil's.

The village residents were angry with Phil and the Glastons; angry for their losses and the damage; angry for the lack of answers and angry for the absence of understanding. Forgiveness was in the future, but not in the near future.

Nick and Stan talked about whether they would attend or not; but concluded that Phil was really screwed up. They attributed his being screwed up to his brothers, they felt they owed it to Phil to say goodbye.

Much to their surprise, Charlie joined them in their pew. Assuming he took the bus, Nick's dad insisted on giving Charlie a ride home.

Phil's asshole brothers, Benjy and Kurt, sat in the front pew with their parents. Nick watched them closely. The more he watched, the more contempt he felt for them. He thought their attendance was only for formality. Benjy actually yawned during the minister's comments. Phil's parents, especially his mom, appeared genuinely heartbroken. Nick felt sad for Phil's parents, but disgust for the brothers.

On Wednesday, August the 6th, service for Thaddeus Artimus Murphy was conducted. Attendance was incredibly high for
an eccentric that experienced limited contact with others. Nick
turned around a couple of times to see people from the village
standing and lining the back of the chapel. The front row was
occupied by the minister, Sally, Stuart and Beth McVee, and an
older couple that Nick did not recognize. Nick's heart was breaking; not for Mr. Murphy, though he felt bad for him, but for the toll
it was taking on Beth. On two occasions, Beth stood; walked to
the closed casket and tenderly placed her hand on the casket and
bawled uncontrollably. On both occasions, Sally gently escorted
her back to the pew.

The minister opened the proceedings with a prayer and a few
comments. To everyone's surprise he asked Mr. Charles Abernathy to give the eulogy. Who the heck was Mr. Charles Abernathy?
Everyone looked around until they saw Charlie step from the second pew and walk to the pulpit. Though no gasps from the crowd
could be heard, they could be felt. Nick and Stan looked at one
another with amazement; they had not seen Charlie enter the chapel. Their Charlie . . . is addressing the village?

Charlie was shaven, groomed and wore a tie and jacket. Nick
thought he might rib Charlie about that later, but he was proud of
him at that moment.

Charlie walked up to the pulpit; looked out as if to identify
everyone in attendance and began, "Most of you might be surprised to see me up here. Frankly, I am a bit surprised myself, but
I am here. For his family . . ." Charlie nodded in the direction of
those in the front pew, ". . . and for those of you that have come to
pay your respects, I am here to say a few words about a man that I
have known for thirty years; that is, as well as anyone could know
Thad Murphy. I feel that a man's life is a combination of many fac-
tors. None of us can fully appreciate who a man is until we learn
what has brought him to this point of his life. We can speculate
and reason, but we will never know the man without understand-

ing his paSt. Thad Murphy is a man who made a mistake. That mistake changed who he was so dramatically that he transformed into what most of you observe him to be; a hermit, a little weird or mysterious, strange, eccentric; certainly reclusive. By the way, those adjectives usually won't win any citizen-of-the-year award."

This caused muffled laughter.

When the laughter died out, Charlie continued, "Allow me to describe a man I once knew. This man was articulate, good looking, a college graduate, gregarious and by most accounts was moving the world in his direction. He enjoyed life to the fullest. But one day he made a mistake; a big mistake. Have any of you ever made a big mistake?" Charlie paused for a second, not expecting anyone to respond, but to give them a moment to think. "I think some of you may have, but I don't know. I do know this man knew he made a big mistake and chose to deal with it the only way he felt was appropriate. He shut himself off from the world that brought him joy. You might call it self-punishment or masochistic thinking, but it was his penance for the sin of a mistake. For thirty years he deprived himself of a life representative of what he once possessed. Sad? Possibly; but, he thought it was necessary; and only he can be the judge of that. Each of us deals with our own mistakes in our own ways." Charlie paused, "Of course you know the man I speak of is Thaddeus Murphy, the recluse on Railroad Street. Few of us can remember the flamboyant, fun-loving, fast-driving, life of the party that he once was, but I assure you that he was all of that and more. He was, until a few days ago, a member of our small community. I have learned in the last day or two that Thad was attempting to make things right during his last couple of months. We will never know what was or wasn't accomplished, but we do know, based on his actions that he was reaching out to the world he chose to turn off. To his family . . ." again nodding toward the front pew, ". . . I offer my sincere condolences. To the rest of you I will close by suggesting a question, 'Does a man have the right to live his life according to his ideals, or must he conform to the ideals of others?' I believe Thad Murphy lived according to his ideals. My hope for Thad is that he will find in the hereafter the peace he so fervently sought here on earth. Thank you." Charlie stepped away from the pulpit.

Nick and Stan wanted to stand and applaud, but that would have been improper. They were proud of Charlie, their friend.

Nick waited outside of the mortuary for the family to come out. When they did, he introduced himself to the McVees, offering his hand to Mr. McVee, nodded at Mrs. McVee. He offered them his condolences. Taking Beth's small hand in his he said "I am so sorry, Beth."

Everyone in the village learned that Beth was secretively visiting her grandfather. Choking back tears, Beth squeezed his hand and said, "Thanks, Nick. I hope to see you before school begins."

Nick's response was immediate and emphatic, "Oh, you will."

CHAPTER 75

As he rode away from the old house on his fat tire Monarch bicycle he felt different somehow. How could so much change that fast? It didn't feel right; he didn't feel right. He headed toward the tracks on Clinton Street on his way to roust Stan out of bed. There was no hurry, but Nick really wanted to sit back with his friend and recount the events of the past week. He'd awakened numerous times throughout the night wishing he could find Stan right then. He wasn't sure what he wanted to talk about, but he needed to talk.

After an initial knock on Stan's front door produced no sound or movement inside, Nick entered the house and found his way to Stan's room. Sleepy-head Stan was on his back sprawled across his bed. An open window provided a nice breeze on this hot August morning. Nick smiled. "Man, you just get too comfortable, that's your problem." Stan didn't move; his mouth was open and his breathing was deep and peaceful. Nick walked over and placed the tips of two fingers over Stan's nostril openings. Stan's breathing changed, momentary panic brought his eyes to life. He jerked backwards freeing airflow to his nose, blinked his eyes repeatedly as he focused on Nick. "You asshole! I need to lock our front door. Damn!"

"Quit your bitching, big boy. Let's go for a ride."

They pedaled hard as they turned east on Webster, disregarded the stop sign as they turned onto River Street and sped down the hill; their T-shirts billowing out in back. At Shannon's they dramatically slammed on their brakes sliding their rear tires sideward. On the steps sat Mr. Charles Abernathy, smiling at his friends. "Hey Charlie" said Nick.

"Hey to you Mr. Mayor."

"How about joining us for a talk under the bridge?" asked Nick.

"Under the bridge? You've never invited me to join you under the bridge before. Why, I am honored." Charlie leaned forward to begin his descent down the steps.

"This is right cozy" said Charlie as he carefully selected a boulder to sit on under the bridge.

"Yeah, it's our place" said Stan. "We do our best thinking here, Charlie."

"I'll bet you do. I'll bet you do."

"Charlie, we were proud of you on Wednesday. It was like . . . well it was like you let the rest of the world know who you are. We've always known, but it was like you opened the curtains to let the rest of the world peek in" said Nick, feeling a little embarrassed.

Charlie smiled, "Thank you. Thank both of you. You boys are my friends and it means a lot to me to know that you think nicely of me. It was Bob Woodyard that asked me if I would offer the eulogy. I had to think about that one. Most folks would not think to consider me as a spokesman for anyone, but Thad Murphy and I shared commonalities, so I thought who better to speak for Thad than me?"

"What commonalities, Charlie?" asked Stan.

Charlie pulled a pack of Pall Malls from his shirt pocket and offered one to each boy. Out came the wobbly top Zippo. The boys knew something important was pending so they remained silent. Charlie sucked in a huge inhale of the Pall Mall, held it so long that the boys began to wonder if he stopped breathing. With a rewarding exhale he looked at the boys and said, "Do you boys remember when I said to know a man, I mean really know a man, you have to know about his past?"

They both nodded.

"Well, I guess to know me; you have to know about my past."

"We know a lot about your past, Charlie. You've told us the stories" said Nick.

"Yes and the stories are all true; maybe embellished a little to make them more interesting, but they're all true. Most of them are a result of something that happened a long time ago. You see, I grew up on a farm a little ways out of town. We were dirt poor; so poor it was a wonder that any of us survived. If it wasn't for what we could raise on the farm, we would have starved. I resented being poor, I hated this village of Montgomery and everything it represented. I wanted to get more out of life, I wanted what others had and I didn't; so without notifying my folks I slipped off in my bib overalls, my brother's shoes and the little money that was kept in a cookie jar and set out to find my fortune. The money in the cookie jar wasn't mine, but I felt I deserved it. That's where all the stories come in. I went to Chicago and worked in the slaughter houses; did debt collecting for unsavory characters on the Southside. Socked away a little money and took a train out west. I learned to ride the ranges, I worked in mines, I befriended an Indian and learned the ways of nature. Everything I did elsewhere was better than what I did here. For a while it was exciting and adventurous; I even took up studies. I would read books anywhere I could find them. I learned a lot from my adventures and from the books. But, in my quietest moments I wondered about my family. They were good folks; hard-working, dumb, lovable folks that made the best of what they had, which was nothing. As I was driving around Chicago in a touring car, that belonged to someone else, or riding a horse on a range, or working in a gold mine, or riding a train to who-knows-where I would think, 'Wouldn't it be great if they could see me now? Me in ordinary clothes, with a little jingle in my pockets', but the thoughts always ended in sadness. Something was wrong. So, after years passed, I decided to come back to check on the family. I accumulated savings; I was going to share that with them to make up for the money in the cookie jar. I came to the realization that I should not have taken the money."

Charlie paused to light another Pall Mall. "I got off the train in Aurora, hitched a ride to Montgomery; walked the few miles to find the farm house empty and the yard over-grown. The fields were not tended. I couldn't understand; the farm was their life. Where were they?"

Charlie paused for a long time and began again, "I learned from a neighbor farmer that shortly after I left, my dad, a big brute of a man, came down with sickness and died; the farmer thought it was lung related. That left only my mom and my brother to run the place. According to the farmer, they tried. He said he hated to see my mom doing the work in the fields and he would help when he could, but he was as poor as they were and needed to tend his own property. My brother found my mother out in the field; she'd died of heat stroke. My brother couldn't farm it all by himself, so the bank took the farm. He said my brother moved off, but he didn't know where. Boys, I am not looking for sympathy, but the weight of the world came down on me. No one needed to tell me that if I had not left, things might have turned out differently; I know that. So I began to drift, only this time I didn't have a goal to achieve, I wasn't looking for adventure or fortune; I was looking for peace. Every night I was haunted by the memories of my mom, my dad and my brother. I came to the conclusion that my joy in life had died. I continued to read books; some days I would spend the entire day in public libraries reading to soothe my aching soul. Surprisingly, I came back to Montgomery. I don't know why, but I was pulled back. I worked in Aurora for a while, but came to the conclusion that I valued the simple life. That's all that I wanted. So, here I am; living above a tavern, serving others, and frankly, I am pretty happy. Besides, I have the best friends in the world." Charlie smiled.

The boys were awestruck with the story. Neither could find the words to respond. Charlie sensed their discomfort, "Now hold on here a minute, that wasn't supposed to make you feel bad, I thought you deserved to know. You are my friends, and friends should know."

Nick cocked his head and spoke, "Charlie, so some of what you said for Thad you said for yourself."

Charlie's grin spread across his face, "You boys are making progress. Thinkers run the world, and you are thinking. Yes, some of what I said for Thad I said for myself, we shared commonalities. But a dime will get you a donut that most that heard never grasped any of it. I am thrilled that you did."

"Thanks, Charlie. Did you ever find your brother?" asked Nick.

"Nope; never have. But I hope he's out there enjoying the simple life."

"Thanks for telling us Charlie. Does anyone else know about this?" asked Nick.

"I doubt it. I regard this a personal matter" responded Charlie.

They gazed at the flowing river; a bird snatched a crawdad in the shallows and flew to a tree to feast. The comforting breeze under the bridge was all that was necessary and they individually dealt with their thoughts. Then Stan asked, "Charlie, what do you think was wrong with Phil?"

Charlie put his hand on his chin, "Based on what you told me about his brothers, I'd say they were a significant influence. I was appalled as I watched them at Phil's funeral. They are either heartless or simply don't care; either way I wish to be anywhere they aren't. But, aside from his brothers, strange as it may sound, Phil justified his actions somehow. He created a false world that allowed him to do what he did. We can all justify what we do if we want to; but the ultimate test must be 'is it right or is it wrong?'. Deep inside we know. That's the test Phil missed."

"Charlie, will things get back to normal around here?" asked Nick.

"In time; time is a healing balm that brings life to areas that are stagnant, hope to those that are discouraged, and peace to those that seek it. It will be a while, but what happened over the past week will simply become a story that will be told many times over the coming years; it will likely grow according to the teller's delight and take on proportions beyond the truth. But, yes things will be normal again, and quicker than you think."

"Is this the biggest mystery you've ever encountered, Charlie?" asked Stan.

Charlie smiled, slowly nodded his head, "Yes, it probably is. It involved so many possibilities; a real mystery from the start. We were all convinced that Thad Murphy did a horrendous act in his cellar, somebody's heartthrob goes missing, our buddy Butch is attacked, you boys confront Phil, somebody's heartthrob is returned, and sadly Thad Murphy is vindicated. Yes, this is the biggest mystery I have encountered. Would you like to know how I sum it up?"

"Yeah" responded both boys.

"You know, I have lived a lot, seen a lot, done a lot and have tried to learn something each step of the way. I kept searching for the lesson as all this developed, but other than being able to watch you boys do a fine job of exploring, I couldn't find it. Yesterday it came to me."

"What came to you?"

"Well, we have a pretty nice little village here. The people are good people. For the most part, they take care of one another; they tend to one another's needs. It's a good place to live. It's a village; and they say it takes a village to raise a child. My conclusion is - that it works most of the time, but not all of the time. Sometimes it might take more than a village."

EPILOGUE

Charlie was right; things returned to normal quickly in Montgomery. The DeSenza Brothers Carnival Company brought the carnival to the VFW the week after the funerals. The carnival, the Ferris wheel, the Tilt-a-Whirl, the hawkers, the barbequed beef sandwich topped with cole slaw, the bingo ten, the crowds, and the general air of excitement rejuvenated the atmosphere; it provided the merriment the village deserved.

On the second day of the carnival, Nick decided to walk to Beth's house to invite her to go to the carnival with him that night, or any night that she could go. He'd saved enough money to take her on rides and buy snacks, maybe even win her a Kewpie Doll from one of the game stalls.

She was uncomfortable seeing him at the shack, but got over it when she explained that they were buying a home in town. She was thrilled with Nick's invitation. Sally had quit her job at the diner and said that she would take Beth to the carnival, but promised to stay out of their way.

Mr. Corrie took Nick and Stan to the hospital to see Butch again. Other than the fact that they shaved away his flat top, Butch looked about the same. Mrs. Miller told them the doctors relieved some of the pressure from the brain and they would know within a couple of weeks as to the outcome. Nick and Stan thanked her for allowing them to see Butch. Nick said, "Mrs. Miller, Butch is going to pull through. He wouldn't ditch Stan and me. He'll be back." That made Mrs. Miller cry. Mr. Corrie encouraged the goodbyes and guided the boys to the door.

The McVees received a call from the Kane County Probate Court. They were asked to come to the courthouse for the reading of Thaddeus Murphy's will.

It turned out that Thad Murphy's estate consisted of substantial holdings of stocks, bonds, cash, and the real estate on Railroad Street; all of it willed to his only daughter, Sally Thomas McVee of Montgomery, Illinois. Along with the inheritance, Sally was given a sealed envelope addressed to her. Across it was written, *'To be opened by addressee only.'* When she opened it she found a hand-written letter dated July 15, 1958:

Dearest Sally,

If you are reading this, I have passed. I will try to say things that should have been said many years ago, but I, for my reasons, chose another avenue to wander at that time. Nothing I offer is to be misconstrued as an excuse, but merely an explanation.

I am not sure where to start, or that I have the right to start at all, but I must say that seeing you, even occasionally and from a distance, made my life complete. Your mother would have been so proud of you.

I am sure that Betty and Grover told you about my Sara, your mother. You are a spitting image of her in every way. When I lost her, I felt I had no right to live or enjoy life again, or to enjoy the things that I should have enjoyed with her. I cannot justify those feelings; I can only say that I foolishly took her life from her, and mine from me.

The years passed, but the thought of you haunted me constantly. My saving grace was the knowledge that Betty and Grover would be wonderful parents to you. Based on what I have seen, I was right on that one. Please thank them for me.

This may sound out of place, but I love you, I have always loved you. You may not want to accept this, but it is true. As strange as I may seem to others, I have maintained the ability to love; even those things beyond my reach. Thoughts of you occupied many empty moments for me over the years, and gave me hope that one day I would see you again. My hope was rewarded.

Getting to know Beth has been beyond my imagination. What a beautiful and charming young lady; I can only assume that her charm, her wit, and her personality are a reflection of you. Beth and I shared many stories; I hope you allow her to share them with you.

In my bedroom you will find a box of photos I think you will enjoy. The box is in the bottom drawer of my dresser. Some may show wear because I touched them often.

By now you know that you are my sole heir, it has always been that way. My hope and prayer is that what I have left you will help you raise your family as I should have raised mine.

Love,

Thaddeus Murphy, your father

Sally sobbed. Stuart pulled her close with his left arm while holding Beth with his right arm.

THE END

Author's Notes

Yes, growing up in the 1950's was magical; kids left their homes early in the morning and wouldn't be seen or heard of until dinner, and parents didn't worry about it. Doors to homes were rarely locked, cars were left open with the keys in the ignition, people trusted others, innocence seemed to be acceptable well into the teen years and the entire world was there to be explored. Untainted heroes existed in comic books, on the movie screens, on television and crawled out of the radio to set an example for followers to live by. Except for Saturday mornings, television was reserved for evening enjoyment. The time was purely magical and I hope I have successfully captured some of it majesty in this novel.

While preparing this novel, I went to great lengths to create characters not resembling people I have known. Nick and I grew up in that little house, our fathers repaired automobiles, we were explorers, but that is where all resemblance stops. Nick is much brighter, much quicker, more compassionate and a better thinker than the Gove kid. If it helps, think of Nick as my alter-ego. Stan, Butch, Phil, Beth, Sally, and Thad are figments of my imagination and reside solely within the pages of this novel. No murder or kidnapping ever took place; at least as far as this explorer knows.

A wise man did sit on the steps of Shannon's tavern; unfortunately I can't remember his name; so I gave him the name 'Charlie'. He was regarded as the town drunk, and maybe he was, but he impressed the young explorers that visited with him; his stories were captivating. His talent of asking questions to encourage others to find their own answer was borrowed from my father.

Most of my references to Montgomery relied on memories over 50 years old. I moved away from Montgomery in 1966 to go off, as many did, to the service of my country. For most of my adult life I have made Colorado my home, but Montgomery, Illinois is my hometown. My 50 year old memory knows there was more than just one house on the west side of Railroad Street; but it made for a more mysterious setting as a lone dwelling. Two explorers lived in one of the other houses on Railroad Street, but at different times, John Brunner and Gary Harbin; both became casualties of the Vietnam War. All references of Montgomery are offered through the eyes of a 12 year old explorer. As you have learned, explorers see the world differently.

I took fictional liberties with Thad's wedding reception hosted in the Leland Hotel in 1926. The Leland wasn't built until 1928. I had to include its grandness in my story.

Chief Bob Woodyard and Officer John Rively represent two men that helped form who I am. They were the real cops in Montgomery in 1958. I chose not to use their real names in the novel without permission. My reference to them is an expression of my thanks. Their positive impact on my life is felt yet today.

Made in the USA
San Bernardino, CA
22 December 2013